More Than a Mistress

When an affair is not enough…

Three passionate novels!

*In October 2006 Mills & Boon bring
back two of their classic collections,
each featuring three favourite
romances by our bestselling authors...*

MORE THAN A MISTRESS

His Virgin Mistress by Anne Mather
Claiming His Mistress by Emma Darcy
Mistress on His Terms
by Catherine Spencer

RED-HOT REVENGE

The Greek Tycoon's Revenge
by Jacqueline Baird
The Millionaire's Revenge
by Cathy Williams
Ryan's Revenge by Lee Wilkinson

More Than a Mistress

HIS VIRGIN MISTRESS
by
Anne Mather

CLAIMING HIS MISTRESS
by
Emma Darcy

MISTRESS ON HIS TERMS
by
Catherine Spencer

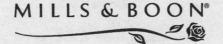

MILLS & BOON®

*MILLS & BOON and MILLS & BOON with the Rose Device
are registered trademarks of the publisher.
Harlequin Mills & Boon Limited,
Eton House, 18-24 Paradise Road, Richmond, Surrey, TW9 1SR*

MORE THAN A MISTRESS
© by Harlequin Enterprises II B.V., 2006

His Virgin Mistress, Claiming His Mistress and *Mistress on His
Terms* were first published in Great Britain by Harlequin Mills &
Boon Limited in separate, single volumes.

His Virgin Mistress © Anne Mather 2002
Claiming His Mistress © Emma Darcy 2001
Mistress on His Terms © Kathy Garner 2001

*ISBN 10: 0 263 84971 6
ISBN 13: 978 0 263 84971 4*

05-1006

*Printed and bound in Spain
by Litografía Rosés S.A., Barcelona*

HIS VIRGIN MISTRESS

by

Anne Mather

New York Times bestselling author **Anne Mather** has written since she was seven, but it was only when her first child was born that she fulfilled her dream of becoming a writer. Her first book, CAROLINE, appeared in 1966. It met with immediate success and, since then, Anne has written more than 140 novels, reaching a readership which spans the world.

Born and raised in the north of England, Anne still makes her home there with her husband, two children and, now, grandchildren. Asked if she finds writing a lonely occupation, she replies that her characters always keep her company. In fact, she is so busy sorting out their lives that she often doesn't have time for her own! An avid reader herself, she devours everything from sagas and romances to mainstream fiction and suspense.

CHAPTER ONE

'Is that her?'

'Yes, sir.' Spiro Stavros gave his employer a faintly sardonic look. 'Not exactly what you'd anticipated, is she?'

Demetrios Kastro arched a dismissive brow. As yet his arrival had not been noticed, and he was able to look across the crowded salon to where his father and his companion were standing without being observed. They were surrounded by the guests who had been invited to welcome the old man back to Theapolis, and Demetri watched with a tightening of his jawline as his father put a possessive arm about the woman's shoulders.

'Perhaps not,' he conceded at last, aware that Spiro knew exactly what he was thinking. He had expected her to be younger. A 'blonde bimbo' was how she had been described to him by his sister, and because it was what he had wanted to hear he had believed her. But the woman his father had adopted as his mistress didn't look like a bimbo. There was intelligence as well as beauty in the high-cheekboned face, with its wide-set eyes and mobile mouth, and, although she was undoubtedly a blonde, she wore her hair drawn up into a severe knot that, whatever its purpose, tended to draw attention to the slender column of her neck. 'She is certainly older than I had imagined.'

'And more sophisticated?' suggested Spiro drily. 'I have the feeling she is not going to be as easy to get rid of as you thought.'

Demetri cast his assistant a dark look. 'You think not?' He was cynical. 'In my experience, my friend, everyone has their price. Man or woman. It makes no difference. If the rewards are great enough, they all succumb.'

5

Spiro's snort was disbelieving. 'Do you include me in that assessment?'

Demetri sighed. 'We were not talking about you, Spiro.'

'That does not answer my question.'

'All right.' Demetri scowled. 'I would hope not. I consider you my friend as well as my assistant. But few people are as scrupulous, Spiro. You know that.'

'Not all women are like Athenee, Demetri,' the other man reminded him gently. Then, aware that he was in danger of overstepping the mark, he added, 'I suppose I must consider myself honoured.' He grimaced. 'So? What are you going to do now?'

'Now?' Demetri's dark, tanned features smoothed themselves into an urbane mask. 'Why, now I am going to announce my arrival to my father, and ask to be introduced to the delightful Kiria Manning.'

Spiro's mouth compressed and, taking a chance, he put a detaining hand on Demetri's sleeve. 'Be careful,' he said, risking a rebuff. But although his hand was shaken off, Demetri merely gave him a mocking smile.

'Am I not always?' he enquired, loosening the button on the jacket of his dark blue silk suit. 'Calm yourself, Spiro. I am not likely to show my hand so early in the game.'

Nevertheless, as Demetri made his way across the room he was aware of an intense feeling of irritation. Dammit, his father had only been out of hospital for a few weeks; weeks that he had spent in London, ostensibly to avoid the blistering heat of Theapolis in mid-summer. The old man had been ill; seriously ill. In God's name, when had he found the time to meet this woman, let alone become intimate with her?

He would find out. Offering a word of greeting here, an acknowledgement of welcome there, he gradually covered the space dividing him from Constantine Kastro and his mistress. What was her name? Manning, yes. But what was her first name? Demetri frowned, thinking. Joanna! That was it. Joanna Manning. Was it her real name? If so, it was elegant, just like the woman herself.

'Do not tell me that frown is because you are sad to see me back, Demetri.'

His father's chiding words—spoken in English for the woman's benefit, Demetri assumed—were delivered in a mocking tone. Demetri realised he was allowing too much of his feelings to show in his face and he hastily schooled his features. Then, finding a polite smile, he shook the old man's hand and submitted to the customary embrace with genuine warmth.

'Forgive me, Papa,' he said disarmingly, and no one could tell from his expression that he was anything but delighted with the present situation. 'Naturally, I am relieved your physicians consider you well enough to return to us at last.'

Constantine looked less than pleased now, his narrow features mirroring his discontent. 'I am not an invalid, Demetri,' he declared irritably, even though his wasted body belied the fact. 'The doctors have given me a clean bill of health, and I do not appreciate you behaving as if I had only just got out of hospital.'

Demetri made no response to this. Instead, his eyes moved to the woman standing at his father's side, and, because they were surrounded by interested spectators, Constantine was obliged to introduce his companion to his son.

'My dear,' he said and Demetri stiffened at the implied intimacy in the term. 'Allow me to present my son to you. Demetrios: this is Joanna. Joanna Manning. My—my friend.'

'How do you do?'

The woman didn't make the mistake of calling him by his first name and Demetri's thin lips stretched into a tight smile. 'It is my pleasure to meet you, Kiria Manning,' he responded politely. 'I trust you are not finding our weather too trying for your English tastes?'

'On the contrary.' Despite the faint film of perspiration on her upper lip, she denied it. 'I love the heat. It's so—sensual.'

Sensual?

Demetri had to work hard to prevent himself from show-ing his incredulity. He had heard his father was besotted by the woman, but he hadn't expected her to disconcert him. And why was she watching him with that air of amused speculation? She was taller than most of the women of his acquaintance—easily five feet eight or nine—and, although he was still almost a head taller than she was, she didn't have to tilt her head too far to look up at him. If he hadn't known better he'd have wondered if she wasn't deliberately trying to irritate him. But that was ridiculous. Nevertheless, there was a definite look of challenge in her face.

'Katalava.' I see. Conscious that his father was enjoying his confusion, Demetri inadvertently spoke in his own lan-guage. But he quickly corrected himself. 'You are familiar with our Greek weather, Miss Manning?'

'It's Mrs Manning, actually,' she corrected him. 'But please call me Joanna, or Jo, if you prefer it.' Then, with an affectionate look at Constantine. 'Not yet. The weather, I mean. But I hope to be.'

Now, why am I not surprised?

It was all Demetri could do to prevent himself from say-ing the words out loud. But at least he knew a little more about her now. No one had seen fit to tell him that she'd been married. But it figured. And if he'd had any doubts about her relationship with his father they'd been dispelled by the familiarity of that look.

'Do you live on the island—um—Demetrios?' she asked suddenly, surprising him again. 'Or do you have your own home?'

'This is my home,' replied Demetri, unable to quite dis-guise his indignation. 'This house is our family home.' He paused. 'But do not worry, Mrs Manning. It is quite big enough to accommodate us all without any—what is it you say?—stepping on toes?'

He was pleased to see that her soft mouth tightened a little at this rebuff. The upper lip was drawn between her teeth and the lower, which was so much fuller and more vulnerable, curved protectively. Then he scowled. When had he started thinking that her mouth was soft, or vulnerable, for that matter? She was a kept woman, for heaven's sake. Hardly better than the sluts who plied their trade on the streets of Athens. He had no need to feel sorry for her. It was his father who was the vulnerable one. Vulnerable, and foolish. What on earth did he think she saw in a man at least thirty years her senior?

'Demetri has his own apartments in the house,' Constantine put in now, the look he cast at his son promising retribution later. 'As do Alex and Olivia. As my son says, this is our family home. Our island fortress, if you will. I regret you will discover that security is paramount in our situation.'

Joanna nodded. 'I understand.'

'I doubt you do,' put in Demetri pleasantly, though his feelings were anything but. 'My father is a constant target for terrorists and paparazzi alike. Only on Theapolis can we—usually—ensure that he is not at the mercy of unscrupulous men—and women.'

Her eyes flashed then, and he noticed how deep a blue they were. 'I trust you are not suggesting that I am any threat to your father?' she demanded coolly, her earlier amusement all gone now. He could hardly suppress a smile.

'Of course not,' he said, but when his dark eyes strayed to his father's taut face he saw he was by no means convinced by his son's denial. 'I am sure you and my father must have a lot in common. Tell me, Mrs Manning, do you have children, too?'

'No.'

Her answer was almost curt, but it didn't have quite the effect he'd expected. Instead of showing surprise, his father put his arm about her shoulders and drew her closer to him. Demetri was almost sure Constantine was reacting to something she'd told him, and he wondered what it was. He didn't like the idea that their relationship might be more than a temporary aberration on his father's part. A desire to prove his masculinity was one thing; a threat to his mother's memory was quite another.

But, before he could say any more, Constantine himself severed the conversation. 'Come,' he said to Joanna Manning. 'I see Nikolas Poros over there. He is a friend as well as a business colleague. I would like you to meet him.' He looked briefly at his son. 'You will excuse us?'

It was hardly a question. Although Demetri bowed his head in silent acknowledgement they both knew he wasn't being given an option. Instead, he stepped back to allow them free passage, aware as he did so that Joanna gave him a covert glance as she passed. Was it a triumphant glance? he wondered broodingly, watching them make their way across the room. He couldn't be sure. But one thing seemed apparent to him: his father's infatuation with her went deeper than the sexual fascination he had anticipated.

'Demetri! Demetri, *pos iseh*?' How are you? *'Na seh keraso kanena poto?'* Can I get you a drink?

With an effort, he became aware that there were other people around him. Neighbours; friends, relatives. They had all gathered to welcome the old man home, and his own absence until just a few minutes ago had not gone unnoticed. Forcing himself to put the problem of his father and his mistress aside, he accepted the greetings he was offered with a grim smile, aware that for the moment he was obliged to play the devoted son.

And he was devoted, dammit, he thought, taking the glass of champagne he was offered with controlled grace. But he was also his father's son, his deputy, and he couldn't help thinking that the last thing the old man needed at this time was the respect he'd always enjoyed among the shipping community weakened by some woman taking advantage of his vulnerability.

'She is beautiful, is she not?'

Spiro was at his elbow and Demetri turned to give the other man an impatient look. 'Yes, she's beautiful,' he agreed. 'But what does she want, Spiro? More importantly, what does she hope to gain from this liaison?'

'Perhaps she loves him,' suggested Spiro, accepting a glass of champagne in his turn and smiling at the dark-eyed waitress who had proffered the tray.

'And perhaps she sees him as a very convenient meal ticket,' retorted Demetri. 'My father is sixty-seven, Spiro. A woman like that does not attach herself to a much older man for love.'

'How cynical you are, Demetri.' He had been unaware that his older sister Olivia had joined them, until her soft words were whispered in his ear. 'Mrs Manning does not look like a gold-digger, you must agree.'

'How do gold-diggers look?' enquired her brother shortly, looking down into Olivia's olive-skinned face with a softening of his expression. 'Surely you are not championing her, Livvy? With only a week to go to Alex's wedding, I'd have expected you to feel as I do. After all, what is Alex going to think when she discovers our father has invited a stranger to what is essentially a family occasion?'

Olivia's lips thinned. 'Alex will not care,' she said. 'But that does not mean we can ignore the influence Mrs Manning has with Papa. And making an enemy of her may not be the wisest decision. You have seen them together. Only briefly, I admit. But you must have noticed that they seem very—absorbed with one another.'

'Absorbed, yes.' Demetri watched his father and his companion over the rim of his glass. 'How did they meet? Do we know? Where has the old man been since he got out of hospital to find a woman like her?'

Joanna's apartments adjoined Constantine's. Each suite comprised a comfortable sitting room, a spacious bedroom, and an adjoining dressing room and bathroom.

And they were sumptuously appointed. Sofas in blue and green striped linen, decorated with matching cushions, were set against walls hung with silk damask. A delicately carved writing bureau, a comprehensive entertainment centre contained in a rosewood cabinet; all were illuminated by heavy brass lamps that stood on every available surface. Long windows, closed at present, opened out onto a wraparound balcony that served all the rooms on this floor, and Turkish rugs, or kilims, splashed colour onto polished floors. There were pictures everywhere: in the sitting room, in the bedroom, even in the bathroom. And floor-length mirrors, also in the bathroom, disdained any attempt at modesty.

But it wasn't just the beauty of the things surrounding her, or their obvious value, that convinced Joanna of their exclusivity. It was the incidentals that reminded her of where she was and why she was there. The sheets being changed every day, for example; the expensive cosmetics and toiletries removed and replaced as soon as she used them; the knowledge that she had only to touch the bell for her smallest wish to be granted.

This was Constantine's world, she thought ruefully. The way he lived. She had never known such assiduous attention to detail, and although she had agreed to come here for Constantine's sake, she had never imagined anything like this. She couldn't help wishing he had not been so *rich*.

Not that his son would believe that, she thought drily, wondering if Constantine had glimpsed the momentary flash of hatred in Demetrios's dark eyes. He probably had. Constantine must know exactly how his son was feeling. After all, that was why he had persuaded her to come here. He'd known that nothing short of grim hostility would blind Demetrios to the truth.

There was a light tap on the panelled double doors that connected her apartments to Constantine's. Joanna, who had been trying to decide what she should wear for dinner that evening, hurried to answer it. She'd guessed that it was Constantine, and it was. But, just in case, she'd wanted to make sure before inviting anyone else into her room.

'May I come in?'

'Of course.' Joanna stood back to allow him into her sitting room, gazing at him intently. He'd shed his formal clothes, as she had, and he looked so frail now that the necessity to appear invincible was gone. She indicated one of the overstuffed sofas. 'Sit down. You're supposed to be resting, you know.'

'You are not my nurse, Joanna.' Constantine's smile was warm but defensive. He was wearing a white towelling bathrobe and the colour accentuated his pallor. 'As a matter of fact, I am feeling a little stronger this evening. Now that Demetri is home I can relax.'

'Oh, right.' Joanna closed the door behind him, tucking the folds of the scarlet wrapper she'd put on after her shower closer about her. 'I suppose that's because you think the worst is over.' She shook her head. 'I wouldn't hold my breath, if I were you.'

'Joanna, Joanna.' Constantine sighed, but he took her advice and subsided onto the nearest sofa. 'Do not be so cynical, my dear. Just because Demetri is not entirely happy with the situation—and, I admit, I believe he does have doubts about the suitability of our relationship—he will do nothing to jeopardise the peace of the household. Not with Alex's wedding to consider. I am his father, Joanna. I think I know him better than anyone else.'

'Do you?'

Joanna wished she could feel as sure. Her own encounter with Demetrios Kastro had left a decidedly unpleasant taste in her mouth. She was convinced that he had nothing but contempt for her, that he believed she was only with his father for what she hoped to get out of him. He had been polite, but cold; saying little, but implying a lot. She was glad he hadn't deceived his father, but she was afraid Constantine was deluding himself if he thought Demetrios had accepted her presence.

'Anyway,' Constantine said now, reaching out to take her hand and urge her down beside him, 'how are you? Are you happy here? Do you have everything you need?'

'Need you ask?' Joanna was rueful. 'This place is amazing. It's everything you said it was and more.'

'I am glad.' Constantine raised her hand to his dry lips. 'I want you to enjoy your stay. I want you to feel at home here. I know Demetri may be difficult for a while, but he will get over it. Besides, so long as I am ostensibly recuperating he will have little time to fret about our relationship. Between now and the wedding there may be occasions when he has to leave the island. With my work to do as well as his own...' He allowed the words to trail away. 'You understand?'

'I can't wait.' Joanna pulled a wry face. Then, withdrawing her hand from his, she got to her feet again. 'But are you sure about this? What is Alex going to think when she finds out I'm here?'

'Alex will love you,' said Constantine firmly. 'She is not like Demetri or Olivia. She is younger; less cynical, shall we say?'

'All the same...' Joanna lifted the heavy weight of her loosened hair from her neck, enjoying the coolness of the air-conditioning on her hot skin. 'I can still go back to England, Constantine. I wouldn't mind.'

'I would.' His response was unequivocal. 'My dear, the reasons I asked you to come to Theapolis have not changed. I need you. I need your strength and your companionship. And, most of all, I need your support.'

'You have that, of course.' Joanna sighed. 'I'm just not sure whether I can go through with it.'

Constantine pushed himself to his feet. 'Because of me?' he asked. 'You find me so repulsive?'

'Don't be silly.' Joanna touched his cheek with a tender hand. 'You're a very attractive man. I've always thought so.'

'You have?' He was sceptical.

'Yes.' She hesitated a moment, and then cupped his face between her palms and bestowed a warm kiss at the corner of his mouth. 'Now, stop fishing for compliments and tell me what you think I should wear for dinner this evening.'

'What you are wearing at present seems eminently suitable to me,' declared Constantine gallantly, his hands reaching for her waist to hold her in front of him. 'You always look beautiful.'

Joanna shook her head, but before she could think of a response there was a knock at the outer door.

'*Beno mesa!*'

Almost automatically Constantine replied, bidding the caller to enter, and Joanna turned her head as the foyer door opened.

Demetrios appeared moments later, pausing on the threshold of the sitting room. He, too, had evidently taken a shower. Water sparkled on the sleek darkness of his hair, contrasting with the pearl-grey elegance of his suit. A dark blue, body-hugging tee shirt completed his outfit, and Joanna was instantly conscious of the intimacy of the scene he had interrupted. Both she and Constantine were scantily clad, and Constantine's hands on her body looked undeniably possessive.

She didn't know which of them was the most disconcerted by Demetrios's arrival. To his credit, Constantine seemed only mildly curious about his son's purpose in coming here, but Joanna was definitely uneasy. And Demetrios himself was evidently taken aback by his father's presence in her suite.

Yet, what had he expected? she asked herself a little wildly. Why did he think Constantine had brought her here, if not to enjoy her company? Surely he didn't think his father was too old to enjoy female companionship? And, most pertinently of all, what was he doing coming to her apartments uninvited? If anyone had any explaining to do, it was him.

CHAPTER TWO

'DEMETRI?'

His father was obviously waiting for an explanation, but right now Demetri didn't have one to give him. He was still stunned by the sight of his father's hands on Joanna Manning's hips. Brown hands, already showing the spots of age, were dark against the scarlet satin of her wrapper. A wrapper that he suspected was all she was wearing. *Khristo*, what had they been doing? Taking a shower together?

His imagination ran riot. He hadn't realised her hair would be so long, but she had evidently washed it and now it tumbled pale and silky about her shoulders. The scarlet wrapper, too, was unknowingly provocative, drawing his attention to the slender shapeliness of her body, outlining her hips and the long, long length of her legs.

To his disgust, his body stirred. He could feel his arousal pushing against the hand he'd thrust into his trouser pocket, and he quickly withdrew it. Then, angry at the immaturity of his reaction, he tried to pull himself together. His father was waiting for a reply and he had no wish for the old man to guess he was in any way attracted to his—he sought for a suitably insulting description—his paramour.

'I—good evening, Papa, Mrs Manning,' he essayed politely. 'I trust you have found everything to your satisfaction?'

His father's brows drew together. 'We have been here two days already, Demetri,' he reminded his son shortly. His hands fell away from Joanna's body. 'I cannot believe that concern for our welfare is the reason you have chosen to invade our privacy at this time.'

It wasn't, of course. But then, he hadn't expected to en-

16

counter his father at all. It was Mrs Manning he had come to see. He had hoped—rather foolishly, he acknowledged now—that they might have a few moments of private conversation before his father interrupted them.

'I—wanted to speak to you, Papa,' he said, improvising swiftly. And perhaps it was just as well that his father was here after all, he conceded. His reaction to this woman had been totally unexpected, and it would have been horribly embarrassing if Constantine had not been there and she had noticed his discomfort. *Theos!* The back of his neck was sweating. What the hell was the matter with him?

'And you surmised I would be here, with Joanna?'

His father was not a fool, and Demetri had to think fast to find an answer. 'I—tried your apartments, but could get no reply,' he muttered, hoping that Philip, his father's manservant, wouldn't contradict him. 'But it doesn't matter now. I can see you are—' the words almost stuck in his throat '—occupied with other things. It can wait until tomorrow.'

'I am sure it can.' Constantine was clearly waiting for him to leave, and Demetri permitted himself only a brief glance at Joanna before striding out of the room.

In the hall outside, Demetri paused for a moment, breathing deeply and running decidedly unsteady hands through the thickness of his hair. He felt unnerved, shaken, and although he knew he should get the hell away from there, he was strangely reluctant to do so. It felt as if the image of the two of them together was emblazoned on his memory, and he knew it was going to take more than the slamming of a door to get it out of his head. And how sensible was that?

He glanced back over his shoulder, half-afraid that he was being observed, but the door was still firmly closed and no sounds were audible from within. His father and his mistress had evidently resumed whatever it was they had been doing before his arrival, and he didn't need a crystal ball to guess what that was.

Na pari i oryi!

He swore silently, and then, gathering himself, strode back along the corridor to the galleried landing at the head of the stairs. He was going to have a great influence on his father's behaviour if he started lusting after Mrs Manning himself, he thought contemptuously. When had he begun thinking with his sex instead of with his head?

The salon had been cleared in his absence. The huge reception room, which had earlier been thronged with the guests his sister had invited to welcome his father home, was now restored to its usual appearance. The furniture, which had mostly been moved aside during the reception, had now been gathered into small groupings, with tall crystal vases and porcelain urns spilling glossy blossoms onto every available surface. The scent of the flowers was pungent, dispelling the smells of tobacco and stale perfume. Someone had turned up the air-conditioning so that the room was decidedly chilly, but he wished it was earlier in the year so that he could fold back the long glass doors that opened onto the floodlit terrace. It would have been nice to allow the soft evening air to cool his overheated senses, but that wasn't an option. At this time of the year there were too many insects flying about, and he didn't wish to be bitten half to death.

'Can I get you anything, sir?'

Demetri swung round to find a member of the household staff hovering behind him. He was tempted to order a bottle of Scotch and take himself off to the farthest corner of the estate and get thoroughly and disgustingly drunk. But he was not his father's son for nothing, and Kastros did not make fools of themselves, particularly not in front of the servants.

'Nothing, thanks,' he responded now, waving the man away. Then he flung himself down into a cream velvet armchair and stared broodingly out of the windows.

Spiro found him there perhaps ten minutes later. The lamplit room was shadowy, and Demetri had chosen to sit in the darkest corner, but Spiro's eyes were sharp. Like his employer, he, too, had changed for the evening, wearing a shirt and tie instead of the casual polo shirts he preferred.

'I believe your sister and the other guests who are staying for dinner have gathered in the library,' he said, advancing across the room. 'What are you doing in here? Sulking?'

'Watch your tongue,' said Demetri shortly, and Spiro arched a wounded brow.

'I gather you were sent away with your tail between your legs,' he observed, ignoring the reproof. 'What is the matter? Did she tell you she was playing for bigger stakes?'

'Do not be stupid!' Demetri placed his hands on the arms of the chair and pushed himself to his feet. He glanced around. 'Is there anything to drink in here?'

Spiro pushed his hands into his trouser pockets and swayed back on his heels, surveying the large room with a considering eye. 'It does not look like it,' he said. 'Why do we not join your father's guests? There is a bar in the library.'

'Thank you, I know that,' retorted Demetri, scowling. 'Look, why do you not go and join the party? I am—not in the mood for company.'

'Why not?'

'*Theos*, Spiro, mind your own damn business!' Demetri heaved a frustrated breath. 'You are not my keeper, you know.'

Spiro shrugged his shoulders. 'So you did lose out?'

'No!' Demetri stared at his friend with angry eyes. Then, when Spiro didn't back down, he gave a resigned shake of his head. 'All right. I did not even get to speak to her. No pain, no gain. Does that answer your question?'

'Not really.' Spiro waited. 'Was she not in her own apartments?'

'Oh, yes.' Demetri was sardonic. 'She was there. She just was not alone, that is all.'

Spiro's mouth formed a pronounced circle. 'Oh,' he said drily. 'Well, there is always tomorrow.'

'Yeah.' Demetri was ironic. 'And tomorrow and tomor-

row,' he acceded flatly. 'Come. Let us go and find a drink.
I do not want the old man to think I have got anything to
hide.'

'Do you think he has?'

'Who knows?' Demetri made a careless gesture. 'I wonder why he has brought her here.'

Spiro pulled a face. 'I think I can hazard a guess,' he
remarked, and Demetri gave him an impatient look.

'Yeah, right,' he said shortly. 'She is to be his guest at
Alex's wedding.' He frowned. 'I wonder where Mr Manning
is.'

'If there is a Mr Manning.'

'You think she is lying?'

'No.' Spiro shook his head. 'But she is not wearing a
ring. Do you think she is divorced?'

'Who knows?' Demetri was weary of the whole conversation. 'Rings do not mean a lot these days. Besides, what
does it signify? She is here. That is the only thing that matters.'

'Do you think their relationship is serious?'

Demetri was taken aback. 'Do you?'

'Perhaps.' Spiro looked pensive. 'Your father seems to
care about her. Do you not think so?'

Demetri scowled. 'So what are you saying? That he in-
tends to marry her?'

'Hardly that.' Spiro drew in a breath as they started towards the door. 'But serious illness can do strange things to
people, *filos mou*. Being reminded of your own mortality
can leave you with a desperate desire to embrace life.'

Demetri snorted. 'Since when did you become a philos-
opher?'

'I am just trying to be objective,' Spiro protested. 'And,
despite reports to the contrary, Mrs Manning does not give
me the impression that her relationship with your father is
purely for financial gain.'

'You feel you know her that well?' Demetri was scornful.

'No.' Spiro was defensive now. 'But I have been here

since yesterday, when they arrived. I have watched them together. And, if I was scrupulously honest, I would say that they have known one another a considerable length of time.'

'Have you known my father long?'

The question was asked by a slim dark woman, whose resemblance to her father was unmistakable. Constantine had told Joanna that Olivia, too, had married when she was nineteen. But the marriage hadn't lasted. In Constantine's opinion Olivia had been too spoilt, too headstrong, to submit to her ex-husband's needs. Within months of wedding Andrea Petrou she had returned to Theapolis, and since then she had shown no serious interest in any other man.

Joanna knew that Olivia was the eldest of Constantine's three children. At thirty-six, she considered herself the mistress of his house, which was perhaps why she was viewing Joanna with such suspicion. Maybe she saw the other woman as a challenge to her authority, and Joanna was glad that her ankle-length beaded sheath bore favourable comparison with the froth of chiffon that Olivia was wearing.

She had cornered Joanna beside the polished cabinets that housed her father's collection of snuffboxes. She had chosen her moment, and Joanna realised she had been a little foolish to walk away from Constantine and lay herself open to cross-examination.

'Quite long,' she responded now, directing her attention to the jewelled items that had drawn her across the room in the first place. She had delivered many of these boxes to Constantine herself, and it was fascinating to see them all together in the display case. Aware that Olivia was still beside her, she added, 'Aren't these beautiful?'

'Valuable, certainly,' said Olivia insolently. 'Are you interested in antiques, Mrs Manning?'

Joanna ignored the implication and, taking the woman's words at face value, she replied, 'I—I work with antiques, actually.' She paused. 'As a matter of fact, that is how I met your father.'

Olivia's thin brows elevated. 'Really?'

'Yes, really.' Joanna chose her words with care. 'I work for an auction house.'

'An auction house?' Olivia immediately picked up on the information. 'In London?'

'That's right.' Joanna allowed a little sigh to escape her. 'What do you do, Mrs Petrou?'

'What do I do?'

Olivia was clearly taken aback, but before she could say anything more her father came to join them. Slipping an arm about Joanna's waist, he said, 'Well, let me see: she is a fabulous dancer, an expert at water sports, and extremely good at spending money. My money,' he added drily. 'Is that not so, Livvy? Have I missed anything out?'

'Because you will not let me do anything else,' retorted Olivia shortly. Then, struggling to contain her anger, 'In any case, I do not think it is any of Mrs Manning's business.'

Joanna was unhappily aware that she had made another enemy. It was obvious that none of Constantine's offspring would blame *him* for his indiscretions. As far as they were concerned, she had instigated this whole affair.

Deciding there was nothing she could say which would placate Olivia, she turned to Constantine instead. 'How are you?' she asked, before he could remonstrate with his daughter. 'You're looking tired. Are you sure you wouldn't rather eat upstairs?'

'I am sure *you* would,' murmured Constantine, for her ears only. But, for all his attempt at humour, he was looking drained. The day had taken a toll on his depleted resources and he should have been resting. But she had always admired his strength of spirit, and he demonstrated it again now. 'How could I desert our guests? Besides, I am ready for my dinner,' he averred, his smile warm and enveloping. 'Are you?'

Knowing better than to argue with him, Joanna tucked her arm through his. 'Is it time to go in?'

'When I have finished this,' agreed Constantine, indicating the remnants of the spirit in his glass. He held the glass up to a nearby lamp. 'Do you know, you can only get real ouzo in Greece? I have tried it elsewhere, but it is never the same.'

'Ought you to be drinking alcohol, Papa?' Olivia had been observing their exchange in silence, but now she took his other arm. 'You have been ill, Papa. I worry about you.' She glanced disparagingly at Joanna. 'It is important that you do not overstretch your strength.'

Constantine's lips tightened. 'I am delighted that you are so concerned for my welfare, Livvy. But I am sure Demetri has told you I am very well. Besides, I have the beautiful Joanna to look after me. I have to tell you, she can be as strict as the most costly physician.'

And twice as expensive. Joanna could practically hear what Olivia was thinking, but she held her tongue. And then Demetrios entered the room, and his sister's eyes turned in his direction. Joanna grimaced. Was she conceivably going to be grateful to Constantine's son for diverting Olivia's attention from herself?

Spiro Stavros was with his employer. Both men were in their early thirties, but Spiro possessed none of Demetrios's brooding good looks. Nevertheless, they were both tall and powerfully built. But Joanna decided she preferred Spiro's open countenance to Demetrios's cold eyes and dark beauty.

Olivia left her father's side to greet her brother, and Constantine took the opportunity to speak privately to Joanna. 'Do not let anything Livvy or Demetri say upset you,' he murmured softly. 'They are curious, that is all. So long as you play your part, and do not allow anyone to coerce you into some unguarded admission, all will be well.'

Joanna wished she could feel as confident. She wasn't used to any of this, not to Constantine's wealth, or his in- fluence, or the feeling that every other person she met thought she was a fortune-hunter. She wasn't. She wasn't interested in Constantine's money. But she'd also realised that the doubts she'd had in England had been justified.

Indeed, they were rapidly developing into a full-blown belief that she shouldn't be here.

'Do you think they believe we're lovers?' she asked in a
low voice, and Constantine grinned with a little of his old
arrogance.

'Oh, yes. They believe it,' he said, permitting himself a
brief glance in his son's direction. 'And do you know what?'
He arched a teasing brow. 'I am beginning to enjoy it.'

Dinner was served in what Constantine told her was the
family dining salon, but it seemed awfully big to Joanna.
She was sure her whole apartment back in London would
have fitted into this one room, and she thought it was just
as well that the Greek islands didn't suffer the extremes of
temperature that England did. Heating this place would be
a nightmare, she reflected, glancing round the high-ceilinged
room with its imposing furniture and marble floor.

Last evening she and Constantine had dined in his suite,
and that hadn't been half so intimidating. Although it had
been her first evening, and the assiduous attention of the
servants had been a little unnerving, she had enjoyed the
meal. She had still been entranced by the beauty of her
surroundings, and she'd managed to persuade herself that
this wasn't going to be as bad as she'd thought.

How wrong she'd been!

Nevertheless, Olivia's claws had been sheathed at that
first meeting. With Alex away at her fiancé's home in
Athens, and Demetri meeting with bankers in Geneva,
Olivia had been alone and unprepared for Joanna's arrival.
Joanna had wondered if Constantine had really warned his
family of his guest's identity. He'd insisted he had, but
there'd been no doubt that Olivia had been shocked by their
relationship.

Joanna sighed. She had spent most of the day avoiding
the other woman's questions and now she had Demetrios to
contend with as well. She wondered if Constantine had realised how hostile his family would be. Despite his reassur-

ances about Alex, she thought that was little consolation now.

The food, as she'd already discovered, was exquisitely prepared. There were *dolmades*—lamb and spiced rice wrapped in vine leaves, and *souvlakia*—which were tiny chunks of pork grilled on skewers. There were tomatoes stuffed with goat's cheese, cold meats and salads, and retsina, the clean aromatic wine of the region, which was flavoured with pine resin and was, to Joanna, an acquired taste.

As well as Constantine's son and daughter, and Spiro Stavros, of course, they were joined at the table by three other people. They were Nikolas Poros and his wife, who Constantine had introduced her to earlier, and an old uncle of Constantine's second wife, who also lived at the villa. Panos Petronides was in his eighties, but he seemed years younger. He was still as alert and spry as he'd been when he'd first left his native Salonika.

Conversation during the meal was, to Joanna's relief, sporadic. She suspected that for all his assertions to the contrary Constantine was tired, and she found herself watching him anxiously, ready for any sign that he needed to escape. Demetrios had been more right than he knew when he'd questioned his father's return to the island. Constantine was very weak, and Joanna hoped he could keep up the pretence until the wedding was over.

Coffee, strong and black, was served in the adjoining drawing room. Joanna had hoped that Constantine might make their excuses and allow them both to escape to their own apartments. But, instead, he settled himself on a silk-cushioned sofa, drawing her down beside him to prevent Olivia from taking her place.

He indicated the silver dishes of sticky sugar-coated pastries on the low table close by. 'Please,' he said. 'Help yourself.'

Joanna, who had eaten little of her dinner, shook her head. 'I don't want anything else,' she said, aware of Demetrios hovering close by, ostensibly studying the rich desserts. She waited until he had chosen a cheese-filled pastry dusted with cinnamon sugar and then retired to the nearest armchair before she felt able to continue. 'May I get you something instead?'

'Not to eat,' murmured Constantine archly, provoking a scowling look from his son. Then, to Demetrios, 'We will talk in the morning. You can brief me on all that has happened since I have been away. For instance, I understand from Nikolas Poros that two of our tankers are lying idle at Piraeus. I hope you have an explanation for that.'

'They are not lying idle,' retorted Demetrios, hot colour filling his angry face. 'Did not Poros explain that—?'

'Tomorrow, Demetri,' said his father finally. Then, to Joanna's relief, he turned to her. 'I am a little tired, *agapi mou*. Are you finished?'

'I—yes, of course.'

'But surely you are not going to deprive us of Mrs Manning's company also?' Demetrios broke in, earning his father's displeasure yet again. Joanna felt Constantine stiffen beside her.

'You have something else in mind, *agori*?' he asked, and Demetrios offered a courteous smile.

'I wondered if Mrs Manning might enjoy a stroll in the gardens,' he suggested mildly, but Joanna detected the look that passed between him and Spiro Stavros as he spoke. 'I believe the English are very fond of gardening. Am I not right, Mrs Manning?'

'I'm afraid I live in a high-rise, Mr Kastro,' Joanna returned carefully, but Constantine intervened before she could say anything more.

'Joanna is tired, too,' he declared, but Demetrios was determined to have the last word.

'Are you sure, Papa? Dare I say it? She is—considerably younger than you are.'

'You overstep yourself, Demetri.' There was no mistaking Constantine's anger now, and Joanna wished she could warn the younger man to back off.

'Perhaps you should let Mrs Manning decide for herself,' he persisted smoothly, and Joanna heaved a heavy sigh.

'I fear your father is right,' she told him coolly, aware that he probably thought she was taking the easy way out. 'I am tired. It has been a—demanding day.'

Demetrios's lips twisted. 'I am sure it must have been,' he remarked, and although his words were polite enough his meaning was plain. He got abruptly to his feet. 'Then, if you will excuse me...' And without waiting for his father's permission he stalked out of the room.

CHAPTER THREE

DESPITE the heat in the early-morning air, the pool was cold. Later in the day, when the sun had done its work, the temperature of the water would rise. But right now it was decidedly chilly, and Demetri welcomed its cooling surge against his hot skin.

He had not slept well. Indeed, he had slept exceedingly badly, tormented by dreams the nature of which he preferred not to dwell on now that he was awake. In fact, he was frustrated by his own inability to control his subconscious mind, and only several vigorous lengths of the pool offered some escape from his tortured senses.

He swam swiftly from one end of the pool to the other, somersaulting beneath the surface to swim back underwater. He broke through the waves his body had created, desperate for air, and then saw that he was no longer alone.

A woman had emerged from the villa. She hadn't seen him. It was obvious from the unhurried way she crossed the sun-splashed patio to rest her hands on the terrace wall. Obvious, too, from the uninhibited way she tilted back her head and allowed the sun to kiss those pale exquisite features.

She thought she was alone, and Demetri felt a momentary pang of shame in observing her this way. But dammit, he thought, he had more right to be here than she had, and it wasn't his fault if she didn't have the sense to ensure she was on her own before behaving like a pagan goddess, worshipping the dawn.

She was beautiful, though. Given this opportunity to study her without her knowledge, Demetri had to admit he understood his father's fascination. She was wearing a sleeveless vest this morning, something soft and silky that clung to her rounded breasts with a loving attention to detail. He caught his breath as she cupped her ribcage and arched her back, driving her taut nipples against the thin fabric. A loosely tied sarong circled her waist, a transparent thing of purples and greens that exposed the bikini briefs she wore beneath. It parted to reveal the slender length of her legs, and, despite the coolness of the water, Demetri felt himself harden.

Theos! He was like a callow youth, he thought exasperatedly. She was beautiful, yes, but he'd seen beautiful women before. He hadn't reached the mature age of thirty-four without making love to a number of them, too, and it irritated the hell out of him that he desired *this* woman, his father's mistress.

She was sliding her fingers into her hair now, scooping its loosened weight back from her face and winding it into a coil on top of her head. Soft tendrils tumbled from the impromptu knot, spiralling down against cheeks that were as smooth and velvety soft as a peach. Realising he couldn't stand much more of this without disgracing himself completely, Demetri sprang out of the water and grabbed a towel to wrap protectively about his hips.

She heard him, of course. Although the ocean surged constantly onto the beach only a couple of hundred yards from the villa it was a muted sound, heavy and rhythmic. His vaulting out of the pool was a much more abrasive sound, and she swung round almost guiltily to confront him.

'Oh...' She was clearly taken aback by his sudden appearance. 'Um—Mr Kastro. I didn't see you there.'

'No.' Demetri acknowledged the fact, and, accepting that they couldn't go on addressing each other across the width of the terrace, he pushed his damp feet into his deck shoes and walked towards her. 'Did you sleep well?'

She managed a faint smile. 'Like you care,' she said drily, and he admired her courage. 'Did you?'

Demetri shrugged his bare shoulders. 'Not very,' he conceded, just as candidly. Then, dragging his eyes back to her face, 'Where is my father?'

'Where do you think he is at this hour of the morning?' she asked, a delicate flush invading her cheeks. 'He's still in bed.' She paused a moment and then added significantly, 'Asleep.'

Demetri's mouth compressed. 'So, what are you doing up so early? Or is this your only chance to escape?'

'To escape?' Her blue eyes flashed with anger. 'To escape from what, Mr Kastro? Your father and I have a perfect understanding.'

'Do you?' Demetri was annoyed to find he half believed her. But he couldn't let her know it. 'That must be very convenient for both of you.'

'It is.' She turned away from him then, bracing her hands on the terrace wall again and gazing purposefully out to sea. 'Oughtn't you to go and get some clothes on, Mr Kastro? I shouldn't like you to catch a chill.'

'Oh, I am sure you would,' he corrected her, making no move to go back into the villa. 'But I would hate to waste this opportunity for us to get to know one another better.'

'We don't need to get to know one another better, Mr Kastro,' she retorted, and although she wasn't looking at him he could see the tension in the slender cords of her neck.

'Well, there, you see, you are wrong,' he argued softly, resisting the temptation to run his finger along the sensitive curve of her nape. He drew a steadying breath. 'And I think we can dispense with formality, no?'

She licked her lips then, and his stomach twisted with sudden emotion. *Theos*, he thought, the intensity of his reaction reminding him that he was playing with fire here. Why was he persisting with this? It was his father he should be harassing, not her.

'What formality are you talking about?' she asked now, and he had to concentrate hard to remember what he'd said.

'I—think you should call me Demetri,' he essayed at last,

congratulating himself on his memory. 'May I call you Joanna?'

Her lips were pressed together when she turned to give him a doubtful look, and Demetri guessed she had expected some kind of accusation. Long lashes, several shades darker than her hair, shaded her expression, however, and instead of feeling any sense of triumph Demetri found himself imagining how they would feel against his lips. He wanted to kiss her, he realised suddenly. He wanted to press that slim luscious body against his own and ease his aching need between her legs…

'I don't think that's a very good idea, Mr Kastro,' she said, and his arousal abruptly deflated. 'You don't like me, so why pretend you want to get to know me?'

Why indeed?

'Because I do,' he insisted, deciding that he had nothing more to lose. 'Why are you so afraid to talk to me?' His dark brows elevated. 'I am not so terrifying, am I?'

She turned then, resting her hips on the low wall behind her and folding her arms across her midriff. 'I am not afraid to talk to you, Mr Kastro,' she said, and once again he had to admire her spirit. 'What do you want to talk about?'

Demetri's hair was dripping onto his neck and he lifted one hand to wipe the moisture from his nape. He refused to accept that it was done to buy himself a little time, but there was no doubt that she had caught him off guard.

'*Entaxi.*' It was an indication of his state of mind that had him lapsing into his own language for the exclamation. 'All right. Tell me how you met my father?'

There was a perceptible hesitation when that tempting tongue appeared again, and then she seemed to straighten her spine before saying slowly, 'We met in London.'

Demetri gave her a dry look. 'Yes. I had gathered that.' He paused. 'I asked how you met my father, Mrs Manning. Not where.'

She looked down at her feet then, and Demetri found himself doing the same, watching as she crossed one slim bare foot over the other. Until then he hadn't realised she wasn't wearing any shoes, and there was something infinitely sensuous about the way she rubbed the sole of one foot across the arch of the other.

To distract himself, he spoke again, his words a little harsh as he struggled to sustain his composure. 'Were you his nurse?'

'His nurse?' She smiled then, and he was treated to the sight of a row of almost perfect white teeth. 'Heavens, no!'

'What, then?' Demetri was impatient at the way she could apparently best him at every turn. 'His doctor?'

She shook her head, and her hair dipped confidingly over one shoulder. 'I am not a member of the medical profession, Mr Kastro.'

Demetri's nostrils flared. 'Do not play with me, Mrs Manning. You might just get more than you—what is the expression you use?—bargained for, no?'

Her smile disappeared. 'I wouldn't dream of playing with you, Mr Kastro,' she declared coolly. 'I just wonder why you are so interested in what I do for a living.'

'I am not.' But he was and she knew it, damn her. 'I am merely curious to know how a man who has spent the last two weeks in hospital could have acquired such a—close relationship with a woman his family knew nothing about.'

She took a deep breath. 'As you say, your father has been in hospital.'

'Where I visited him,' put in Demetri shortly. 'On more than one occasion. Yet he apparently chose not to mention your existence to me.'

Her slim shoulders lifted. 'I suppose he preferred to wait until we could be introduced.'

'You are prevaricating again, Mrs Manning.' Demetri's temper was slipping. 'I suggest that, far from knowing my father for some considerable time, as you told Livvy, yours has been what a kinder person might call a whirlwind romance, no?'

'No.' She was angry now. 'What I told your sister was—

is true. I work—I have worked—for Bartholomew's for several years. They're—'

'One of the foremost auction houses in London,' Demetri inserted tersely. 'I have heard of Bartholomew's, Mrs Manning.'

'Good.' Her eyes challenged his. 'As you're aware, your father is a keen collector of antique snuffboxes. He has been a regular customer there for many years.'

Demetri was stunned. He was ashamed to admit that, because of her beauty, he'd been inclined to dismiss her as an airhead. Now, learning that she had a career far removed from any cosmetic pursuit disturbed him more than he cared to admit. It also made her relationship with his father that much more serious somehow.

'And now, if you'll excuse me...'

She was leaving him, and Demetri could no longer think of an excuse to keep her there. But what troubled him most was that he should want to do so, and he abruptly stepped aside, opening her path to the villa.

'Until later,' he said, but she didn't answer him. If he hadn't known better he'd have said she was trembling with apprehension. Only it wasn't apprehension, it was rage.

Joanna made it to her apartments before she gave in to the fit of shaking that had threatened her downstairs. Dear Lord, she thought, she would never have ventured outdoors if she'd even suspected she might run into Demetrios Kastro on the patio. A naked Demetrios Kastro, moreover. Her mouth dried again at the thought.

But she'd looked over her balcony and there'd appeared to be no one about. Oh, she'd seen a couple of men working in the gardens, and a youth of perhaps fifteen sweeping the steps. Yet even he had disappeared by the time she'd stepped out of the villa, and she'd walked to the boundary wall with the first feeling of freedom she'd had since coming here.

And the view was so beautiful. Acres of flower-filled gardens falling away into dunes of sun-bleached sand. A wooden jetty pointed into the blue-green waters of the Aegean, a two-masted schooner bobbing at anchor, all gleaming steel and polished teak. A millionaire's plaything in a million-dollar setting.

Then Demetrios had emerged from the pool and everything had changed. Her sense of wellbeing had vanished, replaced by the tension that man always evoked. She'd known him for less than twenty-four hours, yet he'd already succeeded in setting her nerves on edge whenever he was near. She had the feeling he looked at her and saw right through her. He didn't like her: that much was obvious. But, more than that, he despised her for what he thought she was doing with his father.

Now Joanna wrapped her arms about herself and crossed the room to the windows. Despite her revulsion for the man, she felt compelled to see if he was still enjoying his swim. She had only interrupted his pleasure. He had destroyed hers.

But the pool was empty. Although she waited half apprehensively to see if he was briefly out of sight, hidden by the lip of the deck, he didn't appear. The water was as smooth and unbroken as a mirror, reflecting only the sunlight and the waving palms that grew close by.

Stepping back into the room again, she looked bleakly about her. And then, annoyed that she had let Demetrios sour her mood, she walked through the bedroom and into the adjoining bathroom.

She felt a little better after a shower. The cool water had washed away the perspiration that had dried on her skin, and she felt more ready to face the day. Constantine had said he would take her to the small town of Agios Antonis this morning, and she was looking forward to seeing a little more of the island. Since their arrival two days ago they had spent all their time at the villa. Constantine had been weary after the flight from London, and yesterday he had had the reception Olivia had organised to contend with.

Joanna knew he would have much preferred to stagger the celebrations for his homecoming, but Constantine hadn't wanted to disappoint his elder daughter. Besides, until his younger daughter's wedding was over he didn't intend to discuss his illness with any of his family.

Joanna finished drying her hair and paused on the threshold of the dressing room that was next to the bathroom. Floor-to-ceiling closets lined two of the walls, but the clothes she had brought with her looked lost in their cavernous depths.

Nevertheless, Constantine had insisted on equipping her with several new outfits for the trip to Theapolis. And, although Joanna still felt slightly uncomfortable about that arrangement, she had to admit that the clothes she usually favoured would not have borne comparison with the designer fashions she had seen since their arrival.

The fact that she normally shunned anything that emphasised her femininity had not been lost on Constantine. And, despite the fact that he respected her preference for severe skirt- and trouser-suits, he had persuaded her that they would definitely look out of place in the hot dry climate of the island in late summer.

Besides, they would have detracted from the image he wanted her to present. It was because she could do what he asked that he'd chosen her, and in the circumstances Joanna had been unable to refuse.

Perhaps she'd wanted to do it for her own sake, she reflected, riffling through the rail of expensive garments, all of which were designed to inspire and provoke masculine attention. Flimsy shirts and tight-fitting basques; low-cut bodices and clinging skirts; hems slashed to expose her legs from thigh to hip—items that until two weeks ago she'd have avoided like the plague.

But it hadn't always been so. Once she would have revelled in their style and beauty. Oh, she had never owned anything too revealing, but she had appreciated her own body and dressed in a way to make the most of her assets.

She'd spent so many years believing she was worthless that when the opportunity had come to make the most of her appearance, she'd taken it. She'd wanted to be admired. She'd wanted to know the thrill of feeling beautiful.

And then she'd met Richard Manning...

But she didn't want to think about Richard now. He was history. He'd hurt and humiliated her for the last time. But perhaps by downplaying her looks she'd been subconsciously denying their relationship. Maybe it was time to come out of her shell.

She viewed her appearance cautiously when she was ready. It would take some time before she was able to look at herself with uncritical eyes, and although the lime-green crêpe shell and cream silk shorts were very flattering, she couldn't get used to exposing such a length of thigh. Still, she was sure Constantine would approve and, for the present, that was all that mattered.

Which reminded her—where was Constantine? He had said he would order breakfast to be served on the balcony again, as he had done the previous morning, but when she stepped outside again there was still no one about. The wrought-iron table wasn't even laid, and she knew a moment's apprehension. What was going on? Surely Demetrios hadn't delayed him. His son had been eager to speak to him, it was true, but all the same...

Turning back into the room, she crossed to the connecting doors and tapped lightly on the panels. It was the first time she had had to initiate their meeting, and she felt a little awkward when Philip, Constantine's valet, opened the door.

'*Kalimera*, Kiria Manning.' The man greeted her politely enough, though she sensed a certain reserve in his manner. '*Boro na sas voithisso?*'

Joanna contained her impatience. Constantine had told his valet that she didn't understand his language, and therefore the man's behaviour was a deliberate attempt to disconcert her.

However, she had taken the precaution of learning one

phrase, and with smiling courtesy she said, 'Then *katalav-eno,*' which she knew meant, I don't understand. '*Signomi.*' Sorry.

Philip's thin lips tightened. He was a man in his late fifties, who Constantine had said had been with him for more than thirty years. Gaunt and unsmiling, he was the exact opposite of Joanna's idea of a genial manservant, his only concession to vanity the luxuriant black moustache that coated his upper lip.

'*Kirie* Kastro is not— up, *kiria,*' he said at last, in a thick barely comprehensible accent. '*Then sikothikeh akomi.*'

Joanna frowned, looking beyond him into the living area of Constantine's suite. The door to the bedroom was ajar, but she couldn't see into the room, and she could only take Philip's word that Constantine was still in bed.

'Is he all right?' she asked, not much caring if the valet cared to stand here trading information with her. 'Can I see him?'

'I do not think—'

'*Pios ineh*, Philip?' Who is it?

Constantine's voice was frail, but he had obviously deduced that the manservant was talking to someone, and, ignoring Philip's attempt to bar her way, Joanna sidestepped him into the apartment. 'It's me, Constantine,' she called, crossing the floor to the bedroom door. 'Can I come in?'

'Please…'

Constantine showed no reservations about inviting her into his room. And why should he? she asked herself drily. When they were deemed to be lovers.

All the same, she halted in the doorway of the huge, distinctly masculine chamber, briefly shocked by his appearance. Constantine was lying propped against the pillows of the massive bed, his face as white as the linen sheets that covered him from chest to foot. Brown hands, slightly gnarled with veins, were a stark contrast to the bedlinen, his nails scraping against the fabric in a mute display of frustration.

'Come—come in,' he said weakly, lifting his hand to point at the tapestry-covered chair beside the bed. 'Do not look like that, *aghapitos*. I am not dying yet.'

Joanna came swiftly to the bed, but she didn't sit in the chair he'd indicated. Instead, she edged her hip onto the bed beside him, taking one of his hands between both of hers and gazing down at him with troubled eyes. 'Don't even suggest such a thing,' she reproved him sharply. Then, hesitatingly, 'Have you sent for a doctor?'

'What can a doctor do for me?' Constantine was dismissive. 'I am already sick of the cocktail of drugs I am forced to swallow every day, without inviting a handful more. No, Joanna, I have not sent for a doctor. A few hours' rest is all I need. Will you tell Demetri and Olivia that I am being lazy this morning?'

Joanna sighed. 'Shouldn't you tell them yourself?'

'And have them see me like this?' Constantine moved his head from side to side on the pillows. 'I know what they are like, Joanna. I would have no choice in the matter. Demetri would have Tsikas here immediately, and it is totally unnecessary.'

'Tsikas?' Joanna frowned. 'I assume he is your doctor.'

'He is the island doctor, yes,' agreed Constantine wearily. 'Look, Joanna, I do not wish to worry anyone. Livvy has enough to worry about, making the final preparations for Alex's wedding, and Demetri is already working flat out, trying to cope with my work as well as his own. Let him go on thinking that I am waiting for his explanation as to why two of my ships are not making me any money. Do not, I beg of you, put any doubts in their minds.'

Joanna shook her head. 'I don't think they'll like me making your excuses,' she said unhappily. 'But I take your point about worrying them unnecessarily. If it is unnecessarily,' she added doubtfully.

'It is.' Constantine was determined. 'You can tell Demetri I will speak with him this afternoon. I have taken my medication and in a few hours I should be as good as new.'

You wish, thought Joanna uneasily, but she knew better than to argue with him. Despite his physical weakness, Constantine's will was as strong as ever.

'All right?' he prompted when she didn't say anything, and Joanna gave a resigned shrug of her shoulders.

'I'll do what I can,' she promised, not looking forward to telling either of the Kastro offspring what their father had said. 'Now, get some rest, hmm?' She bent to bestow a warm kiss on his dry cheek. 'I'll come back at lunchtime to see how you are.'

Constantine nodded. 'We will have lunch together,' he said, patting her cheek. 'Oh, Joanna, how I wish I were twenty years younger. I would not be lying here like a beached whale while the woman I admire above all others was spending her time with my son instead of me.'

Joanna smiled, but as she got up from the bed she couldn't help thinking she'd bitten off more than she could chew by coming here. Yes, she cared about Constantine. Yes, it was easy to spend time with him. But dealing with his immediate family was another thing altogether. She supposed she had been naïve in imagining that they might welcome her into their midst, but she certainly hadn't expected them to be so openly hostile.

Though hostility was not what she had initially felt when Demetrios had surprised her on the terrace that morning. When he'd wrapped a towel about his nakedness—and she was pretty sure he had been swimming in the nude—and walked towards her, she'd felt a most unhostile surge of emotion. Indeed, for the first time in years she'd been physically aroused by a man's body. And although she'd later dismissed it as an aberration, now, faced with the prospect of confronting him again, Joanna knew she was apprehensive of the effect he had on her.

Philip was waiting for her outside the bedroom door. She wouldn't have been surprised if she'd discovered him with his ear pressed to the panels, but her exit had been sufficiently telegraphed to allow him time to move away.

'Mr Kastro is going to rest this morning,' she said coolly, deciding she was going to take no guff from him. 'I'll come back at one o'clock. Perhaps you'd ask the housekeeper to serve a light lunch on the balcony.'

Philip gave her a mutinous look. 'For one, *kiria*?'

'No, for two.'

She managed to keep her cool, but Philip wasn't finished yet. 'What would you like?' he asked, probably knowing full well that Joanna wasn't familiar with Greek food.

But she refused to let him confuse her. 'I suggest an omelette and some salad,' she answered sweetly. 'Mr Kastro is very fond of omelettes, you know?'

'*Veveha, kiria.* I know,' he muttered, as she headed towards her own rooms, and Joanna breathed a sigh of triumph as she closed the connecting doors behind her.

CHAPTER FOUR

DEMETRI was having breakfast on the terrace when Joanna appeared. At this hour of the morning the air outdoors was extremely pleasant, and the view from this elevated position never failed to lift his spirits.

And they'd needed lifting, he conceded grimly, picking at a currant-filled roll between generous gulps of the strong black coffee he favoured. His earlier encounter with his father's mistress had left him feeling piqued and morose. And provoked; definitely provoked. Though not in any way he wanted to acknowledge.

Now here she was again, slim and alluring in a sleeveless top and clinging silk shorts which had surely not come off the peg in some downtown department store. Her legs were bare and her glorious mane of hair had been secured in one of those loose knots atop her head. Strands of white-gold escaped to caress her cheeks, and although when she saw him she made a half-hearted effort to tuck them back behind her ears, they refused to be tamed.

Oh, she was beautiful, he thought bitterly, forced to push back his chair and get to his feet as she came towards him. But what the hell was she doing with his father? He simply didn't buy into May and December love affairs. She wanted something from this relationship, and he'd swear on a stack of Bibles that it wasn't sex.

The morning mail had been spread out on the table in front of him, but he shuffled it together at her approach. He guessed his father wouldn't be far behind her, and the last thing he wanted to do was talk about private business matters with her present.

He was pleased to see that she wasn't wholly relaxed

41

about meeting him again. He wondered if she'd told Constantine about seeing him earlier that morning. If she had, he could probably look forward to his father's displeasure as well. Particularly if she'd mentioned that he'd been swimming in the nude.

Perhaps she hadn't noticed. After all, she hadn't noticed he was there at all until he'd vaulted out of the pool. Thank heaven for towels, he reflected drily. They could hide a multitude of sins.

'Mrs Manning,' he greeted her politely, inclining his head, and she managed a faint smile in return. But she was definitely antsy, and he decided to take pity on her. 'Are you and my father joining me for breakfast?'

'No,' Her denial was swift. But then, as if realising she had been a little hasty, she added, 'That is, your father won't be joining us.'

'Why not?' Demetri's eyes moved past her almost accusingly. 'Is something wrong?'

'He's—tired, that's all,' she told him quietly, apparently not knowing what to do with her hands. She finally folded them together over her midriff, inadvertently drawing his attention to the narrow strip of pale flesh exposed between her top and her shorts. 'He asked me to tell you he'll see you later today.'

Demetri's jaw clenched. He wasn't used to being given news about his father from a third party. He'd had to comply while his father was in the hospital, but being given information by a doctor was vastly different from hearing it from her.

'Are you sure you are telling me everything?' he asked, regarding her from beneath lowered lids, and he felt rather than saw the quiver of emotion that rippled over her at his question.

But, 'Of course,' she said quickly. Then, to his surprise, 'May I join you?'

Demetri frowned. 'Please,' he said without expression, but his thoughts were busy as she hurriedly seated herself in the chair across the table from his own. Was it only his imagination, or was this a deliberate attempt to divert him? He subsided again into his own chair. 'Have you eaten?'

'I—no.' She moistened her lips. 'But I'm not hungry. Perhaps I could have some coffee—'

She broke off as a white-aproned maid appeared at Demetri's elbow. The girl—for she was little more—gave her employer's son a proprietary smile before saying in their own language, 'Can I get you anything else, *kirie*?'

Demetri hesitated. And then, deciding that Mrs Manning couldn't be allowed to starve, he replied, 'Yes. Some toast and coffee for my guest, if you will? Thank you.'

The maid withdrew and Demetri, feeling a little more in command, lay back in his chair. *'Tora,'* he said pleasantly, 'perhaps you will now explain to me why my father is really not joining us for breakfast.'

A hint of colour entered her face. 'I've told you—'

'No.' His denial was soft but implacable. 'You have told me nothing. Are you saying he is not well enough to get out of bed?'

Her cheeks were definitely pink now. 'He said to tell you he was going to be lazy this morning,' she insisted. 'I've explained that he's feeling tired. The journey from England, yesterday's reception, and then dinner last night. He's not used to so much activity. Not—not all at once.'

'And entertaining a much younger woman?' suggested Demetri dangerously. 'Let us not forget your role in his recovery—or lack thereof. Whatever. Perhaps you are tiring him out, Mrs Manning.'

His words were unforgivable, and he knew a moment's remorse at his own cruelty. He had no excuse for blaming her for his father's weakness. Cancer didn't discriminate between its victims, and he should be grateful that she had brought the old man some comfort during his convalescence. Grateful, too, that to all intents and purposes his father had beaten the disease. And who knew that she hadn't had some part in that, as well?

Nevertheless, he despised himself for the sudden sympathy he felt when she turned her face away, blinking rapidly. She could be acting, of course, but he suspected he had upset her, and common sense told him that that was not the wisest thing to do. He had told Spiro he would handle this with kid gloves, but instead he was trampling finer feelings underfoot.

The return of the maid put an end to his self-admonishment. And if Joanna had been thinking of walking out on him, her actions were baulked by the serving woman setting a steaming pot of coffee and a linen-wrapped basket of toast at her elbow.

'Afto ineh entaxi, kirie?' Is that all right? the maid asked, looking at Demetri, and he drew a deep breath.

'Ineh mia khara, efkharisto.' It's fine, thanks, he responded, but Joanna was looking at him now, and she looked anything but pleased.

'Did you order this?' she demanded, uncaring that the maid was still standing beside the table, clearly understanding the tone of her voice, if not the words.

Demetri wasn't used to being embarrassed in front of his staff, and a muscle in his jaw jerked spasmodically as he strove to hide his anger. 'You have to eat something, Mrs Manning,' he said, aware that he no longer thought of her that way. Her first name was becoming far more familiar to him, and that was dangerous. *'Efkharisto*, Pilar. You may leave us.'

A gesture of his hand sent the young maid scurrying back into the villa, but he was going to have no such swift compliance from Joanna. 'I said I only wanted coffee,' she said, her blue eyes glittering now, her earlier emotion banished by a surge of indignation. 'I am not hungry, Mr Kastro. In fact, I can't think of anything I'd like less than sharing a meal with you!'

Demetri was outraged. 'You asked if you could join *me*, Mrs Manning,' he reminded her harshly, and her lips twisted in sudden distaste.

'That was a mistake,' she informed him, reaching for the pot of coffee and pouring herself a cup. Her hand was unsteady, he noticed, but he got little satisfaction from it. 'It was before I realised what a small-minded, selfish boor you are!'

Her voice was shaking by the time she'd finished, but with an admirable dignity she got to her feet. Then, picking up her coffee cup, she turned away, evidently intending to drink it in more congenial surroundings.

'Wait!' Despite the resentment he was feeling, Demetri was loath to let her go like this. '*Signomi,*' he said through clenched teeth. 'I am sorry. I did not mean to offend you.'

'No?' She'd paused, regarding him with scornful eyes. 'You virtually accuse me of exhausting your father with my demands and then try to tell me you didn't mean to offend me? Come on, Mr Kastro. Surely you can do better than that?'

Demetri breathed deeply. 'I spoke—without thinking,' he declared, but he could see from her expression that she didn't believe him.

'On the contrary,' she said, 'I think you knew exactly what you were saying. You might wish you hadn't exposed your feelings quite so openly, but that's all. Don't worry, Mr Kastro. I shan't tell your father what you said. I, at least, have more respect for him than that.'

She would have turned away then, but he moved swiftly round the table to detain her. 'All right,' he said tersely, aware that she was looking up at him now with a certain amount of apprehension. 'All right. You are right and I am wrong. It was a deliberate attempt to provoke you.' He paused. 'But, *Theos*, Joanna, you cannot have expected to come here without arousing some resentment.'

'Why not?' She blinked, and then said faintly, 'You called me Joanna. Was that another mistake?'

Demetri stifled an oath. 'No,' he said impatiently. Then, wearily, 'You must surely see that it is ludicrous for us to call one another Mrs Manning and Mr Kastro? My name is

Demetri. Only my enemies call me Demetrios. And if we are to come to any kind of an understanding we should perhaps try and be civil with one another.'

Joanna hesitated. 'I notice you didn't suggest that we might be friends,' she remarked drily, but she was definitely thawing.

'Let us take each day at a time,' Demetri ventured, gesturing towards the breakfast table. 'Please. Will you sit with me?' He paused, and then added ruefully, 'My coffee is getting cold.'

She was reluctant, but her obvious desire to be accepted by her lover's family seemed to persuade her to give him a second chance. For his part, Demetri was grateful to have avoided an open rift between them. Despite the fact that even the thought of this woman and his father sharing a bed together filled him with revulsion, until he knew how much influence she had over the old man he would be wise not to make an enemy of her.

As if you could, a small voice inside him mocked contemptuously. Even knowing who she was and what she was doing didn't seem to make a scrap of difference to the unholy feelings she aroused inside him. However unscrupulous she might be, he wanted her. And that was something else he intended to change.

But, for now, she'd seated herself again and he was obliged to do the same. And there was no doubt that in other circumstances he would have enjoyed her company. She was good to look at, she made no demands on him, and her slightly husky voice gave everything she said a sensual intonation.

'This is a beautiful place,' she murmured after a few moments, and, acknowledging her effort to behave naturally, he gave a nod of assent.

'Beautiful, yes,' he agreed, his eyes lingering on her delicate profile. And then, when she sensed his regard and turned to look at him, 'My father built this house twenty-five years ago.'

'Twenty-five years?' She arched brows that were much darker than her hair. 'He must love the island very much.'

'It is where he was born,' remarked Demetri simply. 'Did he not tell you that?'

'No.' She bent her head to study the coffee in her cup. 'I suppose I assumed he'd been born in Athens.'

'Because his business was established there?'

'Maybe.'

'Or perhaps you think that Theapolis seems an unlikely place for a successful man to have his roots?'

Joanna looked up, her clear eyes mirroring a faint suspicion that his question hadn't been entirely innocent. 'We all have our roots somewhere, Mr—Demetri.' She paused. 'Even you.'

'And where are your roots, Joanna? London?'

'England, certainly,' she said evenly. Then, when he showed he expected her to go on, 'Actually, I was born in Norfolk. But my parents were killed in an accident when I was quite young and an elderly relative brought me up.'

He was surprised. Somehow he'd expected her to have a different background. Or was he only painting her with the brittle strokes of sophistication because it made it that much easier to despise her?

'Were you born on the island, too?' she asked, when he didn't say anything, and Demetri gathered his thoughts.

'No,' he conceded flatly. 'I was born in Athens. Olivia and me both. My younger sister, Alex, is the only one of us who was born here.'

She inclined her head. 'Alex,' she said thoughtfully. 'I haven't met her yet.' She waited a beat. 'Is she like you?'

Demetri's eyes narrowed. 'In what way? In looks? In temperament?'

'I suppose I meant, is she likely to resent me, too?' observed Joanna quietly. 'What are you afraid of, Demetri? I mean your father no harm.'

He was taken aback. He had never expected her to broach her relationship with his father so openly. But perhaps he had been naïve in thinking he was in control. After all, he had always believed his father to be a shrewd judge of character, yet he had apparently been attracted to her. She had infatuated him. Why should he be any different?

But he was!

'I do not know what you mean, Joanna,' he said now, his smile as guileless as his words. 'I understood we were to attempt a reconciliation.'

'A reconciliation—or an inquisition?' she demanded shortly. 'Why don't you come right out and ask me what you want to know?'

Demetri's lips twitched with reluctant amusement. 'I thought I was,' he admitted. Then, dispassionately, 'As to your enquiry about Alex, I think you will like her. She is nothing like Olivia, if that answers your question.'

'And you?'

'Me?' He pushed his cup aside and lay back in his chair. 'Modesty prevents me from making any comparisons.'

'Really?'

Joanna was sceptical, and he felt a momentary dislike of his own duplicity. What he would have really liked to do today was to go sailing and escape the machinations of both his father and his mistress. It was weeks, *months*, since he had had a completely free day, and although he knew he was being selfish in thinking this way when his father had been so ill, he was only human.

His eyes were drawn towards the jetty where the sailboat rocked at anchor and, as if sensing his frustration, Joanna murmured, 'Whose boat is that?' in a different, gentler tone.

'She is mine,' Demetri responded, with some satisfaction. 'The *Circe*. She is a two-masted schooner, but one person can handle her with ease.'

'And you do?' she prompted, and he was aware of her eyes on him rather than the yacht.

'When I can,' he conceded, turning to meet her gaze and surprising a faintly envious expression on her face. He considered for a moment, and then added, 'Do you sail?'

'Unfortunately not.' Her eyes moved to the sailboat again. 'I envy you. Where I used to live when I was young, people sailed dinghies. Nothing as sophisticated as your boat, of course. But it looked fun.'

'The Broads,' he said, after a moment, and she was startled into looking at him again.

'You know Norfolk?'

'I spent a year backpacking around Europe,' he told her lightly. 'Naturally I spent some time in England. Then, later, I spent a year at the London School of Economics.'

'The LSE?' She was obviously surprised. 'Did you enjoy your time there?'

'I liked London.' Demetri realised he was in danger of becoming too familiar with her. 'Small world.'

'Isn't it?' She hesitated for a moment, and then said, 'You know, I think I will have a slice of toast, after all. Do you mind?'

Demetri could think of few things he'd like less at this moment than to sit here and watch her consume her breakfast. To see those even white teeth digging into the toast, to observe the delicate tip of her tongue emerging to lick a crumb of bread from the corner of that luscious mouth: that was the stuff of fantasy and he wanted no part of it. But civility demanded that he at least ensure that what she ate was hot, so he glanced round, saying quickly, 'I will have Pilar bring you some fresh—'

'No!'

Her denial was instantaneous, and accompanied by an instinctive reaching for his arm to prevent him from raising it to summon the maid. He was less formally dressed this morning, and his cotton tee shirt left his arm bare. In consequence, her fingers brushed across his flesh with devastating effect.

Her touch seemed to burn his skin, but he knew it was just his own unwelcome attraction to her that caused the sensation. Those cool, slim fingers couldn't burn anything, but that didn't prevent an answering flame of awareness from spreading along his veins like wildfire.

The blood surged to the surface of his skin and it was all he could do not to act upon the impulses that had him in their grip. The desire to stretch out his hand, loop it around her nape and bring that parted tantalising mouth to his was almost overwhelming. He could almost taste her sweetness; almost feel the softness of her lips and the satisfying invasion of his tongue. His eyes dropped to her breasts and saw, as if through a haze, the hard nubs straining at the cloth. *Theos*, he thought dizzily, if he didn't get out of here soon he was going to do something he'd definitely regret.

Thrusting back his chair, he got abruptly to his feet. Escape, he though unsteadily. Like everything else in life, escape was relative. He'd imagined his only escape was in getting away from his responsibilities, but it wasn't true. Now, he knew, he needed quite desperately to get away from her.

'As you wish,' he said politely, as if all he'd been thinking about was her satisfaction. He pushed slightly unsteady fingers through his hair. 'And now I am afraid I must leave you. Spiro will be waiting for me. If you do change your mind about the food, Pilar will be more than happy to serve you.'

CHAPTER FIVE

'TO SERVE *you*,' muttered Joanna under her breath as he walked away. She'd seen the way the young maid had looked at Demetri, and the hunger she'd exhibited had been unmistakable. She wondered if he practised *droit de seigneur* with the female staff, and then scoffed at the thought. It was sour grapes. She didn't even like him, but that didn't stop her from being aware of him in a purely sexual way.

She scowled, suddenly losing all taste for the toast she'd put on her plate. She couldn't be attracted to him, sexually or otherwise, she told herself severely. The man despised her, for God's sake, and he made little effort to hide it. He'd been civil to her this morning, but she didn't delude herself that he was doing it for anyone other than his father. And she'd agreed to come here for Constantine's sake, she reminded herself. How convincing would their relationship seem if she allowed herself to be seduced by his son?

But that wouldn't happen. She didn't want another man in her life, period. She was twenty-six, but in terms of experience she sometimes felt she was twenty years older. Which made her a suitable companion for Demetri's father. He had thought so, and, what was more, he wouldn't make any demands on her that she couldn't fulfil.

A shiver slid down her spine and she gave herself a little shake to dispel it. How long was it going to take her to put her marriage to Richard out of her head? Occasionally she had the depressing feeling that it would never happen.

A soft breeze blew up from the water, cooling the damp tendrils of hair that clung to her temple, bringing a reassuring wave of awareness of where she was and why she was there. Constantine wouldn't approve of her sitting here feeling sorry for herself. He wanted her to enjoy this trip. Apart from what he'd asked of her, he'd wanted to give her a holiday to remember—an opportunity to escape once and for all from the psychological walls she'd built around herself.

And she would enjoy it, she assured herself, reaching for the butter and spreading it thickly over the now cold toast. She was not going to let the young Kastros spoil it for her. She was tougher than that. She had had to be. And the sooner they realised it, the better.

To her dismay, Constantine was weaker at lunchtime.

She had spent the morning avoiding any further confrontations with members of his family, but when she presented herself at the doors to his suite at a little after twelve, Philip let her in with a decidedly anxious look on his face.

'*Khriazomasteh enan yatro, kiria,*' he exclaimed as soon as the door was closed behind her. '*Stenokhori-emeh!*'

Joanna made a helpless gesture. 'I'm sorry—' she began blankly, and to her relief Philip seemed to understand.

'A doctor, kiria,' he said urgently. 'We need a doctor. Kirie Constantine—*ineh arostos, kiria.* He is—ill!'

Joanna pressed an anxious hand to her throat. 'Why do you say that?' she demanded in an undertone, glancing towards Constantine's bedroom door, which was, mercifully, closed. 'What's happened?'

Philip shook his head. 'I have—I know Kirie Constantine *pola*—many—years, *kiria.* He—he sleeps—too much.'

'He's tired,' protested Joanna, not altogether convinced she was right, and Philip waved an impatient hand.

'I think we ask Kirie Demetri, *kiria.* He know what to do, *ne*?'

'*Ne.* I mean, *okhi.*' Joanna remembered just in time that *ne* meant yes and not no, which was what it sounded like. 'That is,' she continued, trying to think, 'is that what Kirie Constantine said?'

'*Then katalaveno, kiria.*'

Philip looked mutinous and Joanna suspected he knew exactly what she'd said. 'Have you spoken with Kirie Constantine?' she persisted, speaking slowly so he had no excuse for saying he didn't understand, and the manservant shrugged.

'*Okhi, kiria,*' he said offhandedly, and she hoped he wasn't going to insist on speaking Greek. Then, with a slight softening of his expression, 'I tell you, *kiria*. He sleep all the time.'

Joanna tried not to feel too anxious. Ever since Constantine had got out of hospital he had spent much of the day resting. And, as she'd thought earlier, yesterday had been a particularly strenuous day for a man in his condition. Especially as it had followed on from another tiring day. It was surely reasonable that he was sleeping. It was probably the best thing for him.

But...

'I think I'd better see for myself,' she declared, hoping she sounded more confident than she felt. Then, not really caring whether Philip had understood her or not, she crossed the room to Constantine's bedroom door. 'Give me a few minutes,' she said, opening the door. 'Then I'll speak to you again.'

'*Ne, kiria.*'

Philip shrugged again, turning his head away, but she felt him watching her out of the corners of his eyes as she went into Constantine's room. She sighed. She supposed the man had a right to his feelings. He had known his employer a lot longer than she had.

She closed the door behind her, mostly to prevent the uneasy sense that Philip was peering over her shoulder, and approached the bed. Constantine had his eyes closed, but as she looked down at him they opened, and she took an involuntary step backwards, ashamed to admit that she'd allowed the manservant's words to spook her.

'Hi,' she said, the word coming out a little higher than normal, and squeaky. 'How—how are you?'

'I have to confess I am a little more weary than I anticipated,' Constantine answered her ruefully. 'I am sorry. What time is it?'

Joanna inched her hip onto the bed and took his hand. 'It's about half past twelve,' she said. 'Do you want some lunch?'

'Lunch?' Constantine's expression was revealing, but he quickly hid his revulsion. 'Oh, Joanna, my dear, I do not think I am very hungry just now.'

'That's all right.' Joanna squeezed his hand reassuringly. 'You just take things easy. Have you had your medication? Is there anything I can get for you?'

Constantine shook his head. 'I am fine, really,' he insisted, though it was obvious he was not. 'In a couple of hours I will be up and about again. But I am afraid we will have to postpone our outing until tomorrow.'

'No problem,' said Joanna, wishing she felt more confident about the situation. She hesitated, and then added persuasively. 'Wouldn't you like me to tell Demetri—?'

'Nothing!' For the first time since she'd entered the room, Constantine looked positively animated. 'I want you to promise me you will tell Demetri nothing. If he knew—if he were to suspect that I have not made a full recovery, he would cancel the wedding. I know my son, Joanna. He is a good man, and I love him, but in this instance I will not allow him to treat me as an invalid and destroy Alex's happiness.'

Joanna was very much afraid that Alex's happiness would be destroyed anyway, when she discovered what was wrong with her father, but she couldn't argue with Constantine now. Nevertheless, she couldn't help feeling a certain amount of sympathy for Demetri. However selfless Constantine thought he was being, his children were going to be devastated when they found out the truth.

'He—I think he's expecting to speak to you this afternoon,' she ventured, remembering how insulting Demetri had been about her role in Constantine's recovery. 'He's bound to ask me what's going on. He wasn't very happy with my explanation this morning.'

'Then you will have to improvise,' declared Constantine wearily. 'Come, Joanna. I am sure you can think of some way to divert my son from becoming suspicious.' He paused, his thin lips twisting a little bitterly. 'Use your imagination.'

Joanna stared at him 'I hope you're not asking me to—'

'No. No.' Once again Constantine grew restless beneath her gaze. 'I would not do that. I meant—' He considered. 'Ask him to take you to see the ruins of Athena's temple. Demetri is quite well-versed in the history of the area, and the temple is the highest point on the island. The view is—' He broke off, his energy depleted. 'I am sorry,' he said again. 'I so much wanted to show you my island.'

'You will,' insisted Joanna encouragingly, squeezing his dry fingers once more. She got to her feet, making no promises about asking Demetri anything. 'I'll come back later, when you're feeling more rested.' She smiled, kissing her fingertips and pressing them to his forehead. 'I do care about you, Constantine. I hope you know that.'

He smiled then, but his eyes had closed, and although the smile lingered on his lips she could tell he'd lost consciousness again. Anxiety gripped her. She felt so ill equipped to handle this situation. It was an enormous responsibility Constantine had placed on her, and when Demetri found out—

She decided to have lunch on the balcony. Faithful to her instructions, however unwillingly, Philip was waiting to serve the salad and omelettes she'd ordered when she emerged from Constantine's room. Her explanation that his employer would be getting up later met with a sceptical stare, but the manservant knew better than to argue with her again. Instead, he obediently attended to her needs, ensuring she had everything necessary with polite deference.

And she had, she thought after he'd gone, seating herself at the table and cupping her chin in one hand as she stared at the view. How could anyone find fault with this place? It was heavenly.

A basket of crusty bread accompanied the meal, together with bottles of both wine and water to assuage her thirst. Salad, crisp and green, and liberally threaded with sliced avocados, peppers and olives, nestled in an ice-cooled container, and golden-brown omelettes rested beneath a heated dome.

Turning her attention to the food, Joanna did her best to enjoy it, but she'd spent most of the morning in a state of raw anxiety and nothing Constantine had said had eased her conscience.

Nevertheless, she was hungry, and, ensconced here on the balcony, she felt reassuringly secure from either Demetri or Olivia's wrath. They were bound to want to speak to her later, but for the moment she was determined not to let thoughts of them spoil her appetite.

Not that she ever ate a lot, she conceded, picking at a curl of lettuce. It was many years since she'd had the kind of appetite that would have done justice to the meal. She supposed she was lucky that she had the sort of metabolism that meant she could eat what she liked without gaining any weight, but not since she was a schoolgirl had she really looked forward to her food.

But then that was all tied up with her parents being killed in an avalanche in Austria and going to live with her father's maiden aunt, who had had little time for a spirited youngster. Meals in Aunt Ruth's house had hardly been happy occasions, with the old lady constantly bemoaning the fact that what little money she had was scarcely enough for her to live on, let alone provide for a gangling girl who was always growing out of her shoes and clothes.

Joanna, at first grief-stricken and confused, had soon learned that life was never going to be the same again, and by the time she was sixteen she had already been planning what she was going to do when she left school. College or university had been out of the question; she'd known that.

Her aunt would have said they couldn't afford it. Besides, she'd had no desire to be any more of a burden to her aunt, financially or otherwise. Only the knowledge that her parents would have been horrified if she'd insisted on leaving school after her GCSEs had persuaded her to stay on until she'd taken the higher exams.

At eighteen, however, she'd been more than ready to find a job and start supporting herself. But once again fate had intervened. Her aunt had had a stroke, which meant that Joanna had had no choice but to go on living with her and caring for her. For the next four years she had been her aunt's nurse, cking out an existence on the little money the social services provided.

It wasn't until the old lady died that Joanna had discovered the trust that her father had set up for her. For years the money had been collecting interest in a fund which should have been used to pay for her personal needs and her education. But her aunt had chosen not to use it or tell her about it. Instead she'd let the girl think that her parents had left her penniless as well as alone.

Why she'd done it, Joanna had no idea. Perhaps she had been an embittered old spinster, as the solicitor had said. In any event, after her aunt's death Joanna had sold the small semi where she'd spent the last ten years of her life and bought herself a comfortable apartment in Kensington. She'd splurged on a new wardrobe, had her long hair cut and styled, and finally taken a holiday in Sardinia. Where she'd met Richard Manning...

A shadow crossed the sun and she pushed her plate away. Then, sliding her legs to the side, she got up from her chair and crossed to the balcony rail. Resting her hands on the hot metal, she tried to dispel the feelings of inadequacy that remembering the months she'd spent with Richard caused her. But she was always amazed at her own naïvety. Had she never suspected that he was not what he seemed?

Apparently not, she thought bitterly. At twenty-two, she'd been less sexually aware than a girl slightly more than half her age. She'd never had a regular boyfriend. Aunt Ruth had not encouraged her to see her friends outside school. And, because she'd succeeded in instilling a sense of obligation in the girl, Joanna had always felt that she couldn't let her aunt down.

Which was also why Richard had made such a positive impression on her. Tall and fair and good-looking, with a background of public school and an excellent job in the City, he'd seemed everything she could ever have wished for in a man. The fact that he'd been on holiday with another man hadn't seemed so unusual. He'd seemed suave and sophisticated, and she'd been incredibly flattered when he'd singled her out for attention.

The holiday had been everything she'd ever hoped for. Richard had spent much of his time with her, taking her out in the car he'd hired, dining with her at all the best restaurants. When she'd mentioned the fact that he was neglecting his friend he'd insisted that it didn't matter. He wanted to be with her, he'd said disarmingly, and she'd had no reason not to believe him.

She'd been thrilled when he'd phoned her after they'd got back to London. She'd been half afraid it had just been a holiday friendship, and that she'd been too inexperienced to hold the attention of a man like him. The fact that so far he hadn't even attempted to kiss her had made her doubt his feelings for her, but when she'd voiced as much to Richard he'd assured her it was because he had too much respect for her as a woman.

Joanna's lips twisted now. Even with the sun beating down on her shoulders she felt cold. Respect! She doubted if Richard even knew the meaning of the word. He'd used her, that was all. He'd had his own agenda, and she'd just been his pawn.

Unable and unwilling to continue with this train of thought, Joanna left the balcony and went back inside. But the beauty of her sitting room was of little comfort to her and, deciding she needed to escape, she fled the room and went downstairs.

As she crossed the marble foyer she heard voices coming from the terrace. She guessed Demetri and Olivia, and possibly Spiro Stavros as well, were having lunch outdoors, and she envied them their freedom to do as they liked. They were speaking in their own language, so she didn't understand what they were saying, but in any case she didn't want to be accused of eavesdropping so she quickened her step.

'Mrs Manning!'

She'd reached the door which led out onto the crushed shell forecourt at the front of the villa when Demetri's voice arrested her. She didn't know why she recognised his voice so instinctively, but she did, and, although she was tempted to pretend she hadn't heard him, courtesy demanded that she acknowledge his presence.

In the few seconds it took her to come to this decision, however, he had covered the space between them, and when he spoke again his warm breath fanned her neck.

'Joanna.' He had evidently remembered they were supposed to have called a truce. 'Where are you going? Where is my father?'

Joanna turned reluctantly, remembering all too well how disturbing she'd found him earlier in the day. And although she had other things on her mind—not least the memory of how Richard had deceived her—she was instantly conscious of Demetri's dark attraction and the warm male scent of his body.

'I—I thought I might go for a walk,' she said spontaneously, not really knowing until that moment what she'd had in mind. 'It's such a lovely day.'

'And much too hot to venture out without any protection,' observed Demetri drily, raising his hand as if to check that her bare arms were free of any sunscreen and then thrusting it into the pocket of his drawstring pants. 'You do not even have a hat.'

'I don't intend to go far,' said Joanna, realising belatedly that she hadn't thought it through. She was so used to England, so used to cool breezes even in September, that she hadn't stopped to consider the wisdom of her decision.

'You are going alone?' Demetri was persistent. 'My father is not going with you?'

'No.' Once again Joanna was conscious of being between a rock and a hard place. 'I think your father needs to take things easy today. He—er—he apologises for his tardiness. He's not going to make your meeting after all.'

Demetri frowned. 'You have seen him, I assume?'

Joanna's cheeks turned a little pink. 'Of course.'

'Of course.' Demetri's mouth lifted slightly in faint contempt. 'How could I doubt it? He appears to have put all his trust in you.'

'Hardly that.' Joanna couldn't let him go on thinking they were conducting some kind of intimate liaison, particularly when she was already worried that Constantine wasn't responding to his treatment as he should. 'He's just weary, that's all. I think he needs a complete rest.'

Demetri studied her in silence for a moment, and she had the uneasy feeling that he could see right through her. She hoped not. Right now, she didn't think she could cope with another confrontation.

'You have not called a doctor?' he asked at last, and Joanna sighed. She should have known this was coming.

'No,' she said. 'He doesn't want to see a doctor. He has his medication.' She crossed her arms across her midriff. 'That should be enough.'

'You have made that decision?' he enquired tersely, and again she wished Constantine hadn't put her in this position.

'No. He has,' she insisted doggedly. Then, finding inspiration, 'You know your father. He will not take advice from anyone.'

'That is true.' To her relief, Demetri seemed to accept her explanation. 'So that is why you are—how do you put it?—at a loose end?'

Joanna lifted her shoulders. 'No,' she answered, not altogether truthfully. 'I—just thought it would be pleasant to get out of the house.'

'So you decided to go for a walk in the midday sun?'

She glanced at her watch. 'It's hardly midday.'

'The two o'clock sun, then,' he amended. 'Though the distinction escapes me. It is just as hot now as it was earlier. May I recommend that you confine your activities to the villa until later in the afternoon?'

Joanna expelled a weary breath. 'Is that an order?'

Demetri's mouth compressed. 'It is the advice of someone who knows this climate perhaps a little better than you do,' he told her flatly. 'I would not like you to suffer sunstroke. It is what my father would say if he were here. I am sure he would expect me to look after his—his friend.'

Joanna gave in. 'All right,' she said. 'I'll go back to my room.'

'Or you could sit beside the pool,' suggested Demetri, gesturing towards the terrace. 'There are umbrellas there to protect you.'

No, thanks, Joanna thought, not willing to lay herself open to any more questions. But she didn't say it. Instead, she gave Demetri a polite smile and, without giving him an answer, walked swiftly away towards the stairs.

CHAPTER SIX

DEMETRI went to see his father in the late afternoon.

He hadn't seen Joanna since he'd spoken to her just after lunch, and although he couldn't altogether blame her for wanting to avoid the other members of his family, he was irritated that she had chosen to spend the afternoon in her room.

Na pari i oryi. He'd been civil to her, hadn't he? More than civil when he considered how frustrated she made him feel. It might not be her fault that he had a physical reaction every time he was near her, but, *Theos*, it wasn't his either. His father should never have brought her here. Couldn't he see what kind of woman she was? Didn't he realise that she knew exactly how men responded to her sexuality, how she must have used her experience to infatuate him?

Philip let him into his father's apartments. The old man-servant seemed relieved to see him, and Demetri guessed Philip wasn't finding the situation any easier than he was. But, remembering the *faux pas* he had made the last time he was here, Demetri paused in the doorway to the salon, looking about him intently before venturing any further.

'Mrs Manning?' he said, glancing towards his father's bedroom door. His stomach clenched. 'Is she here?'

'No, *kirie*.' Philip twisted his hands together. 'I have not seen her since before lunch.'

Demetri breathed a little more easily. 'And my father?'

'Your father, *kirie*?' Philip looked confused. 'His condition is unchanged.'

'His condition?' Demetri stiffened. 'What condition?'

Philip shifted a little nervously. 'But surely you know, *kirie*? Kiria Manning—'

He broke off, as if afraid he was saying too much, but Demetri wouldn't let him avoid an answer. 'Yes?' he demanded. 'Kiria Manning—what? What has she been keeping from me?'

Philip looked uncomfortable now. 'I do not know what Kiria Manning has told you, *kirie*, but your father is not well. He has spent most of the day sleeping.'

'Oh.' Demetri made a dismissive gesture. 'I know that. Mrs Manning says that he is tired, that the activities of the last two days have been too much for him. Rest is what he needs.'

'He has eaten nothing, *kirie*.' Philip was defensive. 'He was going to have lunch with Kiria Manning, but she was forced to dine alone.'

Demetri frowned. 'Are you sure?'

'I served her myself,' said Philip stiffly. 'Did she not tell you?'

Joanna had told him nothing beyond the fact that his father was weary, thought Demetri impatiently, resenting anew this feeling of being excluded from his father's affairs. But he had no intention of telling Philip that.

'She may have said something,' he said now, hiding his real feelings. Then, determinedly, 'Is he awake?'

'I do not know, *kirie*.' Philip wasn't a fool and he had detected Demetri's unwillingness to confide in a servant. 'Perhaps you should ask Kiria Manning.'

Demetri's dark eyes bored into the old man's. 'You said she was not here.'

'She is not here.' Philip could be awkward, too. 'I merely meant—'

'I think I know what you meant, Philip,' Demetri interrupted him drily. 'I am disappointed in you. I would have expected you to inform me of any deterioration in my father's condition, not Kiria Manning.'

Philip gave him a wounded look, but before either of them could act on their feelings the door to Constantine's bedroom opened and the man himself appeared in the aperture.

'What is going on here?' he demanded, and Demetri was overwhelmingly relieved to see that his father was apparently capable of standing up for himself. 'Demetri? What are you doing here? I asked Joanna to tell you I would see you later.'

Demetri stared at the old man in some frustration. Was it only his imagination, or perhaps the white towelling of his bathrobe that gave his thin face an unnatural pallor? Whatever, now was not the time to take umbrage at anything he said and, forcing a tight smile, he gave a slight bow of his head.

'I was concerned that you could not keep our appointment, Papa,' he replied evenly. 'That is all.'

'But Joanna—'

'Mrs Manning explained that you were—exhausted—after your journey,' Demetri agreed, realising how much easier this would be if 'Joanna' did not continually come between them. 'But I am your son. Do I not deserve the same courtesy as—as your friend?'

Constantine's features seemed to hollow and weariness etched every line of his face. 'Of course,' he said, and now Demetri noticed he was supporting himself with one hand against the frame of the door. 'I am sorry, *mi yos*. Please.' He glanced over his shoulder into the room behind him. 'Come in.'

Demetri exchanged a look with Philip. '*Poli kala*, if you are sure?'

Constantine's thin lips twitched. 'As you say, Demetri, you are my son. My successor, *okhi*? How can I deny you a few minutes of my time?'

Demetri hesitated, but then, after asking Philip to bring them some refreshment, he followed his father into the bedroom. His bedroom? he wondered, his tension mounting as the old man climbed with evident relief back onto the wide bed. Or theirs? He felt impatience grip him. No, dammit, he would not think of that now. Joanna Manning had her own apartments. He should know. Wasn't that where he had found them together?

'So, Demetri…' Constantine's expression had eased a little now that he was resting more comfortably. 'As you can see, I am not yet as strong as I would wish to be. But it will come. Given time.'

Demetri positioned himself at the end of the bed. 'We are all praying for that day, Papa,' he said huskily 'And, if it is of any comfort to you, Kastro International is in safe hands, whatever Nikolas Poros says.'

'I am sure.' His father gave a rueful smile. 'I have great faith in you, Demetri. I know you will never do anything to let me or—or your sisters down.'

Demetri blew out a breath. 'I am glad to hear it.'

'Did you doubt it?'

'Well…'

Demetri hesitated. He could hardly say that since Joanna Manning had come on the scene he was finding it increasingly difficult to be sure of anything.

'Oh, I know it has not always been easy for you, Demetri,' his father went on, evidently misunderstanding his silence. 'And had things been different you would have had a brother—brothers—to share the burden with you. But…' He sighed. 'Regrettably, your mother was not strong, and having Alexandra was simply too much for her.'

'I know that, Papa.' Demetri felt uneasy suddenly. It was as if Constantine was already preparing him for the day when he wouldn't be around to share the burden himself. 'I just wanted you to know—'

The sound of the door opening across the room allowed him a moment to collect his thoughts, but when he turned his head he saw it wasn't Philip who had interrupted them. Joanna had paused in the doorway. Her face flushed with anger or concern, he couldn't be sure which, and she advanced swiftly into the room. She gave him a glowering look before halting beside the bed and taking one of his father's hands between both of hers. Then, in a voice that was filled with an emotion he didn't care to identify, she said, 'What's going on, Constantine? Is—is Demetri supposed to be here?'

Demetri's indignation was instantaneous. 'What are you implying, Mrs Manning?' he exclaimed, forgetting that earlier in the day he had practically demanded that they use one another's first names. 'I would do nothing to endanger my father's health.'

'*Siopi, siopi!*' Quiet, quiet! Constantine heaved a weary sigh. 'Joanna, my dear, there is no need for you to defend me so diligently. And—' he turned to Demetri '—you must forgive Joanna, *mi ghios*. She has only my best interests at heart.'

'As do we all, Papa,' said Demetri fiercely, resenting having to say it yet again. His shoulders stiffened. 'Would you like me to go?'

'No, no.' His father lifted his free hand and then let it fall again. 'Not like this.' He looked at the woman who had now eased her hip onto the bed beside him. 'Joanna, I want you and Demetri to be friends. Not enemies. Please.' Demetri saw the veins in his wrist stand out in stark relief as he squeezed her hand. 'For my sake.'

Demetri said nothing as Joanna turned to look at him again, but he guessed she hid her own resentment from the old man. 'Um—Demetri and I are not enemies, Constantine,' she assured him, squeezing his hand in her turn. Her slim arms were faintly tinged with red and Demetri guessed she had spent at least part of the afternoon on her balcony. He also noticed that she did not say that they were *friends*. That would have been too much, even for her.

'I am glad,' his father said now, but Demetri could see he was visibly weakening. How long was it since he had had any sustenance? He wished he could remember what the old man had eaten at dinner the night before, but he had been so incensed by Joanna's presence that he had paid little attention to details like that.

'I think we should go,' he said abruptly, and once again Joanna turned a cool gaze in his direction.

'Yes, you should,' she agreed, her deep blue eyes calm and dismissive. 'Your father needs to rest.'

'You are not his nurse, Joanna,' he responded, keeping his temper with an effort. 'I think we should both leave my father to Philip's ministrations, *ne*?'

Joanna hesitated. She was obviously torn by the desire to find out what he and his father had been talking about and the knowledge that for once he might have a point.

With an obvious effort she got up from the bed, still retaining her hold on his father's hand as she said, 'Is that what you want, Constantine?'

'It might be for the best, *agapi mou*,' he conceded gently, but as Demetri started for the door his father's voice detained him. '*Avrio*,' he said. Tomorrow. 'If I am still—what can I say? Incapacitated, no?—will you look after Joanna?'

'There's no need,' she began at once, but Constantine was looking at his son and Demetri didn't have the heart to refuse him.

'*Veveha*, Papa.' Of course. Demetri inclined his head, his lips twisting with reluctant irony. 'It will be my pleasure.'

To her relief, Philip informed Joanna the next morning that his employer had swallowed a little soup at suppertime. According to the old man Constantine had had a reasonably good night, and she began to hope that the fears she had entertained the day before might be only that: fears. After all, Constantine's doctors would not have allowed him to return to Theapolis if they had suspected the journey would be too much for him.

Joanna, herself, had spent a less than peaceful night. Despite the fact that Demetri had been painfully polite to her during and after the dinner she had been obliged to share with him and his family the evening before, the prospect of spending any time in his company was daunting. Had she even suspected Constantine might deputise his son to act as his proxy, she would have made sure he knew exactly how she felt about it. As it was, he'd sprung the request on both of them, and she doubted Demetri was any more pleased by the arrangement than she was.

Not that she really knew what Demetri thought about anything. He was far too clever at hiding his feelings for that. Just occasionally, when he looked at her, she had the sense that what he felt towards her was more than just dislike. Did he hate her? Did he hate the fact that his father cared about her? Or did he simply hate what he thought she was? Whatever, she wasn't looking forward to having him as an unwilling companion.

Perhaps she should have asked him to send Spiro in his place, she reflected, checking her appearance in the long mirrors in her dressing room. Not that she knew him any better, but she suspected he might be easier to get along with. As it was, having seen Constantine and assured herself that he was feeling much better this morning, she'd been forced to accept that he was still not well enough to look after her himself. She was therefore committed to spending the morning with a man she neither liked nor trusted, and she wished she had something in her wardrobes that didn't proclaim her sex quite so blatantly.

Still, she couldn't deny that it was good to wear attractive clothes again, and although the cream linen pants clung to the feminine curve of her hip and thigh, at least her legs were covered. But at what expense? Would Demetri understand that the buttoned waistcoat top that went with the trousers was meant to expose an inch or two of lightly tanned midriff every time she moved, or would he imagine she had chosen the most suggestive outfit she could find?

Either way, she refused to worry about that now. Constantine had suggested she should eat breakfast downstairs this morning, instead of skulking in her room. Of course he hadn't used those words, but Joanna knew what he'd meant. He was trying to integrate her into the life of the household, and, however she might feel about it, she owed it to him to go along with his wishes.

To her relief, the terrace was deserted. If Constantine's son and daughter had had breakfast there they were long gone, and only a few crumbs in the centre of the white cloth betrayed that a basket of bread had sat there. A place had been laid at the table overlooking the gardens that fell away towards the beach, and, although Joanna's appetite hardly warranted such a formal arrangement, she pulled out the chair and sat down.

Almost immediately the maid, Pilar, arrived to serve her, and by means of the odd word and quite a lot of sign language Joanna managed to convey her needs to her. The coffee was easy enough; everyone apparently had coffee at breakfast. But the milk and cornflakes were harder. How did you mime the difference between a bowl of muesli and the world's most famous brand of cereal?

'She understands English, you know,' remarked a lazy voice Joanna was beginning to recognise only too well as Pilar sauntered away. Demetri, who had apparently been watching her from the wide glass doors that opened onto the terrace, now strolled towards her. 'Do not be surprised if you get offered porridge instead.'

Joanna pursed her lips. 'If you knew that, why didn't you say so?' she demanded sharply, and then struggled to contain her anger. 'That is—how long have you been standing there, watching me?'

'Long enough,' remarked Demetri indifferently, moving past her to prop his hips against the low wall that edged the terrace. 'How are you this morning? How is my father?'

'Don't you know?'

Once again Joanna found it difficult to be civil with him. Whatever he said, whatever he did, seemed inclined to rub her up the wrong way, and she was fairly sure it was deliberate.

'Obviously not,' he responded mildly now. 'You are his mistress, Joanna. Do you not know?'

'I'm not—' Joanna had to bite her tongue to prevent her anger from betraying her. She licked her lips and began again. 'I'm not—an expert,' she improvised. 'But I think he's a little better.'

'I am relieved to hear it.'

Demetri accepted her reply at face value, lifting one canvas-shod foot to rest vertically against the low wall. It drew her attention to the fact that he was wearing dark blue shorts this morning, and she hated herself for noticing the powerful length of muscular leg that they displayed. Legs that were lightly covered with the same night-dark hair that sprang from the open neck of his collarless cotton shirt and framed the narrow gold watch that circled his wrist. Much against her will, she found herself speculating about the rest of his body, imagining how his skin would feel beneath her—oh, God!—sweating palms.

'So what would you like to do?'

'To do?' With an effort Joanna dragged her thoughts back from the precipice of her imagination and gazed at him blankly. 'I don't know what you—'

'This morning?' prompted Demetri. 'I thought you might like to take a drive around the island.' He pushed his hands into the pockets of his shorts, drawing the cloth taut across his thighs. 'I could show you the ruins of the temple of Athena that dates back to the fourth century B.C.'

'A temple?' Joanna surreptitiously dried her hands on the knees of her trousers and concentrated on the logo on his shirt. Anything to avoid looking anywhere else. 'Well, I— you don't have to entertain me, you know.'

'I want to,' he said, straightening up from the wall. 'Ah, here is Pilar with your breakfast.'

Joanna turned her head to watch the maid's approach, convinced that she wouldn't be able to eat anything with Demetri looking over her shoulder—metaphorically speaking. Her throat felt unpleasantly dry, and it wasn't just the fact that she hadn't had anything to drink yet. What did he really want? she wondered. Why was he being so nice to her? Was it just because his father had asked him to, or did he have some hidden agenda of his own?

Despite Joanna's fears, Pilar had evidently decided it would be unwise to pretend ignorance with Demetri on hand to take exception to any provocation on her part. On the tray she set down on the table were the milk and cornflakes Joanna had requested, along with a jug of freshly squeezed orange juice, a rack of toast, and a pot of coffee. And *two* cups, Joanna noted tensely. Apparently she was supposed to invite Demetri to join her.

'*Ineh entaxi, kiria?*' asked Pilar politely, and, despite Joanna's limited knowledge of Greek, she understood enough to know that the girl was asking for her approval.

'It's—fine. Thank you,' she said, reaching eagerly for the orange juice and pouring some into a glass. She took a grateful sip. 'Delicious.'

'*Efkharistisi mou, kiria,*' responded the maid, her dark eyes seeking Demetri's endorsement, too. '*Tha itheles ti-poteh alo?*'

'Nothing else,' responded Demetri briefly. 'You can go.'

Pilar's mouth turned down, but she turned obediently away and Joanna was left with the awkward dilemma of not knowing what to do for the best. If Demetri was being friendly for a change she would be unwise to oppose it. On the other hand, she was far too aware that he was a dangerous man in more ways than one.

But to her relief the decision wasn't left to her. 'I will leave you to have your breakfast in peace,' he said, and she wondered with a sense of unease if he could read her thoughts. 'I suggest we meet again at—' he glanced at his watch '—half past nine, *ne*?'

Joanna licked a smear of orange juice from her lower lip. It didn't sound as if she was being given a lot of choice. 'I—all right,' she said, wishing she didn't sound so submissive. 'Thank you.'

'There is no need for you to thank me, Joanna,' he replied, his dark eyes narrowed and impenetrable. 'I shall—look forward to it.'

Yeah, right.

Joanna forced herself not to watch him as he walked away. She was such a fool, she thought irritably. He had virtually insulted her before the maid came back, and just because she had almost blown her cover she'd let him get away with it. Again!

She scowled, tearing open the individual carton of cornflakes and tipping them into the bowl Pilar had provided. She had to stop being so—impressionable. For heaven's sake, she might be inexperienced but she wasn't stupid. Constantine was expecting her to play her part and she would. Whatever it cost her.

CHAPTER SEVEN

'YOU are doing what?'

Demetri scowled. 'I am taking her on a sightseeing tour of the island.'

Olivia stared at him. 'But—how can you?' She gave an exasperated little snort. 'Do you want her to think she is welcome here?'

'No.' Demetri felt the heat of the metal at his back burning into his pelvis but he didn't move away from the Jeep. It was important that he appeared as indifferent to his sister's complaints as possible, and lounging here in the sunlight he looked—he hoped—totally at ease with the situation. 'What would you have me do with her? Take her sailing? Or perhaps enjoy a cosy morning beside the pool?'

'Why do you have to do anything with her?' demanded Olivia irritably. 'Let her entertain herself. She will soon get bored if she has to spend all her time in her room. Then perhaps she will leave.'

'I would not hold your breath,' retorted Demetri, keeping a wary eye on the open doors of the villa. 'Mrs Manning is far more intelligent than you might think.'

Olivia gave her brother a scornful look. 'You sound as if you are infatuated with the woman, too,' she declared coldly. 'Have a care, Demetri. Our father may appreciate your taking care of his—' She used a word that even he found offensive, before adding darkly, 'But he will not be happy if you decide to take advantage of his incapacity.'

'There is no question of that,' retorted Demetri harshly, stung into an involuntary oath. '*Theos*, Livvy, what do you take me for?'

'I take you for a hot-blooded man who is deliberately

putting himself in the way of an unscrupulous woman,' replied Olivia heatedly. 'Demetri, you are not going to tell me that you do not find her physically attractive, at least. The woman is sex on two legs. You must have noticed.'

'I—' Demetri was incapable of an outright lie, but he was determined not to allow Olivia to have the last word. Pushing himself away from the vehicle, he swore as the hot metal burned his palm. 'You are crazy,' he said, by way of a distraction. 'Be careful, Livvy, or I shall begin to think you are jealous.'

'Jealous! Of her!' At last he had caught her on the raw, and she gazed at him with fury in her eyes. 'I am not jealous of that creature! But I do worry about the influence she may be having on our father. He is a sick man, Demetri. Who knows what he might agree to in his weak state?'

'Like what?' Demetri was impatient, not least because he was being forced to defend Joanna.

'I do not know, do I?' Olivia sighed. 'We know she is a gold-digger. Go figure.'

Demetri's jaw compressed, but before he could say anything more a woman appeared in the entrance to the villa. It was Joanna, her glorious hair swept back from her face and secured in one of those tight knots she had been wearing the first time he'd seen her. She was still wearing the linen pants and waistcoat, he noticed, but now the vest was open over a tight black tee shirt that successfully hid most of her throat and upper arms.

So much for sex on legs, he thought drily, despising the momentary disappointment he felt. Surely Olivia couldn't complain about her appearance today.

His sister had noticed his distraction, however, and she swung round irritably, biting back the exclamation that sprang to her lips. Then, after giving her brother a contemptuous look, she immediately strode away towards the villa, passing the other woman without even acknowledging her, her whole demeanour one of outraged indignation.

Demetri saw Joanna glance after her with a puzzled look

on her face and, stifling his own misgivings, he strolled with contrived casualness towards her. 'Ready?' he asked, as she came down the two shallow steps towards him. He saw the floppy straw hat she was trying to conceal beside her leg. 'I see you took my advice.'

Her eyes widened, and he wondered if she realised how innocent they made her look. But of course she did, he told himself disgustedly. Livvy was right. He was in danger of becoming infatuated with her. And that was not going to happen.

'The hat,' he pointed out shortly now, and then, forcing himself to look anywhere than at her, he added, 'I thought we could take the Jeep. The terrain inland can be pretty rough.'

Joanna nodded. 'This is an ideal place for an open-topped vehicle,' she said, squashing any hope he might have had that she'd baulk at getting windswept. 'I'm looking forward to it.'

Just who was kidding who? thought Demetri, pretending not to notice the struggle she had to open the door of the vehicle. But the idea of taking her arm, of helping her into the front seat, was not an option. He was doing his father a favour, he told himself grimly. That was all. And if, in the process, he was able to learn a bit more about their relationship, then Livvy should applaud him, not bite his head off.

As he swung himself up beside Joanna a faintly sensual perfume assailed his nostrils, and he realised he might have another reason for being glad that they were not to be confined in a closed cabin. Her nearness was enough of a provocation in itself, without being assaulted by the delicate fragrance of her skin.

Spiro came out onto the steps of the villa as he was driving away and his assistant raised a laconic hand in farewell. Demetri wondered if Olivia had sent him. Perhaps she'd hoped he'd ask the other man to join them. And perhaps he should have, he acknowledged. But it was too late now.

Theapolis was one of the larger islands in a group that lay about a hundred miles off the coast of mainland Greece. Most of the islands were rocky and arid, and depended on tourism for their livelihood, but Theapolis wasn't one of them. Oh, it had its share of tourists: island-hoppers, for the most part, who came one day and left the next, with the occasional artist or hiker thrown in for good measure. But its main source of income came from its citrus orchards and olive groves that terraced the southern half of the island with wooded slopes and lush valleys.

The Kastro estate was situated at the south-western corner of the island, just a short distance from the village of Rythmos. The main port of Agios Antonis was at the other side of the island, and ferries docked there most weekdays during the summer months.

Demetri regaled Joanna with this information as they drove inland, the roads becoming increasingly rugged as they left the cultivated coastal area behind. The land was scrubby here, coarse and primitive, with only a few goats eking out a living on the inhospitable slopes. Craggy cliffs and isolated outcrops of rock marked a barren landscape, but the views more than made up for its splendid isolation. From here, it was possible to see the whole of the island spread out below them, and although Joanna was clinging to her seat as they negotiated the track up to the ruined temple she was evidently impressed.

She had taken off her hat as they drove into the hills, the cooler air moderating the heat of the sun, but now she put up a nervous hand to check the damage. She must be aware that the breeze had played havoc with her chignon, and Demetri tried not to feel pleased with the result. There was no way she could restore it without a mirror and, as if she'd realised this, too, she tugged the rest of the hairpins out of the knot and shook her head.

Her hair tumbled down about her shoulders in glorious profusion, softening her expression and making Demetri's fingers itch to bury themselves in its silky coils. The wind lifted several strands to blow them about her face, and she attempted to twist them back behind her ears without much success.

'Damn,' she said, as he brought the Jeep to a halt on the pebbly plateau beside the ruins of the temple. She grimaced and, picking up her hat, she jammed it down onto the unruly mass. 'That will have to do.'

Leave it, Demetri wanted to say, but he didn't. Instead, controlling the urge to snatch the hat away again, he switched off the engine and vaulted out of the vehicle before temptation got the better of him. Then, walking to the edge of the plateau, he stood gazing out at the view, struggling to contain emotions that were as unwelcome as they were unfamiliar.

The door opened behind him. He heard it. Heard her canvas-booted feet land on the gravelled sweep of the plateau and then the silence as she looked about her. What was she thinking? he wondered. It was a fair bet that she wasn't fighting an unwanted desire to pull him down onto the rough grass beside the ruin's walls and tear his clothes from him. Why had he ever thought that black tee shirt was a concession to modesty? *Khristo*, she wasn't even wearing a bra.

The silence went on too long. He'd expected her to say something, maybe even come and look at the view. He had the feeling she was as eager to stay away from him as he was from her, though for different reasons. Still, he had to know what she was doing, and, glancing behind him, he found that she was waiting for him to make the next move.

Expelling a breath, he turned and walked back to the Jeep, pocketing the keys before nodding towards the windswept site of the temple. 'Do you want to look around?'

Joanna shrugged. 'Why not?' she said evenly. 'Is there much to see?'

Demetri's lips twisted. 'I suppose that depends on your point of view,' he remarked drily. 'I should tell you that any valuable artefacts have been moved to an archaeological museum in Athens, as Theapolis does not have a museum of its own. But the sacrificial altar is still here. Despite the fact that the island was converted to Christianity in the second century A.D.'

Joanna looked at him. 'You know quite a lot about the island's history, don't you?' she asked. 'Is that because you have a personal interest in antiquities, like your father?'

Demetri's expression hardened. 'I am nothing like my father, Joanna,' he said tersely, brushing past her to stride over the crumbling wall that marked the boundary of the ruins. 'If you will follow me...'

He thought for a moment that she wasn't going to go with him. Looking back, he saw that her cheeks were pink, and from her appearance he guessed she was fighting the urge to tell him to go to hell. But did she have to bring his father's name into their conversation? Didn't she understand that he was only here on sufferance? That the last thing he needed was to be reminded of who—and what—she was.

After a few moments she seemed to come to a decision, however, and, wrapping the strap of the small haversack she was carrying around her wrist, she stepped over the wall. Then, throwing back her shoulders, she tramped across to where he was waiting, meeting his wary gaze with cool, appraising eyes.

'I'm here,' she said unnecessarily. 'Shall we get this fiasco over with?'

Demetri sighed. 'I am sorry if I have offended you,' he said politely, but she wasn't having that.

'No, you're not,' she said, looking past him to where the crumbling columns of what had been the sanctuary guarded the stone altar. 'Why pretend? We both know how you really feel.'

'I doubt that,' murmured Demetri, aware that she had no idea how he really felt. 'But I apologise if I have given you the wrong impression.'

Her brows arched mockingly. 'Is that possible?' she countered. But then, as if she was not entirely sure of her ground, she added, 'Did people actually live up here?'

'I do not think so.' Demetri decided to take his lead from her. 'But, naturally, the temple was erected on the highest point of the island. It emphasised the differences between gods and goddesses and the commoners like ourselves.'

'How things have changed,' remarked Joanna in a low voice, but Demetri heard her.

'Your point being?' he prompted.

'Oh—nothing.' She moved away from him, going towards the inner courtyard. 'It's amazing that anything has survived.'

'It has not exactly been overrun in recent years,' observed Demetri, going after her. Then, 'What were you implying just now?'

She shrugged, not looking at him. 'About what?'

'You know,' he insisted, resisting the temptation to put his hand on her shoulder and swing her about to face him. 'You have a problem with me calling myself a commoner?'

'Did you?' she countered. 'I didn't notice.'

Like hell!

Demetri took a deep breath. 'Not in so many words, perhaps,' he conceded flatly. 'Look, can we stop all this sparring? If I had wanted a fight, I would have gone to the gymnasium.'

Joanna shrugged again, mounting the steps and stopping to admire the remains of a moulded pediment. 'I didn't start it.'

'But you are determined to finish it, *ne*?' suggested Demetri in exasperation. '*Theos*, Joanna, let us call a truce.'

'Another one?' she enquired at once, and then, as if acknowledging his argument, 'Tell me about Athena. Who was she?'

Demetri drew a deep breath. Then, levelly, 'She was the daughter of Zeus. His favourite, I believe. She is said to have been seated at her father's right hand in the council of the gods, *etsi ki alios*.'

Joanna glanced back at him. 'Impressive.'

'Yes.' But Demetri wasn't at all sure what she was referring to. 'She is also reputed to have invented the olive, the plough and the rake, and taught men how to build ships for peace as well as war.'

Joanna frowned. 'Wasn't she a goddess of war, or something?' she asked. 'Or was that someone else?'

'No, she was that also.' Demetri spoke tolerantly. 'She apparently inherited the weapons of thunder and lightning from her father and she is said to have used them. Against him, too, on occasion.' He gave a wry smile. 'A very formidable lady.'

Joanna smiled now. 'You don't approve?'

Demetri merely shook his head, moving past her, picking his way across the uneven ground, where the remains of marble slabs and broken friezes were half hidden in the grass. He was finding himself increasingly intrigued by her candour and he didn't trust himself to exchange this teasing banter with her. Somehow she had got beneath his guard, and his attraction to her was no longer just a physical thing.

He heard her following him, heard the sound of the wind whistling round the stunted columns, and wondered how he could have been such a fool as to bring her here. Away from the villa it was fatally easy to forget her relationship with his father, fatally easy to pretend that they were just a man and a woman spending time together, enjoying each other's company.

He swore under his breath. Where the hell had that come from? He couldn't possibly get any joy out of being with her. She was his father's mistress; at best an opportunist, at worst a gold-digger. Olivia was right. He was being reckless. He should take her back, right now.

'Your sister doesn't like me, does she?'

Joanna's voice came from right behind him, and he turned to find she was squatting down, examining some words she had found carved on a slab of marble propped against a pillar.

'I—she—'

Demetri was annoyed to find her words had disconcerted

him. It was as if she'd instinctively sensed what he'd been thinking, and for a moment he was at a loss for a reply.

'What does this say?' she asked, changing the subject. 'Is it ancient Greek?'

Demetri's nostrils flared, and he was tempted to say, What else? But he realised in time that it wasn't wise to provoke her. Provocation led to stimulation and stimulation led to an arousal he didn't want to feel. So, instead of making some slick remark, he squatted down beside her to read the inscription on the plaque. His education had given him some knowledge of classical languages and, without emotion, he said. 'It is a dedication to Athena. It was probably part of the pediment that formed the portico of the temple.' He studied it for a moment, before adding, 'It extols the virtues of the virgin mother goddess.'

Joanna's head swung round to face him. 'The *virgin* mother goddess?' she echoed disbelievingly. 'Isn't—isn't that a contradiction in terms?'

Demetri found himself gazing into wide blue eyes, dark lashes—probably mascaraed, he chided himself scornfully—casting delicate shadows on her cheeks. Cheeks whose colour deepened to a rich crimson as he stared at her.

She was obviously as startled by his nearness as he was by hers, and before he could think of a satisfactory answer to her question she attempted to get to her feet. But she had acted without taking the unevenness of the ground into consideration and would have stumbled had he not lunged forward and grabbed her arm.

His action unbalanced him, however. With a feeling of helplessness he felt himself falling, and moments later he found himself on a rough bed of gravel with Joanna on top of him.

He didn't know which of them was the most dismayed by what had happened. Judging by the horrified look on Joanna's face as she endeavoured to struggle off him, she had to be in the running. But, hell, he was shocked, too. His spine had taken quite a beating, and it irritated him enormously that she probably thought he was to blame for the whole incident.

Which wasn't true, he thought frustratedly. It wasn't his fault that she hadn't taken care where she put her feet. The outraged expression she was wearing only increased his aggravation, and he couldn't understand why she was looking so annoyed.

'Will you let go of me?' she snapped, and it was only then that he realised he was still gripping her forearm. During the fall he must have held on to her, and now she was behaving as if it was all his fault.

'I did not instigate this, you know!' he exclaimed, feeling a particularly sharp stone digging into his hip. 'I was trying to save you from falling flat on your face.'

'Really?' Patently, she didn't believe him. 'Well, why don't you let me go and we'll say no more about it?'

Demetri's lips parted. Her insolence infuriated him. She was behaving as if he had engineered the whole thing. What did she expect him to get out of it, for God's sake? What pleasure did she think he got from acting as a cushion for her not inconsiderable weight?

The answer came as a treacherous stirring in his groin. Beneath her flailing arms and legs, his unwanted arousal hardened to a throbbing shaft. Thick and muscular, it thrust against the thin confinement of his shorts, an unmistakable stiffness against the softness of her stomach.

He knew the moment she felt it, too. Like a rabbit caught in the glare of headlights, she froze to an unmoving stillness, her eyes wider yet filled with a revulsion he neither knew nor understood. *Theos*, she wasn't a child. She knew something like this could happen. What did she expect when he could feel the pebble-hard pressure of her nipples against his chest?

The most sensible thing would be to push her away from him, to let her get up and hope against hope she didn't tell his father what he had done. He was fairly sure that Constantine, not to mention Olivia, would find his explanation somehow lacking in conviction, but the quicker he dealt with the situation, the less damning it would be.

Yet the panic he could see in her eyes was getting to him. Dammit, he wasn't a monster, he thought angrily. He was just a man—an attractive man, if what most women told him was true—and not someone of whom she need be afraid. He knew that somehow, some way, he had to convince her—convince himself!—that he was not to blame for what had happened. And, ignoring both her resistance and his own misgivings, he raised his arm and ran the back of his hand down her cheek.

Her skin was hot; so hot. Even the casual brush of his fingers left a livid whiteness on her flesh. A whiteness that was soon overtaken again by the heated blush that was so unexpected. But her skin was soft; so soft. It was like the smoothest satin he'd ever touched.

She didn't move. She seemed incapable of doing so now, or perhaps she was afraid of what else her unguarded actions might provoke. His arousal hadn't subsided; on the contrary, it felt as if it had increased. His whole body ached for fulfilment, his erection pulsing heavily against her hip.

Theos, he had never wanted a woman as much as he wanted her, he realised incredulously. The vision he had had earlier, of pulling her down to the ground and tearing the clothes from her, was still with him. But now it had been reinforced with an urgent desire to make love to her. To bury himself inside her and teach her how desirable it could be.

But he wanted her to want him, too. The thought of her wrapping those long, long legs about his hips, arching up beneath him, of him spilling his seed in her tight sheath, was enough to drive him almost to the edge. And why? Because he wanted to show his father what a faithless bitch she was? Or because he wanted to prove to himself that she couldn't prefer the older man?

That suspicion sickened him. What was he doing, for pity's sake? How could he even think of making love with

Joanna Manning and profess to love his father as a son should? It was unforgivable. He was unforgivable. He should have taken Olivia's advice and avoided any chance of something like this happening. Olivia had been right. He was a hot-blooded man, and Joanna was just as unscrupulous as Olivia had said.

Or was she?

He stared up at her and then, hardly knowing what he was doing, he gripped her face between both hands and brought that soft, luscious mouth to his. Just one kiss, he told himself, rolling onto his side and taking her with him. If she kissed him back he'd know he'd been right all along. With her flat on the grass at his side he felt infinitely more in control of the situation, and, just for good measure, he traced the curve of her lips with his tongue.

Theos! His breath caught in his throat and, almost involuntarily, he deepened the kiss. Her lips parted and his tongue dipped irresistibly between her teeth. Heat and sweetness; warmth and wetness; she tasted as delicious as he'd anticipated. And, instead of sobering, Demetri's head swam at the first hint that she was kissing him back.

He struggled to hold onto his sanity. But when her arms rose to circle his neck he felt his control slipping away. With a little moan of submission Joanna abandoned herself to his lovemaking, surging up against him, her tongue tangling with his, her fingers curling into the hair at his nape.

It was heaven and it was hell—and it was wrong. No matter how tempting it would be to abandon his own scruples, as she had apparently abandoned hers, he told himself he couldn't do it. He had been crazy to let things get this far and he had to stop it now. With a groan of anguish, he brought his hands to her shoulders to push her away.

But his own needs betrayed him. When he touched the tight-fitting tee shirt, and realised that it was all that was between him and her breasts, good sense slid away. His fingers slipped down her arms to grip the soft curve of her midriff. With his thumbs stroking the undersides of her breasts, it took very little effort to move higher and palm the swollen peaks.

Khristo! He dragged his mouth away from hers to look at what he was doing, his breath constricting in his throat. She was so responsive, her heart palpitating wildly beneath his hands. Her chest rose and fell with the urgency of her arousal, and her scent, warm and seductive, rose to his nostrils. What was more, he thought he could happily drown in the wanton languor of her eyes.

But the look in her eyes was changing. As he watched, almost drugged by his own emotions, a look of horror returned to her face. Perhaps if he'd still been kissing her, perhaps if he'd still been plundering her mouth with the hunger he hadn't been able to deny, she wouldn't have had the chance to come to her senses. As it was, her hands at his nape became claws that tore him away from her, her flailing legs nearly unmanning him as she fought to scramble to her feet.

Before he could beat her to it, her angry tongue lashed out at him. 'How—how dare you?' she cried. 'How could you? You're—you're despicable!'

'And you are…?' suggested Demetri, in a dangerously bland tone. He got to his feet with a contrived lack of haste and regarded her with an amazingly calm look of enquiry. 'What are you, Joanna? Apart from my father's—' He broke off, knowing full well that she would finish the sentence for him. 'I would like to hear your interpretation of what just happened.'

Joanna swayed. She was obviously distressed, and he despised himself for suddenly feeling sorry for her. She had had no shame so why should he?

'Go—go to hell!' she said at last, somehow summoning the strength to answer him, and, after bending to rescue her hat, she stuffed it into her haversack, and strode unsteadily away towards the car.

CHAPTER EIGHT

DEMETRI left for Athens early the next morning.

Constantine gave her the news when she joined him in his suite before breakfast, and Joanna realised that Demetri must have been on board the helicopter she'd heard circling the island as she was getting dressed. She felt a shiver of relief at the knowledge that she wasn't going to have to confront him again that day, and wondered if his trip had been arranged for the same purpose.

But, no. Demetri was unlikely to let anything she did influence his actions, and Constantine's explanation—that he was going to bring his sister and her fiancé back to the island—was a bleak confirmation. He was completely without honour or conscience, and she despised herself for being a party to his betrayal of his father.

The journey back to the villa the day before had been fraught with tension. They hadn't spoken to one another after what had happened at the temple and Joanna had made a concerted effort not to look at Demetri either. She couldn't have borne to see the smug expression she'd been sure he'd be wearing, and she'd been overwhelmingly relieved when the stone gateposts that guarded the entrance to the villa had loomed ahead of them. She'd leapt out of the vehicle as soon as Demetri had applied the brakes, offering him only a muffled 'Thanks' before hurrying inside.

Thanks! That had hardly been warranted, she'd chided herself later, when a maid had come to ask if she would be joining the family for lunch. Her excuse for refusing—that she had a headache and was going to rest for a while—had been just as mendacious, and she'd guessed that Demetri would see it for what it was. But she hadn't cared. She honestly didn't know how she was going to face him again, and she'd spent half the night wondering if she should tell Constantine that she couldn't continue with this charade.

But what excuse could she give? She couldn't tell Constantine what had happened, not without destroying the faith he had in his only son. Besides, the truth was her behaviour had only reinforced Demetri's opinion of her. He thought she was only using his father for her own purposes and he believed he'd proved it. But, like her, he couldn't use the argument. Not without implicating himself.

Still, Constantine did look considerably better this morning, which was a blessing. He wasn't dressed yet; when she'd joined him in his apartments he'd been resting in his chair beside his bed, wearing only his dressing gown, flicking through some of the letters and reports that Demetri had handled in his absence. Now they were sitting out on his balcony, enjoying fresh fruit and coffee and warmly scented rolls in the open air. He was still not dressed, but Joanna wasn't worried. It was so good to see him up and about again.

Buttering a roll, Joanna realised it was the first food she'd been able to face since the previous morning. The night before she'd only picked at the *mousakas* Constantine had insisted on ordering for her, and, although he had complained, she'd noticed his appetite had been sadly lacking too. Now, though, he seemed to be enjoying the peach she had peeled for him, laughing a little ruefully as the juice from the fruit insisted on dribbling down his chin.

'Um—when will—Demetri be back?' she asked at last, finishing the roll and reaching for her coffee. She had to know. She had to prepare herself for their eventual confrontation, whenever that would be.

'Ah...' Constantine wiped his mouth with his napkin and set it aside. 'Probably tomorrow,' he replied thoughtfully. 'The wedding is in less than a week, as you know. Alex will want to spend some time in her own home before Costas spirits her away to Penang.'

Joanna took a breath, trying not to think about how short-lived her respite was going to be. 'Penang?' she said, as if she'd never heard of it before. 'Is that where they're going for their honeymoon?'

'Indeed.' Constantine smiled. 'You have never been to Malaysia, Joanna?'

'No.' In fact, she had been hardly anywhere. Except Sardinia, she reminded herself bitterly. She would never forget Sardinia. 'Is it nice?'

Constantine covered her hand with his. 'It is beautiful,' he told her gently. 'Very beautiful.' He paused. 'Like you, *agapi mou*.' He paused again, and then said perceptively, 'What is wrong?'

'Wrong?' Joanna hoped he would attribute the slight tremor she could detect in her voice to astonishment. 'What could be wrong, Constantine? I am here, in one of the most perfect places in the world, with probably the kindest man I could ever hope to meet. What could I possibly find wrong with that?'

'*Veveus.*' Indeed. But Constantine was still regarding her with concerned eyes. 'So, tell me more about your outing with Demetri. Last evening you seemed a little tired, and I did not press it. Oh, you said you had enjoyed the visit to the Temple of Athena, but you said little about Demetri himself. Was he polite to you? Did he conduct himself in a way I would have approved of?'

If the situation hadn't been so serious Joanna thought she might have laughed out loud. But it would have been a hysterical laugh, and at herself, not at his words. Dear God, how was she supposed to answer him? What was that expression about being economical with the truth?

'Demetri isn't entirely happy with—with our relationship,' she said carefully. 'But you know that.'

Constantine's mouth tightened. 'You are saying he was rude to you?'

Rude? Once again the urge to laugh was almost irresistible, but she fought it back. 'Um—not rude, no,' she managed weakly. Then, hoping to change the subject, 'He—he's very knowledgeable about the island, isn't he? I was especially interested in the stories about Athena and what she is supposed to have done—'

'*Arketa!*' Enough! With an abrupt cutting gesture of his hand Constantine silenced her, his lined face dark with anger. 'I am not interested in what my son had to say about our myths and legends, Joanna. I want to know what he had to say about me—about *us*.'

Joanna's lips parted in alarm. In her haste to reassure him she had obviously said the wrong thing, and somehow she had to convince him that nothing untoward had happened.

'He—didn't say anything about—about you, Constantine,' she protested urgently. 'I—I just get the feeling he doesn't like me. He thinks I'm a gold-digger. That's all I meant.'

'In other words, Demetri does not consider his father is still capable of attracting a beautiful woman,' retorted Constantine shortly. 'In his eyes I am just a pathetic old man, trying to boost his ego in the company of a trophy mistress!'

'No...' Joanna realised she had only worsened the situation, and she wished she had had more warning of what was to come. But then, she hadn't taken Constantine's insecurities into consideration. 'It's me he despises, not you.'

'Those were his words, were they?'

'No.' Joanna was floundering now. 'That's not what I meant.'

'What did you mean, Joanna?' Constantine looked weary now. '*Then pirazi*, so long as he does not suspect the truth I suppose that is all that matters, *ne*?'

'Yes.' Joanna breathed a little more freely. 'And I can assure you, he believes every word you say.'

'Good.'

Joanna hesitated. 'You're not upset, are you, Constantine?'

'Upset?' His hand fell away to his lap, and to her relief a rueful smile touched his lips. 'I suppose my ego has suffered a blow,' he admitted drily. 'But, no. I am not upset with you, my dear. I am just sorry that you had to bear the brunt of my son's displeasure. Demetri's tongue can be very—wounding. I know.'

Joanna looked down at her coffee. She didn't want to think about Demetri's tongue at that moment. Didn't want to remember what he had done with that tongue, or how warm and hungry it had felt in her mouth. He'd used his tongue to captivate her, to give her an indication of how easy it would have been for him to seduce her. And she'd let him. She'd actually encouraged him. And, whether his lovemaking had been hot and spontaneous or cold and calculating, she'd surrendered any right to judge him.

Oh, Lord…

'You would tell me if there was anything else?'

To her dismay, Constantine was still watching her and he had interpreted her expression in an entirely different way. 'Of course,' she replied hurriedly, thanking the saints that he couldn't read her mind at that moment. She picked up her cup in both hands to avoid any chance of spilling her coffee. 'Um—tell me about Alex's fiancé. Is he handsome? Has she known him long?'

Constantine heaved a sigh. 'Long enough,' he said, and she thought at first he was still preoccupied with Demetri's behaviour. But then he added, 'Costas is the son of Andrea Karadinos. Andrea is a friend as well as a business associate. Our children have known one another since they were young. It is fortunate that they appear to love one another. But Alex knows she is cementing our relationship by marrying Costas.'

Joanna stared at him. 'So it's an arranged marriage?' She didn't know why she should feel so surprised.

'In a way.' Constantine's lips twisted. 'Ah, Joanna, I can see that that troubles you.'

'No.' But it did.

And he knew it. 'You have to understand,' he said. 'Alex is my daughter. As such, she is a target for every fortune-hunter she meets. That is not to say that if she had fallen in love with a man I did not know I would necessarily have prevented her from marrying him. I am not so cruel. But it is much easier that she has chosen a man I like. I was happy to give my permission. *Etsi, kanena provlima*! No problem, *ne*?'

Joanna shook her head. 'I didn't realise you were so—so—traditional.'

'Do you not mean conventional?' enquired Constantine drily. 'I have to admit, I do have certain expectations as far as my children are concerned. Olivia went against my wishes and divorced the man I had chosen for her, and you can see how aimless her life has become. I do not want that to happen to Alex.'

'And Demetri?'

Joanna could have bitten out her tongue. Why had she asked that? After trying so hard to put thoughts of Demetri behind her, she'd said exactly the wrong thing.

Constantine was frowning now. 'Demetri?' he echoed. 'Did he mention a *filenatha* to you?'

'I—no.' Joanna was flustered again. She had heard that word before. It meant girlfriend. 'I just wondered…' …*what you had in store for him*, she finished silently. She didn't want to acknowledge that the idea of Demetri marrying a woman of his father's choosing was a disturbing thought.

'My son knows his duty,' Constantine replied at last—which could have meant anything. 'He knows what I expect of him. He will not let me down.'

By getting involved with a woman he believes is sleeping with his father, Joanna added under her breath, still not knowing why that should matter to her.

She forced a smile. 'I'm sure you're right,' she said, assuming a lightness she didn't feel. 'Now, what shall we do this morning?'

In the event, Joanna did very little.

Constantine insisted on examining his mail before joining

her on the patio downstairs, and after about half an hour he sent a message with Philip, asking that she forgive him if he didn't join her until later. There were business matters to be dealt with, Philip explained stiffly. Phone calls to be made. A backlog of decisions to be sanctioned.

The arrival of Nikolas Poros a little while later was another diversion, and signalled the death knell of any hopes she might have had of them spending the morning together.

In consequence, Joanna went back to her room, changed into her swimsuit and a wraparound skirt, and returned to the patio. She'd brought a magazine with her and, taking up a position on one of the cushioned loungers beside the pool, she tilted her face to the sun.

She'd been sitting there for perhaps fifteen minutes when she heard footsteps crossing the terrace. Olivia, she thought depressingly, wondering how she could have been so stupid as to think that Constantine's daughter would miss a chance like this. But she was pleasantly surprised when a male voice said, 'I would advise you to wear suncream, Mrs Manning. It would be unwise to risk burning such delicate skin.'

Spiro. Joanna turned her head to find Demetri's personal assistant standing beside her chair, his expression one of good humour mixed with mild concern. He was dressed in khaki shorts and a short-sleeved cotton shirt worn outside his trousers, his dark hair still damp—from his shower, she suspected.

'I did put some cream on my arms and legs before leaving my room, Mr Stavros,' she replied now, shading her eyes to look up at him. 'But thanks for the advice.'

'My pleasure,' he said smoothly, his smile revealing a row of even white teeth. 'And, please: call me Spiro.'

'All right. Spiro.' She smiled, realising that most women would find him very attractive. 'And I'm Joanna. I'm not used to answering to Mrs Manning.'

'Why?' He hooked the adjoining lounger with his foot and seated himself on the end of it. 'Is it not your name?'

Joanna's mouth drew in. 'If you're asking whether I've been married or not, then, yes. It's my name. It's just—well, most people call me Joanna.'

Spiro shrugged. 'I was curious, that is all.'

'You were? Or was it Demetri?' she countered, realising that she should not be deceived into thinking that Spiro was any more likely to want her here than his employer. 'Did he ask you to speak to me?'

'Demetri has gone to Athens.'

'To bring his sister home. I know,' said Joanna tersely, without pointing out that that wasn't what she'd asked him. 'Why aren't you with him?'

'We are not—how do you say it?—joined at the hip, *ne*?' remarked Spiro drily. 'I am his assistant, not his bodyguard.'

'His bodyguard?' Joanna caught her breath. 'Does he need one?'

Spiro studied her expression for a moment and then glanced away towards the pool. 'Perhaps,' he said. 'Sometimes.' He drew a breath. 'It is a beautiful morning, is it not?'

'Beautiful,' agreed Joanna a little dazedly, remembering what Constantine had said about security when she'd first arrived. She'd forgotten what a dangerous place the world could be, and had taken the men who surrounded Constantine for granted. He'd always dismissed them as nurses or chauffeurs, but now she realised she'd been naïve in not seeing them as bodyguards, too. This was a very wealthy family, after all. They were bound to have enemies. *Demetri* was bound to have enemies. Oh, God, why hadn't she thought of that before?

Aware that her palms were sweating, she quickly swung her feet off the lounger and sat up. The idea of Demetri needing a bodyguard had ruined her mood. She was antsy; anxiety tugged at her solar plexus. At least Constantine wasn't here to witness it, but she didn't trust Spiro not to see that she was spooked.

'I—think I'll have a swim,' she said, even though until

that moment she'd had no thought of going into the water. She rubbed her arms as if they were burning. 'As you say, it is very hot.'

'He will be back tomorrow, Joanna,' Spiro remarked, getting to his feet with her and reminding her briefly of Demetri, with his superior height and muscled frame. 'He does not take chances.'

'And why should that be of any interest to me?' she asked, stepping towards the edge of the pool, then glancing back at him. 'I'll remember what you said about the sunscreen,' she added. 'Have a nice day.'

CHAPTER NINE

IN FACT Demetri didn't return to Theapolis the next day. It was two days later when the helicopter landed at the small airfield near Agios Antonis, and he couldn't deny he was glad to be back.

To make sure that Joanna hadn't caused his father any grief in his absence, he defended himself irritably. Even though he'd had Spiro's nightly reports to reassure him, he needed to see for himself. Spiro was not family, after all. How could he know what Constantine was thinking, what he was feeling? How could Spiro know what went on behind his father's bedroom door?

How could he?

Scowling, Demetri hauled off his own suit carrier and waited with some impatience for his sister and her fiancé to debark from the aircraft. *Theos*, he swore to himself, how many suitcases did they have? They were going on honeymoon for three weeks, not three months.

It was because of Alex that he'd had to delay his return to the island. She'd insisted that she'd been unable to find exactly the right headdress to wear with her wedding veil. Consequently one had had to be made for her, but it hadn't been ready until the following day.

In Demetri's opinion one headdress looked much like another, but he'd been obliged to humour her in this. It was Alex's big day, after all. If Costas was prepared to indulge her, how could he do anything less?

Costas's mother and father, and his three sisters, who were to be Alex's attendants, would be arriving the next day. And the day after that—the day before the ceremony—many more relatives and friends would be taking up temporary residence at the villa. Demetri wondered how Joanna would cope with so many strangers in the house, and then chided himself for caring what she thought about anything. She shouldn't be here; she didn't belong here. And he sure as hell shouldn't be suffering withdrawal symptoms just because he hadn't seen her for more than forty-eight hours.

The villa was ominously quiet when they arrived there in the late afternoon. Spiro had despatched the car to pick them up, but even he was absent when Demetri walked into the reception hall. Somewhere a bee was buzzing, probably trapped against the glass of the arching atrium, and the sultry scent of lilies and roses and other more exotic blossoms was strong on the air.

With a feeling of disquiet Demetri left Alex and Costas to offload their luggage and vaulted up the stairs to the first floor. The absence of servants wasn't a cause for concern. Most of the staff were free between the hours of three and six. He strode along the corridor to his father's apartments, assuring himself that he was overreacting.

He hesitated at the door. Once he would have walked in without knocking, but recent events had made him more cautious. Clenching his teeth, he raised his hand and tapped on the panels, feeling a mingled sense of relief and aggravation when Philip opened the door.

'Kirie Demetri,' the old man exclaimed warmly, in their own language. 'You are back at last. Thanks be to God!'

'Why?' Demetri brushed past the old manservant and glanced quickly about him. 'What has happened? Is my father all right?'

Philip wrung his hands. 'I wish I knew,' he said, setting all Demetri's nerves on red alert. 'I have been so worried.'

'Worried?' Demetri was sure Spiro would have told him if his father had had a turn for the worse. Or perhaps not. 'What do you mean?'

'Oh, Kirie Demetri!' Philip shook his head. 'That woman—she is no good for him.'

The fact that Demetri agreed with him made it harder for

him to say tersely, 'I am sure my father knows what he is doing, Philip.' He saw his father's bedroom door was closed and took a deep breath. 'Is he resting? I would like to have a word with him—'

'He is not resting.' Philip licked his dry lips. 'They are out, *kirie*. In the heat of the day they went out. I could not stop them.'

Demetri wondered why he felt so deflated. *Na pari i oryi.* He ought to be glad his father was feeling well enough to go out. He had obviously recovered from the setback he'd been suffering when Demetri left for Athens, and it was a short step from there to presuming that, far from being no good for him, Joanna had had a favourable effect. Philip was jealous, that was all. And Demetri—well, he preferred not to dwell on his own feelings in the matter. Far better to go back downstairs and find Spiro, and try to submerge himself in the only part of his father's affairs that should concern him: the Kastro empire.

It wasn't until dinner that evening that Demetri encountered Joanna again.

He wasn't absolutely sure what time she and his father had returned from their outing—Spiro, who had been answering a call from one of their clients when Demetri and his sister had got back, had been annoyingly vague about their whereabouts. He thought they might have driven into Agios Antonis to do some shopping, but he couldn't be sure. As he'd said, Constantine hadn't consulted him before leaving the villa.

In consequence Demetri had had to cool his heels until the evening. He hadn't tried to see his father again before dinner. He was too aware of what he might find if he did. Besides, Spiro had business matters to discuss with him, and until his father was fully recovered—or he allowed Olivia to assist her brother, as she wanted to do—it was Demetri's responsibility to see that there were no foul-ups in the operating process.

His first thought, when he walked into the salon that evening and found Joanna and his father seated on a sofa, laughing together over a book Constantine had open on his lap, was that she looked even more beautiful than he remembered. In his absence the sun had given a golden glow to her fair skin and added lighter streaks to the pale glory of her hair. She was wearing a thin wraparound gown in shades of dark blue and turquoise that left one shoulder bare and clung to the lissom contours of her shapely body. A soft chignon allowed shining strands of hair to curl about her jawline, drawing his unwilling attention to the high cheekbones and the pure line of her throat. In short, she looked delectable, and Demetri knew an unforgivable urge to stride across the room and drag her away from the possessive arm his father had placed about her waist.

'Ah, Demetri.' Constantine greeted him pleasantly, and, despite his misgivings, Demetri was obliged to cross the room and bend to accept the customary salutation. But he drew the line at giving Joanna any kind of welcome, and permitted himself merely a tight smile in her direction.

He saw, to his satisfaction, that she was looking less confident now. Her lids dropped, and she made a play of being absorbed in the book. He realised now that it was a photograph album. *Theos*, he thought furiously, his father was showing her pictures of himself, Olivia and Alex when they were children. Did he have no shame?

'You will forgive me if I do not get up,' Constantine continued, shifting into a more comfortable position on the sofa. 'We have had rather a busy day, eh, Joanna? And I confess I am a little tired.'

'Busy, yes,' murmured Joanna, her eyes flickering briefly to Demetri's taut face. Then, because Constantine obviously expected more of her, 'We—er—we've been visiting a friend of your father's.'

'Marcos Thexia,' put in Constantine smugly, mentioning the name of his lawyer. 'And we did a little shopping, too.' He lifted Joanna's wrist to display the diamond-studded bracelet that encircled it. 'What do you think, Demetri? Is it as beautiful as its wearer, do you think?'

'Constantine!'

Joanna's protest sounded convincing, but Demetri was not deluded by her tone. 'Not nearly,' he said gallantly, but the fleeting look she gave him revealed that she wasn't deceived by his insincerity either. Nevertheless, Demetri was more concerned with why his father should have been visiting his lawyer. In God's name, what had he done now?

'That is what I thought,' said Constantine happily, apparently immune to any undercurrents between them. 'Ah, here is Uncle Panos. *Pos ineh simera to vrathi, Panos*?' How are you this evening?

The old man's intervention allowed Demetri to withdraw to the other side of the room. Finding a tray of drinks on a half-moon-shaped table, he poured himself a generous measure of Scotch before turning back to face the others. He didn't know what he'd expected exactly. Perhaps that the unwelcome emotions Joanna had inspired in him before he went away had been exaggerated in his own mind. He'd assured himself that she couldn't be half as desirable as he remembered, but he'd been wrong. She was just as desirable, just as—

But his mind baulked at the ugly word that had entered his head. He didn't just want to have sex with her; he wanted to make love to her. Using her to assuage his frustrations wouldn't come close to how he was feeling. If it wasn't so bloody ludicrous he'd have wondered if he didn't want to have a relationship with her himself.

'Will you put the album away, *agapi mou*?'

As Panos seated himself in the chair closest to him Constantine asked Joanna if she'd return the photograph album to the cabinet. Then, as the two older men fell into conversation about the political situation in Athens, Joanna got to her feet and, with obvious reluctance, came towards Demetri.

Of course, he thought, with grim satisfaction. The cabinet

was right next to where he was standing. To reach it she was obliged to run the gamut of his narrow-eyed appraisal, and it irritated him no end that she appeared so composed when he felt so tense and on edge.

'Did you enjoy looking at pictures of my father's off-spring?' he enquired in a low voice, unable to help himself. 'Some of them must have been taken before you were even born.'

Joanna bent to slide the album back into place and his eyes were irresistibly drawn to her cleavage. Then she straightened to face him. 'You flatter me,' she said, and for a moment his mind went blank. But she enlightened him. 'I'm not as young as you apparently imagine.'

'Oh. Right.' Demetri struggled to collect his thoughts. 'Well, perhaps you have some photographs of your own family to show us, *ne*? Your husband, *isos*?' He paused. 'If there ever was such a person.'

'There was.' She spoke in a low voice. 'I wouldn't lie about something like that.'

'No?' He paused. 'But that begs the question of what you *would* lie about, *okhi*? Perhaps you have lied about something else.'

'No.' She was indignant. 'Why should you think I would have anything to hide?'

Demetri shrugged. 'I suppose because I only know what you have chosen to tell me. This sad story about your parents being killed when you were a child and having to be brought up by your aunt: do you not think it smacks a little of a fairy story, *ne*?'

She stared at him with wide, accusing eyes. 'It was no fairy story, Mr Kastro,' she told him coldly. 'My parents were killed in an avalanche in Austria and I was brought up by my father's elderly aunt. Believe me, I wouldn't make that story up.'

Demetri's brows drew together. 'You sound very sure.'

'I am.'

'Do I take it that it was not a happy time for you?'

'A happy time for me?' Joanna's face contorted. 'Mr Kastro, my whole life has not been a—a happy time for me. Does that answer your question?'

Demetri frowned. 'And with your husband?'

'My ex-husband?' Joanna clasped her hands together at her waist and stared down at them. 'Then most of all,' she added bitterly.

'What are you saying to Joanna, Demetri?'

Constantine's querulous voice broke into their exchange, and Demetri suppressed an oath when Joanna turned her head to meet his father's gaze. Immediately she seemed to realise she'd been less than discreet in discussing her personal affairs with him, and without another word she hurried back to Constantine's side.

'We were just chatting about my childhood,' she said, letting Demetri off the hook even as she proved she was as capable of bending the truth as anyone else. 'Is it nearly time for dinner?'

'When Alex and Costas get here,' agreed Constantine drily. 'Ah, here they are at last.' With her help he got heavily to his feet. 'My dear, allow me to introduce you to my younger daughter and her fiancé. Alex, Costas—this is my very dear friend, Joanna Manning.'

Dinner went reasonably well. Perhaps it was because Olivia was absent for once, but Demetri had to admit that the atmosphere was considerably less tense than when she was present.

Alex was much different from her sister, of course, and she seemed to see nothing wrong in the fact that their father should be choosing to have an affair with a much younger woman. Indeed, in an aside to her brother she observed that Constantine looked quite well for a man who only weeks ago had undergone a serious operation. Her opinion was that Joanna must be doing him some good, and Demetri was forced to concede that she might be right.

Not that that was any consolation to him. It didn't please

him to realise that he was beginning to find excuses for Joanna's involvement with his father. Listening to her talk about herself, about her marriage, he'd actually felt some compassion for her. So much so that he'd resented his father for interrupting them when she'd been on the verge of telling him why her marriage had broken down. Or rather, he thought she had, he reflected wryly. Perhaps she hadn't intended to confide in him at all. Perhaps everything she'd said had been a carefully orchestrated attempt to gain his sympathy. If so, she'd certainly achieved her aim.

He scowled. Dammit, when was he going to stop thinking with his emotions instead of his head? It didn't matter if she'd lied to him or not. She wasn't his concern.

But she was.

'Is something wrong, Demetri?'

Alex's low voice, speaking in their own language, was troubled, and he realised that although she was sitting beside him he'd hardly spoken a word to her throughout the meal. Which was unusual for him. He'd always felt he had more in common with his younger sister than with Olivia. The fact that Alex was getting married in a couple of days should have been the foremost thing on his mind.

'Nothing,' he denied now, forcing a teasing smile for her benefit. 'So...how do you think it will feel to be Kyria Karadinos?'

'Pretty good, I hope.' She answered him in the same light vein. Then, more seriously, 'How about you? Not having second thoughts about your break-up with Athenee, are you?'

Demetri's smile deepened. 'No,' he said drily, aware that only Alex would have dared to bring up his affair with Athenee Sama at the dinner table. Indeed, most people avoided talking about Athenee at all—believing, quite rightly, that it was a sore subject with him.

Or it had been. He realised with a jolt of amazement that since his father had introduced him to Joanna he hadn't even thought about Athenee. Now he was, but he felt nothing. Nothing at all.

'I am glad.' Alex was nothing if not persistent. 'I never liked her. She was always so vain, so full of her own importance. She would not have made you happy, Demetri. You need someone warm; someone—sympathetic.' She dimpled, her face—with its straight nose and deep-set dark eyes—so like his own. 'Someone like Joanna,' she added mischievously. 'What a pity Papa saw her first.'

Demetri managed to retain his smile, but only just. As always, Alex had rushed in where angels feared to tread. 'I do not think Mrs Manning likes me,' he said, with what he thought was admirable restraint. He took a deep breath and changed the subject. 'Costas.' He leaned past her to speak to her fiancé. 'I hope you intend to keep my sister in order. I regret she has the unforgivable tendency of poking her nose into places where it is least wanted.'

'Well, I had to be sure that you were not pining for Athenee,' protested Alex indignantly. 'I am sure you know that Papa has invited Aristotle Sama to the wedding, and it is not beyond the realms of possibility that Athenee will come with him.'

Demetri's scowl returned. 'And Benaki?' he enquired, with rather less sanguinity.

'Oh, did you not know?' Alex gave a nervous little shrug of her shoulders. 'Athenee and Peri Benaki are no longer an item. Sara, Costas's sister, told me.'

CHAPTER TEN

IT WAS early evening before Joanna had the chance to escape from the wedding party. Avoiding the marquee, where earlier in the day a sumptuous lunch had been served to over a hundred guests, she went down the steps towards the beach, taking off her heeled sandals when the sand started to ooze between the straps.

From Alex and Costas's point of view it had been a successful day. Although Alex had confided that the guest list had had to be pruned because of her father's illness, Joanna couldn't help thinking that getting on to one hundred and fifty witnesses was fairly generous by anyone's standards. Another ceremony was already being planned, to take place in Athens when the young couple returned from their honeymoon, to include all the people they had not been able to invite to the island. But for the present the celebrations were over; Alex and her new husband had left for Malaysia, and all that was left to do was bid goodbye to the guests who had stayed at the villa.

Half an hour ago Joanna had escorted Constantine to his apartments, aware that he had been exhausted by it all. Despite his grim determination to give Alex a day she would remember, at the end he had had to admit his weaknesses. Without Joanna's help he would never have got up the stairs, but he was adamant that no one else should be involved.

Demetri had been concerned, of course. Joanna had been aware of him keeping an eye on his father, like herself, during the service, ready to rush to his aid if he'd looked in danger of imminent collapse.

But Constantine had drawn on strengths even Joanna

hadn't believed he possessed. He'd escorted his daughter to the ceremony, stood by while she'd taken her vows, and given his speech at the lunch that followed with every indication that he was enjoying the occasion just as much as everybody else.

And he had. He'd kept Joanna at his side, of course, despite the many disapproving looks from his older daughter. It was the only intimation Joanna had had that perhaps he didn't feel as confident of his stamina as he pretended. But, apart from that, he'd behaved like any other father, proud of his daughter and eager to demonstrate his approval of her choice of husband to the world.

Thankfully, it was all over now. Joanna could feel her own tension easing as she trod across the still warm sand. Constantine had achieved his objective, and there'd been no doubt of his gratitude towards her as she'd helped him out of his jacket and shirt and replaced them with a silk dressing robe.

Subsiding with evident relief onto his bed, he'd clung to her hand for a moment longer than was necessary, saying weakly, 'You do not think anyone suspected, do you, *agapi mou*?' and Joanna had assured him that he'd done as he'd intended.

'Alex suspected nothing,' she'd assured him. 'Demetri...' She'd hesitated. 'Demetri was concerned that you might be over-taxing your strength, but none of them guessed the truth. However...' She paused again. 'You've got to tell them now, Constantine. It's only fair.'

Constantine's nod of understanding had hardly been a promise, but Joanna had had to be content with it. The old man had already been drifting into unconsciousness, and she'd left his room feeling that she'd done all she could for the present.

She took a deep breath of the salt-laden air. It had been a good day, she told herself determinedly. Constantine had enjoyed it; everyone had enjoyed it. Even she'd felt a twinge of emotion when Alex had appeared, slim and enchanting in the wedding gown that a famous designer had made especially for her. She'd been forced to admit that not everybody's wedding day was doomed to end in disappointment and humiliation. Costas loved Alex; anyone could see that. And she had only to look at them to know that the intimacy they shared was real, not imagined.

It had all been so different from her own wedding day. Oh, she had been just as eager, just as excited, but she hadn't had any idea that the day would end in the way it had. She'd never dreamt that the reason Richard had refrained from making love to her before their marriage was because he couldn't; that the man she'd thought was his friend was in fact his lover.

If only Richard could have been honest with her; honest with his parents. Goodness knew, being homosexual was not something to be ashamed of. Why couldn't he have faced his real identity instead of involving her? Was it only, as he'd said, because she'd been so trusting? Or rather because she'd been so incredibly easy to deceive?

She felt a lump come into her throat at the memory. She *had* been trusting, and naïve. Aunt Ruth had seen to that. She'd treated her niece like a servant. No wonder Joanna had been so eager to escape to a better life.

The holiday in Sardinia had been her first chance to act like a real woman. An attractive woman, moreover. One capable of appealing to a sophisticated man like Richard. Meeting him had seemed like a dream come true. He'd been so charming; so handsome. So kind that she'd fallen headlong in love with him almost on their first date.

Of course she hadn't been looking for his faults. And in the beginning she'd felt only gratitude when he'd expected so little from her. She'd had no experience with men. No experience at all except the admiration of boys when she'd been at school. The prospect of getting married had been a big step for her. It had been enough to be going on with.

Richard's parents had been kind to her, too. A much older couple than her own parents would have been, they'd virtually given up all hope of having a child of their own when Richard was born.

Naturally, they doted on him. Nothing was too good for him. He could do no wrong. Afterwards Joanna had had to acknowledge that his parents were partly to blame for what had happened. They'd expected so much of him. If they'd been younger, more worldly-wise, Richard might have found the courage to tell them the truth.

Perhaps they had suspected, Joanna reflected now. But if so they had never voiced their suspicions to her. They'd let her go ahead with the wedding, insisting on paying for everything in spite of her protests. It was the least they could do, they'd insisted, for the woman who was going to make Richard such a wonderful wife.

The day itself had gone remarkably smoothly. Richard's cousin had been best man, and much later Joanna had realised why he'd seemed so detached from the ceremony. She guessed he knew the truth and had tried to reason with Richard himself. But, for whatever misguided reasons, Richard had been determined to go through with it. Nothing was going to stop him from being the son his parents thought he was.

They'd spent the first night of their honeymoon at a hotel at Gatwick Airport. They were to spend their honeymoon in Antigua, compliments of the older Mannings, but their flight hadn't been until the next morning.

In consequence, it had been comparatively early in the evening when they'd gone to bed. Joanna had been wearing a white lace nightgown, she remembered, bought especially for the occasion. When she'd emerged from the bathroom and found Richard apparently already asleep she'd stifled her own disappointment and got obediently into bed beside him.

She hadn't gone to sleep, however. The excitement of the day and her own unsatisfied expectations had kept her awake. That had been why, when Richard had got out of bed at about half past eleven to go to the bathroom, she'd spoken to him. She'd caught his hand as he'd crept around the bed, and discovered that he wasn't at all pleased that she was awake.

She'd excused his irritation on the grounds of over-tiredness, but when he'd climbed back into bed she'd moved towards him eagerly. His pyjamas had been a little off-putting, but she'd consoled herself with the thought that he'd soon feel differently when he'd kissed her.

But Richard hadn't wanted to kiss her. To her intense humiliation he'd told her that he just wanted to go to sleep. He wasn't a physical person, he'd added, when he'd sensed her mortification. There'd be plenty of time for them to get to know one another in that way once they reached the Caribbean.

It hadn't happened. Oh, Richard had tried to make love to her on several occasions, but even Joanna, innocent as she was, had been able to see that he simply wasn't inter-ested in her. He'd apologised, of course. Made excuses about the heat and various other irritations, which she didn't want to remember now. And still she hadn't realised what was really wrong. That her woman's body repelled him, just as another woman's body would have repelled her.

With the honeymoon over, life had returned to normal, or as near normal as possible in the circumstances. Richard had gone back to work and Joanna had managed to get a job at Bartholomew's. To all intents and purposes—cer-tainly so far as Richard's parents had been concerned—they'd had a happy marriage.

Until Joanna had come home early from work one day and found Richard with John Powers, the young man with whom he'd been on holiday in Sardinia.

God, she thought now. How could she have been so stu-pid for so long? How long would she have gone on believ-ing that Richard was simply not a physical person, as he'd said? She liked to think she'd have found out eventually, but she'd been so busy convincing herself and everyone else that he was a wonderful husband that she might well have overlooked the most obvious explanation.

With his exposure, Richard had taken another tack. She mustn't leave him, he'd insisted. He'd be devastated if she walked out on their marriage now. And if his parents found out... The threat had been implicit in his words. He hadn't actually said that he would do something desperate, but even Joanna had been able to understand how awful that would be.

So she'd stayed. For a little while, at least. Until the day Richard had suggested she should find herself a lover and get pregnant. It was the only way, he'd insisted. She'd been amazed at his insensitivity. His parents had already started asking when they were going to start a family, he'd continued, and she wanted children, didn't she? He'd paused then, before adding that he could always fix her up with somebody he knew if finding a partner would be too difficult for her...

'Where is my father?'

Joanna started violently. She'd been so absorbed with the painful content of her thoughts that she'd been unaware that she was no longer alone. But she realised now that Demetri had come up beside her, his tread keeping pace with her bare feet, his suede boots already stained with seawater.

'You're ruining your boots,' she said without answering him. 'You should have taken them off.'

Demetri's stare was almost palpable. 'Has he retired for the night?' he asked harshly, ignoring her words, and she was reminded that she had spent the days since his return from Athens avoiding any personal contact with him. In fact, apart from a compulsory greeting now and then, voiced for his father's benefit, she had had no conversation with Demetri at all since their visit to the ruined temple.

'He's having an early night, yes,' she replied at last, not looking at him. 'Do you want me to give him a message?'

'No. No, I do not,' he retorted shortly, and she guessed he resented her for asking.

But why should she care? It wasn't as if it mattered what Demetri thought of her. In a few days, a week at most, she'd be leaving the island and she'd never see him again.

Oh, God!

Her stomach hollowed and she pressed a nervous hand to her midriff. It was what she and Constantine had planned, she reminded herself. What she wanted. But her stay on Theapolis had proved far more devastating than she could have imagined.

'How is he?'

Demetri seemed determined to pursue this conversation and Joanna expelled an unsteady breath. She wished he would go away, back to the women of his own nationality, many of whom had shown their willingness to share his company. Young and old alike, all had seemed to blossom in his presence, faces flushed and excited lips parted in anticipation, ready to agree with him whatever he chose to say.

It had sickened Joanna. She hated to admit the fact that she'd noticed, but, seated at Constantine's side for most of the day, she'd found it impossible to avoid seeing that Demetri attracted women like a magnet. And she was just like them, she acknowledged bitterly. She was just as gullible. Despite her experience with Richard, she couldn't deny that Demetri had stripped away her defences and shown her she was just as vulnerable as anybody else.

And why now? she asked herself depressingly. Why after all these barren years was she attracted to a man whose only emotion was contempt? Was this her fate? Was this destiny? Was she the kind of woman who must always be a victim?

'He's tired,' she said at last, forcing herself to continue walking along the shoreline. At least her feet were cool, she thought, even if the rest of her body was burning up. 'Surely you expected that?'

'I expect nothing, Joanna,' he responded coldly. 'Then I am not disappointed.' He paused. 'How about you? Did the day live up to your expectations?'

'Like you, I have no expectations.' Joanna answered him just as coldly, convinced there was a hidden meaning behind his words. Then, because she felt too brittle to indulge in any kind of infighting with him, she added, 'Why don't you go back to your guests? I'm sure at least half of them must be suffering withdrawal symptoms by now.'

She heard his swift intake of breath. 'Jealous?'

Pain filled her. 'Yeah, right,' she managed, with just enough irony in her voice. She quickened her step to get away from him. 'Grow up, Demetri!'

He came after her. His breathing matched hers in pace, but she doubted his heart was palpitating in his chest. All the same, when he gripped her upper arm to halt her, and swung her round to face him, she was surprised by the sudden anguish in his expression.

'Oh, yes,' he said, his tone harsh and unforgiving. 'I had forgotten. You prefer your men to be older—much older. Why? Can you not—what is the word?—*hack it* with someone of your own age, *ne*?'

Joanna pressed her lips together so that he shouldn't see how his words had upset her. 'Well, there's no fear of that with you, is there, Demetri?' she countered scornfully, not caring what she said, just so long as she hurt him as he was hurting her. 'Young or old; they're all alike. They can't wait for the heir to the Kastro fortune to put his hand up their skirts!'

She had shocked him. Dear Lord, she had shocked herself. What she had said was unforgivable, and his face briefly mirrored his disbelief. Then, with an oath, he lifted his hand, and she winced in anticipation of the blow that she was sure was to come.

But he didn't hit her. Instead, his hand settled heavily on the back of her neck and, drawing her towards him, he ground his forehead against hers in a helpless gesture of what she suspected was frustration.

Yet when he spoke, his words sounded tortured. 'Why do

we do this?' he demanded, his voice low and impassioned. 'I know you want me, and heaven knows I want you.'

Joanna didn't know what to say, how to answer him. She was afraid this was just another attempt to prove he was right about her, to humiliate her, to satisfy himself that she was as unprincipled as his accusations implied.

But before she could say anything a light laugh disturbed them. 'Demetri?' came a teasing voice. *'Ti tha kanateh?'*

Joanna felt Demetri's hand tighten convulsively for a moment, and then she was free. With admirable self-assurance, he'd turned to confront the woman—what else? Joanna derided herself bitterly—who had interrupted them. Speaking in his own language, he evidently gave some explanation for what he had been doing, and the woman's smile thinned only briefly before returning as confidently as before.

Joanna recognised her now. Even in the fading light it was impossible not to remember her. Her name was Athenee. Athenee Sama. Her father, Aristotle Sama, was a friend of the Kastros, and Constantine had confided to her that he and Athenee's father had had high hopes that their offspring might make a match of it.

She was certainly beautiful, thought Joanna, feeling a pang of envy. She didn't see how Demetri could fail to be attracted to her. The woman was gazing at him with such a look of admiration in her eyes that for all Demetri had said he wanted *her*, Joanna felt sure she must have misunderstood him. Beside Athenee's sweep of night-dark hair and vivid complexion, she felt pale and insignificant. A not-unfamiliar emotion for her, she conceded dully, but not one she had experienced since Constantine became her friend.

She would have escaped then. Taking several careful steps, she tried to slip away without being noticed, but Demetri had other plans. She wasn't sure whether he'd heard her—her feet had sunk into the damp sand—or he'd just remembered she was there. Whatever, his hand shot out and captured her wrist, imprisoning her beside him. Then, with casual courtesy, he asked her if she and Athenee had been introduced.

'But naturally.' It was Athenee who answered him, and the eyes she turned on Joanna weren't half as friendly. 'She is your father's—um—confidante, *ne*?' She made it sound like a dirty word. 'Constantine introduced us himself. He is, I think, very enamoured of her, is he not?'

Her meaning was obvious, and Demetri wasn't indifferent to the implication, Joanna saw at once. His hand dropped from her arm and she was left with an unwarranted feeling of isolation. And of being despised on all sides, she thought. Athenee didn't like her; that was apparent. And she had no doubt that, if he heard of it, Constantine wouldn't approve of the strangely clandestine relationship Joanna was having with his son.

'It is getting dark,' said Demetri abruptly, without answering her question. 'Come.' He included Joanna in the invitation. 'People are leaving. We should get back to the villa.'

'I'd rather stay here,' Joanna declared, determined not to lay herself open to any more insults from his girlfriend. 'You go.' Her lips twisted. 'Both of you.'

Demetri's eyes darkened. 'Joanna—'

'I'll see you in the morning,' she said, turning away. 'Goodnight.'

CHAPTER ELEVEN

IT WAS after midnight before Demetri went to his own apartments.

He told himself it was because there'd been a lot of clearing up to do after the guests who were leaving had departed, but in all honesty his father's staff were more than capable of dealing with the aftermath of the wedding party. Indeed, they'd probably seen his presence as something of an encumbrance. No doubt they'd wished he would just go away and leave them to it.

But the truth was, Demetri dreaded going to bed. So long as he was with other people he could put the turmoil of his thoughts to the back of his mind. He couldn't forget them, but he could ignore them, and that was almost as good. However, he knew that once he lay down and closed his eyes he'd have no defence against their torment.

Of course it needn't have been that way. Athenee, the woman he'd once believed he desired above all others, had shown him quite clearly that she wanted to renew their relationship. She would have been happy to stay on at the villa. Her father had had to get back to Athens; his helicopter had left earlier in the evening. But Athenee hadn't wanted to go with him. If Demetri had said the word she'd have been waiting for him now, the ideal antidote to what was wrong with him.

Yet Demetri had offered no invitation. After leaving Joanna on the beach, he and Athenee had walked back to the villa in total silence. He doubted if he'd have spoken to her at all if she hadn't caught his arm as they were crossing the terrace, and even then he'd left her in no doubt of his irritation at her interference.

114

'Yes?'

No warmth there, and Athenee had responded to it in her own arrogant way. 'You cannot have her, Demetri,' she'd said carelessly, and he'd known a moment's panic that his feelings were on display for all to see. But then her next words had reassured him. 'You were going to kiss her just now. I know it. But I interrupted you.' Her lips twisted. 'Be grateful to me, Demetri. Do you want your father to cut you off without a cent?'

'I do not know what you are talking about, Athenee,' he'd replied swiftly, glad of the fading light to hide the dark colour that had flooded his cheeks. 'And if this is an attempt to persuade me that you are here to console me for imagined temptations, then I regret to say that I must disappoint you.'

'Are you sure?' Athenee's eyes had flashed angrily.

'I am sure,' he'd told her. 'Nice try, Athenee, but you are wasting your time.'

'As are you, *agapitos*,' she'd retorted, determined to have the last word. 'Constantine would kill you if he ever found out.'

Would he?

Demetri posed the question to himself now, and then dismissed it. He had no intention of finding out so it didn't matter either way. But Athenee was right about one thing. He had been going to kiss Joanna, would have done so if Athenee hadn't interrupted them. He wouldn't have been able to prevent himself from tasting that sweet tempting mouth again. And how sensible was that?

Throwing off his jacket and tie, he raked frustrated fingers through his hair. Dammit, what was wrong with him? Had it been so long since he'd had a woman that he was willing to do anything, no matter how reckless, to get laid? But if that were the case why hadn't he taken up any of the invitations he'd been offered today? He wasn't a conceited man, but he knew when women were coming on to him. Yet he'd blanked them all. Including Athenee.

He scowled, and, unlatching the glass doors, stepped out onto the balcony.

It was a beautiful night. An arc of stars wheeled overhead. Although sometimes the days at this time of the year could be uncomfortably hot, the nights were infinitely more inviting. Even the insects seemed to have taken a breather and the air was overwhelmingly sensual.

Sensual.

He stifled a groan. The word reminded him of the first time he'd met Joanna. He was trying not to think about her, but just a word like that brought a stream of images pouring into his head.

It was the way she'd described the heat on Theapolis, he remembered. Sensual, she'd called it, challenging him with those deep blue eyes that seemed capable of seeing right into his soul. He'd thought she was trying to provoke him, and perhaps she had been. But he knew her better now, and he sensed that, for all her sexy clothes and striking beauty, she was not flirtatious. In fact there was something almost innocent about her at times. And there was no denying that when he'd kissed her at the temple her response had been deliciously unrehearsed.

Or perhaps he was only fooling himself, he thought irritably. He believed it would take a clever woman indeed to deceive him, but what if she was that woman? Was he being blinded by his own unwilling attraction to her? Was she using that to disguise a character that was far more complex than even he could imagine?

He didn't know. In fact, he knew precious little about her. His father seemed to have great faith in her, but what did that mean? Constantine had been ill; very ill. How did he know she hadn't used his illness to get close to him? It seemed mightily suspicious that from being some kind of clerk in an auction house she had graduated to wearing designer clothes and flaunting the friendship of a man like Constantine Kastro.

Friendship!

Demetri's stomach felt hollow. Friendship wasn't the half of it, he thought angrily, deliberately feeding his revulsion in an attempt to dispel the bitter jealousy that was gripping him. She wasn't his father's friend; she was his mistress. Did Constantine have any idea of what he was risking, getting involved with a woman like her?

Probably not, he decided grimly. And now that the wedding was over perhaps it was time he made more of an effort to find out all there was to know about Mrs Joanna Manning. Where did she live, for instance? Had she really had an unhappy childhood? And where was this elusive ex-husband who, according to her, had made her life so miserable? How long had they been married? Why had the marriage broken up? Did Constantine know? Did anybody know? Or was her past, like her present, shrouded in mystery?

He supposed he could put Spiro onto it. His assistant was a computer genius, and it would take him only a short time to discover everything Demetri wanted to know. All he needed was an address and the place she banked, and Spiro could hack into the appropriate records. In a matter of hours he'd have a file that even the secret police would be proud of.

The trouble was, that was illegal. He could hire a private detective, of course. But if his father ever found out that someone had been checking up on Joanna without his permission there'd be hell to pay. It wouldn't matter if the investigation was justified. Constantine demanded total loyalty from his employees and his family, and Demetri would bear the brunt of his father's wrath.

No, if he wanted to learn anything about Joanna he would have to do it himself. But how? How did one investigate someone about whom he knew so little? And whatever he decided to do, it had to be fairly soon.

He didn't know why, exactly, but he had the feeling that time was running out on him. He still didn't know why his father had been to see his lawyer, and the possible implications of that visit filled him with suspicion. Spiro had asked him at the beginning of the week whether he thought his father planned to marry Joanna, and he'd dismissed the idea at the time. But now it wasn't half so unimaginable as it had seemed then.

He walked to the rail that edged the balcony and stood for several minutes staring down at the gardens below his windows. Though mostly in darkness, one or two bulbs were still burning, lighting the paths and giving an eerie radiance to the shrubs that surrounded them.

The marquee was still standing on the lawns below the terrace. The contractors would be coming to take it down in the morning, but until then it stood there like a ghostly shroud. He didn't like the metaphor and turned away abruptly. It would be morning soon enough, and he had to get some sleep.

Sleep! His lips twisted. How could he sleep with the knowledge that Joanna was sleeping with his father at the other side of the house? In fact, the balcony he was standing on now wrapped right around the upper floor of the villa. He had only to turn a couple of corners and he'd be standing outside the very room where Constantine and Joanna slept.

His nerves tightened as a thought occurred to him. If Joanna was sleeping with his father, it followed that her room would be unoccupied right now. It was separated from his father's apartments by a sitting room and double panelled doors, as he knew only too well. If she'd left the window unlatched—and it was possible—he'd have an opportunity to go through her belongings without anyone being any the wiser.

He didn't know what he expected to find, though there was bound to be some identification among her papers. Her passport, for instance. He'd find her address, at least, and then it would be up to him whether he took it any further; whether he told Spiro what he'd done.

His nerves tingled as he went back into his bedroom and stripped off the white shirt he had worn for his sister's wedding. He replaced it with a short-sleeved black tee shirt that, together with his dark trousers, made him a much less conspicuous target in the moonlight.

His lips twisted. *Theos*, he wasn't used to this. No matter what justification he gave to himself, he didn't like it. It smacked too much of attempted voyeurism, and, although he wasn't planning on invading his father's bedroom and checking that they were together, if he was caught—

But he wouldn't be caught, he assured himself. As well as Joanna's sitting room, his father's sitting room lay between him and his father's bedroom. They'd never hear him. And if the window was locked it was all hypothetical anyway.

The window wasn't locked. In fact it was standing slightly ajar, and there was a lamp burning in the room. Demetri saw the light shining out onto the balcony and cursed his ill luck.

He was tempted to turn back, but something—some intuition, perhaps—urged him to go on. There was no sound and, flattening himself against the wall, he took a surreptitious glance into the room.

It was empty. The doors to his father's apartments were closed, and although the door to Joanna's bedroom was open there was no light in there. It looked as if leaving the lamp on had been an oversight. He pressed himself back against the wall again, trying to decide what to do.

This was ludicrous, he thought. She wasn't there. He was so attuned to Joanna's presence that he felt sure he'd have sensed it if she'd been in her own bed. Okay, leaving the window open had been foolish, but there had never been any real danger on the island. Constantine had probably told her that the grounds were patrolled after dark, and maybe she'd had other things on her mind when she'd left the sitting room.

He scowled. This was not the time to be thinking about what those things might be. Pull yourself together, he ordered impatiently. He didn't have a lot of time. It was already after two a.m.

Pushing the window wider, he waited only a second before easing into the room. His heart was hammering in his chest and he had to suppress a gulp of harsh laughter. *Theos*, what had she brought him to? Here he was, breaking into his own home!

Well, hardly breaking in, he amended, crossing the room on cautious feet. He frowned. But he ought to have an explanation prepared in case one of the servants disturbed him. What excuse could he give for being here? That he'd heard an intruder? Did that sound feasible? All right, his rooms were nowhere near Joanna's, but he could always say he'd been taking an evening stroll along the balcony when he'd seen someone enter this room.

He shook his head. An evening stroll at two o'clock in the morning? Who was going to believe that?

Well, it didn't matter what anyone else believed. They didn't have to believe him. He was doing this for his father, no one else. He deserved to know if the woman who had his confidence was worthy of the honour.

Yeah, right!

His deviousness appalled him. He wasn't doing this for his father; he was doing it for himself. But it wasn't sensible to be conducting an inquest on his character right now. He was here for a purpose, and the sooner he found what he was looking for, the sooner he could get back to his own room.

The sitting room offered no solutions. Apart from the sandals she'd been wearing earlier, which she'd kicked off near the balcony doors, there was nothing to show that this was Joanna's room. Any personal items must be in the bedroom and, stifling a feeling of apprehension, he moved to the bedroom doorway.

He would have to turn on a light, he realised. Although he'd regretted the lamp in the sitting room, it had made searching the place that much easier. In here, with the blinds drawn, there was no illumination whatsoever. Tiptoeing over to the bed, he listened intently for the sound of breathing, but he couldn't hear anything. Expelling a sigh of relief, he stepped back and turned on the lamp.

As he'd expected, the bed was empty. But—and this was disturbing—the sheets were tumbled and there was the definite imprint of a head on one of the lace-trimmed pillows.

His brows drew together. She must have gone to bed before his father had sent for her. The old man had returned early, after all. He'd probably been asleep when she'd come upstairs. So what, then? Had he woken up? Or was she the one who'd decided she needed his company?

That was harder to stomach. No matter how often he told himself he shouldn't be surprised by anything she did, he always was. He wanted her to be something she was not, he realised painfully. But what?

He didn't know what made him glance behind him just then. He'd observed her handbag lying on the ottoman at the foot of the bed, and he should have been moving towards it. But instead he looked round—and found Joanna herself standing in the open doorway.

He supposed he ought to be grateful that she hadn't screamed. Finding a dark-clad man in her bedroom would have been enough to spook most women, but not her. How long had she been standing there watching him? And why, when he should have been refining his story to explain this intrusion, could he only stare at her with undisguised hunger in his eyes?

She looked so beautiful, he thought, his own forbidden passion for her never more acute than at this moment. She was wearing a silk negligee over a matching nightgown in a particularly subtle shade of gold that complemented her skin. The cord was tied loosely at her waist and her hair tumbled, soft and lustrous, about her shoulders. She looked like his every dream—and his every nightmare. He wanted her—but he couldn't have her. She wasn't his. And that knowledge was tearing him apart.

'Demetri.' She said his name softly, with a disconcerting lack of surprise. 'What are you doing here? Did Constantine send for you?'

Constantine!

The mention of his father's name brought him briefly to his senses. 'Does he know I am here?'

She blinked. 'Don't you know?'

Demetri shook his head to clear it. 'No,' he said in a low voice. 'That is—I did not come to see my father. I came to see you.' He paused, but he had to know. 'Where have you been?'

'I was with your father,' she said, her voice barely more than a whisper. Her words crucified him. 'Why did you want to see me? I—' She broke off, as if just realising what time it was. 'It's the middle of the night!'

'I know what time it is,' muttered Demetri, wondering what had possessed him to tell her the truth. He should get out of here right now.

'Then—?'

He threw caution to the winds. 'We did not finish our conversation earlier.'

He saw at once that she knew what he was talking about, but he saw just as clearly that she chose not to admit it. 'What conversation would that be?' she demanded contemptuously. And then, as if realising their voices might carry on the still night air, she lowered her tone. 'I think you'd better go.'

'No.' No matter how unwise this was, he had to have some answers. 'We need to talk.'

'Without being interrupted by one of your many girl-friends?' she enquired coldly. She stepped aside from the doorway. 'Go! Go now! Before I decide to start screaming that there's an intruder in my room.'

'You would not do that.'

'No?'

'No.' He took a deep breath. 'I believe you have more—respect for my father than that.'

'But you don't,' she retorted in a low angry tone. 'Have a care, Demetri. I haven't told him about what happened at the temple yet, but that doesn't mean I won't.'

'Joanna...'

He started towards her, but she backed away into the sitting room. She was shaking her head as she groped behind her, trying to avoid falling headlong over the sofa that stood in the middle of the floor. Her hair was a pale aureole in the lamplight, accentuating the sudden colour that was spreading up her throat. She had never looked more lovely, more desirable. Or more untouchable.

Then she parted her lips, and Demetri didn't think before acting. He told himself later that he'd been afraid she was going to scream, as she'd threatened, but that wasn't the whole truth. Covering the space between them, he caught her as she would have whirled away, jerking her back against him and silencing that tempting mouth with his hand.

He didn't know which of them was the most shocked by the experience. She seemed to freeze, her whole body stiffening in outrage and disbelief. For his part, his senses were immediately assailed by the fragrance of her hair, the scent of lemon and verbena mingling with the warm perfume of her body.

But his moment of respite didn't last long. Almost at once she started to struggle against the confining circle of his arm, the muffling indignity of his hand across her mouth. She was stronger than he'd thought, and he had to fight to keep her anchored against him, his own body responding to the spicy heat she was exuding.

'*Efkolos, efkolos,*' he said hoarsely. Easy, easy. 'I am not going to hurt you. I just want to talk with you, that is all.'

Her response stunned him. Instead of giving up the unequal battle, she only increased her efforts to get away from him. And before he had time to assimilate his position, to decide how, if at all, he could reason with her, he felt a searing pain in his hand.

Khristo, she had bitten him!

He couldn't believe it. Letting her go now, without caring for the consequences, he gazed down at the blood oozing out of the soft flesh of his palm. He stared incredulously at the line of teeth marks that defined the bite, and then lifted his head to stare at her. She was crazy, he thought blankly. And he was crazy for thinking she would listen to him.

But she didn't scream.

Although she'd put the width of the room between them, she made no attempt to summon assistance. On the contrary, she was standing twisting her hands together at her waist, and when their eyes met he was almost sure he saw remorse in their depths.

He knew he should go. Whatever was going on here, he wasn't going to solve it by appealing to her better nature. But all the same he couldn't leave without saying incredulously, 'Why?' He lifted his hand and a drop of blood fell onto the rug at his feet. 'Why this?'

She untangled her hands and pressed one to her throat. 'You wouldn't understand.'

'Try me.'

Her tongue circled her upper lip. 'I think you ought to put a plaster on that cut.'

Demetri's mouth twisted. 'Why? Am I in danger of contracting blood poisoning, too?'

Joanna hesitated and then, incredibly, she said, 'You'd better come into the bathroom. I think I've got something you can use in there.'

Demetri's jaw dropped. 'You are offering to tend to my injury?' he asked disbelievingly, and her eyes darted away from his.

'The—the bathroom's through here,' she mumbled, instead of giving him an answer. She sidestepped past him and went through the bedroom to the bathroom beyond. A light went on and, against his better judgment, Demetri cupped his injured hand in his other palm and moved to support himself against the frame of the bedroom door.

He couldn't see into the bathroom itself, but the mirrors that lined the walls threw back the reflection of Joanna riffling through the cabinet, taking out tubes and packets of plasters, extracting cotton wool balls from what he assumed was her own toilet bag. Her industry would have amused him if he hadn't felt such a baffling sense of confusion.

Then she came to the open doorway. 'Are you coming?' she asked, still avoiding his gaze. 'I think you ought to wash it first.'

Feeling a little as if he'd stepped into some parallel universe, Demetri straightened and walked around the bed to where she was waiting. He now saw that what she was holding was antiseptic ointment and, stepping back, she indicated that he should rinse his palm at the sink.

He did as she suggested, and then acquiesced again when she gestured for him to sit on the side of the bath. Taking a swab of cotton wool, she dried his palm first and then, with evident reluctance, took his wrist between her fingers.

'This may hurt,' she said, squeezing a little of the antiseptic cream onto the wound, and he gave her a weird look.

'Tell me about it,' he remarked drily, in an effort to distract himself from the dusky cleavage she exposed when she bent over him. 'Why did you do it?'

She sighed, her warm breath fanning his palm. 'Let's just say I don't like anyone—*any man*—forcing me to—to do something.'

'Is that what you think I was doing?' protested Demetri, horrified. 'For God's sake, Joanna, I meant what I said. I would never hurt you.' Unable to help himself, he used his free hand to lift her chin so that he could look into her face. 'You believe me, do you not?'

He saw her swallow, saw the convulsive movement of her throat as she endeavoured to sustain his invasive stare. Then, with a nervous movement of her shoulders, she lifted her chin out of his hand and looked back at her task. 'You don't understand.'

'No, I do not,' he agreed huskily. 'So why do you not enlighten me?'

She took a deep breath, and after removing the surplus ointment from around the cut she smoothed a plaster over it. He thought she wasn't going to say anything more, but suddenly she lifted her head and looked at him again.

'My—my ex-husband tried to persuade me to—to have sex with another man,' she said, straightening. Then, with a complete change of expression, 'Does that feel all right?'

Demetri was stunned. But not so stunned as to allow her to turn away from him. Capturing her hand, he held onto it. To his relief, she didn't try to resist.

'Your—ex-husband?' he echoed, trying to make sense of what she'd said. 'Joanna—'

'He was gay,' she explained matter-of-factly, not looking at him. 'His parents didn't know. They would have been mortified if they had. They were fairly old, and old-fashioned. Richard was their only son, their only child. They thought he was perfect.'

Demetri's legs were splayed, and now he used his hold on her hand to tug her between them. 'Did you know?' he asked, and now she did cast another, albeit brief glance at his face.

'Not before we were married, no.'

'But—'

'I was naïve,' she said flatly. 'As I told you, I'd been brought up by an elderly aunt. Richard knew that. He used it to his own advantage.'

'Even so—'

Demetri shook his head and looked up into her troubled blue eyes. He knew he should get to his feet, but right now he was too bemused to do it. What she was saying was so incredible. *Theos*, did she expect him to believe her? Did he believe her?

'You don't believe me?'

For a moment he thought he'd spoken his thoughts out

loud, but he knew as soon as he saw her doubtful features that she was merely anticipating his reaction.

'I—did not say that,' he began, but she wouldn't let him finish.

'You didn't have to,' she retorted. A bitter smile crossed her face. 'Richard's parents didn't either.'

Demetri looked down, gathering her other hand so that he held both of hers between his. 'I still do not understand,' he said softly. 'What possible satisfaction could this man get from—?'

'He wanted me to have a baby,' she answered without hesitation. 'It's ironic, really. I'd virtually resigned myself to a sterile marriage, but his parents wanted a grandchild, so...'

Demetri tilted his head to look up at her again. Was it true? Was it possible? Had he been totally wrong about her? He didn't know. What he did know was that his body was treacherously weak where she was concerned.

'And—did he succeed?' he asked, hardly wanting to hear the answer. She had said she had no children, and now he thought he could understand her reaction when he'd questioned her. But that didn't mean—

Her response was as unexpected as her revelations had been. Instead of indulging in some tedious explanation, which he might or might not have listened to, she slid her fingers between his. Then, drawing his hands aside, she stooped to brush a feather-light kiss across his startled mouth.

CHAPTER TWELVE

How Demetri prevented himself from falling back into the bath he never knew. At the touch of her lips his limbs felt boneless, and it would have been so easy to lose what little hold on reality he had. Need, hot and powerful, transmitted itself from her to him, and this time when he reached for her it was in the certain knowledge that she wouldn't push him away.

Between his legs, he'd hardened instinctively, and when her thigh brushed against the swelling in his pants he realised how totally she overwhelmed his senses—and his sanity. With his hand behind her head he crushed her mouth to his, letting her feel the hunger in his kiss. And she met his demand, her lips parting eagerly, inviting the urgent invasion of his tongue.

But Demetri wanted to feel more of her than her hands and the undoubted delight of her mouth. He wanted to feel those full rounded breasts against his chest, her nipples probing the dark hair that arrowed down to his navel. He wanted to touch her breasts, not through the fine silk, as he was doing now, but her naked breasts, warm beneath his hand. He wanted to touch her navel, too, to lick his way down her body to the soft curls he knew he'd find between her legs. *Theos*, he wanted all of her, and he was fairly sure she wanted all of him, too.

With his mouth still glued to hers, he got unsteadily to his feet, releasing her hands to cup her upper arms with fingers that were slippery with sweat. *Khristo*, no woman had ever done to him what Joanna was doing to him, and he hadn't even got her into bed yet.

But he would. He had to. And if the insistent voice of his

conscience was protesting that this was his father's woman, his father's mistress, not his, he refused to listen.

Gathering her against him, he slid his fingers into the silken glory of her hair, revelling in the way it clung to his skin. Everything about her was soft and sweet and desirable, and dizziness assailed him as he edged her back into the bedroom.

It was lucky that the bed wasn't far away. He sensed the moment the back of her legs hit the side of it, and she made an unwary sound against his mouth as she lost her balance. Demetri bore her down onto the tumbled sheets, half afraid of what she might do now that his intention was clear. But to his relief she abandoned any attempt to break away from him, winding her slim arms about his neck and giving herself up to his searching caress.

Dear God. Demetri groaned, feeling the curving form beneath him. Never had a woman felt this good; never had he been so desperate to make love. The cord of the negligee had loosened in her fall, and now all that was between his hand and the sensuous touch of her skin was the virtually transparent fabric of her nightgown. He wanted to tear it from her, to expose the enchanting length of her to his hungry gaze. But, remembering what she had said earlier, he controlled his wilder impulses. There was no hurry, he told himself unsteadily. They had the rest of the night.

Although he was half afraid that in freeing her mouth he might give her the chance to change her mind, the simple need for oxygen had him releasing her lips to bury his face in the scented hollow of her throat. His heart was hammering like a mad thing in his chest and he gulped air into his starved lungs.

But Joanna had her own agenda, he discovered. Her fingers curled into the hair at his nape, pressing his face against her, inciting a need in his lower limbs that was almost impossible to control. One slim leg curved across his thigh and a seductively bare sole inched beneath the cuff of his pants and caressed his ankle.

Demetri's blood pounded through his veins. He wanted out of his clothes, and fast. With unsteady fingers he tore at the buckle of his belt, struggling with the button on his pants that arrantly refused to come loose. Then slim fingers brushed his hands aside, and seconds later he felt the relief of his zip sliding virtually unassisted over his pulsing erection. ⌣

He half hoped she would go on and finish the job, but she didn't. With a breathless little gasp she pulled her hand away, and he was obliged to jerk the trousers over his hips and kick them off. His tee shirt followed them, and this time her reaction was much more positive. Almost tentatively, it seemed, her fingers probed the fine growth of hair that covered his chest, her nails finding his nipples before she rolled them beneath her palms.

Demetri couldn't wait much longer. Unable to stop himself, he found the hem of her nightgown and drew it up to her waist. Long legs, a deliciously flat abdomen, the hollow of her navel: he saw all this in a moment. But his eyes moved swiftly to the cluster of pale curls between her legs, and, as if aware of where his attention was focussed, she shifted almost nervously beneath his gaze.

'*Theos, is' oreos!*' God, you're beautiful! His throat constricted with unaccustomed emotion. 'Ah, Joanna, do you have any idea how much I want you?'

Her lips parted. 'Do you?' she asked, her voice barely more than a whisper. 'Do you really want me? Or—or—?'

'Or nothing,' he said hoarsely, peeling her nightgown over her head as he spoke. His eyes darkened at the sight of her breasts, full and swollen and as rosily perfect as he had anticipated. With a shuddering sigh he bent to take one tight nipple into his mouth. He wet it with his tongue, his teeth digging ever so gently into the soft skin that surrounded it. Then, speaking against her flesh, 'How could you doubt it?'

'You—you could have any woman you wanted,' she protested, her nails digging into his shoulders, and he gave a shuddering sigh.

'I do not want any other woman,' he told her unevenly, and knew amazingly that it was true. 'I just want you.'

'But—'

There was only one way to silence her and he used it. Even as his hand slid down over the quivering swell of her belly to find the moist core of her womanhood his lips closed over hers again, his tongue plunging possessively into her mouth. She opened to him with delicious eagerness, capturing his tongue between her teeth as she opened her legs to admit his probing fingers.

She was ready for him. Her essence wet his fingers, rose in sensual waves of heat and urgency to his nose. And she was tight; so tight that it would be incredibly easy to delude himself that no other man had ever possessed her. She bucked a little as he caressed her, increasing the notion that no man had done this before.

He stifled a moan of impatience, realising he was in danger of losing what little control he had. Her fingers were on his back, exploring his backbone. Then sliding beneath the waistband of his shorts, finding the cleft between his buttocks with mind-shuddering intimacy.

She had no idea how close he was to making a complete fool of himself, he thought dazedly. But she must have. She was no teenager, indulging in her first experiment with sex. She was a mature woman, adult and experienced. She must know exactly what her teasing hands were doing to him.

'My God, Joanna,' he said hoarsely, feeling his shorts snag on his erection. Cool air was a relief against his hot flesh, and somehow he got the shorts down his legs so he could kick them off. He heard her breath catch in her throat when she saw him, and once again he had that feeling of unreality. But she was all woman. She was warm and sexy, and so responsive that she blew his mind.

Taking one of her hands, he deliberately brought it to him. Balancing his control on a knife-edge, he encouraged her fingers to close around him, and gave a groan of protest when she did as he asked.

'What is it? Did I do something wrong?' she murmured anxiously, drawing her hand away again, and he uttered a strangled gasp.

'No,' he assured her huskily. 'You did everything right. It's—oh, *Theos*. I want to love you, Joanna. Let me really love you. Let me show you how incredible you are.'

She rose up then, to cover his lips with hers, and this time it was her tongue that surged into his mouth. Her kiss drove all thoughts of anything—or anybody—else out of his head. Her breasts were crushed against his chest; her stomach was close against his abdomen. Her spread legs, with knees drawn up, made it easy for him to move between her thighs.

He ached with the needs she had aroused in him. Looking down, seeing himself poised at the moist opening to her body, he didn't know how he stopped himself from simply plunging into her enticing heat. He wanted to. God, how he wanted to. Even the knowledge that he had come unprepared for such intimacy was no real deterrent. But something, some inner instinct, perhaps, urged him to take his time.

He'd have liked to explain it as a belated sense of honour that had given him pause. But that wasn't true. He was too obsessed with her, with his own passion for her, to entertain any serious doubts about what he was doing now. He wanted her. He was going to have her. But perhaps it would be good to prolong the expectation.

Good—but hardly sensible. Just the touch of her warmth, of her woman's body, had him trembling like a schoolboy. Senses were heightened, needs refined. This was going to be a life-altering experience. He didn't know how he knew that, but he did.

She was tight, so tight, he thought again. That was his final thought as he eased closer. Making love to her was going to be like making love to a virgin, and he hadn't known many of those in his career.

Her muscles closed about him, gripped him, driving him almost to a climax with their rippling strength. She was amazing, he thought, in his last coherent moment before his control snapped. Having her once was never going to be enough...

Joanna tensed. She couldn't help herself. So far, Demetri's hands and lips and tongue had done a wonderful job of convincing her that she could do this, but suddenly she wasn't so sure. She wasn't what he expected, and although she'd persuaded herself that he need never know how inexperienced she was, that proposition no longer sounded so feasible.

Doubts flooded her mind: doubts about Demetri's real intentions, doubts about what she was doing. Even now she could hardly conceive of how she'd got herself into this situation, and the hot blood swept into her throat at the realisation of how wantonly she had behaved.

Was behaving, she amended unsteadily, trying to draw her legs together and finding the way blocked by hard, muscular thighs. Oh, God, he was really going to do it. He was going to have sex with her. Already she could feel the blunt heat of him nudging the sensitive place between her legs. And while the intelligent part of her brain was telling her that she couldn't go through with this, another part, a reckless emotional entity, was urging her to give in to the needs that even sanity couldn't deny.

She was shaking. More from anticipation than fear, she acknowledged weakly. But that didn't make it right. Yet she couldn't deny that she had started this. It was she who had kissed Demetri; she who had allowed him to push her down onto the bed and make a mockery of the frigidity she had always wrapped around her like a shield.

What was different about Demetri? Why, when she'd seen him standing beside her bed, hadn't she done what any sensible woman would have done and called for help? He'd had his back to her, after all, and just because *she'd* known instantly who it was, no one else would have doubted her panic at finding a dark-clad intruder in her room.

But she hadn't done that. In fact she'd been almost apologetic when he'd asked her where she'd been. Nor had she explained why she had been in Constantine's room. She had no doubt Demetri thought she'd come straight from his father's bed, but of course she hadn't. She'd been in her own bed when she'd felt the need to check on Constantine, and she'd been returning from that unnecessary expedition when she'd found Demetri in circumstances which could only be described as suspicious.

Yet she'd accepted his explanation that he'd wanted to finish the conversation they'd been having when Athenee had interrupted them. A thin explanation at best, she conceded now, when they'd both known that talking was not what Demetri had had in mind. Then or now, she appended silently, her head swimming with so many wild emotions she could hardly think.

So what was different about Demetri? she asked herself again, trying to hold on to her own identity. Why, when Demetri kissed her, when he caressed her, when he crushed her beneath his heavy muscular body, didn't she remember how it had been with Richard? Why didn't she freeze up, as she had with every other man since her ex-husband had made such a travesty of her life?

She didn't know the answer. She only knew that Demetri aroused her in ways she'd never been aroused before. He made her feel like a woman, a real woman. A desirable woman, moreover. Without even being aware of it he had given her back her self-respect. And although she suspected she wouldn't feel half so positive in the morning, right now she didn't have the will—or the strength—to resist him.

However, that still didn't solve the problem of what she ought to do *now*. Though when Demetri sucked in his breath and dipped his head to lave her nipples with his tongue she found she was too bemused to care.

'You are—*apithanos*! Incredible,' he told her thickly, and all thought of trying to explain herself disappeared.

'Am I?' she heard herself say breathily, and instead of drawing away, telling him that he'd made a mistake about her, she arched up to meet him.

And knew at once that it was too late. The thick shaft which she had glimpsed earlier—and which had caused her no small measure of apprehension—was already pushing past the tight muscles that guarded her womb.

Heat, hot and hard and throbbing with life, was invading her lower body. It wasn't painful, but it was unfamiliar, and she knew a moment's consternation that she wouldn't be able to go on. Richard had not been particularly well-endowed, whereas Demetri was—was—

The pain that tore through her at that moment drove any thought of her ex-husband out of her head. Sharp and unexpected, it stifled the breath in her throat and brought hot tears to her eyes. She couldn't prevent the cry that broke from her lips at that moment, and if he had had any doubts before, Demetri was instantly aware of what he had done.

His eyes, suddenly burning into hers, were dark with confusion. And although it was much too late for him to do anything about it, it was obvious he was as shocked as she was. She felt his erection partially subside, and he shook his head as if to clear it. Then he stared at her as if he'd never seen her before.

'*Theos,*' he said in a shaken voice, his hands coming to cup her face. '*Mou lete*—that is, why did you not tell me?'

Joanna was flushed, as much from humiliation as anything else. But inside she felt cold. This was not how it was supposed to turn out. What price now her foolish hopes of hiding her ignorance from him?

'W-would you have believed me?' she asked at last, and Demetri acknowledged the guarded accusation with a rueful nod of his head.

'*Ala*—but you were married!' he exclaimed blankly, and she sighed.

'I told you about that.'

'Obviously not enough,' he said wryly, looking down to where their bodies were still joined. He uttered an oath. '*Signomi*. I am sorry. I should never have done this.'

Joanna's eyes darted to his then, the realisation that this might be her only chance to at least pretend she was like any other woman making her reckless. 'Do you regret coming here?' she breathed, sliding her hands up his chest. Once more she felt him stir inside her. 'You said you wanted me.'

'I did not know,' he said hoarsely, grasping her hands in his to prevent their caressing touch. 'Joanna, you must understand that— Ah, *Khristo*—my father!' He shook his head dazedly. 'I do not understand.'

'Do you have to?' she protested, managing to reach his flat stomach with her fingertips. She gazed up at him. 'Not now, please!' Her tongue appeared in innocent provocation. 'Demetri: make love to me.'

'*Mou Theos*, Joanna…'

The muscles in his wrists tensed as he endeavoured to restrain her. But he didn't try very hard, and it was comparatively easy for her to break free and link her hands about his neck.

Her fingers tangled in the moist hair at his nape, and she exulted in the knowledge that she had done this to him. 'Kiss me,' she said, discovering a confidence in herself she'd never known before. She reached up to him, finding his breathless mouth with hers, and with another muffled oath he cradled her face between his palms and returned the kiss.

The magic had returned. A thrill of excitement swept over her trembling limbs, sending the blood pounding through her veins. She was no longer afraid of what was to happen. She welcomed it as she welcomed the undoubted strength of his passion. Emotions, wild and turbulent, had taken over, and she was all softness, all eagerness, all woman in his arms.

Demetri couldn't resist her. Joanna seemed to know instinctively how to please him. Her teeth dug into his shoulder, drawing a groan of pleasurable protest from him, and then her hands curved over his tight buttocks, bringing him even more fully between her thighs.

The only protest she made was when she thought he was going to draw away from her. But he came into her again, more powerfully than before, and where earlier there had been a nervous frisson of feeling, now she felt a stirring need that was tantalisingly different.

The muscles that gripped him tightened almost automatically, and Demetri slid his hands beneath her to lift her to his thrusting shaft. He said something she didn't understand, some unsteady words in his own language whose meaning was perfectly clear nevertheless, and then added huskily, 'You have no idea how much I have wanted this—wanted you. Dear heaven, you have driven me—crazy!'

She wanted to say, Me, too, but she couldn't. A rising crescendo of need seemed to be building inside her, and only incoherent sounds of both pleasure and protest were issuing from her lips. She wanted to say that it couldn't go on, that *she* couldn't stand it, but apparently she could. Demetri's increasingly urgent body was plunging wildly into hers, and, looking up into his driven, sweating face, she saw a need to match her own.

His eyes were wide, impassioned, and her hands sought the damp skin of his shoulders in a desperate need to anchor herself. She had the feeling she was losing herself, losing her sanity, gradually being absorbed into the being that was him.

Her climax came suddenly. It was as if she had been striving for something that was always out of reach and abruptly found it within her grasp. Shuddering ripples of pleasure swept over her quivering body, and for a few incredible moments she was totally blown away. It was like nothing she had ever felt before, nothing she could ever have imagined, and it took an effort to focus her eyes again and look at Demetri.

He, too, was caught up in the moment. Even as she watched he thrust violently against her, and she felt the flooding warmth of what could only be his seed inside her. *His seed!* Dear heaven, she wasn't on the pill. She could get pregnant. Imagine how he would feel if she found she was carrying his child.

But she had no time to consider those implications. Even as Demetri collapsed upon her, even as he gave himself up to the luxury of pillowing his head in the dusky hollow between her breasts, they both heard the sound of a man's voice from the sitting room next door.

'*Kiria!* Kiria Manning!' called Philip's anxious tones, and Joanna stiffened. '*Kirie* Constantine calls for you, *kiria*. I am afraid he is not well.'

CHAPTER THIRTEEN

DEMETRI stood beside his father's bed, watching the old man sleep. The private hospital on the outskirts of Athens was not where he wished his father to be. Not where *he* wished to be, if it came to that. But so long as Constantine's health was a cause for concern it was the only placc he could be.

And his father was much better. Despite the tubes and wires to which he was still attached, the doctors had assured him that the old man's condition was stable. As stable as it could be, bearing in mind that his father was dying from terminal cancer.

Demetri's stomach hollowed. He knew now that the operation his father had had performed in the London hospital had not been the success he'd told his family it was. Indeed, Constantine had only had the operation in London because he'd been warned by his doctors in Athens that it was already too late for invasive surgery. The stomach cancer had spread to his other organs. Only in a foreign hospital could he hope to keep his condition from his children. And he'd wanted to do that because of Alex. Because he'd had no intention of being the spectre at his youngest daughter's wedding feast.

Demetri expelled a weary breath. He'd believed him, he thought incredulously. When he'd visited him in London his father had always been unfailingly upbeat about his treatment. Even the doctor in charge of his case had apparently been warned not to relay any unpleasant details to the family until after Alex's wedding. As far as they'd been concerned, the treatment he'd received had been successful. After the usual period of convalescence Constantine would be cured.

Demetri's jaw compressed. He realised now why his father had brought Joanna with him when he'd returned to the island. He'd guessed that, without her distracting presence, his children might have been more inclined to question his recovery. It was only because he'd behaved like a besotted old man that they'd overlooked the inconsistencies of his condition. The fact that he'd apparently felt well enough to entertain a much younger woman had blinded them to the truth. They'd believed what he'd wanted them to believe, Demetri conceded heavily. They'd been totally deceived, and that had been Constantine's intention all along.

But Demetri knew the truth now. Shaking his head, he moved to the windows that looked out onto the formal gardens that surrounded the hospital. Beyond manicured lawns, the blue-grey waters of the Aegean surged constantly. It had been raining earlier in the day, and the sea below the cliffs upon which the hospital was situated was still shrouded in mist. Somewhere out there was Theapolis, Demetri mused grimly. How long was it going to be before his father could return to the island? Before *he* could do the same? How long before they could both go home?

His fists clenched at his sides. He needed to go home, he thought impatiently. However painful it was going to be, he needed to talk to Joanna again. Whatever else, he needed to see her. God alone knew, he owed her that much.

It had been three long days and three even longer nights since he and his father had flown from Agios Antonis to Athens. Daniil Tsikas had accompanied them. The island doctor, whom Demetri had summoned as soon as he'd seen his father and realised the old man was having difficulty in breathing, had lost no time in contacting the hospital in Athens and arranging for his patient's emergency admission.

Constantine had been conscious when the arrangements were being made and he'd expressed his objections. He'd insisted he only needed his medication, but Demetri hadn't listened to him. He'd needed a professional opinion, a specialist's opinion, and when he'd learned how ill his father really was he'd realised why the old man had tried to stop him.

Stubborn old fool, Demetri thought now, fighting the unwelcome prick of tears behind his eyes. Dammit, he could have told him; he *should* have told him. He was his father's only son; his heir. He had the right to know what was going on.

Joanna had known. His mouth tightened as he accepted the fact that Joanna had known all along. She had been in his father's confidence. He couldn't have done it without her. And that was something Demetri was finding incredibly hard to swallow.

Yet how could he blame her for something that had been his father's decision? It wasn't her fault that Constantine had chosen to pretend he'd recovered. The fact that she'd gone along with it was surely incidental. But what had she got out of it? What did she expect to get out of it? She hadn't even shared his father's bed.

Thank God!

His hands clenched into fists at his sides. He wondered what she was thinking now. Would she be pleased to see him again? He thrust his fists into the pockets of his leather jacket. Somehow he doubted it. He couldn't help remembering the expression on her face when she'd heard his father's old manservant calling to her from the sitting room of her apartments. There'd been regret there, and remorse. And a certain bitterness. Whatever she'd been thinking, she hadn't said a word. She'd simply fought her way free of him, snatched up her robe and pulled it on before leaving the room.

Of course since then he'd had time to consider the reasons for her behaviour. It was possible that she'd wanted to save him any embarrassment. It was true that by leaving the bedroom she'd prevented Philip from seeing him. It had been a simple matter for him to throw on his clothes and follow her. Philip had accepted his appearance in his father's bedroom without any suspicion. But then, they'd all been too

concerned about Constantine's condition to care about anything else.

It wasn't until much later that Demetri had had the chance
to wonder what would have happened if Philip hadn't interrupted them. The whole experience had been eclipsed by
what had come after, and although there'd been times when
he'd told himself it was all for the best, that what had happened had been the result of over-stimulated emotions and
too much champagne, it didn't always work.

They hadn't had too much champagne that day at the
temple, and he couldn't deny that he'd wanted her then, too.
Indeed, if he was honest, he would have to admit that he'd
wanted her ever since she'd first challenged him with those
incredibly sexy eyes. Seeing her with his father, believing
they were lovers, had torn him to pieces. So much so that
he'd been prepared to betray the old man if he could have
her himself.

Which was something he couldn't forgive.

Couldn't forgive himself, anyway, he amended. Joanna
had done nothing wrong. Not really. Apart from exposing
the charade of her supposed affair with his father, she'd
committed no crime. Whereas he…

He turned back to the bed and gazed at Constantine's
drawn face with a terrible feeling of remorse in his soul.
What kind of a son was he to do such a thing? How could
he live with himself, knowing that if Joanna *had* been his
father's mistress he'd have broken the old man's heart.

So why did he want to see Joanna again? What did he
think could be achieved by talking to her? No doubt she
despised him, too. That would explain her reaction when
Philip had come crying for her help.

She'd phoned every day since Constantine had been admitted to the hospital. Demetri hadn't spoken to her, but the
nurses, who were all thrilled to have such an important patient in the hospital, were always eager to convey every
concerned enquiry to either himself or Olivia.

His sister was here, of course. Olivia had arrived the

morning after their father's emergency admission, chiding Demetri for not waking her and telling her that the old man had been taken ill in the night. She'd berated Joanna, too, for being the undoubted cause of their father's relapse. Even hearing the facts of Constantine's condition from the consultant oncologist hadn't altered her opinion that the demands Joanna had made must have precipitated his collapse. And Demetri hadn't been able to contradict her without involving himself.

He couldn't do that. Not without betraying his father again. So long as the old man wanted them to believe that Joanna really was his mistress he couldn't do anything to refute his claim. Okay, maybe he had his own reasons for not wanting to admit what a bastard he really was, but that was only a temporary reprieve. Sooner or later he was going to have to confess his sins to the family.

Yet why? he asked himself bitterly. What would his confession achieve? Olivia would despise him and even Alex would find it hard to forgive him. It wasn't as if Joanna was going to feel any pride in him baring his soul. The fact that she'd made no attempt to come to the hospital proved that she had no desire to see him again.

His father stirred, and, leaving the window, Demetri approached the bed. The old man looked so frail, he thought uneasily. Makarios, the consultant in charge of his father's case, had admitted that he couldn't give them any guarantees of how much longer he might have. Constantine was already living on borrowed time.

'Demetri?'

His voice was frail, too, and Demetri had to stifle the oath of frustration that sprang to his lips. If only money could buy his father a little more time, he thought despairingly. He'd gladly sacrifice the whole Kastro fortune in his cause.

'I am here, Papa,' he said now, moving closer. 'How are you feeling?'

'Much better,' said Constantine firmly, even though his son knew that couldn't possibly be true. 'Is Joanna outside?'

It wasn't the first time his father had asked for Joanna, but so far Olivia had been able to put him off with excuses as to why she wasn't there. His sister absolutely refused to allow Joanna to be treated as part of the family, and Demetri was now obliged to continue the deception.

'I am sure she would like to be,' he said, knowing as he spoke that his father would put his own interpretation on her absence. 'The weather has been bad since you left the island. Roussos has not been willing to take the helicopter up in such conditions.'

'In other words, you have not permitted her to come,' declared Constantine wearily, and Demetri thought it was par for the course that he should be the one to take the blame. His father hadn't accused Olivia. Only him.

'That is not true,' he insisted. Then, defensively, 'There are other methods of transportation. Ferries, for example.'

He was tempted to go on and say that if she'd really wanted to come she'd have made her own way to Athens, but that would have been too cruel. But it was true, he reflected broodingly. Joanna didn't know that Olivia had taken up guard outside their father's room.

Constantine was not to be put off, however. 'Do not pretend that you would welcome her here,' he exclaimed, and Demetri was alarmed to see the sudden hectic colour that filled the old man's cheeks. 'Nurse Delos tells me she has phoned many times. Is it so hard for you to understand that I want to see her?'

'No.' Demetri conceded the point, aware that his own pulse-rate had quickened at the thought of seeing her again. But his feelings were not important. 'I will see what I can do.'

'Good. Good.' To his relief his father seemed satisfied with his reply. He licked his dry lips. 'I need a drink.'

Demetri stepped forward and lifted a glass from the bedside cabinet, inserting the straw it held into his father's mouth. The old man sucked and a little of the liquid disappeared. 'Thank you.'

Demetri returned the glass to the cabinet and forced a smile. 'I will leave you to rest,' he said, realising that even this brief conversation had tired him. 'I will come back later.'

'I suppose you think I should have told you that I am dying.'

Constantine's words startled him, and Demetri, who had started for the door, turned back. 'Papa—'

'Do not deny it, Demetri.' His father's chest rose and fell with the force of his agitation. 'But do not blame Joanna because I did not.'

Demetri shook his head. This was the first occasion that Constantine had mentioned his illness and he didn't know how to answer him. Until now his father had been too ill to indulge in any serious discussion of his condition, and he didn't want to say anything to upset him.

'I do not blame her,' he replied at last, coming back to the bed. 'I—accept that you had your reasons for doing what you did.'

Constantine's parched lips twitched. 'You are very understanding. That is not like you, Demetri. Do not let this momentary relapse fool you. I will be up and about again before very long and you may wish you had been more honest with me.'

Demetri gave a small smile. 'I think you should rest, Papa.'

'And I will.' Constantine groped towards him and nodded in satisfaction when his son put his hand into his. 'When you assure me that you will make your peace with Joanna.'

'Make my peace with—'

Demetri was confused, but his father wasn't finished. 'You know what I am talking about, *mi yos*. I saw the way you looked at her the night I was taken ill. You thought I would not notice—' Demetri stiffened '—but I could see that you disliked her being there, disliked the role that she was playing. Do you resent her, Demetri? If so, that is a pity, because I had hoped that you two would become friends.'

Friends! Demetri felt a constriction in his chest. If only that were true.

'Papa—' he began, but once again his father forestalled him.

'She has not had an easy life, Demetri,' he said, closing his eyes as if the effort of talking exhausted him. 'Her husband—ex-husband—was totally unsuitable. I cannot go into personal details except to say that he made her very unhappy.'

Demetri inclined his head. 'I understand.'

'I doubt you do.' Constantine held up a trembling hand. 'He hurt and humiliated her, Demetri. He took away every shred of self-respect she had. When I first got to know her she was shy and uncommunicative. She had lost all confidence in herself as an attractive woman.' He paused and opened his eyes again. 'I like to think I changed all that. Slowly, but surely, she opened up to me. We became friends, and when I was first advised of the terminality of my illness it was she I could talk to, she who offered the comfort I could not ask of my own family.'

Demetri sighed. 'Papa—'

'No. Hear me out, Demetri. She is not what you think.' He expelled a weary breath. 'She is a decent woman, Demetri. And I care about her.' He looked at his son with heavy-lidded eyes. 'Do you understand? I care about her.'

Demetri was very still. 'Why are you telling me this, Papa?' Dear God, was the old man saying he wanted to marry her?

'Because I love her, Demetri,' Constantine replied. 'Because she is dear to me. Because when I am dead I want you to promise me that you will see that she never wants for anything again.'

'No! No, I will not allow it!'

Olivia faced her brother in the ante-room that adjoined

their father's suite, her face flushed with anger. Demetri thought it was just as well that all the rooms in the hospital were soundproofed. He could be fairly certain that Constantine wouldn't hear what was going on.

Nevertheless, her obstinacy infuriated him. 'Keep your voice down,' he snapped. 'Do you want everybody to hear that we are already quarrelling over his wishes? It is our father's desire that Joanna should be brought to the hospital. That is all there is to it.'

Olivia snorted. 'His desire, yes. We know all about our father's desires, do we not?'

'Olivia—'

'No, do not attempt to justify this, Demetri.' She wrapped her arms about her waist and stared at him with bitter eyes. 'Why did you not tell him she has gone back to England? Why did you let him think that she is waiting at the villa, anticipating the day when he will return to Theapolis?'

Demetri schooled his features before replying. 'Just because you do not like her—'

Olivia caught her breath. 'Are you saying that you do?'

Off-guard, Demetri was more outspoken than he should have been. 'She is not as bad as you think,' he said sharply. 'At least she cares about the old man.'

'I do not believe this.' Olivia's eyes narrowed. 'She has bewitched you as well as Papa.' She shook her head. 'I warned you what she was like, but you wouldn't listen.'

'You are imagining things,' retorted Demetri, hoping against hope that it was true. 'All I am saying is that you should give her the benefit of the doubt, Olivia. Or do you think our father is such a poor judge of character?'

Olivia wasn't having that. 'I do not think a man in his condition is capable of making rational judgements,' she declared. 'I always wondered why she had taken up with him. Well, now I know. She knew he was ill. She knew exactly how long she would have to play her part.'

'*Siopi!*' Be quiet! Demetri had had quite enough of her vitriolic comments. 'It was not like that. Joanna has known our father for a number of years. Long before—long before he discovered he had a tumour.'

'You believe that?'

'It is the truth.'

'Because she told you so?'

'No, because he did,' Demetri replied heavily. 'Now, if you will excuse me, I am going to ring the villa and arrange for Joanna's transportation to Athens.'

Olivia took a resentful breath. And then she said carelessly, 'She is not there.'

Time seemed to stand still for a moment, and Demetri had to force himself to say, 'What do you mean? She is not there?'

'What is there about that sentence you do not understand?' Olivia enquired coldly. 'Read my lips, Demetri. Joanna is not at the villa. She has gone back to London.'

Demetri mentally shook himself. Joanna had gone back to London? He couldn't believe it. 'When? When did she leave?'

Olivia shrugged. 'Three days ago.'

Demetri blinked. 'But she has phoned every day.'

'I imagine the telecommunications system in England is just as efficient as ours,' said Olivia dismissively, and he felt a violent urge to shake her, too.

Stepping close to her, he said malevolently, 'Am I to understand that you are responsible for her departure?'

For the first time, Olivia looked a little uneasy. 'So—so what if I am?' she asked defensively. 'It is surely what you would have done if you had not been here with our father.'

Demetri scowled. 'If you think that, Olivia, why are you looking so uncertain now?' He was amazed at how furious he felt that she should have done this. 'You—' He heard a faint tremor in his voice and determinedly suppressed it. 'You—had no right!'

'I had every right,' retorted Olivia indignantly. 'You know she was to blame for Papa's relapse. If she hadn't been making—unreasonable demands on his strength, he would not have been so weak when—'

'She was not his mistress!' snarled Demetri, stung into the involuntary admission, and Olivia's hands dropped to her sides.

'Not his mistress?' she echoed faintly. Then, more certainly, 'How do you know?'

How did he know?

Demetri returned her gaze with a flat stare. 'I just do,' he said at last, not prepared to lie even to save himself.

Olivia's lips parted. 'Papa told you?' she prompted.

'No.' Demetri spoke dispassionately. 'Papa did not tell me.'

'You do not mean to say that you believe her lies?' his sister cried scornfully. 'Demetri—'

'Joanna did not lie. Nor did she have to tell me anything,' he grated, through his teeth. 'Do I need to draw a picture?'

Olivia clapped her hands to her cheeks. 'You—you— Oh, I do not believe this.' She took a step back from him, her eyes wide with dismay. 'You—you had sex with her?' She seemed to take his silence as an answer. 'Then surely that only proves the kind of woman she is.'

'She was a virgin, Olivia,' Demetri told her harshly. 'Yes, a virgin.' This as Olivia tried to speak. 'So when you next feel the need to vilify Joanna, I think you should beware of what you say.'

CHAPTER FOURTEEN

THE light was flashing on the answering machine when Joanna got home from work. Her heart skipped a nervous beat. She'd left her number with the hospital in Athens, asking them to let her know if there was any change in Constantine's condition. The few friends she had usually called in the evenings, so who else could it be?

She hurried across the small living room of the apartment and pressed the 'play' button. Then she waited, praying that it wasn't bad news. She didn't think she could take any more bad news right now.

It wasn't the hospital. The voice issuing from the recorder was far too familiar, and she missed the start of the message as she groped for the arm of the nearest chair and sank down onto it. Her legs were shaking as she wondered with a feeling of dismay if Constantine had died. It was the only reason she could think of why Demetri might be phoning her.

'—sister told me how it was,' he was saying, his voice clipped but not unfriendly. 'No matter. My father is asking for you. We would all be very grateful if you could arrange to return to Greece immediately.'

The message cut off and Joanna sat staring at the light that was still flashing for several seconds before switching it off. Then, panicking because she hadn't heard the entire message, she pressed the wrong button and had to sit through half a dozen old messages before hearing Demetri's voice again.

She hadn't missed much. Just, 'Joanna,' and, 'I'm sorry you felt you had to return to England.' She'd tuned in at the point when he'd been saying that his sister had told him how it was, and Joanna pulled a wry face. Knowing Olivia as she did, she doubted she'd been completely honest about their encounter. The Greek girl had been very unpleasant, accusing Joanna of endangering her father's life and ordering her to leave the villa.

Nevertheless, the import of Demetri's message was clear. Constantine wanted to see her and, willing or not, Olivia was being forced to eat her words.

Joanna drew a trembling breath. It wasn't Olivia's reaction that troubled her. If even the sound of his voice could make her legs weak, how on earth was she going to meet Demetri again and behave as if nothing had changed? Because of course it had. For her, at least. Nothing in her life was ever going to be the same again.

In fact, that was why she hadn't taken a stand against Olivia. Spiro, who had been given the task of seeing Joanna off the island, had urged her to wait until Demetri got back. He'd insisted that he was in touch with Demetri every day and that his employer wouldn't be pleased if she returned to London.

But Joanna had insisted on leaving. A small private plane had flown her to Athens, and she'd boarded the London flight there. In a matter of hours after Constantine's collapse she'd been back in her own apartment. If it hadn't been for the rack of totally unsuitable clothes hanging in her wardrobe she might have been able to convince herself that it had all been a bad dream.

Right.

She pulled a wry face. The chance of her being able to put what had happened out of her mind wasn't even an option. The memories were far too real, far too acute. She was never going to be able to forget what had happened. She wasn't sure she even wanted to.

Which was crazy, she knew. Oh, Demetri might have felt some remorse at having misjudged her so completely, but she wasn't fool enough to think that that passionate interlude in her bedroom had meant anything to him. He'd wanted her. He'd told her that. But wanting didn't equal loving, and nothing that had happened between them was going to make the slightest difference to the plans he had for his future. Even Constantine had made it perfectly clear that he expected his son to marry a woman of his own nationality.

Marry!

Joanna caught her breath. Now where had that come from? She must be going senile if she was associating a sexual affair with marriage. As far as she knew Demetri was in no hurry to marry anyone, but when he did decide to make that kind of commitment he would make sure the woman he chose was completely without a flaw. Certainly not someone who had already been dismissed as his father's mistress.

She sighed, not at all sure what she was going to do. She wanted to see Constantine again; of course she did. She would do anything for the man who had been like a father to her; who had been there for her when she'd needed him; who had helped her to get her divorce from Richard. Without him she might still have been married to that creep; might still have been finding excuses why she shouldn't tell his parents what he was really like.

Her association with Constantine had had such an unlikely beginning, she reflected now. When her boss, Martin Scott, had asked her to deliver a Fabergé snuffbox to one of their most important clients at the Grosvenor Park Hotel, she'd had no idea that she and Constantine would become such friends. But the Greek tycoon had taken an immediate liking to the shy English girl, and although it had taken many months and many more deliveries to his hotel for them to get to know one another, they had gradually become close.

Maybe Constantine had guessed how unhappy she was, Joanna mused, walking into the neat kitchen that adjoined the living space. Or maybe she had just needed someone to talk to, someone who could give her an objective opinion of what had been going on.

In any event, it was to Constantine she had confessed the

travesty of her marriage, Constantine who had offered the advice that she should cut her losses and start again.

But that had been easier said than done. Richard had been a master manipulator, and for a long time he had controlled her with threats of what he would do if she left him.

He must have really believed she would never leave him, she thought, carrying the kettle to the sink and filling it from the tap. He must have convinced himself that she was too submissive, too scared to break out on her own. She doubted he would otherwise have dared to bring a string of strange men to their apartment, leaving her alone with them, hoping that she would find one of them attractive enough to go to bed with...

Joanna shivered. Richard had been wrong. With Constantine's support she had gone to see a solicitor and in a short space of time she had moved out of the apartment. Through all the murky days that had followed he had been there for her; the days when Richard's parents had accused her of ruining their son's life. And when she'd finally got her divorce it had been Constantine who had warned Richard not to try and see her again, Constantine who had shared her feelings of sadness and relief that it was over.

Now she looked about her a little uncertainly. Going out to Greece again would mean that she would have to behave as if nothing had happened between her and Demetri, and that wouldn't be easy. No matter how often she'd told herself that she should put it all down to experience, she wasn't that kind of woman. She could never have gone to bed with Demetri without having feelings for him. Feelings she'd fought, goodness knew, but which had only become stronger since her return.

She stood staring out of the window at the darkening street below as the kettle boiled. A row of pots stood on the windowsill, the flowering plants they contained giving a warmth and personality to the small room. Copper pans, hanging above a centre island, were reflected in the tiled walls, but Joanna was in no mood to appreciate the home she'd made for herself at the moment.

What should she do? It was possible that Constantine was worse and that that was why they'd been forced to send for her. She'd phoned the hospital in Athens that morning and been told he'd had a comfortable night, but how reliable was that? She wasn't a member of his family. Any private information would be reserved for the Kastros. They could tell her anything and she'd be none the wiser.

The kettle boiled and she made herself a pot of tea. She had planned on sending out for pizza later, if she was hungry, but now the idea of food choked her. What was she going to do?

Less than forty-eight hours later, Joanna was getting out of a taxi at the imposing entrance to the Oceanis Hospital just a short distance from Athens.

She'd taken that morning's flight from London and checked into a small hotel not far from the Plaka before ordering a taxi to bring her here. She'd wanted to have her own base, somewhere she could escape to if things proved too difficult for her. She didn't want to be dependent on the Kastros for anything.

She hadn't tried to get in touch with Demetri. She'd had enough to do, she excused herself. It hadn't been easy getting leave of absence from her job. She'd just returned from a fortnight's holiday, after all. Then there'd been her apartment to see to. She'd had to arrange for an elderly neighbour to water the plants and take in any mail. Besides, she'd decided that as it was Constantine who had sent for her it was he, and only he, she owed any explanations to. Not that she intended to tell him anything that would upset him. He'd never hear the real reason why she'd returned to England. She was certain of that.

Automatic glass doors gave access to a marble and glass entrance hall, and Joanna approached the reception desk with some trepidation. What if Demetri wasn't here to vouch for her? she worried belatedly. She was loath to involve him, but if they refused to let her see his father she'd have to. She didn't consider Olivia. If she had her way, Joanna guessed she would be on the next plane home.

To her relief, the receptionist spoke English.

'Mrs Manning?' she queried, consulting a ledger lying on the desk in front of her. 'And you are a friend of Mr Kastro's, *ne*?'

'*Ne*—I mean, yes.' Joanna felt awkward. 'I think you'll find he's been asking to see me.'

'*Psemata!*' Joanna didn't have to understand the language to see that this glamorous young woman's raised brows and the pencil tapping thoughtfully against immaculate white teeth indicated some doubt with that assertion. 'I regret only family members are permitted to visit Mr Kastro, Mrs Manning.'

'Nevertheless—'

'I am sorry.' The woman seemed genuinely regretful now, but Joanna guessed she'd been tutored in polite refusals. If Constantine was a patient here, it followed that this was no ordinary hospital. Its staff must be used to dealing with unwelcome visitors. The media, for example. 'I cannot help you, Mrs Manning.'

Joanna heaved a breath. 'Mr Demetrios Kastro, then,' she said quickly, before she could regret the words. 'Perhaps you could tell him I'm here.'

The receptionist regarded her a little impatiently now. 'Mrs Manning—'

'You don't understand.' Joanna was getting frantic. 'I really am a friend of Mr Constantine Kastro. Ask—ask any of his family.'

The sudden presence of a man at her elbow startled her. For a moment she thought Demetri had heard she was here and had come to her rescue, but the man standing beside her was a stranger to her. He was also wearing a uniform that Joanna recognised as matching that worn by the receptionist, but the bulge beneath the left side of his jacket was definitely different. And scary.

'*Apo etho ineh, kiria,*' he said, gesturing towards the glass doors, and Joanna realised he was asking her to leave.

'You don't understand—' she began again, but it was too late. The man had placed his hand beneath her elbow and was gently but firmly drawing her away from the desk.

She was going to have to leave, she thought unhappily. She would have go to back to her hotel and phone the hospital from there. Perhaps she'd have more luck if she warned them she was coming. Surely someone must know about Demetri's call.

They had reached the doors when they opened to admit another visitor. The man—security guard?—who was escorting Joanna drew her aside to allow the woman to pass. But, to the surprise of both of them, she stopped.

'Mrs Manning,' she said, her dark eyes widening in surprise. '*Theos*, what are you doing? Where are you going?'

Olivia! Joanna's spirits plummeted still further. Of all the people to see, it had to be Olivia. The person least likely to do anything to help her.

Olivia's greeting had activated a totally different reaction, however. The security guard had now dropped his hand from her arm and the receptionist, who only moments before had been telling Joanna there was nothing she could do, now came fluttering nervously across the marble floor.

'Oh, Kiria Kastro,' she exclaimed, but that was as much as Joanna could understand. The rest was an unintelligible gabble, even if the gist was fairly plain. She was gesturing agitatedly towards Joanna, and she wondered if the girl was blaming her because they'd been on the point of rejecting her. Whatever, as soon as Olivia could get a word in, Joanna had no doubt she'd be on her way again, albeit without an escort this time.

'*Stamateo!* That is enough.' To Joanna's amazement, Olivia stopped the receptionist's tirade with an impatient exclamation. Then, speaking in English for Joanna's benefit, she went on, 'Are you saying you have not informed my brother that Mrs Manning is here?'

'Kiria Kastro—'

'I will take that as a no, shall I?' Olivia had the enviable knack of reducing the most voluble protest to nothing. She glanced about her impatiently, ignoring the imploring gestures the other woman was making. Then, turning to Joanna, 'I am sorry about this, Mrs Manning. I felt sure Demetri would have left instructions for you to be taken up to my father's suite as soon as you arrived.'

Joanna was taken aback. The last thing she'd expected was that Olivia would want her here. 'I—he didn't know I was coming,' she admitted awkwardly. 'I—just booked a ticket and came.'

'Okhi!' Olivia was looking concerned now. 'So—you have not spoken to my brother?'

'No.' Joanna didn't understand her agitation. 'Does it matter?'

'It may.' Olivia heaved a sigh. 'If Demetri has already left for the airport.'

Joanna didn't know whether to feel glad or sorry. If Demetri wasn't here, her fears of seeing him again would be removed. She might even be able to return to London without ever exchanging a word with him. It was obvious he'd told Olivia that he'd tried to contact her, which surely proved he felt no guilt over what he'd done. She was just a necessary encumbrance; someone his father had become attached to but who would be quickly forgotten once the old man was dead.

Dead!

Joanna shivered again. Constantine dead. She couldn't bear to think about that.

'Demetri was intending to fly to England this evening.'

Joanna realised Olivia was still speaking, and struggled to comprehend what she was saying. 'To—to England?' she echoed, realising she was making no contribution to this conversation. 'I didn't know that.'

'How could you?' Olivia flicked another disparaging glance at the receptionist. 'But he had apparently tried to reach you by phone without any success.'

Joanna swallowed. 'He was coming to see me?'

'Who else?' Just for a moment a trace of Olivia's usual arrogance coloured her tone. Then, turning to the receptionist again, she said curtly, 'Do you know where Mr Kastro is?'

'Mr Demetri Kastro?' The girl was flustered.

'As I doubt my father is capable of leaving his bed, I have a reasonably good idea where he is,' countered Olivia irritably. '*Ne*, I meant my brother. Is he still here?'

The girl licked her lips. 'I— I—'

'I see you are still terrorising the staff, Livvy,' remarked a dry voice from behind them, and Joanna swung round to find the man she'd told herself she least wanted to see striding towards them from the direction of a bank of lifts. In a dark blue button-down shirt and black pants, his jacket looped casually over one broad shoulder, Demetri was at his most intimidating. His eyes held hers for a brief, yet devastating moment, before moving back to his sister. 'What is going on?'

Joanna blushed. She couldn't help herself. The realisation that the last time she'd been with this man he'd been slumped naked across her quivering body caused a wave of heat to envelop her. God, how was she supposed to deal with this? How was she supposed to deal with him?

Thankfully, Olivia wasn't looking at her. Waving the receptionist back to her desk, she said crisply, 'Just a small misunderstanding, Demetri. As you can see, Mrs Manning is here. But if that stupid girl had had her way she would have been ejected from the building.'

'*Mou Theos*, is this true?' His eyes turned back to Joanna, dark and unreadable now in his tanned face. 'Why did you not return my call? I could have arranged for someone to meet you at the airport.'

'Well—'

'I think Mrs Manning prefers to be independent, Demetri,' Olivia broke in smoothly. 'Besides, I doubt she has your number. Unless you left it for her, of course.'

'She could have reached me via the hospital,' replied Demetri shortly. But then, as if realising he was being far too heavy-handed, he switched his attention back to his sister. 'So, Livvy, am I to understand that you have been defending Mrs Manning's right to see our father?' His lips twisted. 'I am impressed.'

'Save your sarcasm, Demetri.' Olivia wasn't amused. 'Perhaps you should escort our visitor upstairs, *ne*? After all, it is Papa she has come to see. Not us.'

Demetri swung his jacket down from his shoulder and pushed his arms into the sleeves with careless grace. 'Why not?' he conceded, his politeness tinged with bitterness. 'It would seem that my journey is no longer necessary. I must ask Spiro to get on to the airline and cancel my ticket.'

'I will do that,' said Olivia, accompanying them across to the lift. 'Is he at the Athens office?'

'He was an hour ago,' agreed Demetri, pausing to allow Joanna to precede him into the panelled cubicle a uniformed attendant had waiting for them. *'Efharisto!'*

'Efharistisi mou,' responded Olivia drily, and walked away.

CHAPTER FIFTEEN

THE attendant's presence in the lift meant any kind of private conversation was difficult, and Joanna told herself she was glad. She and Demetri had nothing to say to one another. She was here to see his father, as Olivia had said. She should be grateful that his sister had chosen to be civil to her. Without Olivia's intervention she would have found her position impossible, particularly if Demetri had left for London.

'You had a good journey?'

Demetri's enquiry caught her unawares. She had been concentrating on the indicator light as it moved up through the floors. It was with some trepidation that she discovered he had come to rest his shoulder against the wall of the lift beside her, successfully blocking her view of the attendant.

'It—was all right,' she replied, not in the mood to explain that her seat had been over the wing and she'd been nearly deafened by the roar of the engines. 'It was delayed for half an hour.'

Demetri's nostrils flared. 'You should have returned my call,' he said with sudden vehemence. 'I would have arranged your flight.'

'That wasn't necessary.'

'No.' A sardonic expression crossed his face. 'You enjoy thwarting my wishes, Joanna. I was beginning to think that Spiro had given me the wrong number.'

Joanna's head felt light. 'I'm sorry.'

'Are you?' To her consternation, he lifted his hand and traced the line of her jaw with his finger. 'Why do you not look at me, *agapitos*? Are you so ashamed of what we did together?'

Joanna's eyes went wide, and this time she couldn't prevent herself from looking at him. 'You shouldn't say things like that,' she protested, her eyes darting round his broad shoulder to where the attendant was standing gazing at the indicator board. 'I—someone could hear you.'

Demetri lifted a dismissive eyebrow. 'He does not speak English,' he declared indifferently. 'And you did not answer my question.'

Joanna's chest fluttered. 'How—how is your father?' she asked, refusing to play his game. 'I'm looking forward to seeing him again.'

Demetri looked as if he would have liked to continue his baiting, but the mention of his father's name brought him upright from his lounging position. 'He is much better than when we brought him here,' he responded formally. 'He is lucky. His determination to keep us all in the dark could have cost him his life.'

It was a challenging statement and Joanna didn't know how to answer him. 'He— I expect he did not wish to cast a shadow over your sister's wedding celebrations,' she said uneasily, and Demetri gave her a sombre look.

'Let us not pretend that you did not know exactly what he was doing,' he said steadily. 'You were his—co-conspirator; confidante. But not his mistress, *ne*?'

Joanna's cheeks flamed again. 'Have—have you told your father that you know?' she asked faintly, and now colour deepened his tan.

'What do you think I am?' he demanded in a strangled voice, and now Joanna knew the most ridiculous desire to comfort him.

But she had to be sensible. 'I—I don't know what you are, Demetri,' she said, and before he could respond to this the lift stopped and the doors slid open. 'Is this our floor?'

'It is the floor where my father's suite of rooms is situated,' he agreed, stepping out of the lift with her. Then, after the doors had closed again, he gestured towards a door at the end of the corridor. 'You will find nurses in attendance.'

He glanced behind him. 'I will wait in the visitors' sitting room. It is along here. Ask the nurse to ring me when you are ready to leave.'

Joanna took a deep breath. 'All right.'

But she wouldn't. If she had her way she'd spend a little time with Constantine and then go back to her hotel. Until she'd spoken to him she didn't know how long he expected her to stay, but, whatever happened, the less she had to do with Demetri the better.

To her relief, Constantine looked much as he had done when they'd first arrived on Theapolis. He looked pale, of course, and tired, but his eyes were bright and became even brighter when they saw her.

'Joanna!' He lifted his hand to beckon her to him. 'Oh, Joanna, I am so glad to see you.'

'And I you,' said Joanna, her eyes misting with tears. 'I've been so worried about you, Constantine. The bulletins I got from the hospital were so—so impersonal.'

'Here—sit here,' said Constantine eagerly, moving so that she could wedge her hip on the side of his bed. He dismissed the hovering nurse with an impatient command, and then squeezed the hand he had captured when she sat down. 'Why did you not come before?'

'Well—'

'No, do not bother to lie to me, Joanna.' He was watching her closely, his dark eyes so like his son's that for a moment Joanna wondered if he could see right into her soul. 'It was Demetri, was it not? He sent you away.'

'No.' Joanna didn't want to take sides, but she couldn't let him think that Demetri was to blame. 'I—my holiday was over,' she said helplessly. 'I didn't know how long you were going to be in hospital and I had to get back to London.'

Constantine looked sceptical. '*Ne?* Well, have it your own way. I know you are only protecting them. I am sure Olivia had her part to play, too. She was never happy with our relationship.'

Joanna hesitated. 'But you have told them now—'

'I think Demetri guessed,' admitted his father wryly. 'Oh, well, it was nice for a time, to have him envy me.'

'Constantine!'

'You do not believe me?' He studied her suddenly pink face with calculating eyes. 'Joanna, I have seen the way he looks at you. I know he is attracted to you, though he may not know it yet himself.'

'Constantine!'

'What? What?' His eyes narrowed. 'You are not flattered that my son considers you a beautiful woman?'

'He doesn't—' Joanna was flustered. 'That is, I don't think this is the sort of conversation we should he having.'

'Why not?' Constantine's greying brows arched interrogatively. 'Would you rather we discussed this wasted body of mine? Would you rather I told you that the doctors are not sure how much longer I have left?'

'Please—'

'Oh, my dear…' His expression was gentle now. 'Do not upset yourself. I have accepted the situation and so must you. We all die some time. I consider I am fortunate to be given the opportunity to prepare for my death.'

Joanna shook her head. 'I don't know what to say.'

'You could say that you will miss me,' he prompted, lifting her chin with a slightly unsteady hand. 'We have been good friends, you and I. Have we not?'

'You know we have.'

'*Poli kala*, it is natural that I should want to ensure your happiness before it is too late?'

'My happiness?' Joanna stared at him now. Then, as a possible explanation occurred to her, she added swiftly, 'I am happy. I have my work. You know I have a decent place to live. I have friends—'

'That is not what I meant, Joanna.' Constantine regarded her steadily. 'I know you have your work, and, yes, I have seen your apartment and it is as attractive as you can make it. But I want to ensure that if you tire of being at Martin

Scott's beck and call you will have the funds to do something else. Whatever you wish.'

Joanna's jaw dropped for a moment. But then, recovering herself, she said firmly, 'No, Constantine.' She took a deep breath. 'I don't want anything from you. Except your friendship. And I believe I already have that.'

Constantine sighed. 'Do not be difficult, Joanna.'

'I am not being difficult.' She didn't want to upset him, but he had to understand that she meant what she said. 'Please, we've discussed this before.'

'Do you remember the day we went to Agios Antonis?' said Constantine obliquely. 'That was a good day, was it not? We went to the jeweller's and I persuaded you to let me buy you a small token—'

'It was hardly a small token,' Joanna interrupted him. 'Even now, I don't think—'

'The bracelet is yours, Joanna.' She could see he was getting agitated now, and she decided not to argue with him. 'I have enjoyed buying things for you, *agapi mou*.' His eyes darkened. 'There is so much more I would like to do, but—'

He broke off then, and Joanna took the opportunity to reassure him. 'You've done everything for me, Constantine,' she said huskily, 'I don't know what I'd have done without you.'

He smiled a little wistfully. 'You are a good girl, Joanna. You have made me realise that I have done things in my life for which I am ashamed. As you know, it was I who encouraged Olivia to marry Andrea Petrou. I knew she was too young, too headstrong, but it was a political coup and that was all that mattered to me. Then, when she told me she wanted a divorce, I was not sympathetic.' He shook his head. 'Do you think she has forgiven me?'

'I'm sure she has,' said Joanna warmly, remembering how concerned Olivia had always been about her father. 'Why don't you ask her?'

'Perhaps I will.' He smiled. 'Perhaps I will. Thank you.'

Joanna stroked the veined back of his hand. 'Just get

strong again,' she said gently. 'That's what we all want. Then Demetri can take you home to Theapolis.'

'Ah, Demetri.' Constantine closed his eyes for a moment and Joanna wondered if that was her cue to leave. But before she could act on it he opened them again and said consideringly, 'Tell me, Joanna: what do you really think of my son?'

Joanna was astounded. It was the last thing she had expected him to ask, and she wondered if Demetri had lied to her after all. Had he told his father about their affair? Had Olivia? Did Olivia know?

'Demetri?' she murmured at last, and Constantine gave her a retiring look.

'How many sons do I have, Joanna?' he enquired mildly. 'What is wrong? Do you dislike him that much?'

'No—' She couldn't allow him to think that.

'I thought not.' Constantine's tone was ironic. 'That is not usually the effect he has on your sex.'

Joanna's tongue circled her upper lip. 'He— I— We hardly know one another,' she mumbled, not altogether truthfully, and saw the mocking glint come into Constantine's eyes.

But, 'No,' he conceded, apparently not prepared to pursue it. Instead, he added, 'I told you, did I not, that he and Athenee Sama used to be close friends? Yes? And when she and her father came to Alex's wedding I think both Aristotle and I hoped...' He shrugged. 'But it was not to be. Something had happened. Demetri had changed. He was no longer interested in Athenee. In fact, he was not interested in any of the young women who flocked around him after the ceremony. Do you know why that should be so, Joanna? Can you explain why a man who has hitherto shown a perfectly natural interest in the opposite sex should suddenly shun even the most innocent of overtures? Can you tell me that?'

Joanna felt hot. 'Have you asked him?' she said, desperately seeking an answer he would accept. She got up from the bed. 'I—perhaps I ought to go. I'm sure your family—'

'Demetri was with you the night I was taken ill, was he not?' Constantine said abruptly, and Joanna couldn't prevent a gasp of dismay. 'Did you honestly think I would not find out?'

Joanna was stunned. 'But—but—'

'How?' suggested Constantine, and she nodded. 'I think you both forgot Philip,' he continued drily. 'He may be old, but his wits are as sharp as ever.'

'Oh, God!' Joanna couldn't look at him. 'And you let me come here knowing—'

'Why not?' Constantine was impatient now. 'We were not lovers, Joanna. I borrowed a little of your time, that is all. You played your part to perfection. How can I be angry with you because my son has allowed his hormones to rule his head?'

She shook her head. 'Does Demetri know?'

'No.' Constantine paused. 'I wanted to tell you first.'

Joanna sighed. 'It wasn't his fault.'

'You would say that, of course.'

'It's the truth.' Joanna was desperate. 'He came to my room to talk. That was all. But, well—one minute we were talking, and the next—'

'Spare me the details,' said Constantine wryly. 'I am sure my son is nothing like your ex-husband.'

'Oh, Constantine…' Joanna pressed her hands to her hot cheeks. Then, remembering, 'But why would Philip tell you something like that? I thought he was your friend.'

'He is.' Constantine gave a twisted smile. 'He thought he was saving me from further heartache. He made a special trip from the island so that he could see me.'

Joanna tried to take it all in. 'And Demetri didn't suspect?'

'Why would he? As far as he and Olivia were concerned Philip was doing what any loyal employee of long standing would do.' Constantine attempted to move his thin shoulders. 'My son has had—other things on his mind.'

'Your illness.' Joanna nodded.

'That, too, of course.' Constantine was looking very tired now, and she realised he had been talking for far too long. 'But—I have noticed a certain restlessness about him, an unexpected desire to get back to the island.' He breathed more shallowly. 'You see,' he persisted, 'until Olivia told him otherwise, he thought you were still there.'

Joanna could only stare at him. 'Constantine…'

But the old man was visibly wilting. 'Not now,' he whispered, his breathing becoming more laboured. 'Later, Joanna. Come back later. Now—I need to—sleep—'

Joanna was waiting for the lift when Demetri came striding along the corridor towards her. His expression revealed his irritation that she had countermanded his instructions, but she was in no mood to care.

'Where are you going?' he demanded, staring at her now pale features with some concern. 'I thought I asked you to let me know when you were leaving. If the nurse had not rung to tell me that my father is resting now I would still have been waiting for your call.'

Joanna didn't want to talk to him now. Concentrating on keeping her voice steady, she said tightly, 'I'm sorry. But I'd prefer to be alone. Do you mind?'

Demetri's dark face tightened with an emotion she couldn't identify. 'Do I have a choice?' he asked tersely. 'At least tell me where you are going.'

Joanna hesitated. 'Does it matter?'

'It might. If I need to get in touch with you,' he replied shortly. 'I suppose you would not agree to me taking you to my father's house in Athens?'

'No.' Joanna knew she was hardly being polite, but she couldn't help it. 'I—er—I have a hotel room.'

'And the hotel's name?'

Realising she had no reason to withhold it, she told him. 'It's a small hotel, not far from the—'

'I have heard of it.' Demetri's tone indicated his opinion of her choice. Then, with a tightening of his jaw, 'You are coming back, *ne*?'

The lift arrived at that moment, and she heard him utter what she assumed was an oath as the attendant held the doors open for her. Joanna had no choice but to step inside, but Demetri detained them.

'You did not answer me,' he reminded her harshly, and Joanna expelled a nervous breath.

'I—probably,' she murmured, supremely conscious of their audience, whether he could understand English or not. 'Um—thank you for letting me visit your father.'

Demetri's mouth thinned. 'You have seen him,' he said flatly. 'Do you think I could have stopped you?'

Joanna managed a small smile. 'You have a point.'

Demetri stepped forward then, startling both her and the attendant by bracing his arms at either side of the lift doors. 'Come back, Joanna,' he said, his voice slightly uneven now. 'For my sake.' He drew a harsh breath. 'If you can forgive me.'

CHAPTER SIXTEEN

JOANNA'S apartment was in north-west London. She'd sold the flat she'd had in Kensington when she and Richard had married. Although it wasn't a particularly fashionable part of the city, the high-rise where she now lived was fairly new, and Demetri had to press the bells of several apartments before someone buzzed him in without querying his identity first.

He'd tried Joanna's apartment, naturally. But she was either out or not answering at the moment, and he wasn't prepared to hang about outside, waiting for her to get home. It was after six already, and November in London was just as chilly as he remembered from his student days. A cold wind probed at his loose cashmere overcoat and he thought ruefully of the more temperate climate of his homeland.

Spiro was waiting in the chauffeur-driven limousine outside, but when Demetri stepped into the carpeted lobby of the building he signalled to his assistant that he could go. He'd contact him on his mobile later, if necessary. And, in the present circumstances, he had to accept that that was likely. Joanna hadn't returned any of his calls, and, although his father's lawyers had received a polite response to their letters, she had refused point-blank to have anything to do with the legacy Constantine had left to her.

That was why he was here, he told himself. Since his father's funeral there had been no contact of any kind between them, and he was growing not only angry but frustrated. Just because she despised him that was no reason to reject his father's last wishes, and he intended to do everything in his power to change her mind.

It was six weeks since he'd buried his father, and this was

the first opportunity he'd had to come here. Becoming the head of Kastro International had not been easy. He'd thought he was prepared for the weight of responsibility he would have to shoulder, but the reality had proved so much harder to bear. Apart from anything else, in those first few weeks he had been grieving, too, and he had been astonished by the sense of bereavement he'd felt—not just at his father's death, but at Joanna's refusal to speak to him. It was crazy, he knew, but he'd badly needed some support and she was the only person he'd wanted to give it to him.

Somehow he'd got through the worst of it. And, despite the fact that Constantine had always jealously guarded his position in the company, Demetri had decided it was time for change. In consequence, much to her delight, he had appointed Olivia as his second-in-command, and promoted Nikolas Poros and another of the directors to positions of real authority at last.

Now, with the knowledge that the company wouldn't fall apart in his absence, Demetri was free to do what he wanted for once. Ever since his father's funeral he'd been desperate to speak to Joanna, and, whether she liked it or not, she was going to hear what he had to say.

Of course, he knew she probably wouldn't like him coming here. Despite the fact that she'd maintained a certain civility between them while she was in Athens, her loyalty to his father had made any real conversation stilted. He had no idea if she knew that Constantine had known they were together the night he'd been taken ill, or that his father had forgiven him for it. There was no way he could have broached that during those tense final days at the hospital, and Joanna had always made it plain that she didn't want him turning up at her hotel. She'd been withdrawn, aloof, only seeming to come alive when she was with his father. He had felt she hated him at times, and he hadn't been able to tell her how he was feeling without risking a total breakdown of communication.

She'd left immediately after the funeral, long before

Marcos Thexia had gathered the family together for the reading of Constantine's will. And, in his position as the chief beneficiary, Demetri had been obliged to assume his role as head of the family. It had been important that there should be no interruption in the chain of command, and by the time he'd reassured his father's investors, comforted his sisters, and assured his great-uncle that he had no intention of asking him to leave the villa, days had stretched into weeks, heavy with responsibility.

There was a lift, he saw now, with some relief. The thought of climbing to the twelfth floor was rather too much to handle at the moment. Despite—or perhaps because of— the amount of work he'd accomplished, he was weary. He didn't feel as if he'd slept properly since the night his father had been rushed to Athens, and he was exhausted.

Spiro was worried about him, he knew. That was why his assistant had insisted on accompanying him on what was, essentially, a personal visit. He'd made some excuse about Demetri not taking sufficient care of his safety, saying that Olivia thought he should have a handful of bodyguards for his own security, and he was making sure Demetri was protected. But Demetri knew that in truth both Olivia and Spiro supported his decision to come here. Olivia had finally accepted the fact that Joanna was important to him, even if Joanna's behaviour had shown he was clearly not important to her.

Whatever happened, he had to find out why she wouldn't speak to him. He had to do this for his own peace of mind, if nothing else. He wanted to see her. He *needed* to see her. He had to know what, if anything, had happened between them that night at the villa…

Joanna had heard the buzzer while she was clearing out her kitchen cupboards. It had seemed to go on and on, and she guessed it was a salesman, trying his uttermost to get into the building. They did that sometimes. Pressed all the buttons until someone lost patience and let them in. Legitimate visitors usually rang a couple of times and then gave up.

She was surprised, therefore, when in a short space of time someone knocked at her door. A salesman couldn't possibly have canvassed the whole building in less than ten minutes, so she didn't hesitate before stripping off her rubber gloves and going to answer it.

She didn't immediately open the door, of course. Although it was some years since she'd seen Richard, there was always the chance that he'd read about Constantine's death and decided to come and tell her he knew she no longer had a protector. It was a twisted thought, and not one she really gave any credence to. But she hadn't lived alone for several years without becoming cautious.

There was another urgent tattoo as she was putting her eye to the observation hole that all the apartment doors were fitted with, and she almost jumped out of her skin. Impatient devil, she thought, half inclined to pretend she wasn't in after all. But then curiosity got the better of her, and she peered out.

It was Demetri!

She stared at him greedily for several seconds, and then turned to press her shoulders back against the door. Demetri, here, she thought incredulously. Oh, God, she'd imagined she'd finished with the Kastros when she'd written back to their solicitors. She didn't want Constantine's legacy. Even though she might live to regret it, she couldn't put herself in their debt. Particularly not now.

She closed her eyes for a moment, and then opened them again to cast a critical glance over her appearance. Loose-fitting jeans; a cotton sweater with its sleeves rolled up; canvas trainers. With her hair drawn back into a ponytail, it was certainly not the appearance she'd have chosen to present at an interview with Demetri, but perhaps that was just as well. He could hardly accuse her of trying to vamp him in this outfit.

Pulling the sweater out of the tightening waistband of her

jeans, she patted it down over her stomach. Then, taking a deep breath and praying she was up to this, she opened the door.

'Demetri,' she said, infusing her voice with just the right amount of cool detachment. Her brows arched. 'What are you doing here?'

His thin smile was forced. 'May I come in?'

No!

'Why not?' She stepped back to allow him into her living room. 'But I think I should warn you that if you've come to try and persuade me to accept any of your father's money you're wasting your time.'

Demetri's lips twisted. 'Just so long as I remember that,' he remarked drily, walking across her oatmeal-coloured carpet. He looked about him with interest. 'This is nice.'

'Thank you.' Joanna closed the door with some reluctance and leaned back against it again. 'I think so.'

Demetri turned, pushing his hands into the pockets of the charcoal-grey overcoat he was wearing. He looked pale, she mused unwillingly, refusing to acknowledge the twinge of anxiety she felt at the thought. Pale, and tired. But still as sinfully attractive as ever.

'How are you?' he asked, and, realising they couldn't continue talking in this stand-off position, Joanna gestured to the sofa behind him.

'Please,' she said, and she guessed it was a measure of his weariness that he didn't wait for her to sit down first before subsiding onto the overstuffed cushions. Then, carelessly she hoped, 'I'm fine.' She paused. 'I expect you're very busy.'

Demetri shrugged. 'We are coping,' he replied, and Joanna guessed that was probably the understatement of the year. If his appearance was anything to go by, he was working himself to death. 'My father is a hard act to follow.'

Joanna thought if anyone could do it he could, but she didn't say that. Instead, she hesitated only a moment before straightening and asking, 'Can I get you anything? Tea? Coffee? A beer?'

'Beer?' Demetri frowned. 'You drink beer?'

She could have said no, that it had been bought for those occasions when Constantine had visited her apartment, but she didn't see why she should explain herself to him.

So, 'Sometimes,' she murmured untruthfully. Then, 'I'm afraid I don't have anything stronger.'

Demetri's eyes were dark and penetrating for a moment, but then his lids dropped and he inclined his head. 'Thank you.'

She went into the kitchen on legs that felt decidedly shaky. Dear heaven, what was she doing, offering him refreshment when she should have been doing her best to get him out of there?

But it was too late now. Taking a beer from the fridge, she collected a glass and returned to the living room. Demetri was still sitting on the sofa, but now he was lying back, his head resting on the cushions, his eyes closed.

Was he asleep? She hovered, not sure what to do, but then he opened his eyes and saw her. '*Signomi*—I am sorry,' he said hastily, pushing himself upright. 'You must forgive me. It has been a long day.'

More than one, thought Joanna, despising herself for caring. It was nothing to do with her if he chose to drive himself so hard he was injuring his health. He was a young man. He'd survive.

Handing over the bottle of beer and the glass, she sought the edge of a nearby chair and perched upon it. 'So, why are you here, Demetri? Are you in London on business?'

He didn't answer her directly. Instead he was looking at the bottle, and a slow smile slid over his face. 'Ah, this used to be my father's favourite,' he said, unscrewing the cap. His brows arched interrogatively. 'Is it your favourite too?'

Joanna sighed and gave in. 'I bought it for him,' she admitted, feeling the pang of loss she always experienced when she thought of Constantine these days. 'He used to come here occasionally. I once made him supper.' She grimaced. 'It wasn't very impressive, but he seemed to enjoy it.'

'I am sure he did.' She decided his response was more rueful than patronising. Then, suddenly realising she wasn't drinking, 'Will you not join me?'

Joanna shook her head. 'I—I'm not a great lover of beer,' she said, wishing she'd thought to bring herself some orange juice, just to give her something to do with her hands. 'Um—you didn't say why you wanted to see me.'

Demetri looked at the beer and the glass, and then set the latter down on the occasional table in front of the sofa. Raising the bottle to his lips, he swallowed at least half its contents in one gulp. Then, savouring its tangy flavour, he wiped his mouth with the back of his hand and looked at her.

'Why did you not answer any of my calls?' he asked at last, when she was wilting beneath his gaze. 'Do you not think you owed me that?'

Joanna moved her head in an awkward little gesture. 'I don't know what you mean.'

'Oh, I think you do.' He put the beer aside and moved to the edge of the sofa. Spreading his legs, he rested his forearms on his thighs. 'Were you afraid? Is that it? Has your experience with your ex-husband made you wary of getting involved with another man?'

'We weren't involved.' Joanna was defensive.

'No?' Demetri regarded her impatiently. 'You are not going to try and tell me you are in the habit of asking a man to make love to you?' he queried drily. 'I was there, Joanna. I know you had never been with a man before.'

'So?' Joanna got up now, unable to sit still under his scrutiny. 'The fact that we had sex together doesn't give you the right to—'

'We did not have sex together,' retorted Demetri harshly, getting to his feet. 'We made love. There is a difference.

As you would know, if you were not trying so hard to hate my guts.'

'I don't hate you.' Joanna folded her arms across her midriff. 'I just think you're attaching too much importance to—to something that—that had to happen one day.'

Demetri's mouth turned down. 'So prosaic,' he said wryly. 'So practical.' His lips twisted. 'If I did not know better, I might even be tempted to believe you.'

'Believe it,' urged Joanna, her nervous hands now groping for the hem of her sweater and tugging it down again. 'I—I wish you would.'

Demetri subjected her to another prolonged stare. And then, when she was on the verge of making a panicked retreat into the kitchen, he closed the space between them and cupped the side of her neck with his hand.

'So,' he said, watching her reaction with narrowed eyes. 'If I were to do this—' His fingers tightened and she felt her own pulse beating against his hand. 'Or this—' He bent his head and bestowed a light kiss at the corner of her mouth. 'You would not object?'

Joanna trembled. 'Wh—why would you want to kiss me?' she asked, determined not to let him see how shaken she was by his behaviour. 'Have you exhausted all the women in Greece?'

He swore then, but he didn't let her go, and she swayed a little unsteadily under his hands. 'You are deliberately trying to provoke me,' he said, pulling her hair loose of the elastic tie she'd used to control it and sliding his fingers into its tumbled softness. 'But you are wasting your time. I will not let you drive me away.'

Joanna tried to remain calm. 'I—I just don't know why you've come here,' she protested. 'I know you probably think I'm ungrateful for not wanting your father's money, but I tried to tell him—'

'Forget the money,' said Demetri, drawing her even closer and nuzzling her neck with his lips. '*Theos*, you have no idea how much I have missed you. It is crazy, no? But I have.'

'Demetri—'

'What?' He lifted his head to look down at her with dark soulful eyes. 'You do not believe me? Well...' he rubbed his thumb over her lower lip '...what was it you said? Believe it? Yes, believe it, Joanna. That is why I am here. Because I find I need you in my life.'

Joanna's jaw dropped. 'You don't mean this—'

'Why not?' Demetri's thumb tipped her face up to his now, making it easy for him to brush her mouth with his. 'You cannot deny that from the minute we met there was an irresistible attraction between us.'

'No—'

'Oh, yes.' He was positive. 'You know it is true. The wonder of it is that I kept my hands off you as long as I did.'

Joanna shook her head. 'You've made a mistake.'

'Really?' He didn't sound convinced. 'So you are not attracted to me at all? When I do this...' He stroked a sensual finger down her spine that had her arching helplessly against him. 'Or this...' His free hand slid beneath the hem of her sweater to spread its cool strength against her waist. 'You feel no answering response?'

'I—didn't say I wasn't attracted to you,' she exclaimed breathlessly.

'Then—?'

'I won't be your mistress, Demetri!'

He let her go then, as she'd known he would. A numbing silence followed her outburst and, unable to stand the anticlimax, Joanna backed away towards the door.

'I think you'd better go now,' she added, groping for the handle. 'It was—good of you to come, and—and I am flattered that you find me att—'

'Skaseh!'

She didn't recognise the word he used, but its meaning seemed fairly obvious—particularly as it was accompanied by a chopping motion of his hand. His face was dark and ominous, and although his features were still drawn with fatigue, a hectic colour had overlaid his pale cheeks. With a muffled oath, he strode towards her, and she had no time to fumble the door open before he slammed angry hands on the panels at either side of her head.

He stared down at her, his eyes searching her face as if seeking answers she couldn't give. Then, with a savage intensity, he said, 'Did I ask you to be my mistress?'

'No.' Joanna couldn't accuse him of that exactly. 'But you're not going to pretend you didn't come here expecting to—to repeat what happened before?'

'What happened before,' he echoed a little mockingly. 'Oh, Joanna, you have a great deal of trouble in saying what you really mean. Of course I came here because I want to sleep with you. But our relationship does not only consist of what we do in bed.'

'We don't have a relationship!' exclaimed Joanna fiercely. 'You want me. You may even believe you want to make love with me. But at the end of the day—'

'At the end of the day, you do not know what the hell you are talking about,' he told her harshly. 'You do not know how many nights I have lain awake, wondering how I was going to function the next day, never mind take responsibility for an organisation my father was reckless enough to put into my hands—'

'Your father was never reckless,' protested Joanna, grateful for something to say that wouldn't engender any more of his anger. But Demetri wouldn't let her go on.

'My father was reckless,' he contradicted her unsteadily. 'He brought you to Theapolis. He introduced me to the one woman I thought I could never have and then pushed us into one another's company, expecting—' But there he broke off, shaking his head. '*Theos*, I do not know what he expected any more. All I do know is that my life has not been the same since you came into it. How can you tell me I do not know what I want?'

Joanna trembled. She ought to stop him. She had to stop him. There were things she had to say to him. But all she managed was, 'What do you want, Demetri?' and with a groan he lowered himself against her.

'You,' he said simply, and in a kind of delirium she felt his mouth open over hers. 'You,' he said again, against her lips. 'I love you, *agapitos*. And I have never said that to any woman.'

Joanna's head swam at the first taste of his tongue in her mouth. She hadn't realised how much she wanted him to touch her until she'd felt the muscled length of his hard body imprisoning her against the door. She hadn't known her breasts had become so sensitive, or bargained for the melting softness in her lower limbs that was only accentuated when he eased his thigh between her legs. The pulsing heat of his arousal stirred against her stomach, and, giving in to the delicious weakness that was enveloping her, she wound her fingers into his hair.

Demetri's kiss lengthened, deepened, robbed her of her breath. Shrugging off his overcoat, he allowed it to fall to the floor at their feet as he drew her across to the sofa and pulled her down on top of him.

'I have dreamed about this, about you,' he said huskily, his hand behind her head, holding her to him. 'But always before I was in control. Sex was just a game to be played, and I played it like everybody else.' He gave a groan. 'No longer.' His fingers slid beneath her sweater, splaying across her back. 'Now I cannot think of life without you. How controlling is that?'

Joanna drew a quivering breath. 'I can't believe this.'

'What?' He rolled over with her so that now she was crushed beneath him, her heart fluttering wildly in her chest. 'What part of this do you not believe? The fact that I have been nearly out of my head because I could not get away from Athens any sooner? Or that I am in love with you; have been in love with you, I think, since your first morning at the villa. You came out onto the terrace and I watched you from the pool. Oh, yes.' This as her eyes went wide with surprise. 'I watched you for quite some time before I chose to make my presence known.'

'Your nude presence,' murmured Joanna daringly, and was rewarded with a rueful smile.

'My nude presence,' he conceded. 'You noticed.'

'How could I not?' she countered, her courage growing. 'You were—well, you know what you were better than me.'

'Aroused,' he admitted huskily. 'You do that to me.' He took one of her hands and drew it down between their bodies. 'Like this, hmm?'

Joanna's cheeks went pink. 'Demetri, I—'

'Do not say anything,' he advised her gently. 'And you need not be alarmed. I do not intend to do anything to frighten you.'

Joanna brought her hands up to his face. 'You don't frighten me, darling,' she whispered, her thumbs brushing his lips now. 'I love you.' She paused. 'But I think you know that already. Isn't that why you're here?'

'I am here because I want to ask you to marry me,' declared Demetri fiercely, pushing himself up and looking down at her with impassioned eyes. 'I do not want a mistress, Joanna. I want a wife. But not just any wife. You. Only you.'

EPILOGUE

'MY FATHER knew about us,' Demetri murmured some time later, drawing Joanna's naked body into the curve of his. Although he had already made love to her he was still half aroused, and she shifted in unknowing provocation as his erection nudged the sensual cleft of her buttocks.

'I know,' she breathed softly, but he sensed a certain ambivalence in the words and wondered if she still doubted the sincerity of his actions.

But surely she believed that he loved her. *Theos*, he couldn't imagine life without her. Hearing that she loved him had been like having a great weight lifted from him. When he'd carried her into her bedroom and stripped the bulky jeans and sweater from her he'd been sure that nothing and no one could harm them. Yet now he could feel an unsettling barrier between them.

But why?

'He told you?' he ventured now, praying it wasn't his father who was his rival. A living man he could deal with. A ghost? That was something else.

'Mmm,' she conceded, heartening him somewhat when she turned her lips against the arm that was cradling her head. 'Philip came to see him. But I suppose you know that?'

'I did hear something about it,' he admitted wryly. 'I would like to say he gave us his blessing, but I would not go as far as that.'

He sensed rather than saw her smile. 'Do you mean Philip or your father?'

'My father,' Demetri assured her firmly. 'He warned me not to hurt you.'

She tensed then. He felt it. And, needing to see her face, he moved so that she rolled onto her back beside him. In the lamplight she was so beautiful, he thought achingly. Her lips bruised from his kisses, her cheeks pink with a mixture of shyness and—what? Apprehension? Surely not.

'He loved you, you know,' he added huskily, needing to reassure her. 'But I am sure you know that.' His hand sought the swollen fullness of her breast that was tantalisingly close to his chest, his thumb massaging the taut nipple. 'He swore he would come back to haunt me if I let you down.'

'And is that why you're here?' she asked abruptly, startling him by the sudden catch in her tone, and he blew out a defensive breath.

'Say what?'

She shifted again, and his hand, which had slipped caressingly over her abdomen, halted at the triangle of moist curls between her legs. 'I asked—' Her eyes were wide and troubled. 'I asked, is that why you're here? Because of what your father said? Because he gave you the impression that I needed—someone.'

Demetri propped himself up on his elbow now, staring down at her with dark, disbelieving eyes. 'Is that what you think?' He made an expressive gesture. 'Is that why you're acting like you wished this had never happened?'

Joanna's face was indignant now. 'I'm not acting like that,' she protested. 'But—but I don't want you to feel that you're responsible for me.'

'Khristo!' Demetri swore. 'Theos, Joanna, I thought we knew one another better than that.'

She looked a little less anxious now. 'Do you mean that?'

'Of course I mean it.' He bent to bestow a sensuous kiss on the curve of her shoulder. 'I love you, Joanna. Me. Not my father. I am crazy about you. How could you even imagine that anything my father said could influence my feelings?'

She shook her head, but one hand came to stroke his cheek. 'I didn't want you to think—oh, you know what I'm

trying to say. What with Constantine making me a beneficiary in his will and all—'

'Hey, I had forgotten that,' murmured Demetri teasingly.
'But it does prove my point. Why should I feel responsible
for a woman who is prepared to turn down a yearly legacy
of—?'

'Shh.' She put her fingers over his lips and he opened his
mouth to bite them instead. 'Don't say any more,' she exclaimed. 'I believe you.'

'In any case, if anyone has a complaint here, it is I,'
Demetri continued drily, smiling as his probing fingers
caused her to catch her breath. She was wet and he was
instantly aware of his own hard response. 'I have tried to
contact you numerous times since you left the island, but
you have persistently ignored my calls.'

Joanna drew her upper lip between her teeth. 'Actually,'
she said carefully, 'you didn't try to contact me for several
weeks. You may have rung me in the last three weeks, but
in the beginning you left contacting me to your father's
solicitor.'

Demetri sighed. 'All right. I admit that in the days—
weeks—following my father's funeral I had little time for
myself. Nonetheless, if you had contacted me, assuredly I
would have returned your call.'

'Would you?'

'Do you doubt it?'

'N—o.'

'Then?' He shook his head. 'Surely you can understand
what it was like? I was inundated with people who required
my decision about this, my signature on that. I wanted to
speak to you. Dear heaven, I wanted to *see* you. But my
life was not my own.'

She nodded. 'I understand.'

'Do you?'

'I think so.'

'So—why did you not return my calls?' persisted
Demetri, stroking her gently. He looked down at her a little

pensively. 'Do you know, I think you have put on a little weight?' He smiled. 'It suits you.'

'That's good.' Joanna drew a breath. 'Because there's a reason for that, too.'

Demetri frowned. 'Too?'

'I—wanted to get in touch with you,' she confessed huskily. 'But—it was difficult.'

'Difficult?'

'I'm pregnant,' she said hurriedly. 'Now do you see why I didn't return your calls?'

Demetri stared at her, feeling as if his breath was trapped somewhere in the back of his throat. 'Pregnant?' he echoed incredulously. 'You are pregnant?'

'Yes.' She licked her lips. 'You're not too shocked are you?'

Demetri didn't know how he felt. Shocked, certainly. Exhilarated, amazingly. But mostly relieved. So relieved. He'd thought for a moment that there was something wrong.

'I cannot believe it,' he said, staring at her helplessly. His eyes strayed to her breasts, still swollen from his lovemaking, to the gentle swell of her stomach, now so understandably rounded. She was expecting his child.

'But you don't mind?' she probed anxiously. 'I mean, I know it's not what you expected—'

'Oh, Joanna!' He suddenly realised how his dazed expression must appear to her. '*Agapi mou*, you have—stunned me, that is all.' He lowered his head and kissed her mouth, his tongue lingering against her lips. 'But as for—what was it you said? Do I mind, no?' He lifted her hand and brought it to his lips. 'My darling, I am overwhelmed, humbled. But—' His brows drew together. 'It is I who should be asking you that question.' He hesitated. 'Perhaps you did not want to tell me.'

Joanna's laughter was tremulous. 'You have to be joking,' she exclaimed, cupping his face between her palms. 'You don't know this, but I've practically spring-cleaned this apartment from one end to the other. Anything to avoid thinking about what I was going to do, what I *could* do. Of course I wanted to tell you. But I didn't know what you'd say, how you'd feel. The last thing I wanted was for you to think that I expected you to marry me because I was having a baby—'

Demetri turned his mouth against her palm. 'Believe me, *agapitos*, it would have been no hardship,' he told her softly. 'As I said before, I have wanted you for what seems like for ever. And now you are mine.' He knew he sounded smug, but he couldn't help it. 'I am content.'

'Olivia may not be so pleased,' murmured Joanna doubtfully, but Demetri only laughed.

'Olivia will not have time to object,' he said wryly. 'As you know, she has always wanted to be involved in the company. Well, now she is. I have made her my deputy. Which means...' He nuzzled her throat. 'We will have all the time in the world to ourselves.'

'But—'

'But nothing,' he insisted, easing his thigh between hers. 'You may be surprised to hear that Olivia encouraged me to come and see you.'

'No—'

'Yes.' He was very certain. 'She has been worried about me. She and Alex both. Unlike you, I have lost weight, and Olivia has finally realised that I need you in my life.' His eyes teased her. 'Does that reassure you?'

'Some,' she admitted, sliding her arms round his neck. Then, 'I suppose I should offer you something to eat, shouldn't I?' Her lips tilted. 'But first—'

Demetri hesitated. 'And—the baby—?'

'Is perfectly content that his daddy is here,' Joanna assured him gently. 'Make love to me, Demetri.' She smiled. 'You see, you have taught me what making love means...'

CLAIMING HIS MISTRESS

by

Emma Darcy

Initially a French/English teacher, **Emma Darcy** changed careers to computer programming before the happy demands of marriage and motherhood. Very much a people person, and always interested in relationships, she finds the world of romantic fiction a thrilling one and the challenge of creating her own cast of characters very addictive.

Don't miss Emma Darcy's exciting new novel
The Playboy Boss's Chosen Bride
out in November 2006 from Mills & Boon
Modern Romance™

CHAPTER ONE

HER hair caught Carver Dane's eye first. Hair like that invariably did—a long lustrous spill of black curls. His mouth twisted self-mockingly. It was said that people were always attracted to the same physical type, but two relationship disasters really should have some deterrent effect on him.

He waited for a negative switch-off.

It didn't happen.

His gaze kept being drawn to her.

Of course it could be a wig since this masked ball was also a fancy dress affair. It was impossible to tell from this distance across the dance floor, especially with the glittery scarlet and purple mask she wore, disguising her hairline. Purposefully he moved his partner in a sequence of steps that brought him closer.

The hair belonged to a woman dressed as Carmen, the femme fatale gypsy from Bizet's opera. Warning enough to stay clear of her, he told himself. Her body was definitely packaged dynamite, poured into a slinky red gown with a provocative fishtail of red and purple frills. The front of the hip-hugging skirt was even more provocative with a thigh-high slit revealing a flash of shapely legs as her partner twirled her around.

Gold bangles on her arms, gold hoops dangling from her ears. A very sexy piece all around, Carver decided, keeping her in view, determined on claiming her for the next dance. The loose tendrils curling down in front of her ears proved her hair wasn't a wig. Third time lucky, he wryly argued, though he didn't believe it. He simply wanted to pursue the desire she stirred.

Katie Beaumont was enjoying herself. She hadn't let her hair down, in a fun sense, for a long long time. Being dressed as Carmen amongst a crowd of people she didn't know, and who didn't know her, was definitely liberating. There was no need to maintain a responsible image. This was a wonderful slice of freedom from any care, especially the care of what others might think of her.

Her toreador partner was sweating rather heavily by the time the dance bracket ended. "That was great!" he puffed, making a grab to pull her close. "Come and have a drink at the bar with me."

"Thanks so much, but I'm expected back at my table," she excused, smiling as she twirled out of reach. "Enjoy your drink," she tossed back at him, not wanting to leave him completely flat. He was an enthusiastic dancer, but she didn't want his company off the floor, and tonight was about pleasing herself.

It was easy to slip away through the milling crowd. She was actually placed on one of the official tables, next to her old school friend, Amanda, who'd set out to marry spectacularly well and had accomplished it with Max Fairweather, a leading stockbroker at Sydney's top financial levels.

Katie was glad to have met her again after so many

years of being out of contact—a lucky coincidence with Amanda placing her four-year-old son at the day-care centre where she'd been working for the past six months. While she had no ambition to slide into the high-flying social scene, having Amanda's amusing company from time to time, definitely put a bit of sparkle in her life.

She grinned at her friend's extravagant gestures as Amanda entertained her other guests at the table with some outrageous story. No doubt about it, she was a great hostess. And looked fantastic tonight, dressed as an exotic belly dancer in vibrant blues and greens, with a gold mask attached to a gold mesh cap, from which hung strings of glittery beads, winding through her long blond hair.

"So how was the toreador?" she archly queried the moment Katie had settled on the chair beside her.

She grinned, knowing she was about to dash Amanda's devious plans to find her a *life* partner. "Good on his feet but a bit too full of himself."

"Mmm…we obviously need a better prospect," she mused with unabashed candour. "The guy I fancy is the very sexy buccaneer. A pirate king if ever I saw one."

"A pirate king?" Katie effected a careless shrug. "I haven't noticed him."

"Well, he noticed you," came the loaded reply. Amanda always had ammunition ready to fire at Katie's single status. "He was eyeing you off during that last dance."

She laughed, aware that many men had been eyeing her off, so one in particular carried no real meaning.

The Carmen costume was blatantly sexy. Amanda lived by the rule—if you've got it, flaunt it—and she'd certainly pressed the principle on Katie tonight. Not that she minded. Tonight she didn't care how many men looked at her. It was harmless enough, letting herself revel in feeling desirable when there was no danger attached to it.

"You're not supposed to be fancying anyone, Amanda," she teasingly chided her friend. "I'm here in place of your husband, remember?"

"Don't remind me. I'm seriously annoyed with Max for missing tonight's ball. Especially when I'm on the fundraising committee for this charity. Him and his golfing weekends," she muttered darkly, reaching for the bottle of champagne to refill their glasses.

"Didn't you tell me the contacts are good for his stockbroking business?" Katie put in politically. "This lifestyle does come at a price."

"Don't I know it!" Amanda sighed. "Still, I'd rather be drinking the best bubbly than worrying my head about setting up a business. Are you sure you want to take on this taxiing kids around, Katie?"

"Yes. I've thought it all out and I've already set up an appointment with the investment company Max recommended."

"I'm sure I could matchmake a suitable husband for you."

Katie shook her head. "I'd really rather support myself."

Amanda heaved another exasperated sigh. "It's not natural." She waved an arm around the ballroom.

"This is what's natural for someone with your looks."

"What? A masked ball in fancy dress? This is sheer fantasy land," Katie mocked laughingly. "But I do thank you for talking me into using Max's ticket. And finding me this costume."

"So you *are* having a good time!" Amanda pounced triumphantly.

Katie grinned. "Yes, I am."

Her friend handed her a glass of champagne and clicked it with her own. "To a night of fun and frivolity! May there be many more of them!"

Katie smiled and sipped, but didn't echo the toast. The occasional bit of fun and frivolity did provide a high spot, but a steady diet of it could soon make it lose its magic.

She suspected Amanda kept her life hectic because her husband, who was a truly nice man, tended to be somewhat staid, and exciting distractions kept a happy balance. She also suspected Max had arranged the golfing weekend because appearing in fancy dress was definitely not his style.

Still, the marriage seemed to work quite well, and Katie wondered if the years of working as a nanny in London had made her cynical about the permanence of any relationship. Observing the intrigues and infidelities that went on behind the superficial glitz of supposedly *solid* marriages had been an unpleasant eye-opener, and guarding the children from them had not been easy.

She loved the innocence of little children. She took more pleasure in their company than the company of most adults. The idea of providing a taxi service for children whose parents didn't have the time to ferry them around to activities had appealed very strongly to her. She was sure it was workable, given enough finance to back the venture.

In any event, she didn't want to be *fixed up* with Amanda's divorced acquaintances, and divorcees seemed to be the only unattached males for a woman looking down the barrel of being thirty years old. Not that Katie was madly interested in getting *attached* anyway. She was used to being independent. There'd only ever been the one great passion in her life, and unless someone, somewhere, could spark those same feelings in her, she'd rather stay single.

Making her own way seemed infinitely preferable to sharing her life with a man she didn't love, even if going into business for herself held more pitfalls than she could foresee at the moment. Just glancing around at the men sharing this table...not one of them was attractive enough to give her even a niggle of doubt about the decision she'd made to invest in a future which she could control.

They were pleasant enough people to spend a few hours with; intelligent, witty, accomplished people who could afford the astronomical price of the tickets to this ball. Maybe it was the effect of the masks and fancy dress, but none of them felt *real* to her. They were all play-acting. But then, she was, too. Silly to judge anyone when tonight was aimed at taking time out from their day-to-day lives.

Fantasy...

She sipped some more champagne and laughed at

the wickedly clever jokes being told. The band started up again and Amanda nudged her in the ribs.

"The pirate king is coming at a stride," she warned gleefully. "To your right. Three o'clock."

Katie turned her head obediently, curious to see the man who had stirred Amanda's interest.

"Now don't tell me he isn't seriously scrumptious," her friend challenged.

It was the wrong word, Katie thought. Completely wrong.

He was striding across the dance floor, a black cape lined with purple satin swirling from his shoulders. The purple was repeated in a dashing bandanna circling his head above his black mask. A white flowing shirt was slashed open almost to his waist, revealing a darkly tanned and highly virile chest. A wide black leather belt was fastened by a silver skull-and-crossbones emblem. His black trousers seemed to strain over powerfully muscled thighs, and knee-high boots accentuated his tall, aggressive maleness.

He looked...seriously *dangerous*...not scrumptious.

Katie's heart started thumping. He was coming straight at her with the lethal grace of a panther on the prowl...and he was not about to be diverted or fended off. She could feel his focus on her, feel the driven purpose behind it. A convulsive little shiver ran down her spine. Before she even realised what she was doing, she was pushing her chair back, drawn to stand up and be facing him properly before he reached her.

He emanated a magnetism that was tugging inexorably on her and she didn't know whether to fight it or succumb to it. All her instincts were on red alert, yet it was more a state of excitement than of fear, like meeting a challenge head-on, compelled to engage whatever the outcome.

She hadn't experienced anything like this since… since her ill-fated love for Carver Dane had swept her into the sexual intimacy that had been so terribly broken.

Shocked at being reminded of a time she had determinedly put behind her, Katie stiffened with resistance when the buccaneer halted a bare step away, holding out an open palm to her in confident invitation. She stared down at it, and the sharp memory of Carver eased back into the darker side of her mind. This man's palm was not rough or calloused from manual labour.

"Will you dance with me?"

The softly spoken question had a mocking lilt to it, drawing her gaze up to the eyes behind the mask. They were too shadowed to see his expression. His firmly etched lips were slightly curved, but she caught the sense that the half smile carried more sardonic amusement at himself than any attempt to persuade a positive response from her.

Resentment stirred at the thought he didn't really want to be attracted to the Carmen persona she was projecting tonight. Yet what was good for the gander was just as good for the goose, Katie argued to herself. His buccaneer costume was also blatantly sexy. In fact, his physical impact was so strong, he was probably well aware of its effect on women, and he was undoubtedly banking on her being an easy target for him.

A perverse streak in Katie urged her to pose a challenge to his overwhelming self-assurance. Instead of placing her hand in his in acquiescence, she propped it on her hip in languid consideration.

"Taking a risk, aren't you?" she drawled. "Men tend to fall desperately in love with Carmen once they give themselves up to her clutches."

Amanda burst into giggles and the rest of the party around the table fell silent to take in this interesting encounter.

He tilted his head to one side, and the hand he'd offered gestured non-caringly. "My life is littered with risks I've taken. One more is neither here nor there."

"You come out...unscathed...every time?" Katie queried disbelievingly.

"No. But I hide my scars well."

She quite liked that answer. It made him more human, less invincible. She smiled. "A fearless fighter."

"More a survivor," he returned blandly.

"Against all odds."

"Would you have me back off, Carmen?"

"That would spoil the game."

She sashayed around him, swishing the frills on her skirt, the exhilaration of being deliberately provocative zinging through her as she turned and extended her hand to him in invitation. "Will you dance with me?"

He'd already swung, following her movements as

though she was now the pivotal magnet. He took her hand in a firm grasp, and with slow deliberation, lifted it to his mouth.

"The pleasure...believe me...will be mine."

He turned her hand over and pressed a hot, sensual kiss onto her palm, completely blitzing any reply Katie might have made to that subtly threatening claim. She stood stunned by the electric tingles running up her arm. Before she could recover any composure at all, he moved, sliding an arm around her waist and sweeping her onto the dance floor with a dominant power that enforced pliancy. He placed her hand on his shoulder and pressed the rest of her into full body contact with him.

"Now we dance," he murmured, his voice simmering with a sexuality that vibrated with anticipation. "We shall see if Carmen can follow where a pirate leads."

CHAPTER TWO

KATIE was swamped by his aggressive maleness. Hard muscular thighs were pushing hers into matching his every step and her feet were instinctively moving to his will. His body heat was seeping into her, arousing a highly sensitive awareness of her own sexuality, and the physical friction of dancing in such intimate proximity stirred feelings she hadn't had in years.

Occasionally a very handsome man with a well-built physique had inspired a fleeting moment of lustful speculation, but that had only ever been a mental try-on... *What would he be like as a lover?* She hadn't experienced any noticeable physical reaction. Her stomach certainly hadn't gone all tremulous. Her breasts hadn't started prickling with excitement. Her pulse rate had not zoomed into a wild gallop.

The pirate was doing all this to her within seconds of her being in *his clutches,* and Katie was so mesmerised by his effect on her, she was following him willy-nilly, taking no control whatsoever over what was happening. Deciding she probably needed a good dose of oxygen in her brain, she took a deep breath. The result was her nostrils tingled with the sharp, tangy scent of whatever cologne he'd splashed onto his jaw after shaving.

It seemed that all her senses had moved up several

intensity levels and were being flooded with some wanton need to pick up everything there was to know about this man. She couldn't get a grip on herself. She didn't even want to get a grip on herself. Her body was alive with all the feelings of being a woman who craved the primitive pleasure a man could give her...*this man,* who might be dressed as a fantasy but was most certainly flesh and blood reality.

"Gold rings on your ears, on your arms, but not on your hands," he commented.

"None on yours, either," she answered, very aware of the strong bare fingers wrapped around hers.

"I walk alone."

"So do I."

"No one owns Carmen?"

"I don't believe anyone can ever *own* another person."

"True. We're only ever given the pieces they choose to give us. Like this dance..."

"You're not counting on anything else from me?"

"Are you...from me?"

"You claimed the role of leader."

"So I did. Which begs the question...how far will you follow?"

"As far as I still want to."

"Then I must keep you wanting."

He executed a masterful series of turns that made wicked use of the front slit of her skirt, their thighs intertwining with every twirl, and the hand pressing into the pit of her back ensuring she remained pinned to him. The deliberately tantalising manoeuvre left her breathless, the surge of excitement so intense she had to struggle to think.

But this wasn't about thinking, she fiercely reasoned.

It was about feeling.

And the desire to indulge herself with what he was promising was too strong to question.

All the long empty years since Carver...nothing. There was a huge hole in her life and this might not be the answer to it but it was *something!*

Free and clear, Carver thought, and the sooner he turned this burning desire to ashes, the better. She was on heat for him. He could feel it. No need for any more talking. The provocative little witch wanted action. He'd give her action in spades.

It had been months since he'd been with a woman, preferring to remain celibate than enter into another affair that didn't satisfy him. But the need for sex didn't go away and the delectable Carmen had it roaring to the fore right now.

Her musky scent was a heady come-on, infiltrating his brain and closing out any reservations about taking what she was offering. The doors were open to the balcony that commanded the multimillion-dollar view over Sydney Harbour. Since it was a fine night, there could be no objection to going outside. She could pretend it was romantic if she wanted to.

He steered her through the dance crowd, revelling in the lush curvaceousness of the body so very pliantly moulded to his. She was ready to give all right. Ready to give and take. He whirled her out onto the balcony. The broad semicircular apron that extended from the ballroom held several groups of smokers but that didn't bother him. It was too public a place anyway.

He danced her down the left flank of the balcony that ran to the end of the massive mansion. The music was loud enough to float after them and there was no word of protest from her, not the slightest stiffening to indicate any concern. She wanted privacy as much as he did.

The light grew dimmer. Huge pots with perfectly trimmed ornamental trees provided pools of darkness. But he didn't want to take obvious advantage of them. Not yet. He took her right to the far balustrade, leaned her against it, and kissed her with all the pent-up need she'd stirred.

No hesitation in her response. Her mouth opened willingly, eagerly, and her hunger matched his, exploding into a passionate drive for every sensual satisfaction a man and woman could give each other. Her arms wound around his neck, pressing for the kissing to go on and on, a wild ravaging of every pleasure possible, a tempest of excitement demanding more.

No artful seduction in this. She was caught up in the same primitive urgency he felt. And that in itself was intensely exhilarating, the direct and open honesty of the craving in her kisses, the hot desire to explore and experience and tangle intimately with him. It reminded him of how it had been with...

No! He wasn't going down that track!

This was Carmen's lust, not Katie's love.

And love was a long-lost cause.

He ran his hands over the body he held. The clinging stretchy fabric of her dress left little to his imagination. He savoured the soft voluptuous curves of *Carmen's* buttocks, the very female flare of her hips, the almost hand-span waist. Her breasts felt full and swollen against his chest. He wanted to touch them, hold them.

Reaching up, he grasped her arms and pulled them down to her sides. Still kissing her, feeding the wanting, he slid his hands up to the off-the-shoulder sleeves and yanked them down, taking the top of her bodice with them to bare her breasts. It shocked her. Her head jerked back. He heard her sharply indrawn breath.

"No one can see," he swiftly assured her, smiling to erase any fear. "The advantage of a cloak."

He moved his legs to stand astride hers, holding her pinned against the balustrade for firm support while he cupped her breasts, lightly fanning her stiffly protruding nipples with his thumbs. She didn't speak. She stared at his mask for several seconds, as though wanting to see behind it. Then slowly she looked down at what he was doing, watching, seemingly fascinated at having her breasts fondled like this, out in the open.

She was still *with* him, still wanting, and her naked flesh was a delight to feel, to stroke, the different textures of her skin intriguing enough to draw his own gaze down. Either his caresses or the cool night air had hardened her nipples to long purple grapes—very mouth-tempting. He gently squeezed the soft mounds upwards, meaning to taste, but was suddenly struck by the size of her dark aureoles, the whole shape of her breasts…so like Katie's…

His rejection of the memory was so violent, his hands moved instantly to pull up her bodice and lift the off-the-shoulder sleeves back into position. It was the long black curly hair, he savagely reasoned, triggering memories he didn't want, playing havoc with what should be no more than a slaking of need. His heart shouldn't be thumping like this. Not for Carmen.

Yet as though she knew it, he saw her gaze fixed on his chest. She slid her hand under his opened shirt, spreading her fingers over the light nest of hair. Her touch on his skin was electric, his arousal almost painful in its intensity.

She was feeling her power over him, Carver thought, and acted again in violent rejection, lifting her off her feet, swinging her over to the shadowed area to the side of one of the ornamental trees, planting her against the stone wall of the house, snatching her hand out of his shirt, and kissing her to reassert his dominance over this encounter.

Again she wound her arms around his neck and kissed him back—following his lead. But Carver now wanted done with the game. He plundered her mouth while he took the necessary packet from his trouser pocket, freed himself and deftly applied the condom. The front split of her skirt had to be hitched higher, quickly effected. Much to his relief, his hand found only a G-string covering the apex of her thighs, easily shifted aside.

He hadn't meant to wait another moment, but the slick warm softness of her drew him into stroking, feeling, *claiming* this intimate part of her and driving her arousal to the same fever pitch as his own. Where he was rock-hard, she quivered, and he knew precisely when she couldn't bear any more excitement. She wrenched her mouth from his, gasping, moaning.

"Put your legs around me now," he commanded, hoisting her up against the wall, one arm under her buttocks as he inserted himself into the hot silky heart of her, thrusting hard, needing to feel engulfed by the female flesh welcoming him.

Her legs linked behind his hips, pressing him in, obviously needing the sensation of being filled by him, every bit as needy as he was for sexual satisfaction. It was more than enough permission for what he was doing. The only thought he had as he continued to revel in the freedom of unbridled lust was... *yes...yes...yes...*

It felt so good...better with every plunge...the tense excitement building faster...faster...his whole body caught in the thrall of it...and finally, a fierce pulsing of intense pleasure exploding from him...the sweet, shuddering relief of it...

He knew she had climaxed before him. Probably with him, as well. He would have liked the sense of fully feeling the physical mingling with her. Impossible with a condom. But protection was more important than any fleeting and *false* sense of togetherness.

Her legs were limply sliding down his thighs. Excitement over. Aftermath setting in. He separated himself from her and helped steady her as she stood once more against the wall. The clasp around his head loosened, her hands dropping to his shoulders. He was glad they were both wearing masks. He didn't want to see the expression on her face. For him, this encounter had run its course, and the sooner they parted, the sooner he could get it out of his head.

He'd wanted her.

She'd wanted him.

They'd satisfied each other and that was that.

The spectre of Katie Beaumont could now be put to rest again.

Katie was stunned out of her mind. It was all she could do to stand on her own two feet. The impression of Carver was so strong—the shape of his head, the texture of his hair, the broad muscular shoulders, the sprinkle of black curls across his chest, the whole feel of him—her head was swimming with it. Her entire body was swimming with the sense of having been...*possessed* by him.

It had to be sheer fantasy, driven by long unanswered needs, yet...

Who was this pirate king?

She could tear off his mask...but if he looked totally different to Carver, how would she feel then?

Wait, she told herself.

It was safer if she waited.

He might say something to reveal more about himself.

Her heart was still thundering in her ears. Impossible to think of anything to say herself. He was readjusting his clothes, all under cover of the cloak that had sheltered their intimacy. Her skirt had slithered back into place when he'd moved away from her. There was no urgent need to reposition the G-string panties. It made no difference to the line of her dress.

Besides, she didn't want to touch herself there... where he had been. Not yet. She wanted to savour the lingering pleasure of all he'd made her feel. Like Carver...

He straightened up. It was difficult to tell if he was the same height as the man she'd once loved, given the boots he wore and her own high-heeled sandals. Was the cloak making his shoulders look broader than she remembered? They *felt* right. She stared at his mouth. The light was dim here, but surely the shape of those firmly delineated lips were...

He compressed them, frustrating her study. He plucked her hands from his shoulders and carried them down, deliberately placing them on her hips as he stepped back.

''The dance is over, Carmen.''

The cold, harsh statement was more chilling than the night air, bringing instant goose bumps to her skin.

Somehow she found her voice. ''So what happens now?'' It came out in a husky slur.

''I told you I walk alone.''

Another chilling statement, striking ice into her heart.

He lifted a hand and ran light fingertips down her cheek. ''This is one man who *can* take what you

give…and leave. But I do thank you…for the pleasure.''

He took another step away from her, his hand gone
from her face but still raised in a kind of farewell
salute. He paused a moment, as though taking in the
image of her—Carmen left against the wall, abandoned by him after he'd taken his pleasure of
her…and after he'd given what she'd virtually asked
of him.

She didn't move.

This was the end of it.

He was going.

''The pleasure was mine, too,'' she said, driven to
match him even now. ''Thank you for the dance.''

He inclined his head in what she thought was a nod
of respect, then turned and strode away, taking with
him the spectre of Carver, the cloak swirling around
his swiftly receding figure.

Fantasy…

She stood against the wall for a long time, needing
the support as she fought the tremors that shook her.
It was better this way, she kept telling herself, better
to have the memory and not the disappointment that
reality would surely bring.

It might be like an empty memory right now…but
it *was* something.

He'd made her feel like a woman again.

CHAPTER THREE

As SHE rode the train from North Sydney to Town Hall for her all-important appointment in the city, Katie did her best to keep her nerves under control by thinking positively.

The facts and figures she had marshalled—costs and estimated profits—for her business proposition were neatly organised in the slim-line black leather attaché case she carried. References from previous employers attested to her good character and sense of responsibility. Trustworthy and reliable were tags that were repeatedly emphasised.

She was wearing her one good all-purpose black suit, having teamed a cherry red sweater with it since red was supposedly a power colour. Her hair was clean and shiny and as tidy as her curls ever allowed. Her make-up was minimal. She wore new stockings and sensibly heeled black court shoes.

There was nothing to object to about her appearance or preparation, so hopefully she would clinch a deal that would give her a more interesting and satisfying future than her current situation. Max Fairweather had told her this particular company matched investors to budding businesses. With luck, her bud of an idea could flower into a fleet of specialised taxis for transporting children.

Because of her fear of being rushed or late, it was

barely nine o'clock when she stepped off the train. Since her appointment wasn't until nine-thirty, she walked slowly along George Street, then up Market Street to the address Max had given her. It turned out to be a skyscraper with a very impressive facade of black granite and glass.

Big money here, Katie thought, even more determined to fight for the investment she needed. She took a deep breath and entered the huge lobby. The directory on the wall gave her destination as the eighteenth floor, with either elevator one or two providing an express ascent.

There were still ten minutes to go before her appointment. Reasoning that being overly punctual was not a black mark against her, and the company would surely have a reception area with chairs where she could sit and wait, she pressed the button to summon elevator two.

A few seconds later the doors opened...and shock rooted Katie's feet to the floor.

Standing inside the compartment, directly facing her, was a man whose identity was unmistakable. She hadn't seen him for almost ten years but she knew him instantly and her heart quivered from the impact he made on it.

Carver Dane.

Carver...who, in her heart of hearts, had been behind the pirate's mask...a fantasy, stimulated by a host of frustrations and the wild and wanton desire to feel what she had once felt with *him*. The mask had let her pretend. The mask had made a dream briefly come true. But that was all it had been. A dream!

The man facing her was the real person!

Shock hit him, too. No doubt she was the last woman in the world he expected to see or wanted to meet. His facial muscles visibly tightened. There was a flare of some violent emotion in his eyes before they narrowed on her in a sharply guarded scrutiny that shot her nerves into a hopelessly agitated state.

Only a few nights ago she'd been fantasising about the intimacy they'd once shared. The raw sexuality she'd indulged in—with a masked stranger who'd strongly reminded her of Carver—suddenly flooded her with embarrassment. Here was her first and only love—in the flesh—and she simply wasn't prepared to face him, especially when *that* memory was so fresh.

"Are you coming in, Katie, or would you prefer not to ride this elevator with me?" he asked.

"I...I was wondering if you were stepping out."

"No." His mouth curled into a sardonic little smile. "I'm on my way up."

She flushed, painful old memories rushing over her embarrassment, making it more acute. The expensive suit Carver was wearing was evidence enough that his status had risen beyond anything her father had predicted, but what he was doing here Katie had no idea. While she wrestled with her inner confusion the elevator doors started to slide shut.

Carver reached out and pressed a button to reopen them. "Well?" he challenged, a savage glitter in his dark brown eyes.

A surge of pride got her feet moving. "I'm going up, too," she declared, stepping into the compartment beside him. She was not her father's little girl any-more. She was an independent woman, all primed to establish her own business, and she was not about to be intimidated by anything Carver could bring up against her.

He released the button holding the doors. As they closed her into sharing this horribly small space with Carver, Katie fiercely hoped the elevator lived up to its promise of being an *express* one. She couldn't bear being with him for long, knowing they couldn't ever be truly together, not how they'd once been.

"What floor do you want?" he asked.

"Eighteen." It was easier to let him operate the control panel than lean across him and do it herself. "Thank you."

"You're looking good, Katie," he remarked as the compartment started rising.

She flashed him an acknowledging glance. "So are you."

"You're back home with your father?"

"No. I'm on my own. How's your mother?" she retaliated, burning with the memories of how each parent had played a critical part in breaking up the relationship they saw as destructive to the best future for Carver and Katie.

"She has to take it easy now. Not as well as she used to be."

And probably plays that to the hilt, too, Katie thought bitterly. Lillian Dane would never give up her apron strings. She wondered how Carver's wife coped with her mother-in-law, and was instantly prompted to add, "And your wife?"

The supposedly polite interest question was not immediately answered. The tension in the silence that followed it was suddenly crawling with all the conflicts left unresolved between them, and the string of circumstances that had kept the two of them apart, preventing any possible resolution.

Katie gritted her teeth as the memories flooded back—the pressures that had forced the break-up, the timing that had been wrong for them, even years later when Carver had come to England looking for her, just when she'd been between jobs and back-packing through Greece and Turkey...the letter he'd left, asking if there was any chance they could get together again, a letter she didn't know about for six months...her phone call, wild hope fluttering through her heart until the call was answered by *his wife*...then the confirmation from Carver himself that he was, indeed, married.

That was the cruellest cut of all!

Five years apart...then six months too late!

Though to be absolutely fair, maybe she'd read too much into his coming to London, too much into the letter, as well. It had only been an inquiry, not a promise. He might simply have wanted to put the memory of her to rest, and her apparent lack of response could well have effected that very outcome. She could hardly blame him for getting on with his life.

He wasn't hers.

He'd never be hers again.

"My wife died two years ago."

The flat statement from Carver rang in her ears,

then slowly, excruciatingly, bounced around her mind, hitting a mass of raw places she didn't want to look at. The sense of *waste* was totally devastating.

She wasn't aware of the elevator coming to a halt.

She was blind to the doors opening.

It took Carver's voice to jolt her out of it. "This is the eighteenth floor."

"Oh! Sorry!" she babbled, and plunged out of the compartment, without even the presence of mind to say goodbye to him.

She found herself in a corridor with a blank wall at one end, glass doors at the other. Her legs automatically carried her towards the doors which had to lead somewhere. It wasn't until Carver fell into step beside her that she realised he had followed her out of the elevator. She stopped, her head jerking towards him in startled inquiry.

"This is my floor, too," he informed her, his eyes flashing derisively at her non-comprehension. "Are you seeing someone here?" he went on, moving ahead to open the way for her.

"Robert Freeman." The name tripped out, though it was none of Carver's business. "Are *you* seeing someone?"

He shook his head, holding one of the glass doors open and waving her through to what was obviously a reception area. "I work here, Katie," he said quietly as she pushed herself into passing him.

Again her feet faltered, right in the doorway next to where he stood, shock and bewilderment causing her to pause and query this extraordinary statement.

What did a doctor have to do with an investment company?

"You work...?" was as far as she got.

He bent his head closer to hers, murmuring, "I'm one of the partners... Andrews, Dane and Freeman."

Not only was she stunned by this information, but she caught a light whiff of a scent that put all her senses on hyper-alert. Recognition of the distinctive male cologne was instant and so mind-blowing, she almost reeled away from it, barely recovering enough to hold her balance and move on into the reception area.

"How...how nice for you," she somehow managed to mutter, though she was totally unable to meet his eyes.

He couldn't have been the pirate, she frantically reasoned, but her gaze was drawn in terrible fascination to the mouth that now thinned at her lame response, and her heart was catapulting around her chest at the possibility that fantasy had crossed into reality.

It was the physical similarities that had got to her at the masked ball. Plus her own sexual response to them. But that didn't make his identity certain. Far from it. Neither did the cologne. It was probably a popular brand bought and used by many men. She was not normally close enough to most men to notice a scent. It was silly to get so rattled by a coincidence that could be easily explained.

"Life does move on," Carver remarked sardonically, responding to her inane "nice" comment.

"Yes, it does," she quickly agreed, hating herself for being so hopelessly gauche.

He hadn't become a doctor but he'd certainly moved up in the world, a long way *up* if this office building was anything to judge by. She didn't understand why he hadn't pursued a medical career, but he certainly had to have become a very successful businessman to be a partner here. His pride had surely been salved by such success. As for *her* pride...

Given the chance, would she have Carver back now that he was free again?

Could one ever go back?

He shut the glass door.

She screwed up her courage to look directly at him, to judge if there was anything left for them.

It was a futile effort.

"Laura will look after you," he coolly instructed, gesturing towards the reception desk.

Having dismissed her into another's hands, he turned aside and headed off down a corridor which ran off the reception area, striding fast as though he couldn't wait to get away from her...like the pirate king after declaring the dance was over.

Katie stared after him, any thought of taking some positive initiative utterly wiped out by the comparison pounding through her mind.

Had it been Carver in the buccaneer costume? A widower, who walked alone, feeling the same compulsive physical attraction she had felt because the chemistry was still there for them? Always would be?

A convulsive shiver ran down her spine.

Even if it had been Carver, he'd made it plain he

wanted nothing more to do with her...at least, not with the Carmen she'd been role-playing. He couldn't have known who she really was.

But the man who'd accompanied her to this office floor did know the woman he'd just left, making it equally plain he was finished with her.

She watched him enter an office and disappear from view, heard the closing of the door behind him, and knew there was not going to be any comeback. He didn't *want* any further involvement with her.

The dance was over.

It had been over for Katie Beaumont and Carver Dane years ago.

CHAPTER FOUR

ONCE inside the privacy of his office, Carver took several deep breaths, trying to clear the insidiously sexy aroma from his nostrils and haul his mind back from the chaos it had evoked.

It was definitely the same musky scent Carmen had worn... Carmen, so like Katie—her hair, her breasts, the whole feel of her, the intensity of her need for him.

Had it actually *been* Katie under that mask?

He shook his head, recoiling from the possibility and all it might mean, yet he couldn't banish it. She was back in Sydney. She certainly had access to the high society crowd anytime she wanted to move into it. Her father's connections and her old school network would open most doors. *It could have been her.*

The need to know drove him to the telephone on his desk. He snatched up the receiver, pressed the button to connect him to Robert Freeman and fiercely willed the other man to pick up. Instantly. Robert was the obvious conduit to immediate information about Katie Beaumont. She was here to see him. He had to know something.

"So how did the breakfast meeting go?" his partner inquired, not bothering with a greeting.

"As expected," Carver answered briefly, too caught up in more urgent issues to go into detail. "I just rode up in the elevator with a Miss Beaumont. I understand you have an appointment with her this morning."

"In five minutes. Some problem with it?"

"Do you know her personally?"

"Never met her. Comes with a recommendation from Max Fairweather. Wants to set up a business and needs cash."

"Needs cash? From *us?*" Carver couldn't stop his voice from rising incredulously. "Do you know who her father is?"

"Beaumont Retirement Villages. Max did mention it."

"The guy is worth millions."

"Uh-huh. Could be he disapproves of his daughter's business plans."

As well as her choice of men, Carver thought acidly.

"Very wealthy fathers can get too fond of flexing their power," Robert went on. "We could reap some benefit here if the daughter is as smart as Daddy at capitalising on a customer need."

"An interesting situation..." Carver mused, recalling Katie's assertion she was on her own, not back with her father. She'd worked as a nanny in England in years gone by but what she had done with her life in more recent times was an absolute blank to him. It could be that everything she chose to do was an act of rebellion against her father...including sexual encounters where she took what *she* wanted...like Carmen.

Every muscle in his groin started tightening at the

memory of her flagrant desire matching his. "Any chance of your passing her over to me, Robert," he heard himself saying, not even pausing to consider the possible wisdom of staying clear of any involvement.

He'd once thought of Katie Beaumont as *his*. The temptation to re-examine the feelings that only she had ever drawn from him was too strong to let go. If she'd been behind the Carmen mask, they could still have something very powerful going between them. They weren't so young anymore and the circumstances were very, very different.

"I'm clear for the rest of the morning," he pressed, "and I must admit I'm curious to hear Miss Beaumont's business plans."

"Mmm…does she happen to be gorgeous?"

"You're a married man, Robert," Carver dryly reminded him, uncaring what his partner thought as long as he turned Katie over to him.

He laughed. "Just don't be forgetting facts and figures in her undoubtedly delectable presence. Go to it, Carver. I'll let Laura know to redirect the client to you."

"I owe you one."

"I'll chalk it up."

Done! He set the receiver down on its cradle, feeling a huge surge of satisfaction. Katie Beamont was his for the next hour or so. The only question was…how to play it to get what he wanted!

Katie was only too grateful that Robert Freeman was occupied on the telephone and not yet free to see her.

She was far from being cool, calm and collected after the run-in with Carver Dane. Her focus on business was shot to pieces, and she was in desperate need of time to get her mind channelled towards her purpose in being here.

The shock of the link between Carver and the pirate king had left her shaky, too, forcefully reminding her of how terribly wanton she had been with the masked man. She had believed that secret was safe. And surely it was. It had to be. She was not normally a wild risk-taker. To have that kind of behaviour rebound on her now...here...no, she was getting in a stew over nothing. Even if Carver had been the buccaneer, he couldn't know she had been Carmen.

It was good to sit down with the option of hopefully getting herself under control again. A few deep breaths helped. If she could just let the past go and concentrate on the future, managing this meeting shouldn't be too difficult. Only the future counted now, she fiercely told herself, and neither Carver nor the pirate king held any part in that. She was on her own.

Definitely on her own.

She had to go into the meeting with Robert Freeman and prove an investment in her business would be worthwhile. All the necessary papers were in her attaché case. She simply had to pull them out and...

"Miss Beaumont?"

Katie's heart leapt at the call from the receptionist, a pleasant young woman with a bright, friendly manner, obviously trained to put people at ease. She had auburn hair, cut in a short, chic style, and her navy suit, teamed with a patterned navy and white scarf knotted around her throat, looked very classy. The perfect frontline person for an investment company, Katie thought, and forced an inquiring smile.

Laura—that was the name Carver had given her—responded with an apologetic grimace. ''I'm sorry. Mr. Freeman is tied up with some urgent business.''

''That's okay. I don't mind waiting,'' Katie quickly inserted, relieved to be given more time to calm her nerves before she had to perform at her best.

''As it happens, that isn't necessary, Miss Beaumont.'' Her mouth moved into a conciliatory smile. ''One of the other partners is free to take over your meeting with Mr. Freeman. In fact, you came in with him... Mr. Dane.''

''Mr....Dane?'' Katie could barely get the words out. Her tongue felt as paralysed as the rest of her at the thought of facing Carver across a desk, spilling out where she was in her life and asking *him* for money.

''He's very experienced at assessing presentations,'' Laura assured her. ''Your time won't be wasted with Mr. Dane, Miss Beaumont.''

''But I don't mind waiting for Mr. Freeman. It's no problem for me,'' Katie babbled, unable to quell a rising whirl of hysteria.

''The arrangement has already been made.''

Without any discussion with her? Didn't she have any right to decide whom she dealt with? Not that she actually knew Robert Freeman, so she couldn't claim an acquaintance with him. And Carver was a partner, so she couldn't very well protest on the grounds of being handed to someone of lesser authority.

Having announced this official decision, Laura came out from behind the reception desk, clearly intending to gather Katie up and deposit her in the appointed place. Katie froze in her chair, her mind in a ferment of indecision, her body churning with sheer panic as her future and past collided head-on.

A benevolent smile was directed at her, along with the words, "I'll show you to Mr. Dane's office."

What was she to do?

Somehow she levered herself out of the chair and picked up the attaché case, grasping the handle with both hands and holding the square of leather in front of her like some shield against the arrows of fate.

"This way..." An encouraging arm was waved towards the corridor Carver had taken.

The past was gone, Katie frantically reasoned. If she didn't take this chance, she faced a future of always being an employee without any prospect of really getting ahead in life. Besides, this was a business deal. There shouldn't be anything personal in it. If Carver turned it into something personal, she could walk out, with good reason to demand a more objective hearing.

"Miss Beaumont?"

Laura was paused in front of her, a slight frown questioning the delayed reaction from Katie.

"Sorry. I'm a bit thrown by the change."

An understanding smile. "There's no need to be, I

promise you. Mr. Dane follows exactly the same company policies as Mr. Freeman.''

Katie expelled a long breath to ease the tightness in her chest. ''Okay. I'm coming.''

Laura nodded approval as Katie pushed her feet into taking the path to Carver's office. The carpet was dove-grey. It felt like sand dragging at every step she made.

She told herself Carver wouldn't want this meeting any more than she did. He'd been landed with it because he was available and Robert Freeman was busy. Which surely meant he would keep it strictly business, totally ignoring the intimacy of their former relationship.

Or was the intimacy the buccaneer had shared with Carmen as sharply on his mind as it was on hers?

Katie instantly clamped down on that thought. But her stomach contracted at the memory and to her horror, some wanton rush of excitement attacked her breasts, just as Laura came to a halt, gave a courtesy knock on a door, and opened it.

''Miss Beaumont for you, Mr. Dane,'' she announced.

''Thank you, Laura,'' came Carver's voice.

It had the same deep timbre of the pirate king's! Why hadn't she noticed that before? Because she'd been in too much of a flap over running into Carver and she hadn't smelled the cologne until he was on the point of leaving her. But now...her heart started thundering in her ears.

Laura stood back and waved Katie forward.

She had to walk into Carver's office, face him, and

pretend everything they'd ever known together was water under the bridge, including a fantasy that was fast gathering too many shades of reality.

Having constructed a somewhat rueful smile to ease her over the next few moments which were fraught with pitfalls, Katie willed her legs to move without wobbling, thanked Laura for her services, then stepped into what she couldn't help thinking of as the torture room.

Like going to the dentist.

Only worse.

No one here was going to give her an anaesthetic to kill pain.

She heard the door shut behind her. Goose bumps rose on her skin at the realisation she was once again enclosed in a space shared only with Carver Dane. At least it was bigger than an elevator, she hurriedly told herself, and there was furniture to keep them separated.

"Hello, again."

The greeting forced her to fasten her gaze directly on the man himself. He'd been on the periphery of her vision, standing to the side of his desk. She'd felt him watching her, probably assessing her reaction to the changed appointment, and a sudden surge of stubborn pride tilted her chin in defiance of any judgement he might have made.

"I wasn't expecting this, Carver," she stated bluntly.

"I do appreciate that, Katie," he returned, his quiet tone aimed to soothe frazzled nerves. His mouth quirked into whimsical appeal. "Will it help if we pretend we're meeting for the first time?"

Impossible! He'd taken off his suitcoat. Her mind's eye was already measuring his shoulders, matching them to old and fresh memories, and her body felt as though it was pulsing to the imprint of every hard muscle in his very male physique.

"Why aren't you a doctor?" she blurted out, totally incapable of putting him in a business frame.

He shrugged and moved to the front of the desk, propping himself against it in a relaxed pose that suggested he was prepared to be patient with her. "That was a long time ago, Katie. I might well ask what you're doing here, seeking a business investment? Why didn't you pursue the course you were taking to become a kindergarten teacher?"

Because I couldn't bear being in the same city as you after the break-up. Not even in the same country! The words screamed through her mind but couldn't be spoken. As he said, it was a long time ago.

"It's just that I always thought of you as working towards that goal," she said to explain her intemperate outburst. "To find you here..."

Carver stared at her, a hard bitterness coiling through him. How *much* had she thought of him? Certainly not enough to bring her back to Australia to find out if anything had changed for them. All those years he'd worked around the clock, needing to prove to himself—and her father—he *could* amount to something...had she given him anything more than a fleeting thought?

Even when he'd gone to England, she'd been off trekking through Greece and Turkey, spending her money on more travel away from him, and staying away so long he'd given up on any response to his letter—given up and trapped himself into a marriage that was bound to be sour before it had even begun, all because he'd been thinking of Katie.

Well, she could think what she liked. He wasn't about to tell her what he'd been through. And certainly not *why!* The sexual attraction was still strong, but he was never going to let Katie Beaumont into his heart again. He'd been there, done that, and any private intercourse between them now would be based on sex, which he very definitely wanted and would find very sweet...*with her.*

He enjoyed her obvious confusion of mind before cutting it off. "So...you want my credentials before dealing with me," he drawled, and enjoyed it even more when a flush rose up her neck and spread into her cheeks, making them almost as red as her sweater...as red as the provocative dress Carmen had worn.

"I'm sure they're everything they should be," she rushed out, discomforted by the doubt she'd inadvertantly projected and retracting it as fast as she could. "You wouldn't be in this position unless they were."

"But it's difficult for you to accept," he taunted, cynically wondering if she'd come to accept her father's view of him—a guy who was screwing a rich man's daughter to make an easy track for himself to a better life.

"No. I..."

Words failed her. Her eyes flickered with confusion. Hazel eyes—grey and green with dots of gold, he remembered. Big, beautiful eyes to drown in... when he was much younger. Her face was still probably the most essentially feminine face he'd ever seen, its frame of black curls accentuating her pale creamy skin, the finely winged eyebrows, a delicately formed nose, and the very kissable, lushly curved lips.

Was she remembering how they'd once kissed?

Were the memories as recent as a few nights ago?

Right now she was boxed into a corner and struggling to get out, realising that referring to the past was a faux pas in these circumstances. She was the one in need of money, not him. Quite a delicious irony, given the background of their former relationship.

Carver noted that her mouth remained slightly parted, the full sensuality of her lips accentuated, and the kisses he'd taken from Carmen were vividly evoked, inciting the desire to taste them again.

She scooped in a quick breath and gestured an agitated appeal for his forebearance. "I'm sorry. Of course, I accept your credentials. I hope you're prepared to accept mine."

They would undoubtedly make fascinating listening, but Carver was not about to reveal any personal interest in them. "I'm here to be convinced that your proposition is well founded and potentially profitable," he assured her, smiling his satisfaction in the concession to his obvious standing in the company. "If you'd like to start..."

He waved an invitation to the chair he'd placed

handy to his desk for her to pass over papers. Without waiting for her to move, he straightened up and strolled around the large desktop to his own chair, a clear signal that he expected business to begin.

Control was his and he intended to keep it, right down the line.

Even when he kissed her.

Which he fully intended to do before she left this office...if Katie Beaumont reacted to the trigger of Carmen!

CHAPTER FIVE

KATIE burned with embarrassment as she took the client chair Carver had indicated. *Client* was the operative word and she fiercely vowed not to forget it again. Her logic had been spot-on before she'd stepped into this office. For Carver, this was strictly business, and if he had been the buccaneer at the masked ball, she could forget that, too. It had no bearing—none whatsoever—on this meeting.

In fact, she wished she knew what Robert Freeman looked like so she could mentally transpose his face onto Carver's. A mask would be very helpful right now. It would save getting distracted again by things that weren't pertinent to this time and place.

As it was, looking straight at the man behind the desk, she couldn't help seeing that ten years had given Carver's handsome face a more striking look of strength and authority. Success certainly sat well on him. But his dark chocolate eyes no longer had a melting quality. No caring in them, she thought. At least, not for her. Which made the past a hollow thing she should discard. Immediately.

"Best to start with a summary of what you're aiming for and why you think it would prove a good investment," Carver directed, making Katie acutely aware that she'd lost all sense of initiative.

"I need to know where you're coming from so I

can assess the probable outcome of where you want to head," he went on, spelling out what she already knew she had to do.

She'd practised it many times. There would be no difficulty at all in rolling it out if Carver was a stranger, so she had to pretend he was one, just as he'd initially suggested...meeting for the first time.

Setting that parameter in her mind as firmly as she could, Katie managed to pull out her rehearsed presentation, beginning with her background in child-care, her current employment at a day-care centre, and her observations regarding the need for a safe, reliable transport service to deliver and pick up children, thereby relieving the stress of working parents who were stretched for time to manage this themselves.

Carver nodded thoughtfully. "You're talking about creches, preschool child-minding centres..."

Katie leaned forward in her eagerness to press her case. "It's where to start distributing leaflets about the service but I envisage much more than catering to the very young age group. I'm thinking school-children who have medical or dental appointments, swimming lessons, dance classes, after-school tutoring, birthday parties. Also picking up teenagers from movies or parties. Parents worry about them using public transport after dark."

"This would encompass a very long working day," he remarked warningly.

Katie nodded and spelled it out. "A 6:00 a.m. start for week days. Before and after school hours will be the busy times. I would expect most days to finish by

9:00 p.m. The weekends would be different—sporting activities and later nights for teenage parties.''

''You do realise the hours you're proposing leave literally no time for a social life of your own,'' Carver commented, watching her intently for some reappraisal of the situation.

''I have no social life,'' she rattled out, dismissing what was irrelevant to her without realising how unreasonable that might seem to him.

''Excuse me?'' His eyes were suddenly very hard and sceptical. ''On any measuring scale you're a very attractive woman, with, I imagine, the normal urges to mix socially. You surely attend the usual parties...*balls*...'

The subtle emphasis on that last word had the jolt of an electric prod. He *knew,* was her first wild thought, and her heart instantly pumped faster, shooting a horribly telling tide of heat through her entire body.

''Only when I want to and I don't often want to,'' she spilled out, frantically casting around for other words to convince him he was mistaken in his view of her. ''It's not important to me,'' she strongly asserted, her eyes flashing a fierce denial at him. He couldn't *know,* she assured herself. Stupid to get flustered.

Silence as he weighed her answer.

Katie sat it out, determinedly meeting his testing gaze, every nerve in her body strung tight, waiting in fearful anticipation of some revealing comment that reason insisted wouldn't come. Carver was intent on avoiding anything on a personal level, especially if it involved him.

"I take it you're currently unattached," he said blandly.

"Yes. And I don't see that status changing," she flashed back, a surge of pride insisting she make it clear that acquiring a man in her life was not a driving need to be relentlessly pursued, and it was her choice to channel her energy into a future of her own making.

His eyebrows rose inquiringly. "You're not looking for marriage? Having children of your own?"

"Would you put those questions to a man, Carver? Are we getting into sexual discrimination here?" she challenged.

"I'm simply questioning priorities, Katie," he answered in a quiet reasonable tone, deliberately defusing the dynamite she'd hurled into the ring. "I'd certainly inquire of anyone seeking to set up a business what balance they envisaged between their private and working lives. I have to make a judgement on how stable an enterprise will be before recommending it for investment."

Still seething over his presumption about her personal needs—of which he knew nothing—Katie eyed him with icy resentment. "Then let me state there is no question that my priority is setting up this business and running it successfully."

"Fine!" He made a concessionary gesture. "As long as you comprehend how demanding it will be. How big a time commitment you're taking on. You are virtually giving up any private life."

What private life? she thought mockingly. Out loud she said, "I expect it to *fill* my life until it grows enough to allow me to invest in more vehicles and employ other drivers."

His eyes sharply scanned hers, assessing her strength of purpose. "So this isn't a one-off enterprise," he said slowly. "You intend to expand."

"Yes," Katie confirmed without hesitation, and pumped more conviction into her voice. "There is a very real need for this service. More and more these days, both parents are working. This is an extension of the caring a nanny can give their children. It takes away the guilt and gives peace of mind."

He nodded. "It's a very saleable idea."

"I'm certain of it."

"But you need the money to set up."

"That's why I'm here."

"Okay." He sat back, both hands gesturing his willingness to pursue the deal as he added, "You've sold it to me so far. Let's see your fact sheets."

Katie tingled with a sense of triumph as she lifted her attaché case onto her knees, opened it, took out the sheaf of papers, sectioned them, and placed three separate bundles on his desk.

"All the information on requirements and costs, the projected rates for permanent and casual bookings, and my references," she instructed, satisfied in her own mind that nothing had been overlooked in her preparation. Any fair-minded person would surely be favourably impressed.

Having set down the now emptied attaché case, she was finally able to relax while Carver meticulously checked the information she'd gathered. He obviously found the material comprehensive as he raised few questions and those were quickly answered to his satisfaction. Her confidence in his approval of the investment grew when he set her detailed planning aside without offering any criticism whatsoever and started perusing her references.

Knowing there could be no objection to anything they contained, Katie's concentration drifted, her gaze inadvertantly dropping to the strong male hands holding and turning the pages. No wedding ring. No sentimental hanging on to the symbol of his marriage, though perhaps he had never worn a ring. Some men didn't.

Were these the ringless hands that had cupped her naked breasts just a few nights ago? A widower for two years…needing sex but perhaps still grieving for his wife. It would explain an aggressive desire, burning briefly and quickly extinguished once satisfied. An anonymous encounter was probably the best answer for someone who wanted to walk away afterwards. It committed him to nothing.

Had he come to the masked ball with that in mind?

If so, why choose her?

She hadn't shown any interest in him, hadn't even seen him prior to his asking her to dance. Yet Amanda had said he'd been watching her. No, watching Carmen in her sexy dress, all inhibitions cast aside as she danced as Carmen would. The moment he'd targeted her, the only question left would be her consent. And because he'd reminded her of how she'd once felt with Carver…

Had he been the pirate king?

His mouth, his hair, the whole feel of him...she'd been totally captivated by the likeness at the time. And today, the same cologne...

"I see you've spent most of your working life in London," he commented, breaking into Katie's dangerously distracting reverie.

She snapped her attention back to the important issue that had to be settled. "Yes. It was easy to get a job as a nanny there and one position led to another," she quickly explained. "My mother was English and I was actually born in England so I have dual citizenship. No problem with staying there."

"You've only been back in Australia for six months. How can you be sure you'll settle here?"

"This is the land of opportunity. I can establish something here that I wouldn't be able to in England."

"So you came back with this business plan in mind."

"And have been investigating its viability ever since."

"You're totally committed to it."

"Totally."

"Ready to sign on the dotted line."

"Unequivocally."

"There are various forms for you to fill in and sign. We can go through them now and complete the deal or you can take them home for further consideration if you prefer to do so."

Katie was stunned at this quick result. "You're approving the investment?"

"Yes. The estimated profit margin comfortably covers the interest you'll have to pay. This is not a high-risk venture. It's simply a matter of how you wish to proceed now."

"Let's go through the forms," she promptly decided, barely able to contain her joy and relief at this outcome.

"I take it you have photocopies of all this documentation?" he said, restacking her papers into one pile.

"Yes."

"I'll file these here."

It was really happening, Katie thought in a daze of excitement. Carver laid out the forms and explained in careful detail what she was about to sign, making sure she understood each clause and what was involved if she couldn't make the repayments. He pointed out the places for her signature, which she duly wrote, then watched him attaching his own, making the agreement a legal contract.

"Is that it?" she asked eagerly.

He smiled. "The money will be forwarded to your account today. You can go shopping for your people-mover this afternoon if you like."

She couldn't stop herself grinning from ear to ear. She'd done it! Her father had refused to lend her the money—unless she toed *his* line—and had derided her chances of getting it elsewhere, but she'd done it!

"Congratulations, Katie," Carver said somewhat whimsically, and rose from his chair.

"Thank you," she breathed ecstatically. Unlike her

father, *he* had been fair-minded, despite their past history and the bitterness of their break-up.

He came around the desk, offering his hand to her. Katie sprang to her feet, happy to put her own hand in his at such an auspicious moment, not thinking of the pirate king at all...until Carver's strong fingers closed around hers.

Suddenly she was back in the ballroom, feeling *claimed,* the heat of his skin sending highly charged sexual signals through hers. His thumb lightly fanned the inner side of her wrist, making her pulse leap at the sensitivity it raised. Her gaze got stuck on the shirt button that closed the fine white fabric over the hair she knew spread across his chest, springy black hair that arrowed down...

"Carmen...unmasked."

The soft, husky murmur was like a thunderclap in Katie's ears.

The pirate king!

No one else *could* say that!

The impact of certain knowledge rocked her mind and thumped into her heart. Her gaze flew up to his. The same certain knowledge was simmering in his eyes, mockingly challenging her to deny it. She felt utterly caught, stripped of any place to hide. But so was he, she thought wildly. No denial possible from either of them now, and that truth blazed between them in a sizzling silence.

He released her hand, lifting his to stroke tauntingly light fingertips down her cheek to her chin. "Will it taste the same...feel the same...knowing it's me...knowing it's you?'' he mused, his eyes locked on hers in burning challenge.

She couldn't move, couldn't speak. The question had been tantalising her from the moment the elevator doors had opened and she'd been faced with the real flesh-and-blood Carver Dane. It pulsed through her mind now with mesmerising force as he stepped closer, his arm sliding around her waist, the hand on her chin tilting it up.

She stared at him...the pirate king unmasked... watching his face—his mouth—come closer, closer, doing nothing to evade the kiss that was coming. The desire to know if it would be *the same* now was a wild rampant thing compelling her into this moment of truth. There was no thought of consequences, any more than there'd been on the night of the ball. Only need...demanding answers.

His lips brushed hers. She closed her eyes, focusing on sensation. He *was* tasting her, no forceful demand in the seductive sipping at all, more a slow and thorough exploration—touch, caress, the sensual slide of his tongue teasing rather than invading, exciting the anticipation for a more intense contact. Yet the very gentleness of this kissing was enthralling—soft exquisite pleasures spilling over each other, inciting a needful *tasting* of her own.

This wasn't a fantasy of Carver. This was the man himself, whom she'd once loved with all her heart, and her heart yearned for him to fill the void of that lost love, to turn back the clock and recapture the joy and wonder and the glorious passion they'd felt for each other. The hunger for it welled up in her. Her hands slid up around his neck, instinctively seeking to hold him to her, to press for a more intimate kiss.

His hand moved to the nape of her neck, his fingers thrusting up through her hair to cradle the back of her head. The arm around her waist scooped her lower body hard against his, instantly arousing the physical awareness of their sexual differences, and the urge to revel in them. She wanted to feel desire stirring in him, reaching out for her, blindly dismissing the years they'd been apart.

Whether she deepened the kissing or he did...Katie was beyond knowing or caring. It happened, just as she wanted it to, the sudden, fierce explosion of passion where they couldn't get enough of each other, the wild need to excite and be excited, abandoning all control in the craving rush to be satisfied, every primitive instinct running riot.

She felt the hard push of his erection and exulted in it, rolling her hips to incite his full arousal, loving the pressure of it against her stomach. His hand clutched her buttocks, increasing the physical sensation of feeling him...feeling her softness accommodate the strong force of a need he couldn't hide, didn't try to hide.

He wrenched his mouth from hers, sucking in a quick breath before he spoke, his words furring against her lips. "We both want this."

"Yes..." The sigh of agreement whooshed from her with the same urgency racing through her body.

"Not here, Katie." The decision seemed to gravel from his throat. "Wrong time, wrong place."

"Oh!" She'd forgotten they were in his office.

Even with his reminder, it was difficult to recollect the reality of their situation. The intoxicating haze of desire, reborn and rampant, still clung to her, reinforced by his unabated arousal. And hers.

He lifted his head back, his dark eyes burning a path to her dazed brain. "Are you free tonight?"

"Yes…" Sweet relief that he wanted to pursue what they were both feeling.

"I'll come to your place. Nine o'clock."

"My place?" How did he know it?

He cut through her bewilderment. "Your address is on the forms you signed."

"Oh!" Belatedly registering the time he'd stipulated, she quickly offered, "Come earlier if you like. I could cook dinner and…"

"No. I'm not free before then."

"Not free?" She was beginning to sound like a mindless parrot echoing his words.

"You won't be in the very near future, either, given you're serious about your business."

"That's…that's true." It shocked her that she had even forgotten the commitment she'd just made to the investment he'd approved. Though time wasn't a problem for her tonight, there was no point in arguing this as Carver had already declared he wasn't free any earlier.

He eased his hold on her, one hand sliding to her hip as he moved back, the other raking lightly through her curls before dropping away. "I always liked your hair," he remarked with a quirky little smile.

It piqued Katie's curiosity. "Is that what attracted

you to Carmen?'' she asked, wanting it to be so as it would mean he had been reminded of her.

He shrugged, his eyes hooding slightly as he answered, ''Carmen presented a very sexy image.''

True, Katie admitted to herself, but she was disappointed in the reply. ''So did the buccaneer,'' she was prompted to comment.

''A fortunate coincidence. And today is another one. But tonight is about choice, isn't it, Katie?'' he said softly, his narrowed gaze glittering with anticipation.

Her stomach clenched over the emptiness he'd left when he'd moved back. ''Yes,'' she agreed, though it suddenly struck her it was sex they were talking about, nothing else.

But tonight would provide more time together, she hastily assured herself, hours of private time in which to come to a broader understanding of where they were and what they wanted of each other. The hope for a new start welled up in her…a chance to mend what had been broken.

Carver stepped past her, picked up the attaché case from beside her chair and set it on the desk. ''You'll need to take your copies of these documents you've signed,'' he advised, prompting her into action.

''Thanks again, Carver,'' she said self-consciously, quickly opening the case and laying her records inside. A nasty thought shot into her mind and agitated her into confronting it. ''You…you weren't influenced by…by…''

His face tightened, his eyes savagely deriding the

doubt in hers. "It's not my habit to buy women, Katie."

"No. Of course not. Why would you?" she babbled, inwardly writhing over another awful faux pas. Women were probably falling over themselves to climb into Carver's bed. Desperate to explain the uncalled-for suspicion, she quickly added, "It's just that my father..."

"I'm not your father," Carver cut in coldly.

She was making things worse, referring to the man Carver had every reason to hate. Her eyes eloquently begged his forgiveness, even as she wondered if they could ever paper over the old wounds.

His mouth relaxed into a wry little smile. "The deal is on the level, Katie. Your idea is soundly based. It's up to you to make it work."

She expelled a long, tremulous breath. "I appreciate your...your faith in me, Carver." Determined not to put her foot in her mouth again, Katie quickly snapped her attaché case shut and picked it up, ready to leave. "I'll see you at nine o'clock tonight?"

"I'm a man of my word," he stated dryly and ushered her to his office door, opening it for her.

She paused, her heart hammering at the idea of leaving like this with so much unresolved between them. She looked at him, a host of questions clamouring to be answered.

"Tonight," he said firmly.

And she knew she had to be content with that promise.

Until tonight.

CHAPTER SIX

CARVER leaned over and pressed a soft goodnight kiss on his daughter's forehead. "Sleep tight, baby," he murmured, his heart filling warmly with love for her.

"I'm not a baby, Daddy," she protested, her big brown eyes chiding him for not recognising how grown up she was. "I'm Susannah and I'm three years old."

He grinned at her. "Of course you are. I keep forgetting you're a big girl now. Goodnight, Susannah."

She huffed her satisfaction, rolled onto her side and closed her eyes. "'Night, Daddy," she mumbled contentedly.

He stroked her silky black curls—tight spirals like Katie's—except this child was no part of Katie Beaumont. She was his, and he'd gone through hell to keep her.

"Sweet dreams," he whispered, loving her innocence, wanting to keep it safe as long as he could.

His baby…she would always be that to him, Carver thought as he rose from the side of her bed, put the books he'd read to her on the side table and moved to switch off the light. He looked back at her—the light of his life—and the realisation struck him that Rupert Beaumont may well have felt this same overwhelming need to protect *his baby girl* and give her the best life had to offer.

60

Had he viewed her first love as a thief who'd stolen her innocence, alienating her from her father? Did that excuse the violence when he'd found them together, intimately naked? Carver remembered the hatred blazing from the older man's eyes, the raging tirade of accusations, the fist swinging, connecting with his jaw, breaking it, Katie's screaming...

He shook his head, sure in his own mind he'd never subject his Susannah to such an ugly scene. As she grew up, he hoped they would develop an understanding that would never encompass harsh judgements about the relationships she chose to have. She wouldn't have a mother to turn to, but he was determined to make up for that—to always be there for her when she needed him. *And* to let her go to be her own person when she was ready to take that step.

Parents could hold on too long, and fathers weren't the only ones guilty of that, he thought grimly, switching off the light and moving quietly along the hallway to his own bedroom, pausing there long enough to pick up his leather jacket before moving on to his mother's apartment—his mother who'd used emotional weapons which were just as powerful and destructive as fists.

Like the old insidious blackmail she had continually pressed—*how much she'd done for him*. It didn't work anymore. She knew that. Nevertheless, the damage done by it still lay between them—a line that was not to be crossed, ever again, if a relationship between them was to survive, given a reasonable amount of give-and-take.

She was in her sitting room, watching television,

already in her nightie and dressing gown, comfortably settled in the adjustable armchair, her walking frame in easy reaching distance. He felt sorry for her disability but he didn't feel guilty. She had chosen to do what she did. He would not carry the burden of her choices anymore. He'd paid too much on that account…was still paying.

"Mum…" he called quietly from the doorway, drawing her attention "…I'm going out."

She frowned. "You didn't say so at dinner."

"No. I didn't want to discuss it in front of Susannah. Would you check on her before you go to bed and leave your door open in case she wakes and needs you?"

He could rely on his mother to baby-sit at night, not that he asked it very often. Though he'd be asking more often if tonight worked out as he wanted.

"Will you be gone long?" she asked, still frowning over the unplanned request. Usually Carver did give her more notice.

He shrugged. "Probably a few hours."

"Where are you going?"

"That's my business, Mum." He wasn't about to open the way to any interference from her this time. "You can always reach me on my mobile telephone if you're worried about anything."

"All right, dear," she quickly backtracked, offering an appeasing smile. "Enjoy yourself."

He nodded. "I'll be off now. Goodnight."

"You, too."

A very good night, he hoped, patting his trouser pocket to check that the packet of condoms he'd bought on the way home was still there. A pity he hadn't had one handy in his office this morning. The temptation to forget protection had been almost irresistible with Katie so obviously willing to go with him, but…nothing was worth the risk of getting a woman pregnant when she didn't want to be. He couldn't face the fight against a convenient abortion again.

And certainly Katie wasn't planning on having a baby in any near future. She was totally committed to building up her specialised taxi service. He might even use it for Susannah on her play-school mornings, though the day-care nanny he employed handled those trips. Still, it was an option he'd keep in mind if the nanny called in sick. Why not put some business Katie's way? Her bid to be free of her father's power deserved respect.

Rupert Beaumont could hardly scorn him now, Carver thought, lifting his car keys from the hook in the kitchen—keys to the Volvo wagon the nanny used for transporting Susannah and his mother, plus keys to the Audi Quattro he drove himself. He might not have as much buying power as Katie's father, but he had more than enough to acquire whatever he wanted.

Like this big house with its large grounds in Hunters Hill, and setting up a specially equipped apartment in it for his mother, employing a nanny, a housekeeper, a gardener, giving his family every material comfort and convenience. Carver felt a deep satisfaction in all he had achieved as he walked through to the garage and settled himself in the powerful Audi sports car.

He switched on the engine, activated the remote control device, and caressed the driving wheel as he waited for the garage door to lift. It wasn't far from Hunters Hill to North Sydney where Katie Beaumont lived, but he'd stop along the way and pick up a bottle of fine champagne to celebrate her new business venture. He could well afford a nice touch, to soften the rawness of what he wanted with her.

Money couldn't buy everything. The wild and wonderful love he'd once felt for Katie Beaumont was irretrievable, yet because of his current position, she was still there for the taking.

And take her he would, whenever it was mutually desirable.

Katie had been in and out of several outfits, the vain impulse to look her best for Carver warring with the suspicion he wouldn't care what she wore and probably would prefer her in nothing at all. But she couldn't bring herself to be quite so blatant about what would undoubtedly happen tonight. On the other hand, she didn't want to appear off-putting, either, not in any sense.

Did Carver want only a sexual affair with her, or did he nurse a hope—a wish—for something deeper to develop between them?

What signals should she give him?

In the end, she put her cherry red sweater back on. Without a bra. No point in making difficulties with undressing, she told herself. Having made *the choice*—as Carver worded the decision to pursue the desire they both felt—she was not about to backtrack on it.

Anyhow, he wouldn't read anything wrong in her wearing the same sweater she'd worn this morning. It might even reassure him that nothing had changed since then. But the black suit was too formal for now and stockings were as much a nuisance for getting off as a bra, so she chose a pair of black slacks and settled on looking casual and...accessible.

She'd dithered over buying wine and beer but wasn't sure either was a good idea since Carver would have to drive home. Besides, she didn't have a lot of money to splash around. Coffee was surely acceptable. And she had bought a pizza to heat up for supper if they got hungry. If they didn't, she could eat it tomorrow so it wouldn't be wasted.

As the minutes ticked towards nine o'clock, Katie grew more and more nervous. Her little bed-sit apartment was tidy; clean towels in the bathroom, clean linen on the bed, the heater on to keep the room warm. Never in her life had she prepared for such premeditated sex with a man, not even with Carver when they'd been so madly in love. It felt...well, not exactly wrong, since it *was* Carver she was waiting for...but not quite right, either.

It would be better when he arrived, she kept assuring herself. It would feel natural then, more...more spontaneous. It was just a long time to wait...until nine o'clock. Sighing to ease the tightness in her chest, she forced herself to sit down and try to relax, though being comfortable was beyond her. Propped on the kitchen stool, poised to leap off it the moment

Carver arrived, she started wondering why he hadn't been able to come sooner.

Did he still live with his mother?

Katie shuddered at the thought. Lillian Dane had been so cuttingly cruel, accusing her of being a spoilt little rich bitch, obsessively blind to anything except what she wanted. At the time, Katie had been too confused and distressed to fight the bitter criticism. And there had been some truth in it, enough to make it even more of a slap in the face.

No truth in it now, she thought, ironically aware of the reversal in their lives. Though she could always go back to her father and…no, she had come too far from all that to ever go back. No going back to what she'd once shared with Carver, either. There was only going forward.

The doorbell rang.

Her heart leapt.

He was here!

Her feet hit the floor and she was off the stool, almost giddy with rocketing anticipation. She barely stopped herself from running to the door and flinging it open…as she had always done in the past, welcoming Carver with uninhibited joy. But this was *now,* not *then,* and she swiftly cautioned herself not to rush *anything.*

Even so, when she opened the door, the sight of Carver took her breath away. The successful business image was totally obliterated. He was dressed all in black, and like the buccaneer at the masked ball, the dark and dangerous impact of him instantly evoked the same sizzling sense of strong male sexuality, ruthlessly intent on claiming her.

Somehow it was more potent with his unmasked eyes raking her from head to foot, desire blatantly simmering in them as he asked, "May I come in?" making the innocuous words mean far more than a request to enter a room.

Her insides were quivering, reacting to a magnetism that was impossible to reject or defend herself against. It was an act of will to step back, her nod giving him silent permission to move forward, which he did, standing right beside her as she shut the door after him and fumbled with the safety chain, finally sliding it into place, wildly wondering as she did so if there was more safety outside than inside.

It was a relief to find him smiling at her when she swung around. "I brought a bottle of champagne," he said, holding it out for her to see. "A celebratory drink seemed in order since you're setting out on a new course in life."

With him?

"It's a hard road, going into business for yourself," he added, deflating that wishful thought. "But very satisfying if you make it work."

"Yes," she agreed, her responding smile somewhat rueful as she glanced down and noticed the Veuve Cliqot label on the bottle, one of the best French champagnes. "Thanks, Carver. I'm afraid I haven't got the proper glasses for this…"

"Doesn't matter."

His gaze skimmed around her small living area, making her acutely aware of the change from the luxurious surroundings and amenities of her father's home, which Carver had to be noting although he made no comment, simply moving to place the bottle on the small counter that was the only serving space in her kitchenette.

The action prompted her to rise above the embarrassment of not being able to match his gift, and deal with it as gracefully as she could. "I do have a couple of wineglasses. If you'd like to do the honours with the cork…"

She flashed an inviting smile as she skirted him and hurried to the kitchen cupboard where the few glasses she owned were stored, mostly tumblers for water or juice. Wine was not part of her daily diet. In fact, the two cheap glass goblets had been left behind by the previous tenants and needed a wash before using. Accomplishing this as fast as possible in the small sink, Katie had them wiped dry and set down on the counter before she realised Carver had not started to deal with the champagne cork.

She glanced a sharp query at him. He was watching her, his gaze lowered to her breasts, seemingly studying their shape. Her nipples instantly tightened into prominence, and an ironic little smile curled his mouth as he refocused on her eyes.

"It wasn't your hair that gave you away, Katie."

The soft words confused her for a moment, until she recalled questioning him in his office about recognising her in Carmen.

"Quite a few women have hair like yours," he went on, the irony becoming more pronounced as he added, "It's something I always notice."

Every nerve in Katie's body tensed at this information. How many women? Had he been attracted to them, and had he acted on the attraction as he'd done with her at the ball? Had it been any different with her?

"But I must admit it did remind me of you," he conceded, stepping closer to her, close enough to rake his fingers through the soft tendrils that framed her face, tucking them behind her ears while his eyes burned into hers. "I don't suppose anyone forgets their first love."

The words poured balm over the emotional wound of being likened to others who had passed through his life. At least she was unique in his memory.

"Did the buccaneer remind you of me?" he murmured, his head bending towards hers.

"Yes," she whispered, unable to find more volume. "In lots of ways."

His lips grazed around one earlobe, raising a shiver of sheer erotic pleasure. "You're still wearing the same scent Carmen wore."

"Oh!" she breathed, instantly picking up on his cologne again...the trigger to her own wild coupling of Carver and the pirate king. Understanding blasted across her mind, followed by the niggle...how could anyone base sure recognition on a scent? But that thought disintegrated as Carver's voice washed over it.

"It wafted from you this morning and I remembered..." His hands trailed slowly down her neck and over the taut peaks of her breasts, pausing to cup the soft mounds. "...I remembered how Carmen's breasts looked and felt just like Katie's…everything about them…but I dismissed the uncanny similarity then. Like hair, I thought. Not unique to one woman. And I couldn't imagine it was you at that ball. To me you were a long way away.''

In time and distance, Katie silently finished for him, having felt exactly the same… *It couldn't be him!* Yet it had been him and he was here, and as his hands reached down and gathered up the soft knit of her sweater, lifting it, her whole body yearned to know him all over again, the intimate reality of him, not fantasy—Carver, the man. Carver…

His name seemed to pulse through her heart. She was only too happy to let him remove her sweater, didn't care that it left her half naked because she wanted his hands on her, wanted to feel everything he'd ever made her feel, and she looked for the heart of the Carver she'd loved in his eyes, but they were lowered, gazing raptly at what had been uncovered.

''It was these that gave you away, Katie,'' he murmured, slowly circling her aureoles with feather-light fingertips, making them prickle with pleasure in his touch. ''And learning you were here in Sydney. The same scent…''

He drew in a deep breath and lifted his gaze, instantly capturing hers with a glittering challenge that pierced the enthralment of intimate memories and evoked an electric awareness of here and now. He took off his leather jacket, tossing it back towards the door. The black shirt was just as quickly and carelessly discarded.

Katie didn't say a word, didn't make a move. There

was no denying she wanted his chest bared—to see, to touch, to feel—and excitement welled up in her as she watched it happen, the emergence of naked flesh and muscle, the strong masculinity that appealed so powerfully to the woman in her, the sprinkle of black wiry curls accentuating his maleness, the gleam of his skin. To her eyes he was beautiful, perfect, and she couldn't resist lifting her hands to press them across the expanse of his chest.

He caught them and carried them up to his shoulders, then grabbed her waist, controlling all movement towards him, bringing her close enough for the tips of her breasts to brush his skin, swaying her slightly from side to side to capture more of the feeling, savouring it, then intensifying the contact, her softness gradually compressing against the unyielding wall of muscle, a slow revelling in the sensation, a build up of heat, and Katie closed her eyes, focusing on the feeling of sinking into Carver, merging with him.

He had meant to go slowly, to enjoy every exquisite nuance of Katie's femininity, to indulge every desire she'd ever evoked in his fantasies over the years, to erase the frustration of not having her when he would have given his soul to have the need for her satisfied. So much to make up for...

Yet he found himself hauling her over to the bed he'd spotted, tearing the rest of their clothes off, barely remembering to snatch the packet of condoms out of his pocket. And there she lay, her legs already spread enticingly, so voluptuously seductive in her abandonment of any inhibitions, waiting for him, wanting him, her eyes swimming over his nakedness, absorbing his maleness, exulting in it, driving him to plunge inside her, to make her take all of him.

And somehow…feeling her welcome him unlocked a mad fever in his brain, and the name, Katie, accompanied every thrust, a wild rhythmic mantra—Katie…Katie…Katie…the sweet convulsive heat of her enveloping him, squeezing him, urging him to spill himself into her.

But it wasn't enough. There was so much more he wanted, needed…the long, long hunger of years seizing him, demanding satiation, compelling total immersion in the whole sensual experience of Katie Beaumont…the feel of every line and curve of her body, the taste of her, the scent of her, the intoxicating excitement of her mouth, her sex, the variation in sensations with having her on top of him, tucked together spoon-fashion, any and every position that appealed.

He didn't know how many condoms he reached for and used, glad there was always another one, no reason to stop. Her passion for more of him—her kisses and caresses and erotic teasing—was constantly exhilarating, and Carver was loath to bring this night of such intense pleasure to a close. But Katie Beaumont was not the be-all and end-all of his life and eventually the call of responsibility could not be ignored any longer.

He kissed her one last time, reluctantly lifting his mouth from hers to murmur, ''It's time for me to leave, Katie.'' Then he heaved himself off the bed and started hunting for his clothes, knowing he had to resist any further temptation to stay with her.

"What time is it?" She sounded slightly stunned, bewildered by the somewhat abrupt separation.

"Midnight."

"We...we've hardly talked."

He slanted her a satisfied smile as he fastened his trousers. "I thought our communication was perfect."

Having slid his feet into the soft leather loafers he'd worn, he swiftly crossed the room to where he'd dropped his shirt and jacket near the door. He had his shirt on and was thrusting his arms into the sleeves of the jacket when Katie spoke again.

"Is *this*...all you want from me, Carver?"

He frowned over the emphasis she gave the words and the tone of voice she used...cold, not warm. Having shrugged on his jacket, he spun around to face her. She was lying on her side, her head propped up on one hand, her eyes half veiled by her long thick lashes, her expression tautly guarded, no longer exuding sensuality.

"No, it's not," he answered, unable to stop his gaze from skimming the lush curve of waist and hip and thigh. "I'll call you...set up another time for us..." He raised a challenging eyebrow. "...Unless this is all you want from me."

His confidence in their mutual desire was instantly affirmed.

"It's nowhere near all I want."

"Fine!" He smiled. "We'll meet again."

She didn't smile back. "Just remember I'm a person, too, Carver."

Was there a slight wobble of vulnerability in her voice? What *did* she want from him? ''I do know that, Katie,'' he assured her quietly, thinking of how she was standing up for herself in spite of her father's opposition—a person in her own right.

''Then make me feel like one,'' she burst out, jerking herself up to a sitting position, her face flushing as she glared at him in angry pride. ''Tell me why you must go now. Don't just pick me up and put me down.''

Her fierce resentment stirred his. She'd run away, stayed away...all these years. Given their history, he didn't want to tell her anything about his family. She hadn't been there when it had mattered, when it would have meant...what he'd wanted it to mean. Too late now. Yet, if they were to keep on meeting, he would have to reveal his circumstances sooner or later, and like her, he hadn't had enough. Not nearly enough.

''I do have others to consider, Katie. My mother might need pain-killers to sleep...''

''You still live with your mother?'' she cut in incredulously.

He felt his face tighten and hated her ignorance. ''She had a stroke some years ago and is...disabled,'' he stated grimly. ''Should I dump her in a nursing home?''

Shock and shame chased across her face. ''I...I'm sorry, Carver.''

''She's minding my daughter for me.''

''Your...*daughter?*'' More shock, almost strangling her voice.

From the marriage I wanted with you, but you weren't there, he thought bitterly. Out loud, he laid out the situation that circumscribed his free time, keeping his tone flat and matter-of-fact, not caring what Katie Beaumont thought about it.

"The pain-killers usually induce a deep sleep and my mother won't take them until I get home, in case she doesn't wake if there's some need to. Susannah is only three and sometimes has a disturbed night."

"Three…" she repeated distractedly.

"Yes. So…will you excuse me now?"

"I…I didn't know, Carver," she appealed.

He looked at her pleading face, the erotic tumble of wild black curls around it, the infinitely desirable body that had pleasured him so much tonight, and deliberately softened his voice, though a thread of irony crept through. "How could you? You've been away."

"You will call me?"

For a moment, her uncertainty stirred a vengeful streak, but what was the point of paybacks when he wanted what she could give him. "Yes. Soon," he asserted decisively. "Goodnight, Katie."

He turned to the door, removed the safety chain, and opened it, ready to exit.

"We…we didn't drink the champagne."

He glanced at the bottle, still on the counter where he'd set it down. Another time, he thought, and looked back at her, a whimsical little smile playing on his lips. "Yes we did. We drank it all night. The very best champagne there could be between us."

To him it was true. No bad memories taking the

fizz of pure pleasure away, no complicated demands being made on each other, just a man and a woman fulfilling a natural desire, revelling in the blissful taste of it, letting the sweet intoxication simply take over and bring all the physical joys of loving without any of the emotional burdens. There had been nothing bad about this. Nothing bad, nothing flat, nothing bitter.

"The very best," he repeated softly, nodding his satisfaction as he closed the door on a night he would always remember as *good*.

CHAPTER SEVEN

AFTER a hellishly restless night, Katie tried hard to focus her mind on all the things she had to achieve *today*. It was almost impossible to switch off the treadmill of thoughts Carver had left her with, but somehow it had to be done. The only sensible course was to keep pursuing the goals she'd set herself, goals that were attainable.

As she arrived at the entrance gate to the day-care centre, where handing in her notice had to be the first item on her agenda, Katie's determined purpose was waylaid by her old friend, Amanda Fairweather.

"Katie! Wait up!" Amanda was hauling her four-year-old son, Nicholas, from his car seat in the back of the BMW she drove. "I want to know how your interview with Robert Freeman went."

Carver instantly dominated Katie's thoughts again—her meeting with him and all that had ensued from it. "I didn't see Robert Freeman," she blurted out.

"What?" Amanda looked stunned. She set Nicholas on his feet, closed the car door and herded him towards the gate, her expression swiftly changing to delighted surprise. "You decided not to tie yourself up with it!"

"No. I am going ahead," Katie corrected her. "I've got the money I need."

Amanda's eyebrows rose. "Your father came good with it?"

Katie shook her head as she opened the gate to let Nicholas through. "I went to the investment company Max recommended."

"But you said…"

"Robert Freeman was busy. One of the other partners took over the meeting."

"And agreed to the deal?"

"Yes."

"Who?"

Katie shrugged. "Does it matter?"

"Max will want to know," Amanda insisted.

Realising that the favour Max had done her deserved some return of courtesy, Katie steeled herself to look squarely into her friend's inquisitive blue eyes and flatly state, "It was Carver Dane, Amanda."

"Carver…?" A shocked gasp. "You don't mean… not the Carver Dane you were…"

"The same."

"How? Wasn't he supposed to be going for a medical degree? Working part-time as a landscape gardener?"

Katie gestured helpless ignorance. "I don't know how he got to where he is."

"Well, I'm certainly going to find out. Max will know." Avid interest lit her eyes. "Wow! The guy your father beat up on shelled out the money. Do you think it could be personal?"

"Definitely not!"

Amanda's expression slid to salacious speculation. "I remember him as a gorgeous hunk!"

"Who married someone else," Katie snapped, unwilling to confide the sexual outcome of the meeting, especially since it was far from clear if there could be any other outcome but a sexual one. "I've got to go, Amanda," she quickly added, nodding to her friend's little boy who'd skipped up the path ahead of her.

"Right! I'll see you this afternoon when I pick up Nick." She grinned gleefully as Katie moved onto the path, closing the gate behind her. "I'll talk to Max in the meantime. I'll bet there's more to this than meets the eye, Katie Beaumont."

With a cheerful wave she was off back to her car, leaving Katie with the unsettling certainty that no stone would remain unturned in Amanda's search for *interesting* information on Carver Dane. Whether this was good or bad, Katie had no idea. It might satisfy some of her own curiosity about Carver's move into finance, but it didn't help the personal side.

No doubt Amanda would discover he was a widower and seize on that fact for matchmaking possibilities. She wouldn't understand there were other barriers—like a handicapped mother who'd hated Katie and wouldn't welcome her into a home she shared with her son; and a three-year-old daughter who clearly had first claim on Carver's heart, the child of his marriage to another woman.

Katie's stomach clenched over that last thought. His wife might be dead but she lived on in the child she'd borne to Carver, a constant reminder of what Katie didn't have with him and a lifelong commitment that couldn't be ignored. Carver wasn't *free*.

He'd never be free. Not in the sense Katie would have liked him to be.

He was *morally* free to have sex with her.

Could she accept that limitation, knowing she would always crave more from him? Was more possible, given these circumstances?

Still churning over her dilemma, Katie entered the day-care centre and checked to see that Amanda's son had joined the group of little children already gathered in the playroom. Her gaze lingered on the two- to five-year-olds, happily settling themselves with books or toys until more organised activities began. Carver's pertinent question of yesterday—*You're not looking for marriage? Having children of your own?*—suddenly brought a surge of bitterness.

He'd been married.

He had a child...like one of these in front of her.

While she...

No! It was futile letting such thoughts and feelings eat at her like this! Taking a firm grip on herself, Katie swung away from the sight of the children and moved purposefully to the administration office.

Today she had to start the moves that would hopefully secure some future business. She was now committed to her specialised taxi service and making that work well was top priority. She'd told Carver so. In fact, it was probably that assurance which made him feel free to pursue a sexual connection with her. No strings attached.

Forget him, Katie told herself savagely.

Until he called again.

If he did.

* * *

Soon, Carver had said. Katie lay in bed on Sunday morning, telling herself she was a fool for even thinking about it. After all, it hadn't even been a week since he'd been here, and he'd probably made prior plans for this weekend. Though he could have called and simply spoken to her...

"How are you, Katie?

"I've been thinking of you.

"All your business plans going smoothly?

"When do you have a night free?"

She rolled over and buried her face in the pillow, wishing she could blot out her thoughts. Sunday was supposed to be a day of rest...from everything. As far as the organisation of her business was concerned, that was true. There was nothing productive she could do today. Except take calls and possible bookings from prospective clients who might have picked up the leaflets she'd left at various child-care centres. And that wouldn't keep her busy. Not busy enough to keep her miserable mind from wandering to Carver.

The telephone rang, jolting her out of the pillow and up on her elbows. It was almost nine o'clock, a reasonably civilised time to call on Sunday morning. It could be anyone. Yet her heart was catapulting around her chest as she reached for the receiver and the one name throbbing through her mind made it difficult to produce a crisp, business-like voice tone.

"Hello. Katie Beaumont..."

"Katie..." came the terse cut-in "...now don't you hang up on me."

Her father, commanding as usual. Her jaw tightened. She was not about to be intimidated, dominated, or spoken to as though she were some recalcitrant child. Just let him start down that track and...

"I'm sorry I blew up the last time you were here and I promise I won't do it again," he stated gruffly. "You're my only child, Katie, and I'd like us to be friends. So..." A deep breath.

"I'm not a child, Dad," Katie bit out, warning him he was on fragile ground.

"I know, I know," he swiftly assured her. "I'll respect your independence. I just don't want this rift between us to go on. How about coming over here and having brunch with me this morning? Talk things over..."

Katie sighed over the appeal. "I'm not going to fit into what you want for me, Dad, and I really don't feel like arguing with you."

"No argument. I'll even consider investing in this scheme of yours," he offered handsomely.

"I don't need your help. I've managed to get the money from another source."

Silence.

"So you can't pull that string, Dad," Katie interpreted bitterly.

"Now hold on there! I know I've made a lot of mistakes with you and I'll probably make more because I don't understand where you're coming from or where you want to go..."

"You could try *listening*."

"Okay! I swear I'll listen. Try me out over brunch. Will you do that?"

"You won't like it," she said with certainty.

"Then I'll lump it." His tone changed to a soft

cajoling. "Anything to get us together again, sweet-heart."

Katie closed her eyes and fought the sudden lump in her throat. She'd adored her father all throughout her childhood and teens, loving the way he always called her *his little sweetheart*. Yet his violent rejection of her love for Carver Dane had soured that pet name forever, giving it overtones of unhealthy possessiveness.

"All right. I'll come," she choked out, deciding she needed to clarify her relationship with her father, once and for all. She'd run from it for years, then turned her back on it when he wouldn't support her plans. Maybe it was time to reassess, get a more definitive perspective on where they both stood. "Expect me about eleven."

"Fine! It'll be like old times," he pressed warmly.

"No, it won't, Dad. It can never be like old times. Please accept that," she told him flatly and ended the call.

Two hours later his housekeeper ushered her into the conservatory which was her father's favourite room in the large old English manor-style home he'd bought to please her mother in the early years of their marriage. Never mind that the house overlooked Sydney Harbour on a prime piece of property in the prestigious suburb of Mosman. The architecture and furnishings inside were every bit as British as any house in London. All very establishment correct.

Like SCEGS, the private and very expensive girls' school Katie had attended.

Like everything her father had planned for her

life…until Carver had derailed the exclusive train to the social superiority of wealth and class.

"Katie…" A warm, welcoming smile.

"Hi, Dad. Don't get up."

He was sitting at the wrought-iron table which was strewn with the Sunday newspapers and she quickly stepped forward to drop a kiss on his cheek, avoiding the hug she didn't want to return. The sense of alienation went too deep to pretend uninhibited affection.

"You're looking good, Katie," he complimented, looking admiringly at her as she busied herself getting coffee, fruit and juice from a side table.

She flashed a smile at him. "You, too."

For a man in his early sixties, Rupert Beaumont, was both fit and handsome, his tanned skin somehow minimising his age, making his blue eyes more vivid and his wavy white hair quite strikingly attractive. He was broad-shouldered, barrel-chested, and if his muscular frame had turned the least bit flabby, it certainly wasn't noticeable in the casual grey and white tracksuit he wore.

"Great display of orchids this year," she commented.

The conservatory was lined with the exotic plants, many of them in bloom. Cultivating orchids was her father's hobby and he'd collected a huge variety of them. It was a safe, neutral topic of conversation and he seized on it, chatting away about his success with some newly developed specimens, pointing them out to her, beaming pleasure in her interest.

The housekeeper wheeled in a bain-marie containing a variety of hot breakfast foods; bacon, eggs, sausages, mushrooms, grilled tomato, hash browns, corn fritters.

They served themselves as appetite directed, and it wasn't until they were sitting back replete, sipping more coffee, that her father asked the first leading question, his eyes wary but sharp with speculation.

"So...whom did you interest in your children's taxi service?"

"I went to an investment company." She returned his gaze with steely pride. "It *is* a sound business idea, filling a need that isn't being met."

He grimaced. "It wasn't the idea I objected to. It was the hours you'll have to put into it."

"My choice," she reminded him.

"You're almost thirty, Katie," he said quietly. "Why have you written off marriage and having a family? You're a beautiful woman. It doesn't seem right to..."

"Remember Carver Dane, Dad?" she cut in fiercely. "The guy you thought was a sponger who wouldn't amount to anything on his own? The guy whose jaw you smashed when you found him making love to me?"

He frowned, dropping his gaze and fiddling with his coffee cup. "That was a long time ago, Katie. Surely..."

"I met him again last week. He's a partner in the investment company I went to."

He looked up, startled, perplexed.

The information Amanda had siphoned from her husband poured off Katie's tongue. "He has quite a record of seeing the potential of new businesses and making big money out of them. He started off with a landscape company called Weekend Blitz where a whole team of people come in and create a uniquely styled garden in one weekend. The owners of the property can have the pleasure of watching it happen in front of their eyes.''

Another deeper frown. ''I've heard of Weekend Blitz. Didn't know he was behind it.''

''He sold it off years ago and created other equally successful businesses. Sold them all off at huge profits to himself. And now he's a highly respected financier in the city.'' Her eyes derided her father's judgement of the man she'd loved. ''Not bad for a sponger who saw me as an easy ride to money.''

He shook his head, pained by the revelations she was tossing at him. ''All these years…you've never forgiven me, have you? And you've still got him in your heart.''

''Yes.'' Her mouth twisted. ''But I don't think I'm in his. It's just one of those bleak ironies of life that Carver Dane supplied me with the money you refused to lend.''

''Dammit, Katie!'' He thumped the table as he pushed back his chair and rose to his feet. ''I was only thinking of what was best for you,'' he gruffly excused as he began pacing around the conservatory, too agitated by the situation to remain still.

''You never asked *me* what was best for me, Dad. Not back then. Not now.''

It stopped him. He stood at the far end of the conservatory, his shoulders hunched, seemingly staring out at the view of the harbour. Again he shook his head. ''A man tries to protect his daughter.''

''I was nineteen. Not a child. And now I'm twenty-nine. Even less of a child. I want respect for my thoughts, my feelings, my judgements and my decisions, not protection.''

The vehemence with which she spoke echoed through the silence that followed, pleading for—demanding—a response that acknowledged her as an adult who had the right to make her own choices. Katie sat with her hands clenched with determination, not wanting to fight, simply waiting for the outcome of this last attempt to reach an understanding with her father.

He spun around, eyes sharp under beetling brows. ''Is he married?'' he shot at her.

''What?''

''Carver Dane. You met with him last week. Is he married?'' he asked more forcefully.

''No.''

''Then go after him, Katie. All the business success in the world won't fill the hole he left in your life. If there's never going to be any other man for you, go after him.''

It wasn't as simple as that, Katie kept thinking, long after her father had finished hammering out his advice. The odd thing was, she'd been so stunned by it at the time, she hadn't realised he was still doing what he'd always done…deciding what was best for her.

Though at least he had listened, and weighed what she'd said, which was something gained, Katie decided. And he wasn't about to criticise any relationship she did have with Carver, so maybe their estrangement could be bridged by more open communication and the desire to understand.

Which was precisely what she needed with Carver,

too…if he called…if he came to her again. If he didn't, could she brave her father's advice and go after him? Would there be any happiness in it if she did? Apart from the negative emotional baggage they both carried, there were still his mother and his daughter to contend with.

Tired of her own endless questions, Katie picked up the television guide to see if there were any decent Sunday movies on. She was just settling down to watch the end of the current affairs program, "60 Minutes," when the telephone rang. Having lowered the sound volume, she picked up the receiver and rattled out her name, not really feeling like conversation with anyone.

"It's Carver."

Her heart stopped.

"Are you free this evening, Katie?"

"Yes," rushed off her lips with the breath whooshing from her lungs.

"Okay if I come over?"

"Yes," she repeated, her need to see him obliterating any doubts about the wisdom of it.

"Be there soon."

Click!

Katie put the receiver down, her mind dizzy with anticipation. She didn't have to go after Carver Dane. He was coming to her. And she didn't care what happened.

She wanted him.

CHAPTER EIGHT

SHE wanted him.

Carver barely stopped himself from exceeding the speed limit on his way from Hunters Hill to North Sydney. The power of the Audi sports car could be contained. Not so the power of the desire coursing through his blood, hot, urgent, pulsing with the need to be satisfied, and inflamed by Katie's ready response to his call.

Yes...yes...

No quibbling, no time-bargaining, no game-playing. Just simple, straightforward honesty. Like the Katie of old, welcoming any time with him, whatever he could fit in around the various workloads he'd carried.

Though, of course, it wasn't the same as then. The romantic dreams were long gone. And Sunday night was usually a free night for most people. He'd counted on that. Still, she might have had second thoughts about carrying on an affair with him, revisiting an intimacy that had ended badly.

On the other hand, the sex last Tuesday night had been great. The memory of it had tantalised him ever since. He'd had nothing like it in the ten years she'd been gone. And maybe she hadn't, either. If that were the case, it put a high value on what they could give each other.

Sensational pleasure…

The anticipation of it zinged through him all the way to Katie's door. She opened it and his body instantly reacted at the sight of her wrapped in a red dressing gown, presumably with nothing underneath it. He stepped inside the small bed-sit apartment, hauled her into his embrace and swung her around so he could close the door and apply the safety chain, not missing a second of feeling her against him.

No greeting from Carver. Not a word spoken. Even as he secured the door behind them, his mouth took hers in a hot, hungry kiss, making words irrelevant. He wanted her, and the urgency of his wanting shot a wild exultation through Katie. It meant he'd been thinking of her, anticipating being with her again, and he couldn't wait any longer.

She could feel the hard roll of his erection, pressing for release, and the adrenaline rush of her power to excite him this much was a heady intoxicant. Her mind swirled with memories of how passionately needful they'd been for each other when they were in love. It was no different now…the same avid kissing, the compulsion to feel all there was to feel of each other, revelling in the sheer excitement of the silently promised intimacy.

Where did sexual attraction end and love begin? Wasn't it all mixed up together? Desire like this…was it really only physical? Or was the force of it driven by a host of things that lay unspoken between them?

Go after him…

Yes, she thought on a fierce wave of primitive aggression. This man was hers and nothing was going to come between them. Nothing!

Her hands attacked the buttons on his shirt. He threw off his jacket and no sooner had she succeeded in parting his shirt than he tore it off, as eager as she to get rid of barriers. He pulled her dressing gown apart as she unfastened his trousers. His hands were savouring her nakedness, sliding, clutching, possessing, warm, strong, exciting...but not as exciting to her as feeling his arousal, freeing it of clothes and grasping it, stroking it, savouring the throbbing tension of his need for her.

Go after him...

Kisses down the hot muscular wall of his chest, over his flat stomach and then she was taking him in her mouth, her hands freed to push his clothes lower, to revel in the hard strength of his thighs, to cup him as she teased with her tongue, flicking, swirling, loving him as she so fiercely wanted him to love her.

His fingers clenched in her hair. Need pounded through him, tightening every muscle. She could sense every atom of his body yearning. His back arched as he instinctively thrust forward, blindly responding.

"Katie..." The cry ripped from his throat.

Her name.

No one else ever, she thought wildly, drawing him into herself, intent on possessing his mind and heart as well as all his body would give up to her. Yet just when he seemed at the point of uncontrollable surrender, another raw cry burst from him.

"No…"

He wrenched her head back from him. His face was contorted with the anguish of denial as he reached down and pulled her upright. Even so, his eyes glittered with savage self-determination.

"This isn't how I want it."

"What about how I want it, Carver?" The words spat off her tongue, frustration firing the challenge.

"No one takes me," he bit out and whipped off his trousers, ready for the action he chose, standing apart from her with all the independent pride of a warrior without weakness, flouting his nakedness as though it were impervious armour.

"But it's okay for you to take me," she shot at him, lashing out at the power of mind that somehow diminished hers.

"Have you said no to anything I've done?" The knowledge that she'd hadn't blazed in his eyes as he swooped, scooping her off her feet, cradling her across his chest as he strode the short distance to her bed. "Say no, Katie, and I'll stop right now."

Choice…

He'd laid that out from the beginning.

And, of course, she didn't say no. Cutting off her nose to spite her face was a totally self-defeating exercise. Besides which, she didn't want to say no, especially not when he laid her on the bed and set about kissing her, wreaking erotic havoc wherever his mouth moved, not when he paused to sheath himself in protection—though the action did trigger the same separating sense of Carver keeping himself to himself—and not when he took possession of her because she craved the feeling of him inside her, gloried in it, loving the deep rhythm of union that took them to the shattering bliss of climax.

Except the sweet warm sense of fusion wasn't there. The safe seal of a condom kept it from her, and even as Carver withdrew from their intimate linking and discarded the protective device, Katie found herself resenting it, even more resenting the control behind its use, though the more rational side of her mind argued he was only being sensible and taking care of her, as well. Though, as it happened, any form of contraception wasn't necessary tonight.

"You don't need to use those," she blurted out. "Unless there's a health reason," she swiftly added, realising she didn't know his recent sexual history.

His mouth quirked. "No social diseases?"

"Not on my side."

"Nor mine." He stretched out beside her, seemingly relaxed as he propped his head up on one hand and softly raked the rioting curls back from her face, but his eyes scanned hers with sharp intensity. "Are you telling me you're on the Pill, Katie?"

"No. Though I will get a prescription for next month."

"Then there's a pregnancy risk."

"I'm past my fertile time. My period's due in a day or two."

"Maybe."

She frowned at the hard cynicism that had flashed into his eyes. "Do you think I'm lying to you?"

"No. But mistakes get made. I'd rather be safe than sorry."

No one takes me.

The harsh words he'd spoken earlier zoomed back into Katie's mind, taking on darker shades of meaning. He had once taken a physical beating from her father and she had known then he hadn't fought back for her sake. But it hadn't won him anything in the end, not from her nor her father. Was that at the root of his resolve to hold himself apart, to only do what he felt he had control over, to never again allow anyone to *take* him on any level?

Or was there more grist to that mill?

"You used to trust me with this," she said quietly, searching his eyes for answers.

"It's not a question of trust. It's a matter of ensuring there are no slip-ups. After all, having a baby is not in your plan," he lightly mocked.

"I'll take responsibility for that, Carver. You don't have to."

"And if you fail?"

"I'll take responsibility for that, too."

His eyes narrowed and his voice lowered to a tone that had savage undercurrents. "So what would you do, Katie? Sneak off and have an abortion without telling me? Come to me for help in getting rid of my child? Have you even stopped to think of the cost of failure?"

She stared at him, her heart pounding at the realisation there had to be answers behind the cuttingly derisive words. "Has that happened to you, Carver?" she asked, every nerve in her body tautly waiting on his response.

Bitter venom blazed for his eyes. "Oh yes, I've

been there. It's not an issue I want to get into. Ever again. The woman has all the say, doesn't she? She can hold a man to ransom...if he wants his child. And the cost doesn't stop at mere money.''

The instant leap in Katie's mind tumbled into speech. ''Your daughter?''

It was terrible to want it to be so, but a part of her couldn't bear Carver to have loved his wife. It was much, much easier to accept an accidental pregnancy had led to the marriage. Which would also explain why it had happened so soon after his trip to England.

But it was obvious Carver wasn't about to reveal any more, a cold mask of pride closing off any other expression. ''My daughter is strictly my business, Katie.''

Warning bells clanged. She was on hostile ground and every instinct told her to retreat to what was currently personal between them. Compelled to touch, to bring his mind back to her, she reached up and ran a finger down his cheek to his chin, holding it there in deliberate challenge.

''You asked me two questions. Do I get to answer them or are you going to assume the worst anyway?''

It evoked a glimmer of interest and a quirky little smile. ''By all means speak and enlighten me.''

''Firstly, I have no intention of risking an accidental pregnancy.''

''Given your commitment to the business you're starting, that would seem logical.''

''Should biology somehow defeat normal nature and medical science,'' she drawled, mocking his distrust of her earlier claim of being safe from conception, "and I find myself unexpectedly pregnant, I would not seek an abortion."

He raised a sceptical eyebrow. "Believe me, a child changes everything, Katie. No part of your life remains unaffected."

"Whatever the consequences, I would have the child," she declared unequivocally. "My decision. My responsibility."

"And what about me...the father of the child?"

"How much of a father role you'd want to take on would be entirely up to you, Carver. I wouldn't ask anything, knowing it was a child you didn't want."

He shook his head. "This is all theoretical. The reality is something different. You haven't been through it, and better that you never be faced with it." He took the hand touching his chin and placed it on the other side of her head as he leaned over and grazed his mouth over her lips, murmuring, "Let's keep things simple, Katie, and have the pleasure barricaded against pain."

She didn't know—couldn't tell—if she'd made any opening in the brick wall he'd constructed around himself. He breathed warmth into her with his kisses, built it with his hands, fanned the heat of desire so skillfully and relentlessly, nothing else mattered but the intense waves of pleasure that ebbed and flowed on a tide of enthralling sensuality. She didn't care that he continued to use condoms. She would rather have him on his terms, than not at all.

Yet the issue of trust did linger in her mind, as did the question about his marriage, suppressed by layers of other feelings while the physical magic of their

intimate togetherness lasted, but when Carver called
an end to it—time for him to leave—and moved away
from her to get dressed, those underlying niggles rose
to the surface, demanding more attention.

She watched him getting ready to close the door
on her again until next time. At least she was confident now there would be a next time, though little
else had been achieved in this meeting. The only hint
of new information she had was Carver's references
to the realities of an unplanned pregnancy.

He hadn't actually linked those realities to his marriage and he'd snubbed her attempt to connect them
to his daughter. It was true enough that in all the years
they'd been apart, he might very well have been involved in such an experience, ending in an abortion
and leaving an indelible impression about the wisdom
of safe sex. It might not have anything whatsoever to
do with his marriage, yet...

The need to know welled up in her.

Go after him...

But how?

He was shrugging on his leather jacket, his departure imminent. His face wore the expression of a
closed book. Desperate to open up the hidden pages,
Katie used the only lever she could think of.

''You know...when I called you from London after
reading your letter...it was a big shock to find you
married.''

His hands were on the jacket hem band, fitting the
zipper together for fastening. His fingers momentarily
stilled on the task. He sliced her a hard glittering look.
''Was it?'' Apparently dismissing any reply she could

make, his focus returned to doing up his jacket, which he accomplished with swift efficiency.

The non-response left Katie floundering. Repeating the assertion seemed useless and the sense that she had alienated him rather than prying him open was very strong.

He regarded her with derisive eyes. "Did you think time would stand still for you, Katie?"

"No." She shook her head, not comprehending the intent behind the question.

"My recollection is that it was some six months after I left the U.K. before you bothered to call and catch up with me."

"You left your letter with my aunt," she reminded him.

"Yes. She told me you were expected back from your Mediterranean trip within a few weeks."

"My aunt forgot about it, Carver. Before I got back to London she learnt a dear friend of hers was dying of cancer and between the distress of that news and caring for her friend..." She heaved a rueful sigh. "Anyhow, the letter was mislaid and she didn't come across it until after her friend's funeral. I called you the day she gave it to me."

His stillness this time was so prolonged, it was as though he'd been turned to stone. He was staring straight at her, not so much as a flicker of movement in his eyes, either, yet she was sure he wasn't seeing her. It was as though she didn't exist at all, his mind having travelled to another time and place.

The *nothingness* of it was chilling. Katie wanted to break into it, bring him back to her, but her mind seemed frozen, incapable of producing anything sensible. She waited, somehow afraid to move herself. She'd laid out the truth. It was up to Carver to make something of it…if only he would.

A perceptible shudder ran through him, like a switch being thrown. The glazed eyes clicked into sharp focus. His face cracked into a sardonic little smile. "Well, that's all water under the bridge, isn't it, Katie?" he drawled.

It left her with nothing to say. Her mind screamed, *Why didn't you wait?* But what reason had she ever given him to put his life on hold for her? She hadn't put her life on hold for him, though he'd always been in her heart, the one—the only one—who'd ever captured it.

"Goodnight," he said curtly, and made a swift exit from the apartment, closing off any further chance of reaching him.

Katie heaved a sigh of defeat.

She still didn't know if he'd loved his wife or not. It was probably foolish to let it be so important to her. Yet most of the shock she'd felt at the time of that fateful phone call was centred on the fact that he'd found someone else…and she hadn't. Hadn't even come close.

However, a different picture emerged if an unplanned pregnancy had drawn him into marriage. She could understand that. It was much more acceptable. It made her feel less…discarded. And more positive about getting Carver back. Though how she was going to smash through the brick wall around him, she didn't know.

She buried her face in the pillow that still carried a hint of the cologne he used. The buccaneer's cologne. The masked man. But she would unmask him, given time. If it was the last thing she did, she'd uncover what beat in the heart of Carver Dane!

CHAPTER NINE

CARVER switched off the engine of the Audi. The action triggered the realisation he was home, parked in his own garage, without any recollection of the drive from North Sydney to Hunters Hill. He'd left Katie, got in his car, and now he was here.

The sense of having lost time had him glancing at his watch. It was only just past midnight, not much later than he'd planned. The shock of learning Katie had called him the very day she'd read his letter had totally spun him out. Automatic pilot had got him safely home. But there were still things to do, checking in with his mother...

His mother...

Carver's chest tightened as he climbed out of his car. But for her he would have stayed in England long enough to meet up with Katie when she returned from her trek through Greece and Turkey. Just a couple more weeks. No counting on a response to his letter. One look and he would have known if it was still there for them. And it would have been. No doubt left about that, given their current desire for each other.

A rage of frustration gripped him, lending an angry momentum to every step he took through the house to his mother's apartment. *But for her...*

She'd never liked Katie, always bad-mouthing her,

resenting the time he'd spent with her and the love he'd felt. What he'd wanted was irrelevant. Mother knew best, and any subversive force to her ambition for him had to be pushed away.

Even five years on, after he'd more than proved he could be successful following his own chosen course, she'd been grimly tight-lipped about his trip to England and his intention to bring Katie back with him if he could.

He'd forced her to accept he had a right to his own life, a right to love any woman of his choice, yet had she ever really accepted it in her heart? Had she made herself sick over it? What had brought on the life-threatening bout of pneumonia that had fetched him home from London?

His mother hadn't died.

The only death had been the death of a dream.

And now he knew the dream had been viable, back then...

He found his mother still in her custom-made arm-chair, disarmingly asleep, having dozed off reading a book which lay askew on her lap. Though she was only in her fifties, she looked old and worn and very vulnerable and the anger in his heart drained away.

He couldn't blame her for the mislaid letter. He couldn't blame Katie's aunt, either, for being too distressed about her friend's illness to remember something that would seem unimportant—a message from a man who'd played no part in her niece's life for years. Illness, particularly the illness of someone close and dear, played havoc with everything.

His mother certainly hadn't chosen to have the

stroke that had done so much damage to her physically, weakening her whole system so that it was vulnerable to any virus. He'd done his best to provide her with a safe environment, but inevitably there were trips to medical appointments, doctors' offices where other patients were gathered in waiting rooms. How could he blame her for getting pneumonia at the worst possible time for him?

He should be blaming himself...giving in to the black moment at that stupid party he'd gone to, telling himself to get Katie out of his mind once and for all. Then seeing Nina—Nina with a head of rioting black curls—being blindly drawn to her, using her...so wrong! It was *his* fault he was no longer free when Katie had finally called. Not his mother's.

Sighing to ease the ache of tension, Carver reached out and gently shook his mother awake. Her lashes flew up and the first moment of disorientation cleared into relieved recognition.

"You're home."

"Yes." He picked up her book, closed it, and set it on the table beside her chair. "Would you like me to help you up?"

"No, thanks, dear. I'll gather myself in a minute."

Her frailty suddenly smote his conscience. "Mum, if it's too much for you to mind Susannah when I'm out at night, please say so. I'll arrange for the nanny to come back and sit."

"No...no..." she cried anxiously, reaching out to grasp his hand and press it appealingly. "I need to feel needed sometimes, Carver. You do so much for me and Susannah's no trouble. She hardly ever wakes. Let me do this for you. For both of you.''

He frowned. ''You're sure it's not asking too much? You'd tell me if it is?''

''I promise I'd tell you. I would have woken if she'd called out. It was just a light doze. I wouldn't put Susannah at risk for the world. I love that child, Carver.''

''I know you do, Mum.'' He smiled. ''She loves her nanna, too.''

She smiled back. ''So there you are. Go off to bed, dear. You have work tomorrow.''

''Yes, Mum,'' he said with ironic indulgence. He bent down and kissed her cheek. ''Goodnight, and thanks for staying up.''

''Goodnight, dear.''

He left her and went down the hall to Susannah's bedroom. The door was slightly ajar and he slipped inside the room quietly, moving across to the bed where his daughter was tucked up, fast asleep. From all appearances, she hadn't moved since he had left earlier, the bedclothes unruffled, her head turned to the same side on the pillow. His mother was right. Susannah was a good sleeper, happy to go to bed when the day was over and rarely waking up through the night.

He leaned over to press a soft kiss on her cheek, breathing in the endearing young child smell of her and counting himself lucky to have her in his life. She had been unthinkingly conceived and had cost him dear in many ways, yet no way would he be without her now.

His fingers brushed lightly over her silky black curls and a heart-twisting thought savaged his mind. *She should have been Katie's. Not just his by another woman. Katie's, too.* Given a different set of circumstances, she might well have been, and Katie would have *wanted* the child, not fought him over giving birth to their baby, nor deserting it once it was born.

But that wasn't how it was.

The water under the bridge had flowed another way and it was impossible to go back and change it. Years on…it was Katie's choice now not to have children, to pour her time and energy into a business. Other people's children were an integral part of that business, but looking after them was not loving them.

He couldn't expect her to love Susannah…another woman's child. Not as he did—his own flesh-and-blood daughter—and he'd hate it if she didn't.

Yet…he wanted Katie Beaumont. He'd never really stopped wanting her. Even when she'd fled to England, he'd tried to understand her reasons for turning her back on the love he would have fought anyone for. He'd thought she'd come back when she was ready to face down her father's wrath…but she didn't. In actual fact, he didn't know what her response to his letter would have been if he hadn't married Nina.

Dreams…

At least his daughter wasn't a dream. And she would always be his, a lifelong love that nothing could ever break.

As for Katie…well, time would tell.

Sexual attraction was one thing, love quite another.

CHAPTER TEN

IT WAS ten days before he came again.

The longer span of time between visits had Katie swinging from bitter cynicism—did the mention of her period keep him away until he was sure he wouldn't be denied his sexual fix?—to emotional torment—had she made a bad mistake in bringing up the letter, somehow driving a wedge between them instead of opening up a bridge of understanding?

The problem was she didn't know what had been going on in Carver's life at the time and what effect her delayed response had had. Not good. That was obvious from his reaction to her explanation of what had happened. But how bad…it was impossible to know unless he told her, and he wasn't about to tell her. *Water under the bridge…*

It was a relief when he called again, wanting to be with her. She instantly agreed, needing the chance to sort out some of her miserable uncertainties. This time she *would* get answers and not be so quick to fall into bed with him, thinking that intimacy would soften the brick wall.

Go after him…

If sex was the only bargaining chip she had, then as much as she recoiled from the calculating nature of the tactic, it had to be withheld until Carver gave her some satisfaction on where he was coming from.

He knew what she'd been doing in the years they'd been apart. He'd read her references. Her life had run along a relatively clear path, while his had a number of murky areas that were endlessly tantalising.

She was fully dressed—determinedly armoured— when he arrived at her door, once again emanating the same strong male sexuality and triggering a host of weak flutters that instantly tested her resolve. Katie fiercely resisted the temptation to simply let him come in and take what he wanted—what she wanted. It wasn't enough!

''Hi!'' she said firmly, hanging on to the door while gesturing him inside. ''I've just made a pot of coffee. Come and sit down and I'll bring you a cup, if you like.''

Her skin prickled as he scanned her body language. The simmering anticipation in his eyes winked out, replaced by a mocking wariness as he answered, ''Thank you. I could probably do with a caffeine shot.''

He walked past her without touching, and the rack on which Katie's nerves were screwed tight moved up another notch. She closed the door, at least keeping him momentarily in her company. Panic churned her stomach as she forced herself to walk back to the kitchenette and attend to the coffee, excruciatingly aware that he was making no move to sit down.

Having stepped into her living space, he simply stood watching her, and she could feel the acute concentration of his attention like a burning presence. Her hands were trembling so much, it was all she could do to pour the coffee into the cups she'd set out without slopping the liquid into the saucers.

"Milk and sugar?" she asked.

"Just black," came the flat reply.

While she was adding sugar to her own cup, he stepped over to the kitchen counter and slid his along to the end of it and stood there, virtually blocking her exit from the kitchenette.

"So what's this about, Katie?" he asked quietly. "You've had a long, tiring day? You don't really want me here?"

"No…yes…" She shook her head at her own confused replies and swung to face him, her eyes pleading for patience and some giving on his part. "I want… I need…to talk with you, Carver. To clear up some things between us."

Again the mocking wariness. "Like what?"

Her inner anguish spilled out, too pressing to be held back by any fear of consequences. "You wrote me that letter. You know what was in it. Yet you were married to someone else within six months. That's a bit inconsistent, isn't it?"

He shrugged. "The silence from you seemed remarkably consistent with the silence you'd held for years. Like I no longer existed in your world, Katie."

"So you just went out and found someone else." The bitterness lashed from her tongue before she could even begin to consider his point of view.

It evoked a sharp flash of derision. "I wasn't looking for anyone. I would characterise my connection with Nina as a moment of madness. Hers to me, she told me bluntly, was an act of careless drunken lust."

"Nina…" The name of the woman who'd answered her phone call, as *his wife*. "Why marry if you weren't in love?"

"Because she fell pregnant and there was a child to consider."

His daughter. So the mind-leap she'd made about an accidental pregnancy had been right! "But if the parents don't love each other…I've never thought that provides a good home for a child," she put to him, remembering how shattering the news of his marriage had been, resenting it even now. "I understand that…"

"You understand nothing," he cut in, glowering scorn at her reasoning. "Being pregnant and having a child didn't fit into Nina's lifestyle," he went on. "She was, by nature, a great opportunist, taking chances as they presented themselves. Finding herself pregnant, she came to me for money to pay for an abortion."

"But you…you didn't agree to it."

"I paid her to go through with the pregnancy and I married her so I would have legal claim to the child."

"You *paid* her to have the baby?"

"My daughter is *someone,* Katie," he grated out. "Someone who's an intrinsic part of me. Would you have preferred me to pay Nina to get rid of her?"

Katie shook her head, realising the child was someone Carver could and did love, especially at a time when there'd been no response from her—no response to a love that might have been. Yet she couldn't help thinking if Nina had not told him she was pregnant...how differently the course of their lives would have run.

"Once Susannah was born, Nina left the baby to me and picked up her own freewheeling life, with considerable funds to do whatever she wanted," Carver explained, spelling out the *payment* he'd made.

"She just walked out...on everything?"

"A divorce and paternal custody were already agreed upon. As it happened, she died in a sky-diving accident before the required year of separation ran its course."

The shocking list of facts left Katie appalled by the situation he had been through. "She didn't mind leaving her baby to you?"

His mouth twisted. "Nina didn't like being pregnant. The only feeling she expressed to me was relief that it was over."

What a terrible marriage that must have been, Katie thought, both of them trapped by the life of a child that meant nothing to Nina, and was precious to Carver. "So your daughter has never really had a mother," she mused sadly.

"She has me."

The grim vehemence in his voice instantly drew her gaze up again and she flinched at the cold glittering indictment she read in his eyes. It was as though he was saying only his love could be counted on, and he would never let his daughter down, never turn his back on her, never leave her wanting in any capacity...as he'd been left wanting by Katie Beaumont.

"And she has my mother, her nanna, to give her plenty of love, as well," he added, driving home the point that his mother still lived under his roof. A tight pride hardened his face. "Don't think of my daughter as a deprived child, Katie. She's not."

"I'm sure she's...very special to you."

Taking desperate refuge in sipping her coffee, Katie tried to get her thoughts in some semblance of purposeful order, but her mind kept whirling around the word, *love*. Carver hadn't loved his wife but he did love his daughter, a love that was supported, not destructively undermined by his mother.

"Why didn't you become a doctor, Carver?" she blurted out.

"I lost interest in fulfilling my mother's ambition for me," he stated tersely, then picked up his own cup and drank its contents, grimacing as though the dregs were bitter as he set the cup down again.

Afraid this was a sign he was about to walk out and leave her, Katie plunged into explaining her question. "I used to think of you, moving up through the years it takes to get a medical degree. And you'd talked about specialising in surgery..."

"I'm sorry I've disappointed you," he slid in sardonically, impatient with her memories, uncaring.

After all, how could such memories mean anything to him when she'd never contacted him to make them mean something? He straightened up, poised to move, and the cold rejection in his eyes told her he hated revealing all he had. It was none of her business. She hadn't been here.

Feeling hopelessly guilty and desperate to keep him

with her, Katie plunged into more speech. "You haven't disappointed me, Carver. It was just that your mother was so adamant that I shouldn't stand in your way."

At least that gave him pause for thought. Frowning, he objected to her claim. "You never stood in my way, Katie."

"Perhaps..." She took a deep breath, frantically trying to select the right words, not wanting to offend. "Perhaps, I got it all wrong...at the time."

"If you had such an impression from anything my mother said...why didn't you ask *me* about it?"

When he was lying in hospital, having his broken jaw wired?

Her father hating Carver... His mother hating her...

She heaved a hopeless sigh, recognising belatedly from the harsh tone of his question that there could have been another answer back then...an answer she hadn't sought because it hadn't seemed possible. Having had her justification for fleeing to England swept out of the equation, all she could do was trot out the reality she had accepted.

"I just had it fixed in my mind that becoming a doctor—a surgeon—was important to you. And I used to think...one day when you had all those impressive qualifications attached to your name..." Bleak irony twisted her attempt at a smile. "...I'd come home and congratulate you on the achievement."

"And check if there was anything left between us?" he finished for her, the same irony reflected in his eyes.

"It was…a thought."

A thought that reminded him of what they had been sharing since they'd met again. His gaze slowly raked her from head to toe and back again, making her whole body flush with the memory of the physical pleasure they'd taken in each other.

"So what do you think now, Katie?" he softly challenged, moving towards her. "Is it worth going on with, given the separate directions our lives have taken?"

"Do they have to stay separate?" It was both a protest and an appeal.

He took the coffee cup she was still nursing out of her hands and set it on the kitchen counter. His eyes simmered with sexual promises as he slid his hands around her waist. "I consider this link worth having. Don't you?"

"Yes," she whispered, unable to deny the need to feel him holding her.

"Then let's dismiss the past," he murmured, planting seductive little kisses around the face she automatically turned up to his. "And move on from here."

"To where?" It was a cry from deep within her heart, a cry that the physical desire he stirred didn't answer. She wound her arms around his neck, driven to hold him as close to her as she could. "To where, Carver?" she repeated, desperately seeking some emotional reassurance.

"Who knows?" His eyes blazed with a more immediate fire. "Right now, all I want to know is this."

His mouth covered hers and any further questions

were seared from her mind by a burst of explosive passion. It was all too easy to dismiss everything else, to let herself sink into the enthralling excitement of his aggressive desire for her. There were so many years behind her that had been empty of such intense physical feelings, and the sensations Carver aroused were so chaotically acute, there simply was no room for questioning where or what or how or when or why.

Yet when he kissed her breasts, she remembered what he'd said about them giving away her identity, and felt giddily proud they were unique, at least to him. In her mind, he had always been unique. Best of all, he hadn't loved another woman. She was still the only one. She had to show him, make him believe they were meant for each other, now and forever.

Consumed by her need for him, Katie was just as eager as he was to get rid of their clothes, to move to the bed, to embrace all they could share together with a fervour that knew no limitations. She loved his strong maleness, loved the tautness of his muscles, loved the whole sensation of his body moving against hers, naked and yearning for their ultimate union.

"Katie, did you go on the Pill?"

"Yes."

He didn't hesitate, didn't question further, didn't reach for a condom, but went straight ahead, sheathing himself only with her, flesh around flesh. Her mind almost burst with happiness. He was giving up his protection, giving up the last barrier that kept him apart from her. So maybe the talking had been good…painful but good. He was letting it be as it had been between them when he'd trusted her love.

And it was wonderful, feeling him inside her like this, so hot and hard and *real*, moving them both to exquisite peaks of pleasure. It gave her an ecstatic sense of satisfaction when she felt him climax, the warm spill of him a deep inner caress of total intimacy, the sharing truly complete this time. As though he felt the sweet harmony of it, too, he kissed her with a loving tenderness that filled Katie's heart with hope.

When he held her close to him afterwards, idly caressing her and luxuriating in the sheer sensuality of being naked together, it was as though they had moved into a peaceful truce, with the angst of the past laid to rest and a future yet to be written. She no longer had the sense of a brick wall around him, sealing off any entry to his personal life. He felt… reachable.

She lay with her cheek over his heart, feeling the gentle rise and fall of his breathing, wondering if fortune favoured the brave. All those years ago, she hadn't been brave enough to fight for a love she'd convinced herself was doomed. She'd projected it into some vaguely possible future, letting it become more a dream than a reality. But she was more than ready to fight for it now.

"Carver?"

"Mmm?" It was a drowsy sound of contentment. He was gently tracing the curve of her spine with his fingertips.

"Ten days was a long time without hearing from you."

He sighed and moved his hand into her hair, weaving his fingers through the curls and tugging lightly as he answered, "Don't try to tie me down, Katie. I do have other commitments. And this is new. It needs time."

To Katie's mind, too much time had been lost already, but she didn't feel she had the right to be demanding. "I didn't like feeling I might have lost you again."

He gave a low, amused chuckle. "You can take it for granted you haven't." Then his voice gathered a harder edge. "I've never run away from anything, Katie. Whatever has to be faced, I face...upfront."

Not like her. But she *was* facing issues between them now. The problem was in learning not to push too far too fast. And not be too selfish, either. Lillian Dane might not have been so wrong in calling her a spoilt rich bitch, expecting everything to be handed to her on a plate without earning it, or paying for it.

"I won't make promises, Katie," Carver went on in a softer tone, stroking her hair now, soothing. "You have a business to run. I have a family to hold together. Let's just see what we can fit in."

With that, Katie firmly told herself, she had to be content.

For now.

CHAPTER ELEVEN

KATIE found a parking place for her people-mover behind the Lane Cove public library and double-checked that her precious vehicle was locked before leaving it behind. Since it was expensively equipped with baby capsules, toddler car seats and boosters, she certainly didn't want to invite any thieving by being careless.

It was right on ten-thirty as she made her way up to the mall where there were open-air cafés under the leafy canopy of trees—a really pleasant venue on a hot sunny morning. She was looking forward to spending a half hour or so with Amanda, who'd taken to grumbling that Katie was always too busy to have any *fun.* Which, Katie had to admit, was mostly true these days.

She spotted her friend at a table, easy to do with her bright clothes and bright personality, topped by lovely blond hair and sparkling blue eyes. The moment Amanda saw her, she signalled a waiter and had him at the table before Katie even sat down. They both ordered cappuccinos.

The waiter departed.

Katie relaxed.

Amanda leaned forward, resting her forearms on the small table, her whole body expressing an excited eagerness to impart some news she couldn't wait to share.

"I've done it!" she declared, her eyes twinkling with triumph. "It's taken me a while, finagling the social links to ensure success, but I've done it!"

Katie shook her head, amused by the secretive glee emanating from her friend, but having no clue whatsoever to the achievement she was gloating over. Since it was clearly the key to Amanda's pressing invitation to join her for coffee once the heavily booked morning runs to child-care centres and schools were done, Katie obligingly fed her back the leading line.

"What have you done?"

The grin that spread across Amanda's face beamed conspiratorial delight. "I've got Carver Dane!"

Katie could feel all her nerves clenching. Her mind flashed to the previous night—two sizzling hours snatched with Carver midweek—and a tide of heat started whooshing up her neck.

Amanda laughed as she observed the revealing flush. "Now don't tell me you're not interested, Katie Beaumont. He's a widower, available, very very eligible, and there's no reason why love can't flourish the second time around."

Matchmaking!

Katie didn't know whether to laugh or cry. She took a deep breath to settle the wild hysteria that threatened to spill into a highly questionable response, and concentrated on finding out what Amanda was setting up for her.

"I think you'd better explain just how you've *got*

Carver Dane, Amanda,'' she said, striving for a non-committal tone.

''Well, I started off working through Robert Freeman…'' Her voice brimmed with enthusiasm for the chase as she detailed the step-by-step plan which had drawn Carver into her social net. ''Anyhow, he's accepted my invitation to bring himself and his daughter to the barbecue lunch Max and I are holding for some of our friends this coming Sunday,'' she finished with smug satisfaction.

''His daughter…'' Katie couldn't help picking up those words.

She and Carver had been lovers for three months, yet he had offered no invitation to meet his daughter, not even dropping a suggestion that he might favour introducing them to each other. Katie herself was in two minds about the child he loved so much, sometimes fiercely resenting her existence, other times seized by an avid curiosity to know what she was like.

''Now don't let a child by another woman get in the way,'' Amanda quickly advised. ''You're great with little children, Katie. With all your experience as a nanny, that can't possibly be a hurdle to you.'' Her eyes danced with sexual mischief. ''And he's still a gorgeous hunk! Well worth having!''

She was hardly missing out on *having* him, Katie thought with considerable irony. But meeting his daughter…would that move her closer to him? Or would it bring a divisive element into their relationship?

''Besides,'' Amanda went on reassuringly, ''there will be other children for her to play with. I've invited quite a few families. And my Nick will draw her into games. Meeting the child won't be awkward for you at all."

"The master planner," Katie mocked, not at all sure if she should go along with Amanda's scheming. But it was tempting…meeting Carver's daughter in such casual circumstances.

Amanda preened. "I certainly am. Quite brilliant when I put my mind to it. And don't think you can give me the slip, Katie. I know you're free on Sundays."

Undeniably true. During the first month of building up the highly specialised taxi business, taking every booking she could manage, Katie had realised she was pushing herself too much—to a dangerous fatigue level—and she'd decided Sunday had to be a day of rest.

It was the least demanding day for her services because parents were generally home to drive their own children around. Apart from which, the safe and reliable transport she provided had proved very popular and profitable so she could afford to take a day off.

"I do have a standing invitation to brunch with my father," she remarked, not quite ready to commit herself.

Amanda waved a dismissive hand. "Don't come the dutiful daughter bit with me, Katie." Her eyes narrowed meaningly. "Your father interfered with the course of true love before and he should be grateful to me for trying to put it right. You are not to let him put a spoke in this wheel!"

He wouldn't. Katie knew that. In fact, he would be full of approval for Amanda's initiative.

"Apart from which," her friend ran on, "after all the trouble I've gone to—a very lengthy and delicate campaign—I shall be mortally offended if you don't come and snag the guy as you should."

"He might not want to be *snagged*."

"Nonsense. He probably had a stiff dose of pride at that interview you had with him. But he gave you the money, didn't he?" Amanda pressed eagerly.

"It was a sound business investment," Katie asserted, still hiding what had ensued from the interview on a very private and personal level. She didn't want to confide the truth. Amanda could never resist passing on a juicy piece of gossip and Katie was not about to risk testing her friend's ability to hold her tongue.

"He could have been prejudiced against you," Amanda argued. "Giving you the money proves he's open-minded. That's a plus to start with. And a nice relaxed lunch on Sunday will give his pride time to unbend. You'll see," came the confident prediction.

The waiter brought their coffees and there was a pause in the conversation as they paid for them and stirred in sugar to their taste. Katie tried to envisage a nice relaxed lunch with Carver and his daughter, but could only see problems with it. Amanda, however, was determined on pursuing this course, jumping in again with more persuasion.

"I bet he won't be able to leave you alone. No one forgets their first love, Katie. A little fanning of the embers...?" Her eyebrows arched a challenge. "Why not give it a try?"

The embers didn't need fanning. She and Carver had a significant blaze already going. The problem was its restriction to a very fine line between them. Would it help broaden the line if she met his daughter and managed to establish a positive rapport with the child?

Go after him…

Nothing ventured, nothing gained, Katie argued to herself.

"All right. I'll come." She eyed her friend warningly. "Just don't get too cute with either of us, Amanda."

"Who, me? The very soul of subtlety?"

"And if it goes wrong, don't try to stop any exits."

"I shall facilitate them with tact and grace," she declared airily, then grinned from ear to ear. "Sunday. Twelve noon. Out on the patio by the swimming pool. Bring your sexiest bikini."

Sunday came, bright and sunny, a perfect summer day although it was only mid-November. Katie was in a nervous flutter all morning, telling herself again and again this meeting with Carver's daughter was surely harmless, yet unable to stop worrying over Carver's reaction once he realised Amanda had deliberately engineered their coming together. Impossible for him not to, once he was aware his hostess was an old school friend of Katie's, and Amanda was bound to let that pertinent piece of information drop.

In a way, it was a test of where she stood with him.

But did she want to know the results?

No point in hiding her head in the sand, Katie decided. Either Carver was going to let her into his family life or he wasn't, and what happened today should be a clear indication of future direction with him.

It would also be a test of her feelings about his daughter.

Not that she worried any more about the little girl being a reflection of the woman Carver had married. Nina was completely out of the picture now in any emotional sense. However, Katie's experience had taught her not every child was easy to love. Some would test the patience of a saint. So it was probably good to get an idea of what she faced with Susannah Dane, should Carver decide he would like a relationship between them to develop.

She didn't take a bikini with her. Fanning embers was not what today was about. She wore a pair of deep fuschia-pink jeans with a fitted white blouse embroidered with tiny fuschias. It was a feminine outfit without being in-your-face sexy. It felt right for meeting a child.

The ten-minute drive to the Fairweathers' home in Lane Cove was a smooth run, although possible problems started multiplying in Katie's mind, filling her with so much trepidation there was no pleasure at all in arriving. Quite a few cars were parked in the street outside Amanda's house, which seemed to suggest she was late, but a check of her watch assured her she was not.

Was Carver already here?

His Audi sports car certainly wasn't, but he probably used some other vehicle when taking his daughter out.

Gathering up her frayed courage, Katie forced her legs to carry her to Amanda's front door and she rang the doorbell to make her arrival final. No running away from this confrontation. Stand and fight for what you want, she fiercely told herself.

The door opened.

Amanda, in white slacks and a multicoloured striped top, clapped her hands in excited anticipation—let the fun begin! Katie ruefully interpreted—then grabbed her and hauled her into the house, winding her arm firmly around Katie's to ensure captivity.

"They're here!" she declared, her eyes dancing with gleeful satisfaction. "And you'll be gobsmacked when you see his daughter!"

"Why?"

"You'll see."

"Is there something wrong with her?" Katie pressed anxiously, wanting to be prepared.

"Not at all." Amanda grinned her delight. "In fact, she's absolutely perfect!"

"Then what are you going on about? And how come everyone's here before me? I'm not late."

"I invited those with children earlier. Gives them more playtime before lunch. Then hopefully they tire themselves out and go to sleep in the afternoon, giving the adults more play time," came the wise explanation.

Katie frowned. "Am I the only one late?" she asked, hating the thought of making *an entrance*.

"Only by half an hour. Perfectly reasonable." Then with a mischievous twinkle in her eyes, she added, "I wanted Carver settled in and comfortable before hitting him with you. He can't make an excuse to leave if he's comfortable, can he? Especially if his daughter is obviously having fun. And she is. The moment she saw Nick's little yellow Jeep, it was love at first sight. Hasn't stopped playing with it.''

They reached the kitchen where Max was unloading a tray of iceblocks into a pitcher of fruit juice. He looked up and gave Katie a welcoming smile. ''Hi! Looking good, Katie! And Amanda tells me your taxi business is thriving.''

''Yes. Thanks, Max.''

He really was a lovely man, not exactly handsome but with the kind of looks you warmed to because he was so nice. He was shorter than average height, his greying brown hair was receding at the temples, he was carrying too much weight, but he had friendly blue eyes, an infectious smile and a charm of manner that always put people at ease.

''You can catch up with Katie later,'' Amanda swiftly advised her husband. ''We've got more important business right now.''

He rolled his eyes and mockingly sang, *''Come tip-toe, through the tulips...''*

It paused Amanda at the door, causing her to cast a warning. ''Now you just stop that, Max. This is serious.''

He broke off into a resigned sigh. ''I know, darling heart. Three months of relentless scheming. Do try to give her a pay-off, Katie, or my life won't be worth living.''

''*C'est la vie,* Max,'' she said, grimacing her sym-

pathy, grateful to him for the light moment which had
eased her tension a little.

"Too true," he answered, nodding his head sagely.

"I am acting for the best," Amanda declared emphatically and hauled Katie outside to the patio which
provided a splendid outdoor family entertainment
area.

Part of it had a louvred roof to protect the barbecue
and several tables from inopportune rain. Other sections were shaded by vine-covered pergolas. There
was a large open play area for the children, and beyond that a fenced swimming pool, where Nick and
a couple of other young boys were dive-bombing big
floating plastic toys.

Several children were playing in and around a
brightly coloured cubbyhouse which had a ladder
leading up to one window and a slippery dip coming
down from another, but a quick, cursory glance didn't
identify any one of them as definitely Carver's daughter.

"Now where is he?" Amanda muttered, checking
the various couples who were seated around tables,
enjoying cool drinks and nibbles. Most of them Katie
recognised from the masked ball where the masks had
come off after midnight. Some remembered her and
smiled, raising their hands in greeting.

"There, by the barbecue!"

Katie looked where Amanda directed. Three men
stood by the cooking grill, idly watching sausages siz-
zle as they drank beer and chatted to each other.
Carver, his powerful physique clothed in dark blue
jeans and a royal blue sports shirt looked, as always,

stunningly male, his handsome face expressing interest in the conversation.

There was a burst of amused laughter between the men, then Carver's gaze roved past Katie towards the cubbyhouse. Her pulse leapt as her presence registered and he did a double take. His whole body stiffened with the shock of seeing her. For several moments, he stared, consternation drawing his brows together. Then something else caught his attention and his head jerked towards...

A little yellow Jeep being propelled into view from behind the cubbyhouse.

In the driver's seat was a little girl wearing a pretty pink hat printed with yellow flowers. The Jeep had no pedals. It was pushed forward by little feet in pink sandals. Clearly the child had got the hang of making the wheels take her where she wanted to go and she headed straight towards Carver with a very proficient scooting motion. She stopped the Jeep in front of him, opened the door and stepped out, looking very cute in a pink singlet and a pink skirt printed with yellow flowers—a perfect match for the hat.

Carver's gaze was now fixed on the child. He set his glass of beer down on the serving bench beside the barbecue grill as the little girl yanked her hat off and handed it up to him.

"I don't want to wear this, Daddy," she said very clearly.

He took it and bent down to scoop the child up in his arms.

It was Katie staring now...staring at a mass of black spiral curls, shorter than her own, but exactly the kind of hair she'd had as a child. With a weird sense of déjà-vu, she watched Carver settle the little girl against his shoulder. She had photos of herself with her father, posed just like that, the curls spilling around her face like an uncontrollable mop.

Katie's heart turned over.

This child could be her!

Or her daughter!

Then she remembered Carver saying that her hair wasn't unique...only her breasts. Other women had hair like hers. And since she hadn't given birth to this child and Carver's hair was not curly, then the birth mother...Nina...Nina who had been only too ready to hand when Katie hadn't responded to his letter...Nina with the same hair!

She felt sick.

"There's someone I want you to meet, Susannah," she heard Carver say, the words ringing hollowly in her ears.

He started walking towards Katie and the child turned her head, looking directly at her...definitely Carver's child; big dark brown eyes, straight neat nose, lips that were emphatically delineated though in a softer, more feminine mould. Katie knew she should acknowledge Carver but she couldn't tear her gaze from his daughter...with the hair like her own.

"Got to speak to those boys in the pool," Amanda said, unlinking herself from Katie and shooting off, obviously deciding this meeting could go ahead without her.

She was right to leave.

A spate of bright banter would have been intolerable.

Katie stood like a stone statue, unable to muster even a semblance of social geniality. Carver came to a halt directly in front of her, the child in his arms eyeing Katie with an expression of fascinated curiosity, probably wondering why the strange woman was staring at her as though she saw a ghost.

"Hello, Katie."

Carver's greeting forced her gaze up. His eyes burned into hers with a defiant pride that rang a host of alarm bells. She would lose him if she didn't respond with some positive warmth. The test she'd anticipated—so mistakenly—was here and now and if she failed it, there'd never be another chance.

"This is...a surprise," she desperately excused herself, somehow managing to construct a rueful little smile.

"Yes. Quite a surprise," he agreed. "This is my daughter, Susannah."

Katie flashed a brighter smile at the child. "Hello, Susannah."

"Hello," came the shy reply. "This is my daddy."

"I know."

And the knowledge hurt...hurt more than Katie had ever imagined it would...because she could have been this child's mother...and would have been if only her path and Carver's had crossed at the right time.

CHAPTER TWELVE

"Juice or wine, Katie?" Max called out, emerging from the kitchen with the freshly filled pitcher of fruit juice and holding it aloft.

Grateful for the distraction, she quickly answered, "Juice for me, thanks Max."

"Coming right up." He turned to a serving table where clean glasses and plastic tumblers were set out and started pouring. "What about you, Susannah? Are you thirsty? All that driving around in the Jeep is hot work."

"Yes. Hot work," she repeated, nodding agreement.

"Need a refill on the beer, Carver?"

"No, I'm fine."

He brought over a glass for Katie and a tumbler for Susannah, smiling at all three of them. "Robert told me it was you who gave the green light to Katie's taxi service, Carver, and Amanda tells me she's been a slave to it ever since she started up."

"I did warn her it would be very demanding," Carver answered easily.

"I don't mind being busy," Katie put in, trying desperately to get her shattered mind to focus on carrying off this meeting with some grace.

"Well, it's a good day to put your feet up and laze away a few hours. Come and sit down." He herded them towards an unoccupied table under one of the pergolas. "Maybe you should check up on how your investment's doing, Carver," he ran on. "Katie's probably bursting to brag about how successful her idea has been."

"I'm glad to hear it," Carver said obligingly.

"Good! Take a chair. I'll go and fetch your beer from the barbecue."

Having been deftly paired by their hosts, even given the prompt to a ready conversation, Katie and Carver settled at the table assigned to them, obliging guests who followed the leads handed out to them. Except Carver knew all about the progress of her business and Katie was hopelessly fixated on his daughter.

He set the child on her feet and turned her towards the barbecue. "Better go and get the Jeep, Susannah. Drive it over here so you can show Katie how well you can do it."

She put the tumbler on the table, flashed Katie a big-eyed look, clearly wanting her interest, then ran off to follow her father's suggestion. Katie watched the curls bobbing, her mind too much of a mess to even think of saying anything.

"It seems our hostess fancies a bit of matchmaking," Carver dryly remarked.

"Yes." Her cheeks bloomed with hot embarrassment. She couldn't bring herself to look at him. She gabbled a jerky explanation of the situation. "Amanda and I are old friends. I was on her table at the masked ball. She was trying to pair me off there."

"Ah!" A pause. "Does she know I was the buccaneer at the ball?"

"I don't think so. I haven't told her."

Silence. Katie imagined speculation was rife in Carver's mind. She felt driven to say, "Amanda means well, arranging this opportunity for us to get together socially. She has no idea we're lovers."

But not lovers at the right time, she thought on a wave of bleak misery, her gaze fastened on the daughter who wasn't hers. Susannah manually turned the Jeep around, then seated herself behind the driving wheel with an air of taking proper control. She smiled at Katie, a bright eager plea to be watched, and as Katie automatically smiled back, an assurance of full attention, she pushed off with her feet, steering the toy vehicle across the playing area to the cubbyhouse.

There she alighted, reached into one of the window seats inside the cubby, lifted out a red plastic cylinder, loaded it into the back compartment of the Jeep, then resumed driving the rest of the way to the table where Katie sat with her father. Out she popped again, grabbed the cylinder and carried it over to Katie. She picked out a plastic letter and offered it to her.

"This is an A," she announced proudly.

Katie took it, pretending to examine it. "So it is. An A," she repeated in pleased affirmation.

"And it's red."

Katie nodded agreement. "Yes, it's red."

"That's 'cause A is for apple and apples are red."

"That's true. How clever you are to know that."

Susannah beamed delight and produced another letter. "This is a Y, and it's yellow, 'cause Y is for yellow."

Katie accepted it with an air of surprise. "Do you know all the letters of the alphabet, Susannah?"

She nodded. "Daddy taught me."

Daddy... Katie took a quick breath to counter the pain in her heart. "It's very good that you can remember them. Do you want to show me another?"

"Yes."

The cylinder was being gradually emptied when Max interrupted the game. "Come on, all you kids! The sausages are cooked. Time to eat!"

"Out of the pool, you boys," Amanda instantly commanded, opening the safety gate for them to exit. "You can bring your towels with you to dry off."

Her four-year-old son was first through the gate and was instructed by his mother, "You can go and collect Susannah and help her get some lunch, Nick."

"Okay!" He spotted the three of them and his face lit up. "Hi, Katie! Did you see me diving?"

"Big splash!" she replied with a smile.

He laughed and turned back to his companions. "Hey, guys! Katie's here!"

His loud announcement spotlighted her to several of the children whom she regularly transported to play centres, instantly drawing them to where she sat. They all clamoured for her attention, wanting to tell her what they'd been doing.

"One at a time," she instructed, "and let's go and have some sausages." She stood up, holding out her hand to Susannah. "Do you want to come with us?"

She nodded, eagerly grasping the offered hand, and they all set off to the barbecue.

Behind them Amanda stepped in to attend to

Carver, saying, "Katie's like the pied piper of Hamelin. Children will follow her anywhere."

His reply was lost in the lively chatter being aimed at her. Not that it mattered. Amanda was being rather heavy-handed in driving home the obvious. It was true that most children took to her. Mostly it was about accepting them on their level and giving approval, paying attention to them, projecting an interest that made them feel like people worth knowing.

As a nanny, she'd found a lot of adults—and parents—couldn't be bothered. It was like—when they grow up they might be worth listening to. And, of course, time was a factor. Caring for little children took up a great deal of time and no one seemed to have enough of it these days.

Carver obviously didn't fall into that category. The child holding her hand was very much cared for. *Daddy taught me.* Katie imagined he gave his daughter all the time he had between his work and when she was finally bedded down at night. It wasn't until Susannah was asleep that he ever came to Katie's apartment.

This child—who could have been hers—came first in Carver's life. As she should. But seeing them together made Katie feel even more sidelined. They were a unit while she...well, she was obviously good for sex but it was now painfully apparent she was not needed for anything else.

She helped Susannah get her lunch—two sausages with tomato sauce, some potato salad, a bread roll, all on an unbreakable plastic plate—then directed her back to her father.

The little girl hesitated, big eyes appealing. "You come, too?"

"When I've finished helping the other children," Katie excused, needing time to paste a social demeanour over the pain. "You go on now," she added persuasively. "Your daddy will cut up the sausages for you."

She trotted off, assured Katie would follow eventually, a very biddable child, and completely innocent of doing any wrong against her, Katie savagely reminded herself. Susannah had not asked to be born and she had every right to be loved by her father. *Every right!*

"You don't have to help, Katie," Amanda muttered in her ear. "I'll fix up the kids." She gave her a nudge. "Go on back to Carver."

"I don't want to," she stated flatly.

Amanda frowned at her. "Why not?"

"Just let me have some space, Amanda." She flashed her a fierce warning. "Stop pushing. I'll work it out my own way."

Inevitably all the children were served with as much lunch as they wanted, and short of snubbing Carver and his daughter altogether, which would be hopelessly wrong in the context of forging any kind of future with either of them, Katie had no choice but to join them again and try to make something positive out of this day. She put a scoop of strawberry ice-cream into a plastic bowl for Susannah and took it across to the table where they were seated.

"Do you have room in your tummy for this?" she asked the little girl, setting the bowl down in front of her.

An eager nod and a big smile as Katie sat down with them.

"Say thank you, Susannah," Carver gently instructed.

"Thank you," she repeated shyly.

Max promptly descended on them with two wineglasses and flourishing a bottle of chardonnay. "A reward for your labours, Katie," he declared, pouring her a glass. "Carver?"

"Yes. Thanks, Max."

Alcohol couldn't smooth this path, Katie thought sardonically, wondering if Amanda had worded up her husband on tensions to be eased.

"Steaks are sizzling now. Won't be long before we eat," he cheerfully informed them before heading off to look after his other guests.

Susannah was digging into the ice-cream.

"Don't feel awkward, Katie," Carver quietly advised. "I don't mind our meeting like this."

She looked him straight in the eye and couldn't stop herself from saying, "But it wasn't on your agenda, was it, Carver? In fact, you could have invited me to accompany you here if you'd wanted to. You know I have Sundays free."

"Which you usually spend with your father," he countered, his eyes cooling.

Her father, who had subjected him to irrational and brutal violence when they were last face to face. And no apology had ever been extended.

"I've told him about our...our coming together again. I'm not hiding you from him," Katie blurted out, wanting to clear the air on that score.

He looked surprised. "You've told him?"

"Yes."

His brows creased into a V as he considered what this might mean—like their affair was not quite as private as he had believed, as he probably wanted it. The urge to press him on that point was suddenly compelling.

"My father no longer has any objection to a relationship between us," she stated, watching to see what that piece of news stirred.

Carver's mouth curled cynically. "He no longer has any grounds for the accusations he once made."

"No, he doesn't," she agreed, flushing at his response and defensively asking, "What about your mother? Have you told her about me?"

His eyes glittered a challenge. "What is there to tell, Katie?"

"That I'm part of your life again."

"How much a part?" He gestured to the guests around them. "These people are obviously more your friends than mine. They would have been happy for you to bring someone. Just as they're happy to see you with me now. So why didn't *you* invite *me* to accompany you here today?"

The implication was that he still wasn't good enough for her, which was so terribly wrong—it had always been wrong!—Katie was instantly stung into attacking *his* motives.

"Because you hadn't made any attempt to make me a part of your family, Carver." She nodded to his daughter who was still thankfully occupied with her ice-cream. "And right now I feel your hand has been forced beyond where you wanted it to go."

"That works both ways, Katie."

What did he mean? Did he imagine she was content with the occasional sex on the side? That she didn't want the commitment of a relationship that would demand more from her than just going to bed with him when it was convenient to both of them?

"I don't mind your being here, Carver," she said quickly, disturbed by the impression his comment had evoked.

Again his mouth curled. "You're not exactly demonstrating pleasure in my company."

"I wasn't sure how welcome I was."

"Do you want to be welcome..." His gaze flicked to Susannah and moved back to hers with a sharper intensity. "...to my family?"

"Yes," Katie stated unequivocally, defying the emotional turmoil stirred by his daughter and the prospect of meeting his mother again.

"Will you invite me to meet your father?"

"Yes," she answered without hesitation. "Any time you like."

For several long, nerve-racking moments his eyes studied the belligerent determination in hers. Katie was not about to back down. She'd thrown the ball well and truly into his court now. It was up to him to answer.

"I hope you realise what these decisions mean, Katie," he said with slow deliberation. "Other lives get touched by them, not just yours and mine."

He was prevaricating, probably wanting them to stay private lovers, but the closed doors had been opened today and Katie didn't want to be locked back into that restricted space.

"You face those decisions, too, Carver," she pointedly retorted, resolved on assessing how much she was worth to him.

Yet when his answer finally came, what it told her was something else entirely, something that rolled back the years and silenced any further argument.

"I just hope you're sure, Katie. Very, very sure... *this time.*'

It was in his eyes...the memory of how she had run away when the going got tough. She had claimed to love him then, but what was love worth if it didn't stand fast, for better or for worse? Neither of them had declared *love* this time around. It was an empty word unless it was surrounded by proof of it.

She would show him, Katie fiercely resolved. She would set up a meeting with her father. Regardless of how his mother reacted to her, she would somehow win Lillian Dane over. As for his daughter...

"I'm finished," Susannah declared, catching Katie's eye on her and putting her spoon into the emptied bowl with elaborate care.

Katie smiled. "I think you must really like strawberry ice-cream."

The little girl nodded. "Strawberries, too. Daddy buys them for me." She looked at her father. "They're good for me, aren't they, Daddy?"

His smile bestowed both love and approval. "Yes, they are."

Amanda swept in and picked up the bowl. "Had enough or would you like some more, Susannah?"

"Enough, thank you."

"Good!" A bright hostess smile was directed at Katie and Carver. "Now that the children have eaten, we're going to join some tables together to make one

big party for the adults. Will you give us a hand with
them, Carver?''

"Of course.''

Which neatly broke up their twosome in case it was
not as harmonious as Amanda had hoped. Katie definitely had to give her friend credit for tact and grace.
As soon as the tables were rearranged to her satisfaction, she ensured that Katie and Carver were seated
with other people on either side, as well as across
from them so conversation could be turned wherever
they chose. Clearly this was to diffuse any one-on-
one tension.

They were served with a veritable barbecue feast;
big platters of steaks, sausages and fried onions,
baked potatoes split and heaped with sour cream and
chives, a variety of popular salads, foccacio bread,
warm and crusty from the oven. It should have been
wonderfully appetising but Katie found it difficult to
do justice to it.

Despite the ready distraction of interesting chat,
witty remarks, and clever jokes, with Carver demonstrating he more than held his own in this company,
her mind kept fretting over his lack of trust in her
staying power, and the more she thought about it, the
more unfair that judgement seemed.

It was a long time ago…what had happened when
she was nineteen, only one year out of school and
still living with her father who'd been the dominant
influence in her young life. She was ten years older
now, with obvious proof she was of an independent
mind, making big decisions for herself and having the
strength of purpose to go through with them.

Increasing her inner angst was the endearing yet

tormenting presence of his daughter. All during lunch Susannah kept popping up beside her chair to show her something, choosing to bask more in Katie's attention than in her father's. It hurt. It hurt more all the time, because Carver had committed himself to this child, and because of her, considered committing himself to Katie a risk he was wary of taking.

A sweets course was served. Platters of cheese accompanied coffee. The party at the table broke up somewhat as some parents attended to their children's needs. Susannah was obviously tired, climbing up on Carver's lap and resting her head on his chest—father and daughter.

But she didn't close her eyes. She gazed fixedly at Katie, not saying anything, seemingly content just to see her seated right next to them. There were lulls in the general conversation now, with people moving around more. In one such lull, they were left to themselves and Katie simply couldn't summon the will to break the silence with inconsequential chat. Mentally and emotionally she'd been stretched too far today.

She sat, gazing blindly at the swimming pool until she felt a tug on her sleeve. It was a child's hand, wanting to draw her attention. Until she turned to look, she didn't realise it was Susannah's. The little girl had stirred from her resting position, leaning over from Carver's lap, clearly wanting to quiz Katie on something. There was a hesitant shyness in her big eyes, yet an imploring look behind the uncertainty.

Katie managed one more encouraging smile.

It worked.

The little girl rushed into speech.

"Are you my mummy?"

The soft question was asked so innocently, so appealingly, it pierced Katie's heart with devastating force. Her eyes filled with tears and an impassable lump lodged in her throat.

"Susannah…" Carver's voice was gruff. "I told you your mummy had gone to heaven."

She turned her face up to his. "But you said she had hair like mine, Daddy. And I heard you say to Katie…" She frowned, trying to make sense of it. "…about coming into our family this time."

Katie pushed back her chair and stood up. She couldn't bear this, couldn't bear to hear how Carver would explain it away. She swallowed hard. Impossible to stop the gush of tears but she managed to speak.

"I'll leave you to sort it out, Carver…with your daughter."

He was a blur. Everything was a blur as she fled, too helplessly distressed to stay at the party or even stop to excuse herself to Amanda or Max.

It wasn't until she was almost back at North Sydney that it occurred to her she was running away again, but it was too late to turn back. Probably too late for everything.

Too early…too late…

It summed up the whole story of her love for Carver Dane.

CHAPTER THIRTEEN

CARVER'S gaze darted to the dashboard clock as he backed the Audi out of his garage, hand clutching the lever, ready to change gears the moment he was on the street. Almost half past five—over two hours since Katie had left the barbecue party in tears.

He savagely wished he'd been free to pursue her much earlier, but he couldn't just dump Susannah, nor subject her to the burning issues between him and Katie when she was the focus of them. No, he'd had to deal with her first. He could only hope he wasn't too late to fix things with Katie now.

He swung the car in the right direction and pressed the accelerator, telling himself to control the urge to speed, though he couldn't help feeling control was his enemy. It was eating up time, like the control it had taken to explain to his daughter about Nina and Katie, to make excuses to the Fairweathers for Katie's abrupt departure, to extricate himself from their well-meaning clutches.

Then having to call Susannah's off-duty nanny, pleading an emergency and getting her to come and stay the night, brushing off his mother's shock at his announcement that Katie Beaumont needed him and he was going to her...it had all taken time which his instincts were warning he could ill afford.

He drove as fast as the legal limit would allow,

knowing if he was stopped for speeding, it would delay him further. And there'd been too many delays
already. More critical ones than a traffic policeman
would cause.

A thousand times he'd thought of introducing Katie
to his daughter. If only he'd done it, this crisis would
have been avoided. And he had no excuses. Not now.
The truth was he'd fed himself doubts about the wisdom of letting any attachment form on Susannah's
side.

After all, Katie had claimed her top priority was
getting her business running successfully. Proving her
idea was worthwhile to her father had seemed second
on the list. Besides which, it had seemed eminently
clear that getting married and having children were
not on her agenda. It had been all too easy to argue
what possible good could come from introducing the
child he'd had with another woman.

Wrong! Wrong, wrong, wrong!

Today…so many things she'd said today strongly
indicated she had wanted more involvement with him
all along, that her relationship with him had been
more important to her than anything else.

The pain on her face…the tears in her eyes…

His hands clenched around the steering wheel as
he cursed his blindness in settling for what had
seemed readily available instead of reaching for more.
She'd *wanted* more. And he hadn't even offered it,
let alone given it.

The only thing going right for him at the present
moment was the traffic lights—all green so far. If he

got a red light from Katie, he had no one to blame but himself.

Pride...that had played its part, too. Her father's social prejudice against him had tainted his thoughts about Katie's view of him—fine to take as a lover on the side as long as he didn't assume a prominent position in her life.

Given what she'd said today, that couldn't be true.

And if he was totally honest with himself, there'd been pride behind his vacillation over introducing Susannah to Katie. It was so obvious Nina had shared a superficial resemblance—the hair!—even a three-year-old child had made the link, thinking Katie might really be her mother. He hadn't wanted to lay himself open so far, revealing such an *obsession* with her.

Damnable pride!

For all he knew, it could have been pride that had made Katie dismiss a desire for marriage and children. At their meeting in his office, she could not possibly have foreseen any relationship developing with him. It had been nothing but business being discussed then.

But there'd been no pride in the eyes that had filled with tears this afternoon...tears that had welled because she was not the mother of his daughter. She had missed out, and was still missing out...would always miss out because he hadn't waited for her.

Had that silent, grief-stricken accusation been behind her tears or had his own sense of guilt read it into her pain? All he truly knew was the depth of pain had been very real and he had caused it. Not

Susannah. She was a complete innocent in all of this. *He* had driven away the only woman he'd ever wanted and somehow he had to win her back.

He glanced at the dashboard clock again as he turned into her street. Eight minutes. Record time. He probably had exceeded the speed limit on the way. No matter. He was safely here.

Determination pounded through him as he parked the car, alighting quickly and heading for her apartment door at a swift stride. *It's not too late,* he fiercely told himself. *I won't let it be too late!*

His thumb depressed the doorbell button for several seconds, the urgency he felt driving him to an emphatic summons. He rocked impatiently on his heels when the door remained closed longer than seemed reasonable. A pang of uncertainty hit him. What if she hadn't come home? He had assumed she would.

He backtracked to the foyer of the apartment block to scan the street outside. His tension eased slightly when he spotted the vehicle she called her people-mover, parked in a side lane. She had to be home, possibly too distressed to open up to anyone.

Intensely disturbed by this thought, Carver returned to her door and pressed the bell again, hoping that persistence might pay off. It didn't. Not only was there no response, but he couldn't hear any sound of occupation, either. The silence started to worry him. Badly.

He thumped on the door with his fist with no more success than he'd had with the doorbell. Wild thoughts jangled through his mind. "Katie!" he shouted, banging harder. It occurred to him that she wouldn't be expecting *him* to come by at this hour. He never had before.

"Katie, it's me, Carver!" he yelled, thumping with both fists. "If you don't open up, I'm going to smash this door down!"

The threat was driven by the fear of not getting the chance to fix things between them and he kept bashing at the door until he heard the metallic click of the deadlock being operated. His chest was heaving and he struggled for some purposeful composure as the door opened...to the short span of the safety chain.

There was no face peering out at him. All he saw was a sliver of empty space inside her apartment. Sheer instinct jammed his foot in the small opening, protecting what little territory he'd won until he could think of how else to achieve what he needed to do.

"What do you want, Carver?"

Dull, flat words, half muffled by the door. She was standing behind it, out of any possible line of vision, obviously avoiding eye contact with him.

He took a deep breath, the memory of her tears vivid in his mind, the need to soothe her pain pumping through his heart. "We have to talk, Katie. Let me in."

All his senses were acutely alert now, aware that this was a battleground and he was fighting for his life with Katie Beaumont. His ears picked up the soft shudder of a sigh.

"I don't feel like talking, Carver. And I don't feel like anything else with you, either. You've had a wasted trip."

He would not accept defeat, yet he could not force

her to accept his presence. Persuasion was the only course he had. Yet the words that came expressed the sudden desolation he felt rather than reaching for some possible soft spot that could be tapped in his favour.

"Is it *all* wasted, Katie?"

Heart-squeezing silence.

Stupid, stupid question, Carver railed at himself, accentuating negatives instead of something positive. But what was positive? On the whole, he had come here to have sex with her and she certainly didn't want that now.

"If you don't feel like talking, that's fine," he said in a softer, hopefully soothing voice. "If you'll just listen… Please? I know I've kept too much back. I'd like to put things right between us, Katie."

"Right for what, Carver?" came the weary question. "I won't be your hidden mistress anymore."

Hidden mistress? He mentally recoiled from the demeaning image…yet wasn't that how he'd treated her?

"You can talk until you're blue in the face and it won't change my mind," she went on, her voice carrying a bitter strength. "And if you think touching me will win you anything…"

"No!" he cut in, anguished by her certainty that he'd only ever wanted sex with her and he was intent on continuing down that path. "I just want to explain to you… Susannah…my mother…all the things you brought up today. I'm sorry I've made you think as you do, Katie. It was wrong…and I want to turn that around."

"Wrong?" she echoed, and he didn't know if it was disbelief, derision, or simple uncertainty wavering through her voice.

"I think I've been wrong about a lot of things," he plunged on. "I need you to tell me, Katie. Set me straight."

Another tense silence.

"Then let it be just talking, Carver," she warned, her tone harshly decisive.

"Yes," he swiftly agreed, removing his foot from the gap it had seized.

She closed the door to release the safety chain, then opened it again, allowing him entry. And that was all it was—a permission, not an invitation. She had retreated from the door before he realised he was to push it open himself. By the time he stepped inside and closed it behind him, she was right across the other side of her living room, her back rigidly turned to him.

He stood still, watching her sit on the edge of the bed where they had shared so many physical pleasures. She was still wearing the clothes she had worn to the barbecue, just as he was. No thought of changing. Thoughts too focused inwards. She wrapped her arms around her midriff, hugging herself to herself, then lifted her head and glared defiance at him.

It sure as hell was not an invitation to join her on the bed!

Carver made no movement whatsoever. The burning question was—how to reach across the distance that now lay between them? It bristled with dangerous pitfalls and any step might mean death to what he wanted. Very slowly he gestured an open-handed appeal, then spoke what was true to him.

"I never thought of you as my hidden mistress, Katie. To me it was like having a little world of our own, where nothing else intruded. Where nothing could harm it. There was…just us."

Her mouth curled. "A private love-nest."

"Yes."

"For the purpose of pursuing strictly sexual desires," she mocked. "I might as well have been a whore except you didn't have to pay anything."

"On the same basis, I could have considered myself your gigolo," he retorted, stung by her interpretation of what they'd shared.

Her mouth thinned. Her lashes lowered. The negative jerk of her head expressed disgust at his lack of understanding. Carver instantly realised his mistake. This was not about scoring points off each other. It was about correcting what was wrong.

"I'm sorry. I guess I wanted to believe it was mutually satisfying."

She said nothing. Her gaze remained lowered. Splotches of colour bloomed on her cheeks. He sensed she was hating being reminded of how *sexual* their relationship had been and quickly changed tack to the far more important issue.

"Susannah liked you very much."

Again her mouth curled. "It's my one talent…an affinity with children. I've based my business on it."

Business!

No, he was not going to let that cloud his vision

now! It was a red herring to the critical issue of his daughter.

"How did you feel about her, Katie?" he asked softly, not wanting to cause more distress, yet needing some hint as to whether she could bear a close involvement with Susannah.

She bit her lips. Her thick lashes hid her eyes. Carver suspected tears might be hovering again and cursed his lack of positive action on this front.

"I know it was a shock, seeing her without any warning," he said on a rueful sigh. "If the meeting had been planned, I would have prepared you for...the likeness. Prepared both you and Susannah. She would have known you weren't her mother."

Still, she didn't look up or speak. Her hands clutched her arms more tightly. Hugging in the pain?

What could he do? What could he say to take it away? There was only the truth to hold out to her.

"I wish you were, Katie. In fact, how Susannah was conceived... I went to a party and through an alcoholic glaze, Nina looked like you. It was like... like a substitution...through a dark dream. That's how it happened and I can't take it back. But there's not a day goes past that I don't look at my daughter and think of you, wishing the situation had been different."

She raised tear-washed eyes. "Do you, Carver? Do you really?"

Her torment ripped away the last shreds of pride. "Yes. I've always wished it."

"Then why?" Her anguished cry left no doubt

about how she felt. "Why have you kept her from me all this time?"

He took a deep breath, fighting the urge to charge over to the bed, sweep her up in his arms and hold her tight, giving all the physical comfort he could impart. Such an action was too open to misinterpretation to follow it through. The touching had to be done with words. Yet he didn't have them. Only a welter of feelings that had swirled and tugged like a treacherous undertow, most of them unexamined.

"Lots of reasons," he muttered, trying to find the sense of what he'd felt. "Hangovers from the past. A misconception of what you wanted." It was all he could offer and he shook his head over the paucity of the explanation. "None of it is relevant anymore, Katie."

She sighed and looked bleakly at him. "So what is relevant, Carver?"

He had that answer ready. It had been building to a certainty from the moment she had cared enough to overcome her shock and be kind to Susannah.

"Whether we can get it together so it can be right for us this time," he said purposefully. "All of it right. As far as it's humanly possible."

"And what does that entail for you?" she asked, the bleak expression still holding sway as she wryly added, "You haven't even told your mother…"

"Yes, I have. She knows I'm here with you. And she is well aware of how important it is to me…to keep you in my life."

Surprise lent a spark of life to her face. "You told her?"

"Yes."

"How did she react?"

"It doesn't matter how she reacts. It doesn't change anything for me where you're concerned." He paused, frowning over her fixation on his mother. "It never did, Katie. Not the first time around and certainly not now."

A startled wonderment accompanied the slight shake of her head. There were definitely hangovers from the past on her side, as well, Carver decided. However, only action was going to resolve them now.

"Would you accept an invitation to my home for lunch next Sunday?" he said impulsively.

"Lunch? You mean…with your mother and daughter?"

"Yes. Unless you'd prefer…some other arrangement."

She looked uncertain.

"My mother has a self-contained apartment within the house. She won't mind if…"

"No. No, I *want* to meet her," she said with an air of grim decision.

He sensed it was a big hurdle for her and it was a measure of her wanting their relationship to continue that she was prepared to face it. At last he was winning some ground here. Even if it was only a testing ground.

"So you'll come?" he pressed.

Her brow creased anxiously as she considered the invitation. "Did I upset Susannah this afternoon? Is she worried that I…"

"No. She understands that she was wrong and

thinks you'd be just as good as her real mother anyway.''

Tears blurred her eyes again. ''She's a lovely child,
Carver. A credit to you…the way you've brought her
up,'' she said jerkily.

''She would like to see you again, Katie. Do you
mind…too much?''

Slowly she shook her head, then managed a rueful
little smile. ''Life happens. We just have to accept it
and make the best of what we're dealt, don't we?''

''You managed admirably today. And I thank you
for it.''

She sat there, looking at him as though she was not
quite sure how much to believe of this turnaround of
attitude and direction. The fragility of the lifeline he'd
hung out made him acutely aware of how vulnerable
she was in her hope for something better between
them.

And she was hoping.

He had achieved that much.

Carver again fought the urge to grab her up and
make wild tempestuous love until she was thoroughly
convinced nothing could ever separate them again.
The problem was, he doubted she would be convinced, not by physical means. Best to get her away
from the temptation of that bed.

''Why don't we go for a walk, Katie?'' he suggested. ''It's a pleasant evening for a stroll and there's
a whole row of pavement cafés and restaurants along
Miller Street. We could stop somewhere to eat when
we feel hungry.''

She looked stunned. "You're...asking me to go out with you?"

Carver gritted his teeth as the phrase—*hidden mistress*—hit home with a vengeance. What had he done to her in his own blind selfish desire to hold her to himself?

"Would you like to? I noticed you didn't eat much at the Fairweathers' lunch party."

"No. I..." She jumped up from the bed, looking flustered, one hand lifting to her hair. "I'll need to tidy up a bit."

"Take your time. I'm happy to wait."

She hesitated, her gaze directly meeting his. "Thank you. I would like a walk."

He smiled his pleasure in her agreement and won a tentative smile back. Then she was heading for the bathroom and Carver was heaving a huge sigh of relief. There was serious damage to be undone before they could move forward, but at least he had reached her.

He glanced at the bed. No more, he vowed. Not until he'd given Katie a true sense of her worth to him.

He opened the door and stepped out to the corridor that bisected the block of apartments, making his intentions absolutely clear. No lingering in her apartment. No hiding anything. He was taking her wherever she wanted to go, giving her whatever she fancied, telling her whatever she wanted to know. This was *her* night.

When she joined him a few minutes later, her face was shiny from having been washed, her mouth was shiny from a fresh application of lipstick, and her eyes were shiny…but not with tears. He read hope in them and the tension tearing at his guts eased.

She locked the door behind them, put her key in the shoulder-bag she'd collected for the outing, and turned to him with an air of knowing she was taking a risk but not knowing what else to do.

He held out his hand to her.

She looked at it, then slowly, almost shyly, slid her own hand into its keeping.

Trust, Carver thought, begins with this.

CHAPTER FOURTEEN

ANOTHER Sunday...and this one loaded with as much hope and fear as the last, Katie thought, dithering over what to wear for the critical meeting with Lillian Dane.

It was all very well for Carver to say his mother's reaction didn't matter. Katie did not find it so easy to shrug off the weight of disapproval she had always felt coming from the older woman. Not just felt, either. There had been words spoken that were etched in her memory.

Admittedly that had all been ten years ago, and circumstances had changed, so she shouldn't be stressing out about it, yet Lillian Dane's attitude towards her had cut so deeply, influencing actions that had altered the course of her life, Katie could never forget that. She wasn't even sure she could forgive it. But she *would* try to let bygones be bygones if Carver's mother demonstrated a true willingness to accept her as a fixture in her son's life.

Approval was probably asking too much.

Nevertheless, the need for it swayed Katie into deciding on a modest little dress. The simple A-line shift was black but printed with colourful little flowers— red, pink, violet, yellow and white—making it bright and summery. The mix of colours made it practical for wearing around children, who were apt to have grubby hands at times. It certainly couldn't be called a flashy or sexy or stylishly *rich*. The little girls she regularly transported had said it was pretty.

Maybe Susannah would think it pretty, too.

She stepped into the dress and zipped it up, smiling over Carver's assurance that his daughter was looking forward with great excitement to seeing her again today. All the negative feelings she'd had about the child were gone. As Carver had said, he couldn't take back what had happened, but his wishing his daughter was hers...that made such a huge difference. She didn't feel...*cut out*...anymore.

Not on any level.

Which still amazed her.

Everything was so different.

Having slid her feet into the pink sandals she'd bought to go with her fuschia jeans and checked that they looked all right with the dress, she headed for the bathroom to put on make-up and tidy her hair, proceeding to perform these tasks automatically as the events of the past week kept teasing her mind.

No sex.

She could hardly believe it.

Twice Carver had taken her out to dinner—last Sunday evening and again on Thursday night. Nothing really fancy. She didn't have time for dress-ups during the week. But it had been so nice strolling out together, choosing a place to eat, sharing a casual meal and a bottle of wine...just like any normal couple who enjoyed each other's company.

Best of all, Carver had opened up about areas of his life he'd kept from her before. She hadn't known his initial move into the landscaping business had been triggered by the urgent need for money—fast and big money—to meet the costs of his mother's rehabilitation from a paralysing stroke, the equipment and medical care she needed if there was to be any chance of recovery.

It had happened just a few weeks after Katie had gone to England. In just a few seconds everything had changed. His mother could no longer work. Without her wage coming in, he had to bear the whole financial burden of keeping a home for her to come back to, as well as assuming the responsibility for her recovery. The circumstances were such that even considering pursuing a medical degree was unrealistic.

Working hard, helping his mother, and never any word from the girl he had loved, the girl who'd run away when everything had turned too difficult for her to handle—Katie marvelled that he had ever come to England to look her up. Then no response to his letter…

She understood so much more now, even why he'd kept all this from her. In a way, she hadn't deserved his confidence. And there was pain attached to almost every connection with her. Perhaps that was why he had sought only pleasure with her…a need to balance the scales.

The question he'd asked through her door last week—*Is it all wasted?*—had echoed what she had felt in her heart.

Carver didn't want to let it go any more than she did, and he was trying very hard to make a new start with her, opening the doors into his life for her to enter if she wanted to, offering her the choice, not assuming anything or taking anything for granted.

She was still coming to terms with the sense of freedom it gave her with him. It was so good to feel there weren't any barriers between them. Except those in her own mind. It was now up to her to try hard, too. Today, with his mother. The past had to be buried if they were really looking at a future together.

Satisfied that she had achieved a readily *acceptable* appearance for the critical eyes of Lillian Dane, Katie took a deep breath to settle her fluttering nerves and set about collecting the items she wanted to take with her. She put her lipstick and hairbrush in her shoulder-bag which she laid, ready to hand, on the kitchen counter, then dealt with the pretty bunch of spring flowers she had bought as a peace gift to Carver's mother.

The doorbell rang just as she finished tying a ribbon around the cone of tissue paper. Cradling the bouquet in one arm and slinging the strap of her bag over her shoulder, Katie told herself to approach this meeting with smiling confidence, knowing she had Carver's support. Which his mother had to know, as well. And it was ten years down the track. So it shouldn't go wrong.

Nevertheless, her heart was pitter-pattering as she opened the door. To her surprise, it wasn't only Carver who'd come to collect her. Susannah was holding his hand, looking absolutely adorable in a lime green top and a white bib and braces skirt outfit, printed with violets. Her big brown eyes sparkled excitement at Katie, who instantly forgot Lillian Dane in the pleasure of this child's pleasure in seeing her.

A bubble of inner delight instantly spread into a smile. "Hello, Susannah!"

A big smile back. "Hello, Katie."

"I wasn't expecting you to come for me, too."

"Daddy said I could."

"Waiting was beyond her," Carver said dryly. "Ready to go?"

"Yes."

Somehow Susannah's presence made everything easier. The car trip to Hunters Hill in a Volvo station wagon felt like a family affair with conversation flowing from the front seats to Susannah holding forth from her special seat in the back, a much more confident child in a familiar environment, with her father in obvious control of the situation. Carver's relaxed manner was infectious, and Katie found herself laughing along with him at Susannah's artless enthusiasm in engaging Katie's attention.

Several times she caught herself remembering the old days when laughter had been part and parcel of their relationship—having fun together. Laughter and love should go hand in hand, she thought, sharing joy. *This* was champagne, far more so than great sex, though glancing at Carver in his physique-hugging, cotton knit white shirt, and the blue jeans stretching around his powerful thighs, the physical desire he stirred was as strong as ever.

She shouldn't be thinking about it—especially when he was exercising restraint to prove she meant more than a convenient sexual pleasure to him. But

it was difficult not to be aware of his attractive masculinity and all it promised on a physical level. He
didn't have to keep holding back, she decided. It *was*
different now. Though there was still the meeting with
his mother ahead of her.

She loved Carver's home at first sight, a long
sprawling redbrick house set on large landscaped
grounds. It looked friendly, welcoming, not the least
bit intimidating though she realised it represented a
very solid financial investment. Carver drove straight
into a garage big enough for three cars, and they used
a connecting door to enter the house.

As he ushered Katie into a well-appointed kitchen,
he urged his daughter forward. ''Run ahead,
Susannah, and tell Nanna we're here.''

The little girl was only too eager to carry the news,
which allowed them some private time together. Katie
glanced at him, nervous now at not quite knowing
what to expect.

He smiled, his eyes caressing her with warmth.
''You look beautiful, Katie. I just wanted to assure
you my mother is more than ready to welcome you.''

''That's good to know,'' she said gratefully, though
she couldn't help wondering if he had pressured his
mother to accept what she was in no position to refuse. Clearly he had provided her with so much, what
choice did Lillian Dane have?

''The flowers are a kind thought.''

''I hope she likes them.''

''I'm sure she'll appreciate the gesture.''

The kitchen opened onto a large casual dining area
where the table was already set for lunch with many

covered dishes suggesting everything was pre-prepared for easy service. Double glass doors gave access onto a wide verandah and Susannah's voice floated back to them from outside.

"Nanna, she's here! Katie's here!"

The answer was indistinct.

One of the doors had been left open and Carver waved her forward. Katie stepped out, her gaze catching a fine view of Sydney Harbour, then a wheelchair ramp leading from the verandah to the extensive lawn below it. The ramp was a jolting reminder that Lillian Dane was no longer the formidable figure memory conjured up, and as Katie turned to the sound of Susannah's bright chatter, she was shocked to see how *little* Carver's mother looked, little and white-haired and older than she could possibly be in years.

She was sitting in an electric wheelchair which was angled towards Susannah and slightly away from the table in front of her, a table strewn with Sunday news-papers. She held an indulgent smile for her grand-daughter who was claiming her attention, but her eyes flicked nervously at Katie as Carver escorted her along the verandah.

Nervously!

"Look, Nanna! Katie brought you some pretty flowers. Just like on her dress," Susannah said ad-miringly.

"How lovely! Thank you," she said, accepting them graciously as Katie presented them.

"Mrs. Dane, how are you?"

"Fine! It's good to see you again, Katie." She ges-tured to one of the ordinary chairs at the table. "Do sit down. Carver?'' She looked up at her son. "Will you put these flowers in a vase for me? I'll take them to my living room later. They look so bright and cheerful.''

"Sure, Mum.''

She handed them to him. "And I switched the coffee-maker on so it should be ready by now.'' An anxious flash at Katie who was settling on the chair indicated. "Carver said you liked coffee.''

"Yes, I do. Thank you.''

"Bring it out, dear,'' she instructed her son. "And Susannah, will you fetch the plate of cookies from the kitchen counter?''

"Yes, Nanna.''

Father and daughter went off together, leaving the two women together. Katie sat warily silent, sure that Lillian Dane had just manipulated a situation she wanted. The moment she felt it was safe to speak without being overheard, the older woman leaned forward, her dark eyes determined on the course she had decided upon, but seemingly fearful of it, as well.

"I know you couldn't have told Carver what I did. What I said to you all those years ago,'' she started, clearly searching for answers to end the torment in her mind.

"No, I haven't,'' Katie said quietly, stunned to find Lillian Dane frightened of *her* influence over Carver's feelings.

"Will you?'' she pressed, resolved on knowing Katie's intentions.

"No. That's behind us, Mrs. Dane.''

She shook her head. "The past is always with us.

I know it's my fault. My fault that Carver's been un-happy all these years.'' Guilt threaded her words, yet there was pride and purpose, too, as she added, ''He's been so good to me. The best possible son. I want him to be happy. He deserves to be.''

Katie couldn't think of anything to say. As always, Lillian Dane thought only of what she wanted for her son. It seemed some strange irony that she now saw Katie as a possible source of happiness for him. But then, hadn't her father accepted the same thing—that Carver might be the man who could make her happy?

A claw-like hand reached out and clutched Katie's arm. It stunned her even further to see tears film Lillian Dane's eyes. Yet when she spoke her voice was strong, with the kind of strength that had always driven this woman to do what she had to do to achieve what she wanted.

''I know you wouldn't want me here, Katie Beaumont. How could you?'' The thin fingers dug deeper. ''I promise you I'll go. Being a handicapped person, I'm given a good pension. I can get myself into an assisted-care place…''

''Please, I have no wish to put your out of your home. What kind of person do you think I am?'' Katie cried, appalled by what was being suggested. ''Besides, nothing has been decided between Carver and me.''

''But it will come up. I know it will. And you won't want to live with me under the same roof.''

''Perhaps it's you who won't want to live with me,'' Katie flashed back, the memory of this woman's scathing diatribe slicing through her wish to make peace.

"Don't you understand?" It was an urgent plea. "I don't want to be a factor in stopping what Carver wants with you. Nor will I get in the way. God knows I've learnt my lesson about interfering in what I shouldn't." Her eyes looked feverish with determination. "I can't take back what I did, but I can clear the way this time. That would be some reparation."

"Truly, there's no need for this," Katie asserted, thinking there had to be some better way of resolving this conflict.

"*Listen* to me!" It was a desperate command. "Back then...it felt as though you were taking him away from me. I was jealous...cruel...wanting to get rid of you so I could have my son to myself again. I remember it all, so don't pretend it's not in your mind, too."

She darted a look along the verandah, afraid she was running out of time. Katie held her tongue, realising Lillian Dane had to unburden herself of the torment she must have been going through since Carver had told her Katie Beaumont was in his life again.

Her gaze fastened once more on Katie's, anxious to make the situation clear. "I won't stay and be a bone of contention between you and Carver. All I ask is you don't tell him what I did. I couldn't bear it if..." The strength of her resolution gave way to a burst of emotional agitation. "...if he didn't visit me now and then. With Susannah..."

"You have my solemn promise I won't tell him,

Mrs. Dane," Katie stated emphatically, intent on removing that source of fear.

"You promise..."

"Yes. He will never know from me."

She sagged back into her wheelchair, her hand sliding from Katie's arm. Her eyes were still not at peace. "He has a good heart, Carver."

"I know."

"And Susannah...she's the sweetest child."

"Yes, she is."

"Can you be happy with them?"

"I am happy with them, Mrs. Dane."

She folded her hands in her lap and heaved a deep sigh, looking both relieved and drained. "Take this as my apology, Katie Beaumont...that I'm ready and willing to leave my son and grand-daughter to you."

Katie took a deep breath and stated her own position. "I don't want that apology, Mrs. Dane. What you've been planning is as divisive as anything you've done in the past."

She looked startled, as though she hadn't seen it that way.

Katie ploughed on. "Once again you're making me out as spoiled rich bitch who thinks only of herself."

A negative jerk of her head which only riled Katie further. She wasn't going to let Carver's mother have her way this time. She was going to fight the prejudice and wear it down if it was the last thing she did!

"Do you imagine Susannah will thank me for losing the Nanna who has cared for her since she was born?"

''She'll have you,'' came the flash of blind reasoning.

''And Carver had you when you succeeded in getting rid of me. Did *you* make up for the loss of that love, Mrs. Dane?''

She stared at Katie, a painful confusion of guilt in her eyes.

''Perhaps you want Carver to think that I now want to be rid of you. Another contest between us, Mrs. Dane? Is that the twisted motive behind this offered sacrifice of your home here?''

''No.'' Her shock was genuine. ''I swear it's not!''

''Then make the effort to live *with* me,'' Katie bored in, determined to shake this woman into seeing the real truth. ''Try getting to know me, instead of treating me as a hostile force. Running away doesn't resolve anything. That was the lesson I learnt, Mrs. Dane. Ten years in the wilderness…''

''I'm sorry. I'm sorry I did that…to both of you.''

''Then stay and help to make it better,'' Katie argued with a ferocity of feeling she couldn't temper in the face of the entrenched view Carver's mother had of her. ''What good can it do…making this grand gesture of leaving? Why don't you work at being friends with me? For Carver's sake. For Susannah's sake. Am I so abhorrent to you that you can't stand the thought of even trying for a truce between us?''

''You want…a truce?'' The idea seemed alien to everything she had thought about this meeting.

''Why not? Don't we both care about the same people? Isn't that a bond we can share?''

Carver's and Susannah's voices drifted out from the house, indicating they were on their way back.

"Think about it, Mrs. Dane," Katie urged. "If you're really sorry for what you did, try making it better. For all of us."

CHAPTER FIFTEEN

KATIE had just completed the last booked trip for the morning when her car phone rang, which probably meant a job she didn't want right now. Every day this week she'd been planning to get to the Formal Hire shop at Chatswood, needing something to wear to the FX Ball, but she'd been picking up so much casual business, here it was, Thursday, and time was getting short with the ball happening tomorrow night.

In two minds about accepting any extra work today, Katie activated the receiver, and was instantly relieved to hear a familiar voice.

"Katie, it's your father. Are you finished for the morning?"

"Yes, Dad."

"Then come and have lunch with me."

She frowned, wondering if it could be fitted in. With the last two Sundays having been taken up with very personal business, she hadn't seen her father for almost three weeks. "Where are you?" she asked, thinking of distances to be covered.

"Where are *you?*" came the immediate retort.

"I'm at St. Leonards, heading towards Chatswood. I need to a hire a ball gown for..."

"*Hire?* You mean...get some second-hand dress? You're going to a ball with Carver Dane in a second-hand dress?"

Katie sighed at his outraged pride. "No one will know, Dad."

"Katie, just you turn around right now and head into the city," he commanded autocratically. "You can park under the Opera House. I'll pay the parking fee."

"Dad, that's right out of my way," Katie protested. "I don't have a great deal of time."

"If Carver Dane could make time to have lunch with me yesterday, my daughter can certainly make time today," he declared.

"Carver? You've met Carver?"

"I'll wait for you at the oyster bar on the quay. Fine morning for oysters."

"Dad…"

He was gone. And trying to call him back was bound to be futile. She knew he wouldn't respond. He'd put in the hook to get his own way and the bait was too intriguing for Katie to resist. The ball gown could wait. Knowing what had transpired between her father and Carver couldn't.

It both stunned and alarmed her that her father had chosen to contact Carver at this somewhat delicate turning point in their relationship, probably deciding *he knew best,* as usual, and a push from him would get his daughter what she wanted.

Katie gritted her teeth in frustration at his arrogance. Didn't he realise that interference—especially from him—would be unwelcome? Had he suddenly decided that offering an apology—a very, very late apology—might help? If so, how had Carver responded to it?

With her heart fluttering in agitation and her mind whirling with wild speculation, Katie took the road which would lead her across the Harbour Bridge to Benelong Point. It was a waste of time, wishing her father had left well enough alone. It was done now. But she couldn't help worrying about the effect of his intrusion.

She really didn't need this complication. It had been difficult enough last Sunday, moving into a truce situation with Carver's mother. Lillian Dane's predetermined decisions might have been well-meant, but hardly helpful. Potentially destructive would be a better description. Katie hoped she had set the older woman straight on that score.

Certainly, after their altercation on the verandah, Carver's mother had made the effort to treat her as a welcome guest, though it was impossible to tell if that was more to please her son and grand-daughter than to actually extend the hand of friendship to a woman she'd previously planned on avoiding as far as possible.

Carver had been pleased with the meeting, believing it had established a bridge from the past to a future where rejection was not in the cards. Katie had not cast any doubt on this belief. She hoped he was right. The burning question now was if any hopeful bridge had been established between him and her father?

Since it was almost midday, the traffic was flowing fairly easily and Katie made it to the car park under the Opera House in good time. She hot-footed it to the oyster bar where she found her father settled at one of the open-air tables with a commanding view of Circular Quay. A plate of empty oyster shells implied his appetite was not the least bit diminished by the prospect of confessing his interference in *her* relationship with Carver. Katie hoped that was a good sign.

"Ah, there you are!" he said complacently, smiling as she took the chair waiting for her.

"What did you say to Carver?" she burst out, intent on pinning him down.

"First things first." He signalled a hovering waiter and received instant attention. "A dozen Kilpatrick oysters for my daughter and another dozen natural for me. And some of that crusty bread. Better bring two cappuccinos, as well. My daughter's in a hurry."

Katie barely contained her impatience. The moment the waiter, who'd undoubtedly been liberally tipped already, moved away she went on the attack again. "How could you, Dad?"

"How could I what?" he answered, infuriatingly effecting a sublimely innocent air.

"Stick your nose in," she fired at him.

His eyebrows arched. "You would have preferred me to refuse Carver's invitation to lunch with him?"

"Carver's?"

"*He* called *me,* Katie. I didn't think you'd want me to snub him."

"No, of course not," she said weakly, the wind completely taken out of her sails. "What did he want with you?"

"Oh, I guess you could call it touching base," came the somewhat ironic reply. "Some diplomatic easing around what happened in the past. My equally diplomatic apology was accepted. In fact, it was quite a masterly exercise in diplomacy all around.''

''No fighting?''

''Katie…'' he chided. ''…I promised you I wouldn't put a foot wrong this time around.''

She heaved a sigh to relieve the tightness in her chest.

''Your Carver was clearly prepared to fight with words,'' her father went on, ''but given no opposition from me, we reached an understanding very quickly and had quite a pleasant lunch together.''

''No sparring at all?''

''Merely a little deft manoeuvring until positions were made clear.'' His eyes twinkled amusement. ''We parted on terms of mutual respect so you have nothing to worry about.''

''Mutual respect,'' she repeated, wondering why Carver had taken this initiative. He could have waited until she set up a meeting. On the other hand, maybe a man-to-man talk was better for sweeping problems out of the way, and more easily accomplished without her being present.

''He's turned into a very impressive young man,'' her father commented.

''He was always impressive.''

''Well, I'll not be arguing with you. Just rest assured that your old dad does want to see you happy, Katie. If Carver Dane is your choice, he's my choice.''

She eyed him uncertainly. ''Did you really like him this time, Dad?''

He nodded. "If I were doing the choosing for you, he'd definitely be a prime candidate."

She relaxed into a smile, recognising the accolade as genuine.

"Now tell me about this ball you need a dress for."

"Carver's asked me to partner him to the FX Ball. It's all financial markets people, a networking evening for him."

"When is it?"

"Tomorrow night. It's being held at Sheraton on the Park."

"Uh-huh."

The waiter returned with their lunch order. Now that her stomach was unknotted, Katie attacked her oysters with great appetite, mopping up the Kilpatrick sauce with the crusty bread.

"That *was* good!" she declared, sitting back replete and smiling her satisfaction. "Thanks, Dad."

"My pleasure. And it would give me even greater pleasure if you let me buy you a ball gown."

She eyed him wryly. "Please don't start trying to run my life again. Just because..."

"Now, Katie, you haven't let me buy you anything for a long time," he broke in, frowning his frustration. "A father's entitled to give his daughter a few fripperies."

"A ball gown isn't a frippery."

He waved a dismissive hand, and she knew the cost was irrelevant to him. He wouldn't even blink at tossing away a few thousand dollars on a dress that might only be worn once. Was she clinging too hard to her independence? Her father had put in a huge effort to reduce their estrangement. Maybe it was time to go his way…at least a little.

"You can't partner Carver at a ball like that in a hired gown," he insisted, leaning forward to lay down his law. "He'll be out to impress people and… dammit, Katie! You're my daughter! He'll be introducing you to all these top-level people in the finance world—Katie Beaumont—and I will not have you dressed in second-hand clothing."

Pride!

Well, there was no escaping the fact she was her father's daughter, and if it made him happy…a dress was only a dress.

"I admit I should have backed your business when you asked me to," he rolled on, gathering steam. "I admit I've made a lot of mistakes where you're concerned. But, Katie…"

"All right, Dad."

It caught him off-stride. "All right what?"

She grinned at him. "You can buy me a ball gown. As long as we do it quickly because I've got to get back to work."

His face lit with triumphant pleasure. Action stations instantly came into play. "Waiter! Waiter! The bill?" A finger stabbed at Katie. "Get that coffee drunk right now. We're going shopping, my girl, and *you* are going to *slay* Carver Dane tomorrow night!"

CHAPTER SIXTEEN

IT WAS a fabulous dress—a Versace design that fitted her like a second skin. Fashioned from Shantung silk, a shimmering scarlet shot through with gold, the strapless bodice hugged her curves, and the slimline front view of the skirt accentuated the rest of her femininity and highlighted the lustrous fall of a graceful train at the back. It hadn't cost a million dollars, but Katie felt like a million dollars in it.

A gold bracelet had a special clip to which she could attach the train when dancing, and long dangly gold earrings were the perfect accompaniment to the dress. Katie had fastened her hair back from her face to show off the earrings, and the tumble of black curls behind her ears made a great frame for them.

When the doorbell rang, announcing Carver's arrival, her eyes were sparkling with the pleasure of knowing she couldn't look better. Her father was right about some things. She did want Carver to feel proud of her as his partner tonight, in front of his peers in the business world. Such a *public* outing was another step up in their relationship, and this dress certainly gave her the confidence to carry it off successfully.

She was smiling over her father's words—*You're going to slay Carver Dane*—as she opened the door, but seeing Carver, so strikingly handsome in a formal dinner suit, she forgot all about her own appearance.

177

She loved this man, and her desire for him squeezed her heart, caught the breath in her throat, and shot a tremulous feeling through her entire body.

For several seconds they simply stared at each other, the hunger of years burning slowly to a crescendo of need that pulsed with the sense that at last, *this* was the time, *this* was the moment when everything could be right.

Carver took a deep breath. His dark eyes glittered with an intensity of feeling that pierced Katie's soul. This was how it had once been. This was how it was now. And she revelled in the moment of magic that had leapt the terrible gap of missed chances and brought to life this elated certainty that nothing more could go wrong. Ever!

"You make me feel...very privileged...to be your escort tonight, Katie," Carver murmured.

She took a deep breath and a bubble of sheer joy broke into a smile. "You're the only escort I've ever wanted, Carver."

Her impulsive response seemed to evoke a shadow of pain in his eyes before he smiled back and held out his arm. "Shall we go?"

"Yes," she answered eagerly, telling herself she must have imagined the slight darkening of his pleasure.

Once he tucked her arm around his to take her out to his car, everything seemed perfect again. He saw her settled into the passenger seat of the Audi roadster, carefully tucking in the train of her dress before closing the door. The hood of the sports car was up tonight, and Katie was grateful for the forethought. It saved her hair from being tossed into an unruly mass of curls by the wind.

She watched Carver settle into the driver's seat beside her and close his door, sealing them into an intimate little world of their own. We're on our way, she thought, as he leaned forward to insert the car key into the ignition. On our way together. Really together.

Carver gripped the car key, telling himself to switch on the engine, get going, move on. Katie wouldn't want to revisit the pain of the past. She'd put it behind her. What she'd said to his mother proved that beyond a doubt—wanting it set aside, forgotten and forgiven. And she was here with him, her whole body language poignantly telegraphing this was *right* for her.

Which made it all the more impossible to wipe out the injustice he'd done her in his mind—an injustice that had influenced his attitude towards her, inflicting more hurt. He couldn't turn the key. He had to *put it right* first. This journey tonight had to start with a clean slate.

He sat back, reaching over to take her hand in his before he spoke, needing a physical link to lighten the burden on his heart. Katie was startled by the action, her eyes filling with questions at the delay in their departure. Carver secured his grip on her hand by interlacing their fingers, then faced her with what he now knew.

"I've always believed you didn't love me as much as I loved you, Katie. For you to cut and run as you did..."

She sucked in a quick breath, clearly feeling attacked.

"But it wasn't like that," he quickly asserted. "I know you left me because of all my mother said to you at the hospital when the doctors were working on my broken jaw. Her virulence, coming on top of your father's violence...you thought it was best for me if you took yourself out of my life."

"Yes," she whispered. "I didn't want you hurt because of me, Carver. And your mother..."

"She told me, Katie."

"When?" she asked, clearly perplexed.

"A few days ago."

"Since...Sunday."

"Yes. All these years I didn't know. From the time you left I thought...I imagined you...finding other *more suitable* men..."

"No," she cried, squeezing his hand in agitation.

Realising he'd used a bitter tone, Carver tried to correct it. "I couldn't blame you if you had, after being treated like that by my mother. I'm trying to explain... I lost faith in your feeling for me, so when we met this time, I wouldn't let you close to me."

"But you have, Carver," she said, her relief palpable.

"I wish you'd told me, Katie. I wasn't fair to you."

"She *is* your mother. You wouldn't have wanted to believe me."

It was a truth he couldn't deny. Even from his mother's own mouth, the admissions of her malicious venom had appalled him...how she'd seized the most opportune time to make Katie feel like the lowest of the low, flaying her with vicious names, accusing her of selfishly ruining his life, blaming her for crimes that hadn't even been committed.

"They were lies, Katie. Lies about your effect on me and my studies. Lies about me wanting to drop out because of you. And she hated you because she saw you as being of a privileged class—a silver spoon in your mouth—while she had had it tough all her life, working hard to give me the chances she'd never had. To her, being a doctor represented success on every level and she saw you as getting in the way."

"Perhaps I was," came the sober comment.

"No. I would have worked my butt off at anything to secure a good future for us. My mother simply couldn't bear you being the focus of my life instead of her."

"I think my father felt the same way."

"Possessive parents," he grimly agreed. "But mine was far more destructive. The scathing way she cut you down…"

"I don't want it recalled now, Carver," she pleaded.

"I'm sorry. I just…" He caught himself back. The horror of it was new to him, but she'd lived with it all these years and risen above it. "It's incredibly generous to let it all slide as you have," he said with deep sincerity. "In fact, it was the generous way you dealt with my mother last Sunday that shamed her into confessing the part she'd played in driving you away."

"Part of it was my father, too, Carver. For me, it was shock on top of shock."

"I understand. It all makes sense to me now. And I'm sorry I ever thought harshly about the decision you made."

"Your mother asked me not to tell."

"So she said. I think that promise finally forced her to be fair to you, Katie." He rubbed his thumb over her skin, wishing he could dig under it. "Can you forgive me for doubting your feelings?"

"You had reason to, Carver," she said softly. "I should have talked to you." Her eyes shone with eloquent emotion. "But I promise...this is true. You are—you've always been—the only man I've ever loved."

"And you the only woman I've ever loved," he returned, intensely grateful for her response to him and seizing the moment to press what he most wanted. "I told your father so on Wednesday."

She looked dazed. "He didn't tell me that."

"I wanted him to know I intended to marry you...if you'd have me."

"Marry?" It was a bare whisper, as though she couldn't quite bring herself to believe it, but she wanted to. Her eyes glistened with the inner vision of a dream coming true.

Carver reached into his pocket and brought out the velvet jeweler's box he'd planned to open some time tonight...when it felt right. The sense of rightness was coursing through him so strongly, waiting another second was beyond him. He flicked the top up as he held the box out to her.

"They say diamonds are forever. Will you marry me, Katie?"

She stared down at the ring—a solitaire diamond set on a simple gold band. Then she looked up and there was no mistaking the love swimming in her eyes. "Yes, I will. I will marry you, Carver. And it will be forever."

He had to kiss her. He yearned to make love to her, but that had to wait until later. It was a kiss that filled him with the sweetest satisfaction he'd ever known.

"My fiancée, Katie Beaumont."

Every time Carver said those words, introducing her to the people he knew at the ball, Katie felt as though she would burst with happiness. It was difficult not to keep glancing at the magnificent diamond ring on her finger—the ring that proclaimed to everyone that she and Carver were engaged to be married—the ring that promised this really was forever, symbolising a love that had lasted the test of time and always would, despite anything the future might throw at them.

It gradually dawned on Katie that her father had guessed what Carver intended tonight. That was why he'd been so insistent on buying a special dress—to make the night even more special. A gift of love, she thought, not pride, and made a strong mental note to give her father a big thank-you hug.

Lillian Dane's confession to Carver was a gift of love, too—a setting straight, putting doubts to rest. Katie silently vowed to view her much more kindly in future.

Her father...his mother...both of them had made amends as best they could.

"Katie?"

Amanda's voice?

She turned to see her old school friend on Max's arm, both of them paused on their walk down the ballroom, their faces expressing uncertainty in her identity.

"It *is* you!" Amanda cried in delighted surprise. "Why didn't you tell me you'd be here? And how!" She rolled her eyes down the Versace gown and up again. "You look fabulous!"

"Yes, doesn't she?" Carver warmly agreed, swinging them both around for a more formal greeting. "Good evening, Amanda…Max."

"Carver!" Amanda's eyes almost popped out.

"Good to see both of you," Max rolled out smoothly.

"Good to see you, too," Katie replied, her inner joy sparkling through an extra-wide smile as she held out her left hand. "Look, Amanda!"

"I don't believe it! A rock!" she squealed, then looked goggle-eyed at Carver.

He grinned at her. "Katie said yes."

"You got to a proposal in less than two weeks?" she said incredulously.

"Oh, I'd say it was about ten years overdue," Carver drawled good-humouredly.

Amanda heaved a sigh of triumphant satisfaction. "I just knew it was simply a matter of getting the two of you together." She hugged her husband's arm. "We did it, Max."

The band started playing an introduction to a

bracket of dance numbers. Carver turned to Katie, his eyes dancing with wicked mischief.

"Shall we dance, Carmen?"

She laughed and gathered up her train, clicking the end of it onto her bracelet. "Where you lead, I shall follow," she responded flirtatiously.

"What do you mean...Carmen?" Amanda demanded, eyeing them suspiciously.

Carver slid his arm around Katie's waist, ready to swing her out to the centre of the ballroom. He grinned at Amanda and raised his other hand in a salute to her. "The masked buccaneer thanks you for bringing us together."

"The masked buccaneer?" Amanda gaped as enlightenment dawned. *"The pirate king!"*

Definitely *her king,* Katie thought, as they moved across the dance floor, in tune with the music and beautifully, wonderfully, in total tune with each other. The desire which had been ignited so strongly at the masked ball, simmered between them, their bodies once again revelling in touch and feeling, loving the tease of sensual contact, exulting in the certainty that the most exquisite satisfaction was theirs for the taking.

"This dance will never be over, Katie," Carver whispered in her ear.

"No more walking alone," she sighed contentedly.

He pulled her closer so they moved as one.

Not too early...not too late.

This time was right.

MISTRESS ON HIS TERMS

by

Catherine Spencer

Catherine Spencer, once an English teacher, fell into writing through eavesdropping on a conversation about Harlequin romances. Within two months she changed careers and sold her first book to Mills & Boon in 1984. She moved to Canada from England thirty years ago and lives in Vancouver. She is married to a Canadian and has four grown children – two daughters and two sons – plus three dogs and a cat. In her spare time she plays the piano, collects antiques, and grows tropical shrubs.

CHAPTER ONE

"I'LL be waiting by the baggage claim carousel," Hugo Preston had told her, when they'd spoken by phone the night before. "You'll know me by my gray hair and the bouquet of roses I'll have brought for you—red roses, because tomorrow's a red-letter day for me. I'm counting the hours until we meet, Lily."

But the other passengers had already collected their belongings and gone, leaving Lily standing alone with her two suitcases and carry-on bags stowed in a luggage cart. Although there'd been a number of older men with gray hair waiting to meet the Vancouver flight when it landed on time in Toronto, none had been carrying roses, nor had any come forward to identify himself as her biological father.

Caught between a sense of letdown and resentment—so much for his anxiety to connect with the daughter he'd always known about but never met!—Lily took out the map tucked in the side pocket of her purse.

Stentonbridge, the small town where Hugo maintained a year-round residence, lay some hundred and fifty miles northeast of Toronto, so she supposed that, because of the heavy rains in the area, it was conceivable that the drive had taken longer than he'd expected.

But then, another scenario rose up to haunt her. What if, even as she stood there silently berating him for his apparent parental disregard, a car crushed beyond recognition was being hauled out of a ravine, and the man she'd come so far to meet lay covered by a sheet in an ambulance bound for the nearest morgue?

Refusing to allow the thought to take root, she stuffed the map back into her bag. Tragedy like that didn't strike twice in a row; it was the terrible exception, not the rule. There was some other perfectly plausible reason for Hugo's tardiness, and quite possibly a message explaining it waiting to be picked up at the airline information desk. If not, he'd given her a number where he could be reached.

Wheeling around, she scanned the arrivals terminal again. A lull between incoming flights left the immediate area relatively uncrowded. Apart from a family of four trying to pack a baby as well as their overflowing bags into one cart, a group of students gathered around their tour leader, and a man forging a purposeful path between the lot of them, she remained in conspicuous isolation.

The man was imposingly tall and the crowd, small though it was, fell back to allow him passage in much the same way, Lily thought with dry amusement, that Moses might have parted the Red Sea. Craning her neck, she peered past him, searching for the familiar Air Canada logo.

He, however, appeared determined not only to obstruct her view but also to occupy the one spot in the whole vast place to which she'd laid claim. In fact, the way he was zeroing in on her, he might have intended running her clean into the ground.

"You're looking for me," he announced tersely, coming to a stop so close that she had to tilt her head back to look into his face and the most arrestingly cold blue eyes she'd ever seen.

But *gray-haired, elderly and kindly* hardly fit his description. "Oh, no, I'm not!" she informed him with equal brevity and attempted to push past him.

He had a hold of her buggy, though, and it wasn't going anywhere without his permission. "You're Lily Talbot," he said, and it occurred to Lily that any other man would have couched the words as a question. But this modern-day Moses wasn't subject to the limitations of the rest of humanity. Preferential treatment from on high had blessed him with special powers. No doubt he could have told her what brand of toothpaste she used, if she'd been of a mind to inquire!

Instead she said stiffly, "More to the point, who are you?"

"Sebastian Caine."

He introduced himself as if the mere mention of his name should be enough to start bells of recognition clanging in the mind of even the most dim-witted person. Not about to cater to such a monumental ego, Lily said, "How nice!" and gave her buggy a determined shove. "Unhand my cart, please. I'd like to make a phone call and find out what happened to the person I'm supposed to meet."

"No need," he said, not budging an inch. "I'm your chauffeur."

Clearly he no more relished the idea of driving her to Stentonbridge than she did. "Oh, I don't think so," she said. "I don't climb into cars with strange men."

A flicker of what might have been a smile twitched the corners of his mouth before he wrestled it back into its former severe line. "You haven't known me long enough to label me 'strange,' Miss Talbot."

"It's 'Ms.,'" she said. "And regardless of whatever label you care to hang around your neck, I'm not getting into a car with you. I'll wait until Mr. Preston gets here."

"Hugo isn't coming."

She'd been afraid of that. "Why not?"

"Because I persuaded him to stay at home."

"And he always does as you tell him, does he?"

"Not as often as he should," Sebastian Caine said bitterly. "If he did, you wouldn't be here now and I wouldn't be wasting my time carrying on this inane conversation. Let go of the damned luggage cart, for pity's sake! I'm not about to abscond with it—or you, come to that. But I would like to load up and be out of here before the rush hour gets any worse."

He'd referred to Hugo by his first name without any prompting from her. He'd known who she was. He wore a look of unimpeachable propriety. His clothes, his watch, even his haircut were expensive, and he no more resembled a kidnapper than she did a call girl. But appearances could be deceiving, as she'd learned to her considerable cost. "I'm not going anywhere with you until I've verified your identity with my father," she said.

He stiffened and a grimace of aversion rolled over his face, as if her referring to Hugo as her father was an affront to decent society. Lips compressed in annoyance, he produced a cell phone from the inside pocket of his jacket, punched in a two-digit code and thrust the instrument at her. "Be my guest."

She accepted it warily, still not entirely sure she ought to trust him. But a glance at the illuminated screen showed Hugo's name and number.

"Will you for pity's sake hit Send and get on with it," Sebastian Caine snapped, noting her reluctance. "It's a phone, not a bomb. It won't explode in your hand."

Hugo answered on the third ring. "I'm so glad you called, Lily," he said. "There's been a slight change in plan—an old back injury's flared up to give me grief, so my stepson Sebastian's meeting your flight and driving you up here. He's about six foot three, dark haired, good-looking so the women tell me, and hard to miss even in a crowd.''

Add rude, arrogant and condescending, and the description would be complete, Lily thought. ''We've met,'' she said, glaring at Sebastian Caine and itching to wipe the smug expression off his face. ''He's standing in front of me, even as we speak.'' *Not to mention practically stealing the air I breathe!*

''Excellent! Ask him if we should hold dinner for you.''

She did so, and could have been forgiven for thinking, from the way Sebastian commandeered the phone and hunched one shoulder away from her, that his answer conveyed information pertinent to national security. His voice carried loud and clear, though, as he said, ''Hugo? Better not wait dinner for us. This afternoon's meeting ran late and I've got one more call to make before I head back.''

Whatever Hugo replied had Sebastian casting her another of his disapproving looks. ''I suppose so, if you like that sort of thing,'' he eventually said, ''but I can't say I see any startling family resemblance. She could be anybody from anywhere.''

He made it sound as if she were something unwholesome he'd scraped off the sidewalk! If it weren't that she had no more sense of direction than a drunken field mouse, she'd have dearly loved to rent her own car and tell him to stick his offer to drive her where it would lodge most uncomfortably. Instead she swallowed her pride and allowed him to hustle her and her baggage out to the parking area.

Practically sprinting to keep up with him as he plowed his way to where he'd left his car, she asked, ''How long will it take to drive to Stentonbridge?''

"Normally around three hours. Today, because of the weather and delays, more like four or five."

To say he sounded ticked off gave grim new meaning to the word understatement. "I'm sorry you've been inconvenienced on my account. I'd have been just as happy to take a train or bus."

"None run from here to Stentonbridge and even if one did, Hugo wouldn't hear of it." His voice took on a derisive edge. "You're the long-lost daughter returning to the fold, and he wants you welcomed in style."

"It's rather obvious you don't share his enthusiasm."

He spared her a brief, dismissive glance. "Why should I? Even if you're who you claim you are—"

"There's no *even if* about it," she said. "I have documented proof."

"Which has yet to be verified as authentic." He swung the luggage cart to a halt behind a sports car as long, dark and sleekly handsome as its owner, popped open the trunk and started piling her bags inside. "You want any of this stuff in the front with you?"

"No."

"Then since the door's unlocked, climb in and get settled. I'm in a hurry."

"Well, silly me!" she said sweetly. "Here I thought you were merely in training for a decathlon!"

He raised one winged brow and cast her a look that might have turned a more prudent woman to stone. "Don't push your luck, Ms. Talbot. You've already tried my patience to the limit."

"And how have I done that, Sebastian?"

His pinched nostrils told her exactly what he thought of such untoward familiarity. "You're here, aren't you?" he said. "Isn't that enough?"

"But I'm not here to see *you*. In fact, crushing though

it might be for you to hear this, I didn't even know of your existence until ten minutes ago.''

"You raise an interesting question nonetheless," he said, slamming closed the trunk and ushering her into the passenger seat with more haste than gallantry before sliding his rangy frame behind the steering wheel. "Why, after all this time, do you want to see Hugo?"

"He's my father. What better reason is there?"

"But why now? If you're telling the truth, he's been your father all your life."

"I didn't know that until recently."

"Precisely my point, Ms. Talbot. You've managed without him for the better part of twenty-six years. You're well past the point where you need a guardian. There's no emotional tie between you. So what's the real reason you're suddenly sniffing around?"

He made her sound like an ill-bred bloodhound. "It's highly personal and not something I choose to share with a total stranger."

"There are no secrets between Hugo and me."

"Apparently there are," she said smugly. "Judging by your reaction to my sudden appearance, he never confided to you that he had a daughter waiting in the wings."

"Maybe," Sebastian replied, giving back as good as he got, "because he never missed you. The daughter he *does* know and love more than compensated for your absence."

"I have a...sister?" The concept struck a strangely unsettling, though not unpleasant note. She had been an only child who'd always wanted to be part of a big family, but there hadn't even been cousins she could be close to. No aunts or uncles, and no grandparents. Just her mother and the man she'd known as her father. "We don't need anyone else," he'd often said. "The three of us have each other."

Three, that was, until the September day ten months before, when a police officer showed up at her door and told her her parents were among the fatalities of a multivehicle accident on a foggy highway in North Carolina.

"Half sister," Sebastian Caine said. "Natalie is Hugo's child by his second marriage to my mother."

"So what does that make you and me?" she asked, aiming to introduce a more cordial tone to the conversation. "Half stepbrother and sister?"

He cut her off in a voice as cold and sharp as the blade of an ax. "It makes us nothing."

"Well, praise heaven!" she replied, stung.

"Indeed."

They'd cleared the airport by then and joined the stream of traffic headed through the pouring rain for downtown Toronto. He was probably a very skilled driver, but the memory of her parents as they'd looked when she'd gone to make a positive identification remained too fresh in her mind, and the way Sebastian Caine zipped around slower vehicles left her bracing herself for disaster.

"Keep pumping an imaginary brake like that, and you'll wind up putting your foot through the floor," he observed, zooming up behind another car with what struck her as cavalier disregard for safety.

"I don't fancy ending up in someone else's trunk, that's all."

He sort of smiled. At least, she supposed that was what the movement of his lips amounted to. "Do I make you nervous, Ms. Talbot?"

She closed her eyes as he changed lanes and zipped past a moving truck. "Yes."

"Then you're wiser than I expected."

Her eyes flew open again. "What's that supposed to mean?"

"It means I don't trust you or your motives. It means I'll be watching every move you make while you're here. Put a foot wrong, and I'll be all over you."

"How exciting. Be still my heart!"

"I'm serious."

"I can see that you are. What puzzles me is why I'm such a threat to your peace of mind. I assure you I don't plan to run off with the family silver or murder people in their beds. I have questions that only Hugo Preston can answer, that's all."

"You didn't have to come halfway across the country for that. The telephone was invented a long time ago."

"I'm curious to meet my father face-to-face."

"I just bet you are!" he sneered.

She shrugged. "So sue me."

"Give me reason to, and I will."

She stared at him, unable to fathom his hostility, but his expression gave nothing away and she wasn't about to beg for an explanation. "I'm afraid you're in for a terrible disappointment," she said instead. "I have no hidden agenda in coming here."

His mouth tightened.

"There's nothing unnatural in a person wanting to meet her biological parent."

He glanced in the rearview mirror, stepped on the accelerator and raced past a stretch limo. Prickles of sweat broke out along her spine as he took an off-ramp at alarming speed.

Thrusting both palms flat against the dashboard, she asked, "How many auto accidents have you had?"

The question was ill-advised, to say the least. He speared her with a chilly sideways glare, which glimmered with evil amusement. "None. But there's a first time for everything."

"Well, if it's all the same to you, I'd prefer you postpone the premiere performance until I'm not your passenger."

"Your preferences don't rank high on my list of priorities, Ms. Talbot. In fact, it's safe to say they don't register at all. As for your perceived sense of danger, let me assure you I don't intend risking either life or limb on your account."

They'd turned onto a street lined with elegant town houses by then. Braking to a stop next to a van, he shifted into reverse and began backing into a parking space so tight, it invited disaster. She opened her mouth to tell him so, then snapped it closed again as, without a moment's hesitation or a single false move, he angled the car into place and brought it to rest parallel to the curb.

He reached behind her seat, leaning close enough that she got a pleasant whiff of his aftershave, and hauled out a briefcase. "Wait here," he ordered, climbing out of the car. "I won't be long."

Lily watched as he loped across the street and up the steps to a door three houses down. Before he had the chance to ring the bell, a woman appeared. She was very pleased to see him, if the smile and hug she bestowed were anything to go by, and she was also very pregnant. He slung an arm around her shoulders and the two of them disappeared inside the house.

Ten minutes passed, then twenty. The clouds, which had been dense enough to start with, grew even darker. Not long after, a light came on at an upstairs window of the house into which Sebastian Caine had disappeared.

"Oh, fine thing!" Lily muttered resentfully. "I'm left

cooling my heels in here while he has an assignation with his mistress. No wonder he told Hugo not to hold dinner!''

She twisted around and craned her neck, searching the narrow area behind the two front seats in the hope of finding something to wile away the time—a newspaper or magazine, even a map of the area. But the only item of interest was Sebastian's passport lying open and facedown on the floor.

She prided herself on being an essentially decent person, the kind who returned her library books on time, held open doors for the elderly, and told little white lies only when absolutely necessary. She definitely did not consider herself to be the sort who snooped through other people's medicine cabinets or read their mail. But that darned passport drew her like a magnet and before the full import of what she was doing could properly register, she found herself picking it up and sneaking a look inside.

In line with those of most other people she knew, her own passport picture made her look as if she belonged on North America's *Ten Most Wanted* list, but Sebastian Andrew Caine might have commissioned a portrait photographer to produce his. His face stared back at her in all its direct-gazed, firm-jawed glory.

He'd been blessed with impeccable cheekbones, thick black hair, eyelashes to draw the envy of every woman alive and a disarming cleft in his chin. On top of that, as she knew from firsthand observation, he stood well over six feet and probably sent his tailor into raptures over his trim, perfectly proportioned physique.

Too bad he'd been at the end of the receiving line when God dispensed charm!

Though now a Canadian citizen, he'd been born in Harrisburg, Pennsylvania, on April 23, thirty-four years ago. He traveled often and mostly to exotic places like Turkey, Russia, The Far East, Morocco and Greece.

She thumbed through the pages. His most recent port of call had been Cairo; his most far-flung Rarotonga. He'd visited Rio de Janeiro twice in the last three years and the southern Baja four times. What with jaunts all over the world and house calls to his current ladylove, it was a wonder he found time to work!

Annoyed at being kept waiting, Lily slapped the passport closed and turned to glare across the street at the house he'd entered, only to find her view blocked by Sebastian Caine's tall figure. Completely unmindful of the rain pelting down, he stood beside her window, glaring right back at her.

At the realization that she'd been caught blatantly prying into something that was absolutely none of her business, her whole body blushed, starting at her toes and spreading in waves until the blood suffused her face and left it burning. Even her throat and eyeballs felt parched. She could neither swallow nor blink. She simply sat in paralyzed horror and prayed he was a mirage created by the rain weaving patterns down the glass.

At best, it was an unlikely alternative and one he soon disabused her of by striding around the back of the car and wrenching open the driver's door.

Of course, there was no justifying what she'd been caught doing. Still, she felt compelled to try. "It was lying on the floor," she blustered, the minute he climbed into the car.

He didn't speak. He didn't have to. His raised eyebrows told her plainly enough what he thought of *that* as an excuse.

"So I picked it up. A passport's not something to be left lying around, you know."

He leaned back in his seat and continued his frigid, unblinking regard.

Self-preservation told her she was merely digging herself in deeper with every word and that her best bet was to keep quiet. But his silence, charged with unspoken accusation as it was, unnerved her. "I mean, it could just as easily have fallen out on the road without your noticing, and I'm sure you know what a hassle it is trying to get a replacement.... Particularly if you needed to travel overseas in a hurry... Not to mention the ramifications of some underworld figure getting hold of it and putting it to criminal use...and...well..."

"Are you quite done?" he asked, when she finally ran out of steam.

She looked down, realized she was still clutching the passport and hurriedly dropped it into his lap. "Yes."

"Thank God!"

He tossed the passport over his shoulder, and eased the car out of its parking spot. The rush hour was in full swing by then, which made it a bit easier for her to tolerate his aloof silence since she had no wish to distract him from the job of negotiating the heavy traffic. But when the city limits lay far behind them and the only sound to break the twilight hush was the frenzied swipe of the windshield wipers, she decided they'd both sulked long enough.

"I'm afraid," she said, slewing a glance at him, "that we got off to a rocky start and I'd like to apologize for my part in that."

His shrug of acknowledgment could hardly be construed as encouraging.

Still, she persevered. "I really don't make a habit of going through other people's private possessions, you know. But you were gone longer than you led me to expect and I was just looking for something to read."

He favored her with a scathing glance. "In that case, I suppose I should count myself lucky that you stopped with my passport. There must be at least a dozen legal files back there, which would have provided you with much juicier entertainment and after you'd read your fill, you could have blackmailed me for breaching lawyer-client confidentiality."

"I didn't know you're a lawyer."

"And I didn't know you're a meddlesome busybody, so that makes us even."

She shifted in her seat, the better to observe him. He really was quite outstandingly good-looking. "Why are you so determined to dislike me, Sebastian?"

"I have no feelings toward you, one way or the other, Ms. Talbot. I already told you, you're an inconvenience, but I'll get over that as soon as I've deposited you on Hugo's doorstep." He punctuated his statement with a telling pause before continuing, "Provided you don't hurt him or anyone else I care about."

"It's obvious you think I'll do exactly that."

He swung his head and pinioned her in his cold blue stare, and she almost cringed at the expression she saw in their depths. "Let's just say that, in my experience, the apple seldom falls far from the tree."

She stared at him, more perplexed by the second. "Meaning?"

"Meaning if you're anything like your mother—!"

But then, as if he'd given away more than he intended, he clamped his mouth shut and returned his attention to the road.

Lily, though, wasn't so inclined to let the subject drop. "What do you know about my mother?"

"More than I care to."

"Because of things Hugo's told you?"

"Hugo had no contact with her for more than twenty-six years."

"Exactly! Which make his opinions less than reliable."

"Then for once we're in agreement." He flicked on the right turn indicator and slowed the car as they approached the neon-lit entrance to a restaurant set back about fifty yards from the road. "On which fortuitous note, I propose we stop for something to eat. Stentonbridge is still a good two hours' drive away."

Part of her wanted to tell him she was more interested in having him explain his cryptic remarks than she was in food. But another, more cautious part urged her not to pursue the topic. That he knew more than he was telling was plain enough, but although she'd come here looking for answers, she didn't want them from him. Whether or not he'd admit it, there was too much anger seething beneath his surface, and she didn't relish the idea of it bursting loose on some dark country road miles from anywhere.

She'd waited this long to find out the truth. She could wait a few hours longer.

She wasn't what he'd anticipated. Watching her covertly as she studied the menu, he had trouble reconciling the woman sitting opposite him in the booth with his expectations of a vulgar, money-grubbing fortune hunter. He'd been prepared for flashy good looks, provocative necklines, big hair, fake fingernails and too much cheap jewelry. They fit the image. Lily Talbot did not.

Oh, he supposed she was pretty enough, in an ordinary sort of way. More than pretty, some might say. But the cheapness wasn't there, no matter how hard he searched for it. She had narrow, elegant feet. Her hands were delicate, the nails well-cared for and buffed to a soft shine.

Her features were small and regular. Patrician, almost. Her dark brown hair lay smooth and shining against her cheek. She looked out at the world from wide, candid eyes and she smiled a lot. Her mouth was permanently upturned at the corners, her lips soft and full.

Apart from a watch, her only other jewelry was a pair of small gold earrings. She wore a blue denim skirt, which came to just below her knees, a short-sleeved white blouse buttoned to a vee at the front and sandals. Her legs were bare and, he hadn't been able to help noticing, extremely long and shapely. Her skin was lightly tanned and she'd painted her toenails pink. They reminded him of dainty little shells.

Ticked off, he glowered at her, knowing Hugo would love her, that he'd accept her immediately and not once question her motives for suddenly wanting to make contact with him. But the fact remained that her mother's betrayal, over a quarter of a century before, had nearly killed him, and it was Sebastian's self-appointed job to make sure the daughter didn't finish the job now.

Unaware of his scrutiny, she tapped her fingernail against her front teeth and continued to peruse the menu. She had lovely teeth, a lovely smile. "For Pete's sake, I invited you here to eat, not spend the night," he practically barked. "Make up your mind what you want to order."

"I like looking at menus," she said, rewarding him with a look of pained reproach from her big brown eyes.

"Then you must be a very slow reader. I could have memorized the entire thing in half the time you're taking to get through it."

"Well, I'm not like you."

Hell, no! She was pure woman, and the fact that he couldn't stop taking inventory of her assets was beginning to irk him more than a little! "In case it's slipped your mind, Hugo's been waiting a long time to meet you. If it's all the same to you, I'd as soon not prolong his agony."

She slapped the menu closed and leaned back in the booth. "I'll have a large order of fries and a vanilla milk shake."

"You took all this time to decide on a milkshake and fries?" he asked incredulously.

"With ketchup."

"If that's all you want, we could have stopped at a fast-food drive-in and saved ourselves some time."

She collected her bag and the sweater she'd heaped on the bench. "Okay. Let's go find one."

"Stay where you are!"

He must have raised his voice more than he realized because the next thing he knew, the waitress had come barging over to their booth to inquire, "Your boyfriend giving you trouble, honey?"

Lily Talbot exploded into warm, infectious laughter, as if the woman had said something hilariously amusing. "Heavens, he's not my boyfriend!"

"And I'm not giving her trouble."

The waitress eyed him darkly. "You'd better not be." She fished out her notepad and waited with pen poised. "So what'll you have?"

He relayed Lily's request and ordered a steak sandwich and coffee for himself. "I thought women like you existed on salad and tofu," he said, while they waited for their food.

"Women like me?" She regarded him pertly. "And what kind of woman is that, Sebastian?"

"Under thirty and in thrall to the latest trend, no matter how outlandish it might be."

"You don't know much about women, do you?"

Enough to know you're bad for my concentration, he could have told her.

She leaned forward and he couldn't help noticing the graceful curve of her breasts beneath her blouse. He even found himself wondering if she was wearing a bra. Damn her!

"Real women aren't slaves to fashion, Sebastian," she informed him, her tone suggesting she found him singularly lacking in intelligence. "We make up our own rules."

"What happens if your rules don't coincide with men's?"

"Then we compromise, the way we have since the beginning of time."

"Sounds to me like a convenient excuse to do whatever you want, whenever you want, and not be held accountable for your actions."

She looked at him pityingly. "Don't you know that if you always go looking for the worst in people, you'll eventually find it?"

She was either a complete innocent or a contemptible schemer, and until he determined which, he wasn't about to let down his guard. "I don't have to go looking, Ms. Talbot. I live by the credo *Give a person enough rope and she'll eventually hang herself.*" He paused meaningfully. "You'd do well to remember that."

CHAPTER TWO

LILY shook her head in bewilderment, floored by his unremitting hostility. "Well, so much for striking up pleasant dinner conversation!"

"I'm sorry if the truth offends you. We can change the subject if you like, and talk about the weather instead."

"I'd prefer not to talk to you at all. You've been nothing but disagreeable from the minute you set eyes on me and I'm tired of trying to figure out why. I'm beginning to suspect you don't have to have a reason because you're the kind who makes a career out of being miserable."

"At least we're not harboring any illusions about what each of us thinks of the other."

There was no getting past that steely reserve of his, no hint of humanity or warmth in his makeup. He might be handsome as sin on the outside, but inside he was as dry as the law books he probably considered riveting bedtime reading. "Oh, go soak your head!" she snapped.

He looked mildly astonished, as if he thought he had a corner on the insult market. "Now who's being offensive?"

"I am," she allowed, "because trying to be pleasant about *anything* is a lost cause with you, Sebastian Caine. You're fixated on being as insufferable as possible, whether or not you have just cause."

Their meal arrived then, so she poured a dollop of ketchup on her plate and stabbed a fork into her French fries.

"No need to take out your frustrations on your food, Ms. Talbot. That's not my heart you're impaling."

More's the pity! "Oh, shut up!" she said, wondering why she'd ever thought coming here was a good idea in the first place. Hugo Preston might have sounded eager to meet her, but he hadn't cared enough to pursue the connection until she'd approached him. Given her other troubles, she didn't need the aggravation of having his obnoxious stepson enter the mix! "Just shut up and eat, and let's get this whole miserable evening over with as soon as possible."

But it was not to be. When at last they were ready to leave, the waitress brought more than their bill. "Hope you folks aren't planning to go far tonight. Just got word of flash floods right through the area. Police are asking people to stay off the roads."

"Oh, brother, just what I need to make the day complete!" Sebastian threw down a fistful of money and glowered at Lily as if she were in cahoots with God and had personally orchestrated the storm. "Grab your stuff and let's get moving."

"But if the police are warning people to stay put—?"

He took her elbow and hustled her out to the porch. "We don't have a whole lot of choice, unless you want to spend the night here."

"Perish the thought!"

A small river was running through the parking lot, a fact Lily discovered when she inadvertently stepped in it and felt water splashing up past her ankles. Not that it really mattered; by the time she flung herself into the car, she was soaked to the skin all over.

Sebastian hadn't fared much better. Great patches of rain darkened the shoulders of his pale gray suit jacket, the cuffs of his trousers were dripping, and his hair, like hers, was plastered to his head.

Muttering words unfit to be repeated in decent company, he fired up the engine, started the windshield wipers slapping and inched the car over the rutted ground toward the road. Before they'd even cleared the parking lot, the side windows had misted over and the air was filled with the smell of wet clothes and warm damp skin. In fact, Lily was pretty sure she could see steam rising from her skirt.

To describe the driving conditions as poor didn't approach reality. In fact, they were ghastly. The road ahead resembled a dark tunnel into which they were hurtling with no clear idea of where it might curve to the right or left.

Fists clenched so tight her fingernails gouged the palms of her hands, Lily huddled in her seat and prayed they'd reach Stentonbridge without incident. But they'd covered only about forty miles of the remaining distance when Sebastian brought the car to a sudden, screeching halt.

There was no sign of human habitation; no lights in farmhouses, no illuminated storefronts, no street lamps. Nothing but the driving rain pounding on the car roof like urgent jungle drums, and the dark shapes of trees twisting in the wind.

"Why are we stopping here?" she said. "Or aren't I allowed to ask?"

And then she saw. Where earlier in the day there'd been a bridge over a ravine, there now was a torrent of muddy water cascading down the hillside and taking with it everything that stood in its path. Another twenty feet, and the car would have careened into empty space, then plunged into the swirling rapids.

"Precisely," Sebastian said, hearing her shocked gasp.

It was late July. High summer in that part of Ontario. Even the nights were warm. But suddenly she was freezingly cold and shivering so hard that her teeth rattled.

This was how it happened: one minute people were alive, with the blood flowing through their veins, and their minds full of plans for the next day, the next year…and then, in less time than it took to blink, it was all over. That's how it had been for her parents, and how it had almost been for her.

Tragedy wasn't selective in its choice of victims; it could strike twice.

She tried to breathe and could not. The air inside the car was too close, too drenched, and she was suffocating. With a strangled moan, she released the buckle of her seat belt and fumbled for the door handle.

Her lungs were bursting. She had to get out—out into the open air. With a mighty shove, she sent the door flying wide and half-fell, half-crawled from her seat. Never mind the rain pelting down, or the wind whipping wet strands of hair across her face. Anything was better than being locked in the close confines of that long, low-slung burgundy car, which all at once looked and felt too much like a mahogany coffin.

Blind with panic, she set off through the wild night with one thought uppermost in her mind: to find her way back to the brightly lit safety of the roadside café. She'd covered no more than a few feet, however, before she blundered full tilt into a solid wall of resistance and felt her arms pinioned in an iron hold.

"Have you lost your tiny mind?" Sebastian Caine bellowed, raising his voice above the din of the waterfall. "What the devil do you think you're doing?"

"We were almost killed!"

"And almost isn't good enough? You want to finish off the job?"

"I w-want..." But the irrational, superstitious terror that had propelled her out of the car and sent her stumbling away in the dark refused to translate into words. She tasted salt and was astonished to find tears mingling with the rain on her face. To her shame, a great ugly sob broke loose from her throat.

"Stop that!" he ordered. "Nothing's happened yet. At least have the decency to wait until real calamity strikes before you decide to fall apart." He gave her a little shake, but the hint of sympathy texturing his next remark showed he wasn't as blind to the cause of her distress as he'd first appeared. "Look, I appreciate that your parents' accident must still be pretty vivid in your mind, but letting your imagination run wild isn't helping. Get a grip, Lily, and go back to the car."

"I don't think I can," she wailed.

Even though the night was black as the inside of a cave, she sensed his frustration. "Then let me make it easy for you!"

Before she knew what was happening, he bent down, grabbed her behind her knees and flung her, firefighter-fashion, over his shoulder. Oblivious to her shriek of outrage or her hands clawing at his back, he marched back to the car and tossed her into the passenger seat as if she were a sack of potatoes.

"You've taxed my patience enough for one day," he informed her savagely, yanking her seat belt into place, "so don't even think about pulling another stunt like the last one, or you *will* wind up alone on the side of the road and let me tell you, it won't be an experience you'll want to talk about—always assuming, of course, that you survive the night." Then, as a further inducement to comply with his orders, "You do know, of course, that this whole area's swarming with cougars and snakes. And vampire bats."

He slammed her door, raced back to the driver's side and climbed in.

"You're lying," she said shakily. "Especially about the bats."

In the glow from the dashboard, his grin and the whites of his eyes gleamed demonically. "Prove it."

Unable to drum up an answering smile she huddled down in the seat, listless with defeat. The day, which had started out so full of anticipation, had sunk too far in disappointment to be redeemed with humor and she was beyond fighting to save it. She just wanted it to be over.

As he swung the car around, the headlights sliced across the landscape, turning the rain to long silver darning needles spearing the night. "We passed a motel about ten miles back. Let's hope the road hasn't washed out between here and there, and that they still have vacancies."

Luck was with them, but barely. The motel had been built in the fifties and hadn't seen a dollar spent on it since. A bare bulb hung above the desk in the office. Tears in the vinyl padding on the one chair were held together with duct tape. The manager, Lily noticed with a shudder, reeked of tobacco and had tufts of hair growing out of his ears, which left him looking like a troll.

"Busy night tonight, what with the weather and all," he told them. "Only got the one room left. Take it or leave it, folks. You don't want it, someone else will."

"We'll take it," Sebastian said, slapping down a credit card and filling out the registration card.

"I'm not spending the night in the same room with

you,'' Lily informed him, trailing behind as he marched to their assigned unit.

''You'd rather sleep in the car?''

''*No!*''

He unlocked door number nineteen and flung it open. ''Well, I'm not offering to, if that's what you're hoping, so step inside and make yourself at home while I unload our stuff.''

''Sebastian,'' she exclaimed, still hovering on the threshold when he returned with her luggage, a zippered nylon sports bag, and a newspaper, ''this place is a flea pit!''

He reined in a sigh. ''So sorry it isn't up to the five-star standards you were probably hoping for, but it's warm and dry, isn't it? There's a shower and a bed.''

Exactly. *One* bed! Not a bed and a pull-out sofa, not even an armchair. Just a double mattress that sagged in the middle and was covered by an ugly green bedspread, which had seen better days. The only other furniture consisted of a nightstand holding a fake wood reading lamp, a ratty chest of drawers with a TV on top, and a straight-back chair that matched the one in the office, even down to the duct tape patching.

''I'm not sleeping on that bed!''

He shrugged. ''Sack out on the floor then.''

Not an inviting prospect, either. There were suspicious stains on the threadbare carpet. ''You're the most insensitive creature I've ever met!''

''And you're a spoiled brat.'' Kicking the door closed, he dumped her suitcases next to it, tossed the sports bag and newspaper on the bed, and shrugged out of his jacket. His shoes and socks came off next, followed by his tie.

She watched in sly fascination as he proceeded to peel off his shirt, thereby displaying an expanse of muscular, well-tanned chest and proof positive that his width of shoulder owed nothing to clever tailoring. Well, if he thought flexing his pecs would impress her, he was in for a disappointment! It would take more than that to get a rise out of her.

Just how little more she soon found out. "What do you think you're doing?" she squeaked in horror, when he casually began unbuckling the belt holding up his pants.

"I'd have thought it was obvious. I'm getting out of these wet clothes, and then I'm taking a shower. Close your mouth and stop gaping, Ms. Talbot."

"I don't believe...what I'm seeing!"

"Then don't look."

The belt was off, the zipper of his fly sliding down. The next second, he was shucking his trousers as unselfconsciously as if he were completely alone. And for the life of her, she couldn't look away.

He glanced up and caught her staring. "You're blushing, Ms. Talbot."

Any fool could see that! "Well, one of us certainly should be, and it clearly isn't going to be you."

He had great legs. Wonderful thighs. Lean, muscular, tanned. Long, strong, powerful. And he preferred briefs to boxers. Plain white cotton to silk stripes and fancy colors.

"Don't you *dare* remove anything else!" she said hoarsely. "I'm not interested in seeing you in the altogether."

"Just as well," he said, folding his trousers over the back of the chair. "I don't show my altogether to just anyone."

He draped his jacket over a wire hanger in the curtained recess that passed for a closet then did the same for his shirt. And she, ninny that she was, followed his every move and wondered how it was that God had seen fit to bless men with such trim, taut hips, even if the rest of them was oversized!

"Sure you don't want to use the bathroom?"

"Quite sure, thank you. There's probably an inch of mold growing in the tub."

"No tub," he said, almost gleefully, poking his head around the door to inspect. "Just a shower stall."

"I wish you the joy of it."

"I'm sure you do." He flung a glance over his shoulder and she could have sworn he was biting back a snicker. "No peeking, Ms. Talbot, and no funny business."

"Funny business?"

"There isn't room for two in here. If you change your mind about taking a shower, wait your turn."

"Oh, dream on!" she gasped, flabbergasted by his gall. "Heaven only knows what might come crawling up the drain."

But the truth was, her clothes were sticking to her most uncomfortably, her skin felt unpleasantly clammy and the idea of standing under a hot shower didn't seem such a bad idea, after all. She had fresh underwear and a nightshirt in her suitcase; dry clothes she could pull out for tomorrow. Who was she really punishing by stubbornly refusing to make the best of the situation?

Sebastian reappeared ten minutes later, wearing a skimpy towel draped perilously around his hips and nothing else. His black hair stood up in spikes, drops of water gleamed on his skin, and he smelled of clean, warm man. "The place might be a flea pit, but at least there's plenty of hot water. Sure you don't want to take advantage of it?"

She cleared her throat. "I might." She eyed his makeshift loincloth, then hastily glanced away again.

"There's another towel in there, if that's what you're wondering," he said snidely.

"Good," she croaked and fled with the toiletry bag, nightshirt and panties she'd taken from her suitcase.

In keeping with the rest of the place, the bathroom was basic: a washbasin, a toilet and a fiberglass shower stall with a mottled glass door. An unused towel the same size as the one barely covering the delectable Sebastian Caine lay folded on a shelf, and the management had kindly provided a minuscule bar of soap, a tiny bottle of shampoo, most of which he'd used, and two paper cups.

Fortunately she came fully equipped with hand-milled French soap, body lotion, salon formula shampoo and conditioner and, praise heaven, toothbrush and paste. She wasted no time putting them all to good use.

From the feel of them, the pillows were stuffed with peanut shells, and the mattress wasn't a whole lot better. But it beat a marble slab in the nearest morgue, which was where they'd almost certainly have wound up if he hadn't spotted the washed-out bridge when he did.

He'd been rattled, and he didn't mind admitting it. But her reaction had been over the top! Jumping out of the car like that and racing off without the first idea where she was headed pretty much proved his first impression had been right: the woman spelled nothing but trouble. Still, he hadn't been able to help feeling sorry for her. She'd been trembling like a leaf when he finally caught up with her, and the way she'd felt when he'd picked her up…

Best not to dwell too long on how she felt—or looked. His mandate was to deliver the goods, not sample them! Which reminded him Hugo would be expecting them to show up at the house anytime now.

Jamming a pillow behind his head, he stretched out on the mattress, pulled the top sheet up to his waist and reached for the phone.

Hugo picked up on the first ring. "Sebastian?"

"How'd you guess?"

"I saw the weather report on television. The whole county's under siege with this rain. You'll never make it up here tonight."

"I'm way ahead of you, Hugo. We checked into a motel about an hour ago."

"Thank God! So both you and Lily are safe?"

No point in regaling him with their close call. No point, either, in entering into a debate about the dubious wisdom of daughter and stepson spending the night together. "We're safe."

"So tell me, how do you like her, now that you know her a bit better?"

"She's…" *Nosy. Annoying. Too smart-mouthed for her own good.* And, he was beginning to realize, *sexy as all get-out!* "Hell, you know me, Hugo. I don't jump to conclusions until I've got all the facts."

Hugo laughed. "Just once in your life, could you try not to behave so much like a lawyer?"

And do what? Take advantage of the situation and put the moves on her? Better stick to being a lawyer! "It's who I am, you know that."

"I want the two of you to get along. We're all family here, Sebastian."

"Which is precisely why I'm being cautious. You've always been like a father to me, Hugo. Now it's my turn to act like a son and protect your interests."

"You're worrying about nothing. Lily doesn't have any ulterior motives for seeking me out."

"Uh-huh." No point in stating the obvious: that she

was her mother's daughter. Even if genetics weren't a factor, her role model had been a woman without conscience or moral rectitude. All that being so, who could say what motivated her actions? Only time would reveal that.

"Is she as pretty as she looks in the photo she sent?"

Just then, the bathroom door opened and Lily emerged on a cloud of steamy, flower-scented air. Her skin was flushed—and he ought to know. Enough of it was showing.

"Sebastian?" Hugo's voice came from a great distance. "Are you still there?"

"Yeah." He cleared his throat and dragged his gaze away from the hem of the pale blue nightshirt, which barely covered her backside. How come she didn't smell of cheap motel soap, the way he did? How come she looked as if she'd been polished with moon dust? Why was her damp hair so lush and lustrous-looking that he wanted to take handfuls of it and let it slide through his fingers?

"Well? Is she?"

Dry-mouthed, he said, "Is who what?"

"Is Lily as pretty as her picture?"

She came to the foot of the bed and stood with her hands behind her back, looking for all the world about fifteen years old. Well below the age of consent! "Shall I wait in the bathroom until you've finished your call?" she whispered.

"No," he said, answering them both at once. The photo Hugo was referring to had been a snapshot taken at a distance and had revealed only sketchy details. Addressing his stepfather again, he added, "I'd say 'different.'"

"Better?"

''Different,'' he said firmly. ''Look, Hugo, I'll call you in the morning, once I've checked the road report. Sleep well and don't worry about us. One way or another, we'll make it home tomorrow.''

''Why didn't you say it was Hugo on the line?'' she started in, the minute he hung up. ''I'd have liked to speak to him.''

''He knew I was calling from a motel room.''

''So?''

''I didn't think you'd want him to know you were sharing it with me.''

''Why not if, as you claim, it's an unavoidable and perfectly innocent arrangement?''

''Because I'm not so sure it is innocent. If it were, you wouldn't be parading around half-naked.''

Her pupils flared and she heaved a breath that set her breasts to bouncing gently beneath her nightshirt. ''You've got some nerve! What about you flaunting nothing but a towel?''

He jerked aside the sheet and rather enjoyed the way she reared back in alarm. ''You'll notice I've exchanged it for a perfectly decent pair of swimming trunks.''

Which fit snugly enough to discourage untoward activity in his nether regions!

''I wondered what you had hidden in that sports bag,'' she said, recovering quickly.

''Now you know.''

''And are swimming trunks all you're planning to wear to bed?''

''Afraid so. I forgot to bring a top hat.''

''Very funny, I'm sure!''

He shrugged. ''I aim to please.''

She gave a huffing little sniff, which told him exactly

what she thought of his pathetic sense of humor. "Move over to your own side. You're on my half of the bed."

"I thought you said you wouldn't sully your body by laying it on this mattress?"

"Upon consideration, I've decided the bed's safer than the floor."

She wouldn't want to bet money on it, if she knew the direction his thoughts kept taking!

She turned back the top sheet, using only the tips of her fingers as if she expected something to leap out and bite her. "This isn't exactly the kind of place I expected to be spending the night."

"Relax," he said. "I already chased away the bed bugs."

Her eyes, large and luminous to begin with, widened to saucer size. "Is that another of your feeble jokes?"

"Hell, no! They were marching heel to toe over the pillow, big as fighter jets, some of them—but they didn't hold a candle to the cockroaches tap dancing on the floor."

She yelped and leaped onto the mattress. It creaked ominously, formed an even more pronounced sag in the middle and sent her rolling toward him. One minute, he was lying there keeping his distance, and the next, she was pressed up against him with nothing but her abbreviated nightshirt coming between them.

She smelled even better, up close. As for the way she felt...! Silky, smooth as cream, soft. The way nature intended a woman to feel, with just enough meat on her bones to turn her angles into sweet, alluring curves.

Intending to shove her back where she belonged, he closed his hands over her shoulders and managed to choke out, "You're trespassing."

But that's as far as he got because he made the mistake

of looking at her face. Her features were delicate as porcelain, her brows finely shaped, her lashes so long and thick they looked artificial. And her eyes...

He fought to breathe normally and tried to look away. A man could lose his soul staring into those eyes.

''If you don't like it—'' she began, sounding as if she, too, had just run a marathon.

''I don't!''

''Then let me go.''

Easier said than done! He didn't trust her and he didn't like her, but underneath his lawyerly facade he was still only a man and there were some things beyond his control. Such as his hands, one of which slid from her shoulder to her jaw and from there to her hair, while the other stroked over her bare arm. And his mouth, which suddenly itched to taste hers. And not to be outperformed, an uprising from that singular component of the male anatomy which most definitely sported a mind of its own.

Show a little decency and move away, for crying out loud! his mind commanded.

But beneath the drooping veil of her lashes, her eyes had turned dreamy. Her lips had fallen softly apart. The hard points of her nipples pressed against his chest. Her thighs nested warmly against his.

We're all family, Sebastian...I want you to get along....

But not quite this well!

She was the one to break the spell, if that's what it could be called. ''I told you this wasn't a good idea,'' she said faintly.

''So you did.''

''Perhaps now, you'll believe me.''

Masking his reluctance, he let go of her and rolled onto his back. ''I never disputed the fact. But neither did I expect you'd fling yourself at me the way you just did.''

"That was a regrettable accident."

"The way I see it," he said, glaring at her, "the entire business of your being here at all is regrettable."

He thought himself well-armed against her, that nothing she might say or do would breach his defenses, but the sudden hurt in her eyes stirred him to dangerous compassion. Damn her for invading his part of the world! Why couldn't she have stayed where she belonged?

Gritting his teeth, he snapped off the lamp, folded his hands behind his head and stared at the ceiling. He'd hoped for utter darkness, something to erase his awareness of the shape of her lying beside him, but a floodlight on top of a pole in the parking area shone directly at the window, spearing the thin fabric of the curtains and filling the room with a dim glow.

A silence descended, oppressive with unspoken tension. Time trickled past—fifteen minutes, half an hour.

She lay ramrod straight, arms by her sides, legs held primly together. Only her breasts moved, rising faintly with her every breath, but she wasn't sleeping. Slewing his gaze, he caught the gleam of her open eyes in the murky light, and then, to his horror, saw a tear slip down her cheek.

He pretended not to notice. No more anxious to acknowledge her distress than he was, she turned her face away and he thought the danger had passed. But then a faint sniff pierced the silence, followed by a smothered gulp.

Finally he could stand it no longer. "Why are you crying?"

"Because," she said, after a wrenching pause, "I miss my mother and dad. Just when I think I've come to terms with losing them, it hits me all over again. I guess I must be overtired or something, because I seem to be doing a lot of crying lately.''

Was it her referring to her mother's second husband as ''dad'' that softened him, or was he just a pushover when it came to women in distress? Whatever the reason, he found himself wanting to comfort her. ''I'm sorry if I came across as an unfeeling lout earlier. I know how hard it is to lose a parent,'' he admitted. ''My father died when I was eight.''

Slowly she wriggled onto her back again. ''It hurts, doesn't it, no matter how old a person is?''

''Yes,'' he said, not sure he liked the near-intimacy of skin touching skin the sagging mattress enforced, but not exactly objecting to it, either. ''At first, I refused to believe I'd never see him again. I used to look for him in crowds. Every time there was a knock at the door or the phone rang, I'd expect it to be him. I remember the first Christmas without him, the first birthday, the first vacation, and how much I envied those kids who had both parents around to take them places and do things with.''

''Were you an only child?''

''Yes,'' he said, and went on to tell her how he'd gradually come to terms with his loss.

After a while, though, it occurred to him that he was the one doing all the talking when he should be taking advantage of such a heaven-sent opportunity to learn more about her. ''I gather you were a pretty close-knit family,'' he said. ''Were you still living at home when you lost your parents?''

He waited for her to reply and when she didn't, he raised his head a fraction to look at her and saw that she'd fallen asleep with her cheek lightly brushing his shoulder. She looked young and innocent and totally at peace.

He wished he could drift off as easily, but his thoughts

were too chaotic. Facts on which he'd based all his assumptions about her suddenly appeared less well-founded and he hated the uncertainty it produced.

Part of him wanted her to be exactly as she appeared: a young woman with nothing in mind but coping with personal tragedy and getting to know the man who'd fathered her. But another, greater part clung to the legal training in which it was so well versed and warned him not to be lulled into a false sense of security.

So she'd shed a tear or two and shown a more vulnerable side. What did that prove except that there was more to her than initially met the eye? Underneath, she was still the same unknown quantity; a woman with a questionable agenda.

I'd love to come and stay with you, she'd told Hugo, latching on to his invitation with unsettling alacrity. *There's nothing to keep me in Vancouver right now, nothing at all. Discovering you couldn't have come at a better time.*

Better for whom, and why? Not for Hugo, who'd been put through enough by her money-grubbing mother, and who'd fought hard for the good life he now enjoyed. No prodigal daughter showing up on the doorstep was going to spoil that, not as long as Sebastian Caine was around to monitor events!

She sighed in her sleep and kicked at the sheet so that it slipped down to expose the top of her thighs and the pale line of the panties she was wearing under her nightshirt.

Carefully he lifted his wrist and pressed the button to illuminate the face of his watch. Not yet eleven o'clock. Another six hours before daylight and the chance to assess the storm's damage. Another six hours of lying next to her and feeling her perfumed warmth reach out to touch him.

There was a hell, and the devil ruled!

CHAPTER THREE

THEY reached Stentonbridge shortly before lunch the next day. A small town nestled on the banks of a wide river, it boasted quiet residential streets shaded by old maples and lined with elegant nineteenth-century houses. But nothing quite prepared Lily for the opulence of the Preston estate.

Situated on several acres of riverfront property, the house sat in majestic Georgian splendor on a low rise, amid manicured lawns and lush flower beds. "Why, it's beautiful!" she exclaimed, taking in the spectacle as the car swept up to the front entrance.

"As you very well knew it would be," Sebastian said dryly. "You received photos, I'm sure."

"But they didn't do the place justice. Nothing could. It's...palatial! It must cost Hugo a fortune to maintain these gardens." She shook her head ruefully. "I wish I was the one supplying his stock."

"Try to control the dollar signs dancing in your eyes, Ms. Talbot, and remember why you're supposed to be here. The welcoming committee will descend any minute now, and I'll be seriously ticked off if the first words out of your mouth imply the only thing you're interested in is how much Hugo's worth."

She'd woken that morning feeling well rested and optimistic, with the emotional overload of the past night behind her. Foolishly she'd hoped she and Sebastian had reached some sort of truce and his sly insinuations were at an end. But for all that the new day had brought clear

skies, from the moment he'd opened his eyes his dispo-
sition had been anything but sunny. Perhaps, she'd
thought at the time, he just wasn't a morning person and
his mood would eventually improve.

If anything, though, it worsened. When she'd thanked
him for his sympathetic understanding of the night before,
he'd shrugged her off with a succinctness that bordered
on surly. He'd reacted with near contempt to her enthusiasm for the charming old towns they passed through.
Refusing to let him dampen her spirits, she'd remained
doggedly cheerful. This latest attack, though, was not
something she felt inclined to let pass.

"I resent that remark, Sebastian. It's completely un-
called for."

"Is it? When I woke up this morning, you were pawing
through the money I'd left lying on the dresser in that
motel room."

"I was not! I was looking for your keys so that I could
load my luggage in the trunk of your car and be ready to
leave the second you decreed we should, as you very well
know because I explained it the minute you started lev-
eling accusations at me. And if you'd got up at a reasonable hour, instead of lying around in bed half the morning,
I wouldn't have had occasion to *paw* through anything
belonging to you!"

"I hardly call getting up at eight o'clock and being on
the road by nine 'lying around in bed half the morning.'"

"I was up at six."

"I didn't get to sleep until nearly four."

"Well, don't take your insomnia out on me!" she
snapped, so exasperated she was ready to crown him with
her purse. "It's not my fault."

"Lower your voice and stop waving your arms around

like that," he said. "In case you haven't noticed, we have an audience."

She saw then that the front door of the house stood open and, suddenly, all the silly bickering didn't matter anymore. "Is that Hugo?" she whispered, her gaze glued to the white-haired man coming down the steps with a silky English setter dancing at his heels.

"Afraid so," Sebastian said. "Disappointed it's not the butler?"

"No," she cooed sweetly. "But I wish the dog was a rottweiler and you were its lunch."

"Nice," he said. "Very nice, Ms. Talbot. You're finally showing your true colors."

Smiling determinedly, she hissed, "Why don't you go jump in the river, Sebastian?" and without waiting for him to hurl something equally rude back at her, climbed out of the car and walked toward the man waiting at the foot of the steps.

Hugo Preston was almost seventy but didn't look a day over sixty. Tall and erect, with an enviable head of silver hair and clear blue eyes, he cut a handsome figure. "Well, Lily," he said warmly as she approached, "we meet at last!"

"Yes," she said, all at once awash with conflicting emotions. How did a woman greet the man whose blood ran in her veins but who, for reasons he'd yet to disclose, had chosen to remain incognito until recently? With a kiss, a handshake, a hug?

What did she call him, now that they were meeting face-to-face? Given his dignified bearing, *Hugo* suddenly seemed too familiar, and *Mr. Preston* absurdly formal…but *Dad?* Neil Talbot had been the man who'd filled that role, and her ties to him were too strong to be so easily severed in favor of this smiling stranger.

Seeming to sense her uncertainty, Hugo took her hands and kissed her lightly on both cheeks. "My dear daughter, you have no idea what today means to me. I would be deeply honored if, in time, you could bring yourself to call me Father. Until then, I'm Hugo…and this," he continued, turning to the slender blond woman who'd come out to join him, "is Cynthia, my wife."

Cynthia Preston did not fit the image of The Other Woman. Even less did she look or act the part of resentful stepmother. Tall and elegant in a pale bronze two-piece ensemble with gold accessories, she was, quite simply, beautiful. More than that, she was kind. It showed in her smile, and in her sky-blue eyes.

"I'm so happy to meet you, Lily," she said, enveloping her in a warm hug. "Hugo has hoped for a long time that this day would come. We both have. And we're so grateful to you for making it possible. Welcome to our home and please forgive our dog for pawing you like that. She considers herself one of the family."

Such total acceptance, following on the heels of Sebastian's trenchant disapproval, completely undid Lily and, to her embarrassment, she burst into tears. "Thank you," she wailed, dripping all over Cynthia's fine silk shirt. "I'm really…very h-happy to be here."

"No more than we are to have you." Slipping an arm around her waist, Cynthia guided her up the steps. "What a dreadful time you had of it yesterday. We were so worried when we heard the news. Let's go inside and I'll show you where you can freshen up, then we'll have lunch and start to get properly acquainted. Sebastian, bring in Lily's luggage, will you, and take it up to the Rose Room?"

If she hadn't found herself such an emotional mess, Lily would have enjoyed watching the almighty Sebastian

Caine reduced to the role of porter. But she was too busy mopping up her tears on the linen handkerchief Hugo had produced and trying not to smudge her mascara in the process. She'd taken great pains with her appearance that morning just so that she'd make a good first impression, and here she was, all red-nosed and puffy-eyed within minutes of arriving!

"I'm not normally like this," she said apologetically.

"Nor are we," Cynthia replied. "But look, Hugo and I are both misty-eyed, too. Family reunions tend to have this effect on people."

Unless your name happened to be Sebastian Caine! Lily felt his glare on the back of her neck as he tramped up the stairs with her suitcases, and wondered how he'd manage to sit through the meal and not let fly with one of his barbed remarks.

As it happened, she worried needlessly. He had someone else to occupy his attention. When Lily joined the rest of the family on the terrace after splashing cold water on her face and running a comb through her hair in the guest powder room, she found another woman had joined the party, and that she considered Sebastian her personal property became immediately apparent.

"Hello, I'm Penny Stanford," she said, subjecting Lily to a somewhat clinical inspection. "I wanted to be on hand to meet the long-lost daughter who stole my man away last night."

Oh, please, you're welcome to every miserable inch of him! Lily wanted to say. *Oh, and by the way, did you know he has another girlfriend stashed away in the city, and she looks ready to give birth any day now?*

Instead she confined her reply to a noncommittal "How nice to meet you."

"I think we could all use a little sherry before we sit

down to eat,'' Hugo decided. ''You and Penny will join us, won't you, Sebastian?''

''No, thanks,'' he said. ''I've got a load of paperwork to take care of at the office and Penny's working the night shift tonight so she needs to get some sleep.''

''I'm head nurse on the surgical floor at our local hospital,'' she informed Lily grandly.

''I sell flowers,'' Lily said.

''How nice.'' Nurse Penny swatted at the English setter. ''Do stop sniffing at me like that, Katie! It's so unhygienic. Well, Sebastian, since I left my car at the stables, I'll hop a ride over there with you. Shall we go?''

''Sure.'' His glance skimmed over Lily. ''Enjoy lunch.''

Cynthia looked up from her chaise. ''You'll be here for dinner, won't you, Sebastian?''

''I hadn't planned on it.''

''But it's Lily's first evening here and I'd like the whole family on hand to make it special.'' She paused and sent him a sly little smile. ''I had fresh lobster brought in, and Clara's making your favorite dessert.''

''That's shameless bribery,'' Hugo chuckled, pouring the sherry. ''The man has his own life, Cynthia, and there'll be other nights.''

''And he's already done more than his share to make me feel welcome,'' Lily put in blandly. ''Please, Sebastian, don't feel you have to show up on my account. I'll be perfectly happy without you, so consider yourself excused.''

''Lobster, you say?'' Glacial as a northern sky in winter, his gaze once again settled on Lily.

Cynthia nodded. ''And raspberry tart. With homemade vanilla ice cream. A meal fit for a king, Sebastian—or, in this case, our new princess.''

"Count me in, then. I wouldn't miss it for the world."

The satisfaction in his voice left Lily in no doubt about who'd emerged the winner in this latest go-round. She should have kept her mouth shut, instead of baiting him like that!

"I've got to get to the office and return some calls." He dropped a kiss on his mother's cheek. "What time are you serving dinner?"

"Half past seven, the same as usual. But come early if you can."

"Will Natalie be here?"

"Of course. She can't wait to meet Lily." Cynthia waved Sebastian and Penny off, then turned to Lily. "Natalie's taking extra summer courses at our local college and had a class she couldn't afford to miss this morning. She asked me to pass on her apologies for not being here to greet you, but she'll be home by three o'clock, which gives you time for a bit of a rest after lunch before you meet her."

"I look forward to it," Lily said. "What's she studying?"

"She wants to be a social worker. It's been her dream since she was a little girl. She'd like to work with children. But she can tell you all about that herself. Your father and I are more interested in learning about you. You're a horticulturist, right?"

Lily grimaced self-deprecatingly. "I'm just a florist. Until recently, I was part-owner of a retail outlet."

"So you know your flowers, which makes you very much your father's daughter! I've always said, if Hugo hadn't been in the legal profession, he'd have been a professional gardener."

Rising gracefully from her chaise, Cynthia ushered Lily to the umbrella-shaded table and waited for Hugo to seat them both before picking up the conversation again. "I gather from your remark, Lily, that you're no longer in business for yourself?"

"My colleague and I dissolved our partnership," she said, choosing her words carefully. Despite the warm welcome she'd received, she was among strangers. How would they receive the news that Jonathan Speirs, the mousy little accountant who was her business associate and who took care of all the bookkeeping, had been arrested for fraud, money laundering and connections to organized crime, and that, because of their business connection, she herself had been thrown under suspicion of conspiracy?

Sebastian, she knew, would have a field day, and with some cause!

The trouble with cases like this, her lawyer had told her, when the magnitude of Jonathan's criminal activities had first come to light, *is that people tend to forget which one's the guilty party and you both wind up being splattered with dirt. The police are pretty much convinced you're not involved in Speirs's activities, but you are a material witness, and I'd prefer you put as much distance between yourself and him as possible. It's a good time for you to get out of town until the case goes to trial, which won't be until after the summer.*

Cynthia dipped the bowl of her sterling spoon into her chilled watercress soup. "Does that mean you're working for someone else now, Lily?"

"No. I leased temporary premises from a friend so that I could honor promises I'd already made to do the flowers for several May and June weddings, but now that they're over, my time's my own."

"So there's no urgent reason for you to rush back to Vancouver?"

"Cynthia," Hugo interrupted, pouring white wine into fine crystal stemware, "I thought we agreed not to pressure Lily into making any long-term decisions until she's had a chance to get used to us."

"Letting her know there's no time limit on her stay isn't pressure, Hugo darling," she said lightly. "It's telling her she's family and this is her home. What's so bad about that? Heaven knows, this house is big enough to accommodate one more!"

"Does Sebastian live here?" Lily asked, jumping at the chance to ask a question she'd had in mind ever since she met him.

"Not quite," Hugo told her. "He lives in the old groom's quarters above the stables, which lie quite a distance from the main house. We often don't see him from one week to the next. The only one left at home is Natalie."

Well that, at least, was a bonus! The idea of tripping over Sebastian every time she set foot out of her room held no appeal at all.

Noticing that she'd finished her soup, Cynthia passed her a platter of fat prawns. "Try some of these, Lily."

"They look delicious, but I'll pass, thanks."

"You're not hungry?"

"I thought I was," she confessed, stifling an unladylike yawn, "but the sun and the wine are making me sleepy."

"Then you must rest. Don't blame the weather or the wine, dear. It's all that traveling, and the dreadful time you had yesterday." She put aside her napkin and stood up. "Come with me and I'll show you to your room."

She led Lily through the house and up the grand staircase. "Just let me know if there's anything you need," she said, standing back to allow her entrance to a large corner suite at the end of the upper hall.

"I can't imagine there will be," Lily said, taking in the luxury awaiting her. "This room is absolutely lovely, Cynthia."

Cynthia permitted herself a small smile. "I like to keep things looking nice. If you need anything ironed before you dress for dinner, just let me know."

So the family dressed for dinner! Grateful for the subtle hint and glad she'd brought along a couple of dressy outfits, Lily thanked her, closed the door and set about exploring her new surroundings.

The suite was charming, with four tall windows draped in deep rose taffeta on two of the walls. One side offered a view of the gardens and the river. The other overlooked a swimming pool and, showing through the trees some distance away, the gabled roof of another, smaller building.

The walls were covered in pale pink silk, there were roses in a silver bowl on a small pedestal table next to an armchair upholstered in pale pink velvet, and on the Queen Anne desk in the corner. The off-white carpet was deep and luxurious, the bed an antique four-poster flanked by bow-fronted nightstands of similar vintage, the paintings on the walls exquisite flower prints mounted in gold leaf frames.

Double doors led to a large, equally opulent bathroom. "Good grief!" Lily exclaimed, standing on the threshold. "A person could hold a party in here and still have room to spare!"

She eyed the deep marble tub longingly, but decided to postpone the pleasure of bathing until after she'd taken a nap. Sebastian Caine was coming for dinner, and she wanted to be well rested before they squared off again. Shedding her sandals and dress, she climbed onto the bed, nestled against the soft feather pillows and took stock of the morning's events.

Sebastian found his mother and sister on the terrace when he got to the main house that evening, but there was no sign of Hugo or Lily Talbot.

"Daddy took her off to the library," Natalie informed him. "They're probably talking about the past."

"But you've met her?"

"Yes."

"And?"

"I love her! She's exactly the way I hoped she'd be—so pretty and nice and friendly. I really feel as if we're sisters."

Raising his brows, he glanced at his mother.

"Don't look at me like that," she said. "I happen to agree with Natalie. I know you've got your doubts, Sebastian, but Lily really does seem genuine. Although…"

"Although what?" Suspicions on full alert, he regarded her closely.

"She did mention, in a roundabout sort of way at lunch, that she's out of work. But that isn't necessarily significant."

"You think not, do you?"

"Honestly, Sebastian!" Natalie scoffed. "You're always looking for the worst in people!"

"And you're always looking for the best—even when it's obvious to everyone else that it isn't to be found."

She set her mouth in the stubborn cast he knew so well. "Oh, phooey! Why can't you be like the rest of us and just take Lily at face value?"

"Because somebody around here has to dig beneath the surface."

"Why? What's she ever done to you that you're so set against her?"

"It's what she might do to you that worries me, Nat."

She threw up her hands in disgust. "Such as what? Steal my jewelry when I'm not looking? Poison my food? This isn't a fairy tale, and I'm not Cinderella at the mercy of a wicked stepsister. Your trouble is, you spend too much time around criminals, Sebastian. You need to get a life."

"I'm a divorce lawyer," he said, grinning at her outburst. Natalie had always been a spitfire when it came to defending anyone she perceived to be the underdog. "I don't come across too many felons in my particular line of work, though there has been the odd one, I must admit. But I pride myself on being a pretty good judge of character."

She snorted disparagingly. "If you were, you wouldn't be squiring Penny Stanford around town!"

"Penny's harmless."

"That just goes to show how much you know! She's so busy sinking her hooks into you, I'm surprised you don't need a weekly blood transfusion!"

Penny might be trying to land him, but she wasn't even close to succeeding. More to the point, she was no threat to his peace of mind, whereas Lily Talbot...!

The object of his displeasure chose that moment to swan out to the terrace on Hugo's arm. Although he didn't profess to be an expert in haute couture, Sebastian knew quality when he saw it, and the flame-red chiffon gown clinging lovingly to Lily's curves wasn't something she'd picked up in the bargain basement of the nearest department store. The whole outfit, down to the matching silk pumps, and pearl-and-garnet choker and earrings, was a custom affair designed to make the most of her looks.

She was laughing at something Hugo had said, and he was clearly besotted with her. The animation faded from her face when she saw Sebastian, though. ''Oh, you're here,'' she said, plainly wishing he were anywhere but. ''I half expected you'd change your mind about joining us.''

''Wishful thinking on your part, I'm afraid, Ms. Talbot,'' he informed her, wondering how she managed such an extravagant wardrobe on a florist's earnings. Either she'd inherited a bundle when her parents died, or she had some other source of income, and it was the *some other* that piqued his curiosity!

''Ms. Talbot?'' Nat hooted, oblivious to the undercurrents swirling in the atmosphere. ''What a lot of pompous nonsense! For heaven's sake, Sebastian, why don't you call her 'Lily' like the rest of us?''

''Yes,'' Lily said, playing the innocent for all she was worth. ''Why don't you, Sebastian? After all, we're family.''

He'd have wrung her pretty neck if it weren't that the rest of them would have rushed to her defense. *Because we're not family and I don't intend to roll over and play dead on your say-so,* he thought. ''Neither of you has a drink,'' he said, smoothly changing the subject. ''What'll you have, Hugo? Your usual?''

''Not tonight. In honor of the occasion, I'll join Cynthia and Natalie and have champagne.'' He turned to Lily. ''What about you, my dear?''

''I never turn down champagne,'' she said, practically simpering at him.

Grinding his teeth, Sebastian grabbed the neck of the bottle of Montrachet, hoisted it from the ice bucket and filled two flutes. Under cover of handing one to Lily, he cupped her elbow in his hand and steered her out of hearing range of the others. "What were you and Hugo talking about in the library while my mother and sister were left out here cooling their heels?"

"*My* mother. The *first* Mrs. Preston," she said defiantly, shrugging him off. "In other words, none of your business, Sebastian."

"As long as you're a guest under the roof of the present and *last* Mrs. Preston, I'm making it my business. And I won't tolerate your challenging my mother's right to be in this house."

"If your mother were one-tenth as boorish as you, I'd be staying in a hotel. As it is, I find her an utterly charming hostess and I wouldn't dream of insulting her. Or of hurting her feelings by telling her what I think of her son!"

He'd made her angry. Her cheeks were delicately flushed. Her parted lips were the same color as the flame-red begonias growing on the shaded north side of the stables. Without warning, he found himself wondering if they'd feel as silky smooth as they looked, and what she'd do if he suddenly bent down and kissed her.

Before he could act on such an insane notion, Cynthia joined them. "What are you two whispering about?"

"I was admiring your lovely home," Lily said. "You have exquisite taste. Have you always lived here?"

"Only since I married Hugo. Before that, Sebastian and I lived in Hamilton, in an apartment. Rather a nice one, to be sure, but it didn't compare to this."

"Not many places would, I suspect." Lily smiled, and Sebastian could practically hear the calculator clicking into gear behind those big, guileless brown eyes.

"I'll take you on a tour after dinner, if you like," his mother offered, completely drawn in. "Hugo grew up here, but he gave me a free hand redecorating the place when we married and I'm rather proud of the job I did.''

"So it's been in the Preston family a long time?"

"Yes," his mother replied, blithely ignoring the warning glance Sebastian shot her way. "His great-great-grandfather had the house built in the late 1840s and every generation of Prestons since was born here."

Lily sipped her champagne reflectively, then said, "It's odd to think they were all my ancestors and I didn't even know they existed until recently."

"I know your father would love to tell you what he knows of them, but it'll have to wait until another time. Sebastian, will you take Lily in to dinner? I believe we're ready to be served."

Given little other choice, he tucked her hand under his elbow and led her into the house. Her perfume teased him faintly, an alluring, exotic scent reminiscent of tropical flowers; plumeria or tuberose, he thought. Even though she was wearing heels, his height advantage allowed him a covert glimpse of her cleavage.

A flash of heat caught him off guard, riding over him to settle low in his belly. Furious, he transferred his gaze elsewhere and wished he could as easily divert other, less biddable sections of his anatomy. But the unpalatable truth was, although he mistrusted her, he mistrusted himself more. The more he saw of her, the more desirable he found her.

Well, there was one sure way to put an end to that nonsense. First thing tomorrow, he'd make some calls to the West Coast and initiate an investigation into her background. Hugo wouldn't like it; had openly forbidden any such move, in fact. But in this case, what Hugo might learn could well end up hurting him a lot less than what he didn't know.

"I've put Lily on her father's right, and Natalie on his left next to you," his mother said, taking her customary place.

At least, he'd be spared having to sit next to the woman throughout the meal, he thought, depositing her with relief at her chair and taking his place on the other side of the long table. But sitting opposite her brought its own share of hazards. Try though he might to find diversion elsewhere, he couldn't help watching her.

She had a habit of pressing her lips together after she'd taken a sip of wine. He found himself waiting for that mannerism with absurd anticipation. He had seldom seen a more delectable mouth. It could ruin a man, if he let it.

"Don't you agree, Sebastian?"

"Huh?" Jerking his attention back to safer channels, he realized he hadn't the first idea what had prompted his mother's question.

"Hel...*lo!*" Natalie chanted. "We're talking about Daddy's birthday, big brother, and you get to cast the deciding vote. What's it to be?"

"I'll go along with whatever Hugo wants."

"Then it's settled." Cynthia looked pleased. "We'll throw a joint party here a week from Saturday, to celebrate Hugo's turning seventy and to welcome Lily to Stentonbridge, then go up to the cottage later in the month. I'll get on to the caterer tomorrow."

"I'd love to take care of the flowers," Lily said. "If you don't mind letting me loose in the garden, that is."

"Not in the least," Hugo assured her. "You're welcome to whatever you fancy, my dear, including the greenhouse stock."

"And we need to think of someone to be Lily's escort," Cynthia said. "I'd ask you, Sebastian, but I don't think Penny would be too happy about lending you out for the evening.''

Ignoring Nat's unladylike titter, he said, ''Probably not.''

''Never mind. I'm sure there are plenty of eligible bachelors in town who'd be only too delighted to take on the job.''

He had no doubt about it, either. And the idea was enough to put him off his food, steamed lobster and raspberry tart notwithstanding.

CHAPTER FOUR

IT DIDN'T sit too well with Lily, either. "Heavens, this is the twenty-first century! I don't need a blind date to see me through the evening. I'm quite well able to look after myself." She dabbed her perfect mouth with her napkin and purposefully changed the subject. "You mentioned a cottage, Cynthia?"

"Yes. We have a summer place on the lake, about an hour's drive from here. Unfortunately we don't use it nearly as much as we did when the children were young, but it's a lovely peaceful spot and I think you'll enjoy seeing it."

"I don't know why you don't sell the place," Sebastian said. "The upkeep's more trouble than it's worth."

"I guess for the same reason you don't sell your town house," his mother said. "When was the last time you spent any time there?"

"I stopped by yesterday, as a matter of fact."

He should have thought before he spoke. Lily immediately picked up on the information he'd let slip and said, "I didn't realize that was *your* house."

"You mean to say he took you there?" Natalie exclaimed. "Well, aren't you the lucky one! He's never let me set foot inside the front door."

"Lily didn't, either," he said hurriedly. "I was in and out so fast, it wasn't worth giving her the grand tour. Anyhow, to get back to Hugo's birthday bash, what can I do to help?"

"Show up without Penny Stanford, for a start," his sister replied, dissolving into giggles.

Cynthia smacked her playfully on the wrist with her napkin. "Behave yourself, you wicked child! Lily, how's your lobster?"

She rolled her eyes. "It's wonderful, a real treat. I'm enjoying it thoroughly."

Too thoroughly, he thought, watching her. A minute smudge of melted butter smeared her chin and he itched to reach across the table and wipe it away with his finger.

She caught him staring and laughed. "What's the matter, Sebastian? Do I have dirt on my face?"

"As a matter of fact, you do," he said, irritated with himself, with her, and the whole damned setup. He prided himself on being a take-charge kind of guy and it irked him that she so easily set him off balance. "You've dribbled butter down your chin."

"Sebastian!" His mother looked shocked.

"Well, better she knows and does something about it before it drips on her dress."

"That's the trouble with lobster," Hugo said, ever the peacemaker. "I've always contended the only way to eat it is sitting around a picnic table wearing a bathing suit. That way, a person can be hosed off afterward. Here, Lily, allow me." He blotted her chin with his own napkin. "There you are, good as new."

The rest of the meal progressed without incident. Sebastian kept his eyes to himself, left the others to carry the bulk of the conversation and, when he couldn't avoid responding, confined himself to neutral replies.

As soon as was decently possible, he left the women happily conferring on party arrangements and followed Hugo to his study for an after-dinner drink.

"Well, what do you think of her?" Helping himself to

the one daily cigar his doctor allowed, Hugo settled in his favorite chair and regarded Sebastian curiously.

Weighing the port decanter's heavy crystal stopper on the palm of his hand, Sebastian tossed the question back. "More to the point, what do *you* think of her?"

"I find her very generous. Very willing to forgive."

"She has nothing to be forgiving about, Hugo. You're the one who was betrayed."

"But she doesn't know that. She thinks I walked away from her and left another man to assume my parental responsibilities. In my opinion, Neil Talbot more than proved himself up to the job."

"How did you explain having apparently abandoned her?"

"I didn't." Hugo accepted the glass Sebastian handed to him. "I gave her an abbreviated version of the truth, and told her how deeply I regretted not having exercised my paternal options."

"You have nothing to feel remorseful about, Hugo, and she needs to know that."

"Nevertheless, I've been burdened by guilt for the last twenty-six years." He made a gesture of appeal. "What if Neil had resented being saddled with another man's child? What if he'd deserted Genevieve and she'd fallen on hard times? If she hadn't been able to keep her baby, Lily could have been placed in foster care or adopted by strangers, and lost to me forever."

"Why torture yourself with 'what if's?' None of those things happened."

"But I didn't know that until a few months ago. I didn't even know if Genevieve gave birth to a son or a daughter, and that preyed on my mind a very great deal. No matter how many other good things came into my life, there was always this big empty space where another child should have been.''

"Your whereabouts were never a secret. If things had not gone well for Genevieve, she knew where to find you and you'd have been the first to hear about it.'' He savored a mouthful of the port, before continuing, ''At the very least, she'd have come after you for child support. From everything you've told me about her, she was above all else a survivor.''

"Until her luck ran out.'' Hugo inspected the glowing tip of his cigar critically. ''I've always appreciated your loyalty, Sebastian. More than anyone else, you've been the one who's comforted me the most when the past came back to haunt me. I've been able to talk to you about things I could never discuss with your mother. But you have to promise me you won't let what you know about Genevieve taint your feelings toward Lily.''

"That's a tall order, given the circumstances. It's not as if you never made an effort to get to know her. How old was she when you tried to make contact—fifteen, sixteen?''

"Just turned fourteen. And remember, I addressed my inquiries to her mother and never did contact Lily directly.''

Sebastian shrugged. ''She was old enough to make up her own mind, regardless of any outside pressure that might have been brought to bear on her. And she chose to rebuff your overtures.''

"You're assuming she knew of them, but from what I gathered in our conversation before dinner, clearly she didn't. If you're going to assign blame, Sebastian, then blame me. I could have pursued the matter but I chose not to, and gave up hope of ever getting to know my first born. It's sad that the opportunity to reverse that decision rose out of someone else's tragedy but I'm deeply grateful I've been given another chance.''

"I'm not trying to spoil your reunion, Hugo, but I can't help feeling Lily's turned to you now out of some sort of expediency, and that makes me uneasy. I don't want to see you hurt again.''

"Keep an open mind, Sebastian. You can do that, can't you?''

"Sure," he said. "Until she gives me reason to think otherwise, I'll accept the person she appears to be.''

It was as close as he could come to saying what Hugo wanted to hear, without telling an outright lie. But Sebastian remained more determined than ever to have Lily Talbot investigated.

When they emerged from the study an hour later, they found Natalie alone at the table in the breakfast room, a stack of books and a notepad in front of her. "Mother's in the hot tub,'' she told her father.

"And Lily?'' Hugo asked.

"Walking Katie. She said she needed to stretch her legs before she turned in.''

"Then I think I'll join your mother. A bit of aqua therapy might help my back spasms. Sebastian, we'll see you a week from Saturday, if not sooner?''

"Count on it,'' he said. "I'd never miss your birthday, Hugo, you know that.''

He watched his stepfather head back into the house, noticing the slight limp and the way he paced himself carefully, as if every step hurt. "He's in pain.''

"I know it. He'd never have opted out of meeting Lily's flight otherwise.'' Natalie regarded him slyly. "His bad luck was your good fortune, though, wasn't it?''

"How so?''

"You know…you and Lily. Alone!''

"What the hell is that supposed to mean?" Surely the woman hadn't spilled the beans about their sharing the same bed the night before? If she had, he'd have her head!

"Oh, come off it, Sebastian! You can hardly keep your eyes off her and you practically come unglued every time she looks back at you."

"I *what?*"

Natalie snickered. "Did you really think I wouldn't notice? I've known you all my life, brother dear, and while I admit I haven't seen it happen often, I recognize the signs. You're smitten."

"You've had too much sun," he told her testily. "It's all I can do to be civil to the woman."

"So I noticed. It's what first tipped me off."

"The little boys you run around with might develop infatuations on the strength of twenty-four hours' acquaintance, Nat, but men my age—!" He stopped and banged the heel of his hand to his forehead. "Why am I defending myself against this absurd accusation?"

"I'm wondering the same thing," she smirked.

He yanked gently on a lock of her hair. "Hit the books, kiddo, and leave the psychoanalysis to the experts. You're way off base with this one."

"You're leaving before Lily gets back from her walk?"

"You bet," he said. "I've seen enough of her for one day."

"Do me a favor before you go." She flipped through her notes and handed him a slip of paper. "See if there's a copy of this book in the library, will you? Dad said he thought there might be."

"Sure."

He headed back into the house and crossed the hall. The library door stood ajar and swung quietly open at his touch. Evening sunlight streamed through the long windows, casting a golden patina over the cherrywood desk, and spotlighting Lily Talbot kneeling before the open door of one of the glass-fronted cabinets under the bookcases.

For a moment he watched her, noting her absorption. Several large leather-bound albums lay on the floor beside her, suggesting she'd been there for some time.

"The last I heard, even dogs as smart as Katie aren't interested in learning to read," he said, finally making his presence known.

She almost jumped out of her skin. Her startled exhalation gusted across the room and the book she'd been inspecting slipped from her hands. "Heavens, you scared me!"

"So it would seem. Exactly what are you doing in here?"

"Looking at old family photos," she said. "Hugo's got pictures going back a hundred and fifty years. There are some of my great-great-grandfather when he was a boy. And look!" She leafed through one of the albums on the floor beside her. "This is one of my great-grandmother when she was about my age. You can see the family resemblance. We have the same shaped face and eyes."

He didn't budge. "You were supposed to be walking the dog. At least, that's the impression you gave Natalie."

"I tried, but Katie was more interested in the river and I wasn't sure it was safe for her to be in the water, so I cut the walk short."

"And decided instead to poke around in here and help yourself to whatever took your fancy. Sneaking through other people's private possessions is practically an Olympic sport with you, isn't it?"

"Hugo gave me permission to look through the family albums whenever I please. How else do you think I knew where to find them? And you're a fine one to talk about being sneaky! I didn't notice you being very forthcoming about the fact that the reason you never invite anyone in the family to visit your town house is that you have your pregnant ladylove holed up there."

It wasn't often he found himself at a loss for words, but this latest broadside, wide of the mark though it was, left him temporarily speechless. "My ladylove?" he finally managed to say.

"*Pregnant* ladylove. Let's not gloss over that small fact."

Working hard to keep a straight face, he said, "You mean, you actually deal with fact on occasion—when you're not jumping to wildly inaccurate conclusions, that is?"

"Sneer all you like," she spat. "I know what I saw. All that hugging and kissing, not to mention the length of time you left me twiddling my thumbs while the pair of you…"

She trailed off and gnawed her bottom lip, looking uncertain all at once.

"Well, hell, don't stop now, Lily," he said mockingly. "I can hardly wait to hear the rest."

"You went upstairs." Something fascinating about her left forefinger captured her attention and prevented her from meeting his gaze. "I saw the bedroom light go on."

"Pity I didn't leave a ladder strapped to the top of the car. You could have used it to gain a better view of what was going on up there and blackmailed me with what you witnessed."

She shot him a venomous glare. "No need to be sarcastic, Sebastian. I assume she's married and that's why you're so reluctant to let anyone in the family know about her. Well, don't worry. Your secret's safe with me."

"It had better be," he said, deciding the game had gone

on long enough, "because the woman you saw is indeed married, although she's not my mistress, nor is that my child she's carrying. She happens to be the friend and client of a colleague, temporarily hiding out from a violent, abusive husband who's already threatened her safety and attempted to flee the country with their three-year-old son. The boy happened to wake up from his nap yesterday while I was there, which no doubt explains why you saw a light go on in an upstairs window. Sorry if that's not colorful enough to satisfy your overactive imagination, but it happens to be the truth."

"Oh," she said, sounding as if she'd had the wind knocked out of her.

He eyed her grimly. "Under no circumstances is what I've told you to leave this room."

"Of course not. And…" She worried her lip again. "I owe you an apology. I'm afraid I accused you unjustly."

"You certainly did," he said, strolling to the reference section to find the book Natalie needed. "Afternoon quickies, crammed in between other appointments, aren't my style at all. Where seduction's concerned, I like to take my time.

Her eyes grew big as saucers and she blushed like a rose. Enjoying her discomfiture, he located the book, then made for the door. "Oh, yes, and one more thing," he said by way of a parting shot. "Contrary to what you might have been brought up to expect, not every woman has the morals of an alley cat and jumps into bed with whichever man happens to take her fancy."

The sky had faded to purple but the heat of the day still lay thick on the air when he finally got back to his apartment. A perfect ending to a less than perfect day, he thought, opening all the windows to the night scent of Hugo's flower gardens.

He still had a briefcase full of notes to go over, a string of phone calls to return and a sluggish lack of enthusiasm for tackling either. Too much good food and wine, on top of more irritation than any one man should have to suffer in a day, and not nearly enough exercise, he decided. What he needed was a long run.

Ignoring the flashing light on his telephone answering machine, he changed into shorts and T-shirt, grabbed a towel and set off down the narrow driveway leading from the stables to the road. Settling into an easy stride, he passed through the gates, turned right and jogged up the shoulder of the hill on the first leg of an arduous five-mile circuit.

Such grueling punishment should have been enough to banish Lily Talbot from his thoughts. With any other woman, it would have been. But the memory of her—the sound of her voice, her disturbingly attractive mouth, the sweep of her glossy hair—went with him, buzzing around in his mind like a mosquito and giving him no peace at all.

Because of her, he was deceiving Hugo, if not overtly then certainly by omission. That alone was reason enough to resent her. That he also found himself fascinated by her merely added to his irritation. She was stylish and carefree and unpredictable. She was everything he didn't want in a woman. Left to her own devices, she'd derail his entire life and everyone else's that he cared about.

He was not a man given to fanciful notions; logic, cause and effect—these were the touchstones by which he pursued his profession. Yet he could not rid himself of the superstitious feeling that she spelled trouble. For what seemed like the hundredth time, Sebastian wished she'd never come into their lives.

Hugo and Cynthia had made an early night of it. Natalie was holed up in her room studying. Save for the grand-father clock chiming eleven in the front hall, the house was silent.

It had been an emotionally exhausting two days and she should have been tired, but after an hour of tossing and turning in bed, Lily gave up on sleep. Too many questions about the past still remained unanswered.

Why had her mother never told her about Hugo? He seemed such a decent man, so eager to welcome her into his family. It was difficult to reconcile that with the fact that he'd never come forward as her father until she searched him out.

When she'd tried asking him why he'd let another man raise her, he'd been evasive. There was something he wasn't telling her; she could feel it in her bones. She sensed, too, that there was a hurt in him that ran very deep.

Flinging back the sheet, she climbed out of bed and went to lean on the sill of the open window beside the desk. At the foot of the garden, the river slid silently past, a ribbon of dark silk in the starlit night. By craning her neck, she could see over the treetops to the roof of the building that Natalie had told her was where Sebastian had his apartment. A light glimmered through the branches, showing he was home.

Everyone around her had a sense of place, of belonging. They all knew where they'd sprung from and where they were headed. Only she was adrift in a sea of uncertainty. Despite her warm welcome here, she remained alone. The sense of connection that came from knowing she belonged just wasn't there yet. Maybe it never would be. Maybe she'd never really feel part of this family.

That she was even here at all was a matter of luck. If she hadn't found among her mother's possessions the envelope containing old photographs, a marriage license and her own birth certificate, she'd never have known Genevieve had been married before or that Neil Talbot wasn't her biological father. Given her happy childhood, it shouldn't have mattered. But it did. The people she'd trusted the most had deceived her.

All at once, the spacious, elegant room was too confining, too suffocatingly hot and humid. Her cotton nightshirt stuck to her skin. She ran a finger inside the neck, suddenly longing for the cool Pacific night air of Vancouver; for the gentle sigh of the sea breeze stirring the branches of the western hemlock tree outside her apartment window.

A flicker of light below and to her right drew her attention to the faint prick of stars reflected on the calm surface of the swimming pool. Inspired, she exchanged the nightshirt for a bathing suit, took a towel from the bathroom and stole through the quiet house to the French doors leading to the back terrace.

Except for a series of mushroom-shaped lights lining the path, the garden lay in darkness—until she rounded the corner to the tiled deck of the pool, that was, when a pair of motion-activated floodlights flared to life and, contrary to what she'd expected, showed that she was not the only one bent on a late-night swim.

A seal-dark head broke the surface of the water and a voice, unmistakably Sebastian's and unmistakably ticked-off, echoed across the pool. "What the hell...! Who's out there?"

"Me," she said, stepping forward. "I came to swim."

''Well, forget it,'' he snapped. ''I got here first.''

How like him to think he could chase her off as if she were a common trespasser! ''I think it's safe to say the pool's plenty big enough for two.''

''I'm willing to bet I can change your mind on that.''

She dropped her towel, kicked off her sandals and very deliberately stepped onto the diving board. ''I doubt it. I've never been one to back down to a bully.''

''Hold it right there, Lily!''

''Why should I?''

With smooth, powerful strokes, he swam to the far end of the pool, the water flashing like diamonds around him. ''Because, if you're determined to butt in where you're not wanted, you'll have to get rid of the swimsuit first.''

''That's one of the house rules, is it?'' she said, her words dripping with sarcasm.

''Tonight it is.''

''And why is that, Sebastian?''

''There's an old proverb that goes along the lines of *When in Rome—*''

''*Do as the Romans.* I'm familiar with it, surprising though you might find that.''

''Then you ought to be able to figure out why the swimsuit comes off before you come in. You saw last night how I like to get rid of my clothes the first chance I get, Lily. I'm buck naked in here.''

Her mother had been a stickler for good manners. *It's impolite to stare* had been one of the first rules of etiquette she'd impressed on her daughter. It wasn't enough to stop Lily's eyes from almost popping out of her head now, though. ''You're what?''

''You heard.''

''The almighty Sebastian Caine is *skinny-dipping?*''

"That's right. And if you insist on joining me, you're going to be doing the same."

"Forget it! I'm not putting on a one-woman peep show for your entertainment." She jumped back down to the pool deck and scuttled over to where she'd left her towel and sandals.

She moved quickly, but he was even quicker, stroking powerfully across the width of the pool to where she had bent to retrieve her belongings. He grabbed her by the ankle, a move to which she greatly objected. "Chicken!" he taunted.

She squatted down and faced him eyeball to eyeball. His lashes clustered in wet clumps, his hair lay plastered to his skull and his skin gleamed bronze in the unearthly green light of the pool. "If you're so brave, hop out here where I can get a good look at all I'm missing."

He laughed and without warning switched his hold to her wrist and yanked her forward so that she pitched face first into the water. Her limbs tangled with his; flesh slid against flesh, fabric against fabric.

She came up sputtering and furious. "You lied! You *are* wearing swimming trunks!"

"And you," he said, smiling evilly, "were just about wetting yourself in anticipation of discovering otherwise."

She spat out a mouthful of water. "You wish!"

"Uh-huh."

The way he was staring at her mouth disconcerted her more than a little. For no logical reason, a warmth stole through her that had nothing to do with the balmy night. *"What?"* she snapped, when she could bear his scrutiny no longer.

His gaze scoured the rest of her features. "Still trying to figure out what's really going on behind that innocent face.'' He drifted so close that there was scarcely an inch of water separating their bodies. "Come on, Lily," he murmured, persuasive as a lover bent on seduction, "it's just you and me—no one else around to overhear. Tell me what you're really after."

"I already have," she said, suddenly fighting for breath. He was all rangy, hard muscle; an athlete posing as an officer of the courts. Tanned when he should have been pale and bookish; exciting when he should have been dull and austere. Nearly naked when he ought to have been buttoned up in a three-piece suit and conservative tie.

All right, her heart told her, when her head was insisting he was all wrong!

She tried to back away from him but he forestalled her by bracing both his arms against the side of the pool so that she was imprisoned between them. She tried to *look* away, but his eyes held her captive, their blue flame burning clean through to her soul. "Why won't you believe me?"

"Because I've learned to trust my instincts." He leaned closer; so close she could detect on his breath a trace of some sweet, heavy wine—port, perhaps, or apricot brandy—and almost feel the new beard growth stubbling his jaw. "And they tell me you spell nothing but trouble."

For no good reason at all, she was a mess. Her pulse was fluttering and stalling like a demented butterfly. Her windpipe felt constricted all the way from her lungs to her throat. She didn't know what to do with her hands. If she moved them, she'd make contact with some part of that tanned, toned body hemming her in so effectively. And regardless of how *his* instincts were operating, *hers* were screaming out loud and clear that touching him anywhere would be a very unwise move.

So she sort of hung there in the water, and doing her best to eliminate the silly, adolescent breathiness still plaguing her voice, said, "I hope you like crow because you're going to be eating a lot of it before the summer's over."

He opened his mouth to speak and she cringed inwardly, expecting he'd fire back some pithy retort. Instead their gazes locked and everything around them grew suddenly still, leaving them isolated in a capsule of expectant silence.

Nothing prepared her for what happened next and, afterward, she couldn't have said who took the first step in the agonizingly slow journey that followed. Perhaps neither of them did, and some powerful magnetic current drew them together until their lips were barely touching.

The impact to her senses stunned her. He was so unfeeling in many ways—in his attitude, the things he said to her—that she'd have expected his lips to be cruel. But they settled on hers with such eloquent finesse that she found herself yearning toward him.

At that, the pressure of his mouth increased. His hand meandered down to bracket the indentation of her waist. A thousand sensory pinpoints sprang to life, electrifying the swath of skin grazed by his fingertips. His hips nudged hers, a fleeting contact only, but enough to remind her that what was happening above water had repercussions below the surface.

It was all so unexpected, so foolish, really. They disliked each other. Their short acquaintance was larded with suspicion and wariness. Yet their bodies recognized a rapport their minds refused to acknowledge, and melded with such complete trust that she found herself dangerously close to losing sight of his true objective.

This was not irresistible attraction run wild, nor even rampant lust. It was calculated seduction.

She pulled away just a fraction and met his unblinking gaze. Was it really fire she detected in the depths of his eyes—or the cold blue steel of dedicated hostility?

"Maybe," he said, an unaccustomed hoarseness ruffling his words, "it's time we called an end to this."

"I don't think so," she said. "Not until you explain what you meant by that remark you made earlier tonight, just before you left the library—the one about not all women having the morals of alley cats. Was what happened just now your way of putting the theory to the test?"

CHAPTER FIVE

To HIS credit, he didn't feign ignorance of what she was referring to, but nor did he give her a straightforward answer. "Never mind. I spoke out of turn," he said, then did a neat underwater flip and swam to the other side of the pool.

Before she'd begun to catch her breath or recover from the devastation of his kiss, he'd climbed out and disappeared along a side path toward the stables, moving so swiftly that she was left to wonder if she'd imagined the whole kissing incident.

That pretty much set the pattern for the days that followed. For the most part, Sebastian avoided having to deal directly with her, which wasn't too difficult since his law office was in town. But for a gainfully employed man, he seemed able to take a lot of time away from his clients to monitor her movements.

One morning, she was busy cutting dead heads from the roses and suddenly got the eerie sense she was being watched. She looked around, found the garden deserted, then caught sight of him spying on her from a window in the house. What did he think, she wondered, half amused, half annoyed. That she planned to steal the best blooms and sell them on the nearest street corner?

Another afternoon so soporific with heat that it was all anyone could do to walk six paces without melting, she and Natalie were fooling around in the pool. The glare on the water was blinding, so when she hauled herself onto the tiled deck and raced to the umbrella table to apply more sunscreen, she didn't notice Sebastian lounging in one of the chairs until she almost tripped over his feet.

"Having a good time?" he inquired, his eyes unreadable behind dark aviator glasses but his tone so frosty she almost shivered. At least, that's how she chose to justify the goose bumps popping out all over her skin, because to admit to the other possibility—that being this close to him brought back too-vivid memories of their last intimate encounter—was not to tolerated.

"Yes," she replied, adopting the confrontational attitude that was becoming almost habitual in her dealings with him. "Does that offend you?"

"When it interferes with my sister's studies, it does. You might have nothing else to do but romp in the sun, but Natalie will be writing final exams in another month and her time would be better occupied studying. In case you haven't heard, her ambitions amount to something a bit more intellectually taxing than arranging flowers."

Lily had a very respectable diploma in horticulture to her credit but, "Natalie is an adult, Sebastian," she told him, choosing to save until another time the news that she was not quite the mental lightweight he perceived her to be. "I doubt she needs you to organize her time or remind her of her priorities. And since she happens to be as much my sister as she is yours, you can safely assume I, too, have her best interests at heart."

He whipped off his glasses and subjected her to one of his most imperious stares. It was criminal, she thought, that any man should be blessed with such compellingly beautiful eyes. They put a woman off-kilter, made her forget she was dealing with the enemy and tempted her to dwell on possibilities best left to molder in obscurity. "That kind of sentiment might fool everyone else around here,'' he said flatly, ''but it doesn't wash with me so you might as well save your breath.''

The rejection stung worse than a slap on her wet skin, though heaven knew she should be used to it by now. ''You want to know your trouble?'' she countered, reining in a strong urge to shake her wet hair and drip water all over his immaculately creased dress pants. ''You're jealous because you've forgotten how it feels to have fun. That's assuming you ever knew how in the first place, of course! And I'll tell you something else—you're also unnaturally possessive. You think you own Natalie, and it's been a real shock to your system to have someone else usurp her affections.''

''Don't flatter yourself, Lily,'' he sneered. ''You happen to be the flavor of the week, that's all.''

That he remained so impeccably unruffled by her attack, while she'd worked herself into an outright sweat by his was the only excuse she could offer for what she said next. ''Flavor of the week, hmm? So *that's* what you found so irresistible the other night that you simply had to sample it by kissing me!''

He rose languidly to his feet and towered over her. ''I kissed you to relieve the tedium of your incessant chatter, but it's not a mistake I intend to repeat. Go back to your girlish games with my sister, cupcake. You're out of your league trying to match wits with me.''

''And what are you going to do to pass the time, Sebastian? Continue to play the part of my personal prison warden?''

''I don't know what you're talking about.''

''Of course you do! Or did you think I haven't noticed the way you're always lurking in the bushes like some third-rate undercover agent waiting to catch me in some unspeakable act of espionage?''

"Good God!" he said, a small smile curling his mouth. "I had no idea you numbered paranoia among your other dubious qualities. Thank you for drawing it to my attention."

Having once again had the last word, he brushed off his hands and sauntered away.

And so it went for nearly two weeks: parry and thrust, every time their paths happened to cross. By the morning of Hugo's birthday, she was ready to weep with frustration at Sebastian's unremitting antipathy toward her, and almost dreaded that night's party for fear of how he might try to humiliate her in front of the guests.

She could only hope he'd have eyes for no one but his date, Penny Stanford. When she confided as much to her sister, though, as they worked on the flower decorations, Natalie declared rather ambiguously, "Sebastian might like to pretend that'll be the case but if you ask me, his eyes have been wandering of late and it's my bet someone else has become the object of his affections."

Unwilling to admit that the unpleasant lurch of her stomach could possibly be ascribed to dismay, Lily made a minor adjustment to one of the floral arrangements and said with studied indifference, "Really? Anyone I know?"

Natalie stifled a giggle. "Oh, yes—better than anybody, if you get my drift! But I've already said too much and Sebastian would throttle me if he knew I'd even brought the subject up. He's a very private individual, you know."

"*Secretive's* the word I'd use."

Natalie looked at her curiously. "Don't you like him, Lily?"

The question was simple enough; the answer unexpectedly complex.

Did she? Too much, perhaps, despite their frequent run-ins? And was the feeling mutual? Was the reason they worked so hard at insulting each other nothing but a defense mechanism designed to prevent them from facing up to underlying feelings neither was brave enough to acknowledge? If so, how adolescent!

"I'm not sure," she finally said. "He's a difficult person to read and he's seemed resentful of me from the first."

"It's because of the way your mother treated my—" Natalie began, then turned bright red and clapped her hand to her mouth. "Oh, sorry, Lily! I shouldn't have said that."

Lily's heart gave a peculiar jolt. Hugo had changed the subject when she'd tried to ask him about her mother, Sebastian had clammed up, and now Natalie was behaving as if she'd dragged some horrendous skeleton out of the closet by mentioning Genevieve's name. "Perhaps you shouldn't have, but now that you've started, I wish you'd finish."

"I can't. I promised Dad." She made a big production of checking her watch. "Heavens, look at the time! Eleven o'clock already. Mom and Dad'll be back from the golf club soon, and we haven't even begun on the table decorations! You get started on them and I'll go cut more sweet peas."

Puzzled, Lily watched her leave. What did they all know—or think they knew—that they couldn't share with her?

"Sometimes, marriages fail, especially the May-December kind like mine and Genevieve's," was all Hugo would admit, whenever she pressed him to talk about the past. "There was some bitterness, we parted and I elected to forfeit my right to know my child. It wasn't a wise choice but, at the time, it seemed the best choice.

Enough to say, my dear Lily, that I have lived with the guilt of that decision ever since and welcome this chance to make up for my omission. Let's leave it at that and go forward from here.''

Easy for him to say, when he already had all the answers, but impossible for her! Sometimes, she wished she'd never found out that Neil wasn't her biological father. Just when she was beginning to come to terms with her parents' death, her life had been thrown into turmoil yet again, and she hadn't known a moment's real peace since.

Well, no more! The truth was supposed to set a person free and before the day was ended, she intended to find release from her particular prison.

She waded in as soon as Natalie returned with the sweet peas. ''You know, Natalie, I'd never ask you to betray a confidence, so perhaps you aren't free to talk about my mother, but there's nothing to stop me from telling you what *I* know about her.''

''I wish you wouldn't. I wish you'd forget I ever mentioned her name.''

''I can't. She doesn't deserve to be swept aside like this, as if she were never of any consequence.'' She touched her sister's arm pleadingly. ''She was a wonderful wife and a wonderful mother. I never came home from school to an empty house, the way some children do. She was always there, eager to hear about my day, and always ready to welcome my friends. She made our home a place that was full of love and warmth and laughter, and it hurts me that no one here thinks well of her.''

Natalie plucked at the sweet pea stems uncertainly. ''People aren't always what they seem, Lily.''

''I know that. Why else do you think I contacted Hugo this last May? Because there was an important part of my mother's life that I knew nothing about. I *had* to fill in the blanks."

"But don't you see, there's a problem right there? Your parents died last September, yet you waited eight months before you decided to get in touch with Dad. If it was that important to learn what happened, why didn't you come to him sooner?"

"Because I didn't know he was my father until after the estate was settled, and probating a will takes months. As soon as it was complete, I had access to the safe-deposit box my parents had leased from the bank that looked after their financial affairs, and that's when I found the envelope."

She drew in a steadying breath as she recalled that fateful morning. "I never expected it would be easy, finalizing the last details, but at first it didn't seem so bad. Money is nothing more than figures printed on a statement and can't really hurt a person. Even cash possesses a sort of cold impersonality, having already passed through thousands of strangers' hands before touching ours. But the safe-deposit box…"

"If this is too difficult for you, you don't have to go on."

"Yes, I do! I have to make you understand that I need to find closure before I can get on with my life." Determined to finish what she'd started, Lily blinked furiously to stem the threatening tears. But the same wave of painful nostalgia that had assailed her when she'd opened the box swept over her again as she relived the moment.

"The little velvet bags protecting my mother's more valuable pieces of jewelry retained traces of her perfume, Natalie. One of her fine blond hairs was tangled in the clasp of a gold chain. A cameo locket held miniatures of her and Neil. Their signatures were scrawled on various documents—the deed to their house, a copy of their will, a life insurance policy. It was as if my mother and father were suddenly standing there beside me, encouraging me to go on. I felt their presence so strongly, it was... unnerving. Uncanny.''

She stopped and pressed a hand to her trembling mouth for a moment. ''Then I found the envelope, hidden under everything else at the very bottom of the box, and learned that Neil wasn't my father at all, nor was he my mother's first husband. And I felt betrayed by the people I loved the most.''

''Was it a letter to you?'' Natalie's voice was hushed with sympathy.

Somehow, Lily managed a laugh. ''If only it had been, I might not be pleading my case with you now. But no, there was nothing addressed to me personally. I found a photograph of my mother. She looked very young, but I recognized her immediately. She was wearing a wedding outfit—very formal, all lace and satin, with a train and a veil and everything—and was on the arm of a man a good bit older. He wore a morning suit and I realize now that he was Hugo. There was a photographer's inscription on the back—*Mr. and Mrs. Hugo Preston, Stentonbridge, Ontario,* and the date—two years before I was born.''

''And that's all you found?''

''No. There was a copy of an early birth certificate of mine, naming Hugo Preston as my father, also my mother and Neil's marriage certificate, dated when I was eleven months old, and last, adoption papers making Neil Talbot my legal father.''

She faced Natalie again. ''And that was it. So you see why I came here looking for more information. I know all the 'whats,' but none of the 'whys.'''

"I can't help you," Natalie said. "I wish I could. For a start, I don't have the complete picture, only bits and pieces I've picked up at one time or another. I'm afraid that if Dad won't tell you what you want to know, the only other person you can turn to is Sebastian. He knows the whole story."

"And flatly refuses to discuss it with me." She slumped into a chair at the table. "I don't know where else to turn."

Natalie took a seat across from her. "What if I were to ask Sebastian to talk to you?"

"I doubt he'd listen," she said miserably.

"He might. It's worth a try." Natalie nibbled thoughtfully on her lip for a moment, then slapped the flat of her hand on the tabletop. "I'm going to do it! This afternoon!"

"You'll never pull it off."

"Watch me! Sebastian's basically a very fair man, and I think I can convince him you deserve to know your own history. You're going to have to strike while the iron's hot, though, before he's had time to change his mind, and that means finding some reason to pry him loose from Penny at the party, and getting him by himself, because you know this isn't something he'll discuss in front of a crowd. Oh, yes, and one more thing, Lily." She leaned forward and cupped her mouth close to Lily's ear. "Try buttering him up a bit between now and then, if you get the chance, instead of baiting him all the time. It might make my end of the job that much easier to pull off."

A figure moved out of the shadows on the terrace and into the sunlight flooding through the open French doors. "What's all the whispering about?" Sebastian wanted to know. "I thought the pair of you were supposed to be working on the flowers for tonight?"

A guilty flush swept over Natalie's face. "Oh, we were just…talking."

He eyed her suspiciously, then swung his attention to Lily. "Were you badgering my sister? Is that why she's twitching like a nervous cat?"

Natalie, bless her heart, sprang to Lily's defense. "Stop picking on her, Sebastian! I'm her sister, too, and she wasn't badgering me at all. She was telling me how sweet you were to her the night the road was washed out and you ended up in that awful motel."

Briefly he seemed at a loss for words—a remarkable occurrence, in Lily's experience of the man—but not entirely surprising. She was pretty taken aback herself, given that she'd said almost nothing to anyone about that particular evening. But then she caught the meaningful *butter-him-up* stare Natalie directed at her behind Sebastian's back, and tried to pick up her cue. "Yes," she said brightly. "Exactly."

If anything, he looked more dubious than ever, but before he could pursue the subject, the swish of tires on gravel alerted them to Hugo and Cynthia's return from their early-morning round of golf. A moment later, their voices could be heard as they came around the side of the house.

"Never mind that rubbish. Let's get this job done and out of the way before the caterers arrive." Reasserting control, Sebastian swept up an urn containing a massive arrangement of white gladioli. "Lily, tell me where to put this."

Oh, don't tempt me, Sebastian Caine! she thought. *You wouldn't like my answer!*

He bathed her in a Machiavellian smile. "I just read your thoughts, honey, and they weren't pretty."

She was ready to kick him where it would hurt the

most. To tell him that he was the most arrogant, controlling creature ever to cross her path and that she hated him. *Hated him!* Except it wasn't true. And pretending otherwise wasn't helping her cause any.

Taking a deep breath, she made a sincere effort to banish the antagonism that kept coming between them. "Please let's stop this senseless sparring, Sebastian, and at least try to get along."

"Why?"

"For Hugo, and your mother, if nothing else. I think they'd like us to be friends."

"So what you're suggesting is just for their sakes and has nothing to do with your personal agenda?"

"What are you implying?" She attempted a laugh that came out sounding more like a nervous whinny. "That I harbor a secret fondness for you?"

He looked at her long and searchingly. "Do you?"

Confronted so directly, she hardly knew where to look or how to answer. That he'd detected something she thought she'd kept well hidden left her feeling slightly queasy. "Put the gladioli on the piano," she mumbled, "and don't ask silly questions."

If giving the party a miss had been an option, he'd have taken it. So, once the birthday toasts were over and the dancing heated up, Sebastian put himself at a safe distance on the fringes of the crowd scattered over the lower lawn.

Nursing a glass of champagne, he chatted with Forbes Maynard, the other retired senior partner of the law firm along with Hugo, and tried to keep his attention away from the woman who seemed bent on creating nothing but havoc in everyone's lives.

Even if Forbes hadn't been teetering on the brink of senility, though, she'd have been difficult to ignore. The transformation from working woman in shorts and a T-shirt, with a smudge of dirt on her cheek and her hair tied back in an elastic band, to sought-after belle of the ball, was, to put it bluntly, nothing short of breathtaking.

She wore purple—the kind associated with violets or pansies. Deep and rich and sensual. The neckline fell from narrow shoulder straps to a low vee in front and just about to her waist in the back. The hem swept her ankles. The parts in between were…awe-inspiring.

A pendant on a gold chain nestled just below her throat, with matching earrings suspended from her ears. Though no gemologist, Sebastian knew enough to appreciate the fine quality of the cabochon amethysts pavéd with diamonds, and the hunk of gold on her wrist. Somebody had invested a lot of money in her trinkets. A lover, perhaps? Or was she her own biggest fan?

His thoughts veered to the preliminary report he'd received on her just the day before. *Born to Genevieve and Hugo Preston, August 5. Name changed by adoption to Talbot, July 27. Never married, no known relationships of any significance. Holds annual lease on penthouse in small, older apartment building in West End of Vancouver. Has resided at present address for six years. Drives three-year-old minivan registered to Lily's Flower Nook.*

It had not read like the résumé of a big spender, nor did it give the impression there was a rich boyfriend waiting in the wings. The last surprised him, given the amount of attention she was attracting tonight. When she wasn't charming the women or wowing the old men, she was dancing with younger guys, too many of whom his mother had found to keep her entertained and who were clustered around her as eagerly as flies around a honey jar.

The sight was enough to sour his champagne to vinegar.

But even though they held her in their arms and their eyes damn near popped out of their heads as they tried to get a look down the front of her dress, they didn't know what he knew: that the skin around her waist was taut and satin smooth; or that he'd made her tremble when he'd kissed her, and her eyes had turned huge and dark.

"You were saying, Sebastian?" Forbes was regarding him expectantly.

"Huh?" Feeling as dazed as if he'd walked into a brick wall, Sebastian turned to his companion and struggled to recapture the thread of the conversation.

He'd have had more luck finding a blade of grass in a desert and Forbes seemed to realize it, too. Looking over his shoulder, he followed Sebastian's gaze which, like a magnet attracted to true north, had again fastened on Lily. "Ah, yes," he murmured. "She does tend to make everything else forgettable, doesn't she? I take it she's the long-lost daughter?"

"Uh-huh." He sounded as if he was choking, which he damn near was! *Where the devil did she find that dress? And who sewed her into it? Or had it been sprayed on?*

"Fine-looking woman, wouldn't you say?"

"I guess."

"Looks to me as if she's headed this way." As though sensing he was ready to bolt, Forbes clamped an age-spotted hand over his arm. "Introduce me, Sebastian. I'd like to meet her."

Meet her, my ass! You want to ogle her, you lecherous old goat!

She swayed down the terrace steps and across the lawn, the stuff her dress was made of shimmying over her body like a live thing. The skirt had a mile-high slit up the front, which bared a good three inches of thigh with each step she took. By itself, that was enough to send the fittest man into cardiac arrest and Forbes, who didn't get nearly enough exercise, began panting asthmatically.

A waiter offered her a glass of champagne. Hugo way-laid her and made some remark that had her tipping her head back in laughter. She moved among the guests, look-ing thoroughly at ease, as if she'd been born to the high life and hadn't a care in the world.

Eventually—unavoidably—she came to where he waited with Forbes hyperventilating at his side. "Hello, Sebastian," she burbled, all smiling, deceptive sweetness. "I don't see any sign of Penny. What happened? Did she stand you up?"

"She had to work."

"Even today?" She fluttered her ridiculous eyelashes in patent disbelief.

"Penny's a nurse, remember?" he said. "Unlike you, she doesn't have the luxury of keeping shop girls' hours. Forbes, this is Lily Talbot, Hugo's daughter from a former marriage."

"Nothing wrong with shop girls," Forbes wheezed, his handshake straying until he was mauling her wrist like a mangy old lion gone too long without a decent meal. "I'm the Maynard in Preston, Maynard, Hearst and Caine, my dear. Too old to be of much value around the office these days, I'm afraid, but not so far gone that I don't appreciate a pretty face."

Extracting herself from his clutches, she bathed him in a smile that left him drooling. "So nice to meet you, Mr. Maynard, and I'd love to chat some time, but right now," she cooed, latching onto Sebastian and maneuvering him toward the terrace, "this man owes me a dance. Remember you promised me, Sebastian?"

"I did no such thing," he growled, but there was no real bite behind his answer. His senses were too clouded by her nearness. How was it that she was fooling everyone but him, yet he was the one falling deepest under her spell?

Her hand felt tiny and fragile wrapped in his. Her hair, piled in gleaming curls on top of her head, brushed his chin. Her perfume teased his nostrils.

Turning into the circle of his arm and fitting her steps perfectly to his, she lifted her face up to his. "If I didn't know better, I'd think you've been avoiding me."

"Given the amount of attention you've been lapping up from just about every other man present, I'm surprised you've had time to notice anything but the success of your debut into local society."

She smiled delightedly at him from under heavy lashes. "Why, Sebastian, you almost sound jealous."

"Surprised, perhaps, that you're causing such a stir, but *jealous?* Don't be ridiculous!"

In fact, he wasn't surprised at all. When he'd first met her, he'd thought her pretty enough in an ordinary sort of way, but not exactly the kind to stop traffic. Maybe the sensible denim skirt and plain white blouse she'd been wearing had fooled him because the truth was, she had a surreptitious glamour that crept up on a man and blind-sided him when he least expected it.

What other reason could there be for him to find himself repeatedly drawn to her when every neuron he possessed warned him to steer clear? How come he could dance the night away with Penny and manage to control his libido until they were alone, but he couldn't hold Lily Talbot's hand for five seconds without getting steamed up?

Good thing the evening had faded to night and shadows as purple as her dress swirled around them. If he couldn't help making a public fool of himself, at least she was the only one who had to know about it.

Driven to test the waters even further despite himself, he inched her a little closer, half expecting she'd kick him in the shin for his nerve. Instead she slid her hand up the lapel of his jacket until her fingers were touching the back of his neck.

"Sebastian?" she murmured, tilting her head so that her lips almost brushed his throat and her breath sifted over him as sweetly as a magnolia-scented breeze. "I guess you know why I dragged you away from Mr. Forbes?"

He heard invitation, sweet and simple, in the way she uttered his name. Thoroughly fired up, he folded her hand against his chest and seized the moment. "Because you wanted to be alone with me?"

"Exactly."

'Then what say we slip away and continue this someplace else?"

She tilted one shoulder provocatively. "I was hoping you'd say that. Where do you suggest we go?"

His better judgment blown to smithereens, he allowed his hand to wander past the low back of her dress and caress the silk-clad curve of her hip. Her mouth, he decided fuzzily, had the texture of a rose; soft, beautiful, easily bruised. "My apartment?" he croaked, barely able to hear himself speak over the drumming of his blood.

"If you like. But a quiet corner of the garden will do just as well." She pulled away slightly, just enough to captivate him with a dark, alluring gaze from beneath the sweep of her lashes. "Anywhere, as long as we aren't disturbed."

He looked over to where Hugo and his mother circulated among their friends, with Natalie, looking somewhat trapped, in tow. "You're not concerned you might be missed?"

"It won't take long." She squeezed his fingers persuasively. "We'll be back before anyone realizes we're gone."

He swallowed. The women he knew were usually more bashful and he wasn't quite sure how to handle such a bold approach. But she was Genevieve Talbot's daughter, after all. Still, "You're sure about this, Lily?" he asked.

She subjected him to another slow, seductive blink. "Absolutely."

"No regrets when it's too late to change things?"

She shook her head. "Not a chance."

Her reassurances notwithstanding, a better man might have had the gumption to decline so willing an invitation. But the simmering attraction between them had risen to the point that he was prepared to postpone dealing with his shortcomings until another time. "Then come with me."

Grasping her hand more securely, he pulled her to the edge of the terrace and around the side of the house to the shortcut that led to his apartment. She might be anticipating nothing more than a quick roll in the hay, but he prided himself on knowing how to prolong a woman's pleasure.

Lily Talbot was in for the surprise of her life.

CHAPTER SIX

FOR a man who had shown marked reluctance every other time she'd broached the subject of her birth, Sebastian was in a tearing hurry to talk to her about it all of a sudden. "Could we slow down, do you think?" she panted, almost tripping as one of her high heels caught between the paving stones.

He turned a glance on her which, even by moonlight, seemed to smolder. "Changing your mind already, Lily?"

"I've never been more sure of anything in my life." She shook her head decisively and glanced around. They'd passed through the rose garden and the shrubbery separating the stables from the main house, and were now so completely beyond the perimeter of the party that even the music was barely audible. "But we're safe enough here, surely? No one's going to overhear us."

A tiny frown creased his forehead. "I should hope not! But to be on the safe side, I'd prefer the privacy of my apartment."

"All right." She shrugged. "Just bear in mind I'm not wearing running shoes, though, will you?"

"Sorry. I wasn't thinking." To her surprise, he clasped her hand warmly, and led her the rest of the way as carefully as if she were made of glass. "Better?"

It was better than better! She liked this more chivalrous side of him; liked having him touch her, just as, when they were dancing, she'd liked the strength of his arm at her back and the almost intimate way he'd held her. Under different circumstances, she'd have savored such a rare occurrence and even have thought he was not unmoved, either, because, once or twice, when his hips had accidentally brushed against hers, she'd thought he was…well, *physically affected*….

But no! Given his manifest dislike of her, she had to have been mistaken. The only possible reason he'd held her close had been to avoid having other people bump into them.

Placing his hand in the small of her back now, he guided her inside the stables, through a door and up a winding staircase to his apartment, a spacious, charming area of vaulted whitewashed ceilings supported by dark cross beams, plain white walls displaying a few very good watercolors, and pegged oak floors scattered with jewel-toned Oriental rugs. The living-room sofas were of black leather, deep and luxurious, the tables, desk and tall armoire antique English cherrywood.

A wall sconce on the landing lent a subdued glow to one end of the long room, but most of the radiance came from the opposite side where bands of moonlight speared a wall of open windows bare of any kind of drapery or blinds. "I had no idea you enjoyed such a splendid view of the river," she said, leaning over the broad sill and inhaling the mingled scents of summer. "You're much closer to the water here than we are in the main house."

"And far enough away from the main house to ensure total privacy."

She heard the rustle of fabric, the sound of him moving around the room, the faint creak of the armoire doors being pulled open. Moments later, the mellow tones of a clarinet seducing the night fused with the musical clink of crystal.

"How about a glass of wine?" he suggested. "I don't have any champagne chilling, but I've got just about anything else, including a very respectable sparkling burgundy.''

She turned to find him watching her intently and, despite the music, the room all at once seemed filled with a taut, waiting silence that left her feeling inexplicably uneasy. That he'd shed his jacket, pulled his bow tie loose and undone the top button of his dress shirt, didn't help. It served as too vivid a reminder of how casually he'd climbed out of his clothes that night in the motel, and had her wondering, irrationally, if he was planning a repeat performance now.

Swallowing to relieve her dry mouth, she said, ''I'd just as soon get straight down to business, if you don't mind.''

For the first time since she'd known him, he looked thoroughly disconcerted. Shoving his hands into his pockets, he took a turn across the room and back again, then swung to a stop in front of her. ''I like a woman who knows what she wants, Lily, make no mistake about that,'' he finally said, ''but I confess I'm not keen on one who's in such a hurry to get to the main event that she can't be bothered with a little foreplay, even if it's only the social kind.''

She stared at him, stunned. ''I don't think I heard you correctly. Did you say *foreplay?*''

''I did.'' He closed the distance between them and hooked a finger under the shoulder strap of her gown. ''What would you like to call it?''

''I...I...!'' Realizing her mouth was hanging open, she snapped it closed and blinked. ''I didn't realize straightforward communication required any sort of...*preliminaries!*''

''You prefer to hoist up your skirt and just get on with it, do you?'' He stroked the side of her neck lightly. ''No lingering over the finer points of seduction?''

If she'd confounded him moments earlier, his reply reduced her to utter bewilderment now. "Are you drunk?" she asked nervously, edging away from him and wishing suddenly that she'd insisted they remain in the garden.

He tracked her movement with eyes far too clear and observant for him to latch on to *that* as an excuse for his bizarre behavior. Nor did he try. "I'm beginning to wish I was," he replied, barring her way with one arm braced against the wall. "Exactly what is it you want of me, Lily?"

"What I've always wanted from the first—information about my birth. What did you think I wanted?" Then, seeing the disbelief on his face dissolve into ironic amusement, which he tried to hide by shielding his mouth with his other hand, the disjointed parts of their conversation over the last half hour came together in an interpretation entirely different from the one she'd originally understood. "Oh, my stars, you thought I wanted *you?*"

He looked at her from hooded eyes. "The thought did cross my mind, particularly in light of the way you came on to me."

"*Came on—?* I did no such thing!"

"I think I can be forgiven for believing otherwise." His voice dropped to a mocking whisper. "*I was hoping we could slip away from here, Sebastian...anywhere, as long we're alone and won't be disturbed....*"

"I was referring to our not being overheard by anyone else."

"Well, the next time, don't preface the remark by rubbing up against a man until he's ready to explode. And you can wipe that appalled expression off your face. It's a bit late in the day for a woman your age to pretend you don't know what I'm talking about."

"I didn't! I had no idea...!" She stopped, and bit her

lip, ashamed. Hadn't she entertained the suspicion, however briefly, that when they were dancing, he was *enjoying* having her in his arms? "A lot of people like dancing
close. It has more to do with...with *style,* than sex."

He let out an exclamation of disgust and strode to the
armoire. In seconds, the music came to an end and one
of the doors slammed shut. Reaching inside the other, he
pulled out a bottle of brandy and splashed an inch into a
cut-glass snifter. "Just as a matter of interest, what made
you think I'd break down tonight and give you information I've repeatedly refused to divulge every other time
you've brought up the subject?"

"Natalie promised she'd talk to you this afternoon, and
try to convince you to change your mind. So, when you
suggested we leave the party, I naturally assumed she'd
succeeded since it obviously isn't something either of us
would discuss in front of other people."

He regarded her over the rim of his glass and took a
sip of the brandy.

Dismayed by his silence, she tugged nervously at the
shoulder strap he'd dislodged. "She didn't get in touch
with you, did she?"

"She did not, although she tried several times. I just
never got around to returning her calls." His mouth tightened in annoyance. "Not that it would have mattered,
anyway, because I've already made it very clear I won't
tell you what you want to know, and you had no right
asking my sister to intercede on your behalf."

"Perhaps," she said testily, "it's time *I* made a few
things clear to you, the first being that I won't allow you
to go on dictating my actions. I didn't come here to be
given the runaround, and I'm frankly tired of being told
to butt out of something which, by any sane person's def-

inition, is most definitely my business. I resent your attitude. I'm not the bad guy here, Sebastian.''

''Nor is Hugo.''

''Perhaps not. But if you continue holding to your code of silence, you leave me no choice but to go to him again, and this time I'll insist he answer all my questions, even though I know the fact that he more or less abandoned me as a baby is painful for him to relive.''

''And if he refuses to accommodate you?''

''I'll be out of here within the hour and none of you will ever see or hear from me again.''

She was bluffing, of course, and felt sure he knew it. Blood ties, however tenuous, were not so easily severed, and she could no more walk out of Hugo and Natalie's lives than she could forget her own name.

Surprisingly, though, Sebastian appeared to take her at her word. ''That would kill him.''

''It's a risk I'm prepared to take.''

He swirled the contents of his glass meditatively, then pinned her in one of his famous legal-eagle stares. ''Okay, I'll make you a deal. I'll tell you what you want to know, if you'll answer a question for me, first.''

''Ask away,'' she said, dismissing the tremor of unease that spiraled through her as nothing more than anticipation at finally achieving her goal. ''I've got nothing to lose and everything to gain.''

''If you believe that, you're in for a nasty surprise.''

He sounded almost sorry for her, but she wasn't about to be sidetracked by cheap displays of concern at this point. ''Get on with it, Sebastian. What's your question?''

''Have you never asked yourself why your mother chose to keep you in the dark about events surrounding your birth? Did it ever occur to you that the reason might be that she didn't want you to know?''

"That's two questions, but I won't quibble over trifles since the answer in both cases is, no. Mom and I were very close. There was nothing we couldn't share. I think she was simply waiting for the right time to confide in me."

"You're twenty-six years old, Lily. I doubt there was ever going to be a right time."

"You didn't know my mother."

"And you're quite sure you did?"

"Positive."

He paced to the window and stared out. "What would you say if I told you she was an adulteress who had an affair with her obstetrician and left your father before you were born so that she could be with her lover?"

Another tremor, stronger than the first, shook Lily but she stood her ground. "I'd say you were lying. My mother would never do such a thing."

Still with his back toward her, he said, "I'm telling you the truth. Genevieve Preston ran away with her doctor—Neil Talbot, the man you thought was your father—and left behind a husband who adored her. She stole his child, she humiliated him before the entire town, she broke his heart. And if that wasn't enough, she asked him not to pursue his right to know you after you were born."

"I don't believe you! No man worth his salt would agree to such a demand."

"Hugo did, because he was too proud to beg, and because he sincerely believed you'd be better off not being torn between parents who lived at opposite ends of the country."

"He didn't have to agree to that. He could have insisted on his rights."

"He could have ruined Neil Talbot. Do you know what happens to doctors who abuse their positions of authority and trust? They're stripped of their right to practice medicine. Left without the means to earn a decent living. Disgraced in the eyes of society. If I, as a lawyer, were to behave as your adoptive father did, I'd be disbarred. And I can promise you, if ever I were treated as Hugo was, I'd destroy the man who stole my wife and child, not let him leave me the laughingstock of the area. He'd live to regret messing around with what's mine.''

''Because you're arrogant and vindictive!'' she cried, her insides churning. ''And if Hugo really did as you're suggesting, and made no attempt to enforce his paternal rights, *he* was weak and undeserving!''

In two strides Sebastian was at her side. His eyes were cold, his fingers around her upper arm iron-hard. ''He was the best thing that ever happened to Genevieve Talbot! Before she married him, she was nothing. *Nothing,* do you hear? *Trailer trash!* Slinging hamburgers in a truck stop by day, and hanging around bars at night, offering God only knows what in exchange for the price of a drink.''

Lily's bid to laugh in his face emerged as high-pitched and devoid of amusement as a crow's dying screech. ''Now I know you're lying, because if she was all those things, how did she ever meet such a fine, upstanding pillar of the community as Hugo Preston?''

''A police officer friend of his talked him into representing her when she filed assault charges against one of her barfly associates. Seems that even battered and bruised, she made a beautiful victim. Even though Hugo was twice her age, he fell head over heels in love and married her. It's a familiar enough story—wealthy, sophisticated older man rescues helpless young woman from the wrong side of the tracks, and gives her a better life. But instead of repaying him with loyalty, she dumped him two years later for her young stud of a doctor.'' He tossed back the rest of his drink and swiped the back of his hand across his mouth. "Once a slut, always a slut, I guess."

Lily had never hit anyone in her life; never been hit, either, come to that. Her mother couldn't abide violence in any form. But at Sebastian's last remark, she lifted her hand and landed it flat across his cheek in a stinging slap. The noise cracked the night like a rifle shot.

He didn't flinch. Showed no reaction at all, in fact. He merely continued to hold her glance and said quietly, "That won't change the truth, Lily."

"It has to," she quavered, clinging desperately to beliefs suddenly and shockingly undermined by facts that made a hideous kind of sense. "You're mistaken. It was never like that."

"It was exactly like that. But you don't have to take my word. There's plenty of other evidence. The letter she left behind when she ran away, the others she wrote when she wanted Hugo to agree to a divorce and give his permission for Talbot to legally adopt you. It's all there in black-and-white, with her name signed at the bottom."

"No! You're protecting Hugo. The truth is, he didn't want to be bothered with a child at his age, and that's why my mother left him."

But she was grasping at straws, and even if she hadn't been willing to admit it, Sebastian wasted no time setting her straight. "If that was the case, why, when he married *my* mother four years later, did he not take steps to prevent Natalie's being conceived? And why, for pity's sake, did he take on a stepson who, at twelve, showed every sign of being a royal pain in the rear as a teenager?"

She twisted her face away, beset by the conclusions crowding her mind. Little things she'd taken for granted as part and parcel of her mother's personality suddenly took on new and painful significance. *Genevieve had*

never touched a drop of liquor; had detested overindul-
gence in others. She'd volunteered her time at a shelter
for battered women. She'd insisted on Lily's attending
college because she herself had never finished high school
and the lack of formal education had cost her dearly when
she was young. She'd displayed a compulsive need to bet-
ter herself, taking one night class course after another
until she'd accumulated enough postsecondary credits to
earn a degree in fine arts.

"Well?" Sebastian continued regarding her patiently.
"Why did Hugo take on another man's family, Lily?"

"I don't know," she said, turning aside her face to hide
her brimming eyes, "and I don't care. I just want to know
why he didn't fight to keep me."

Sebastian cupped her cheek and forced her to look at
him. "He made a mistake. He let hurt pride dictate his
actions and by the time he came to his senses, you thought
Neil Talbot was your father. He loved you enough then
to give you up, and he loves you enough now not to want
to tarnish your memories of your mother by telling you
how things really stood."

"My mother!" she wept bitterly, the truth sweeping
over her in huge, unforgiving waves. "Genevieve Talbot,
the elegant, gracious doctor's wife. The accomplished
hostess. The morally upright citizen whose whole life was
built on a lie. And I believed every word that came out
of her mouth. How that must have amused her!"

Hearing the rising hysteria in her voice, he put his arms
around her and drew her firmly to him, even though she
tried to fight him off. "Don't," he murmured, his hands
stroking in long, strong, comforting sweeps up and down
her spine. "Don't beat yourself up like this. You were the
innocent victim caught in the middle. None of this is your
fault."

"No," she sobbed, beside herself, "it's yours. Oh, I hate you, Sebastian Caine, for what you've taken away from me tonight!"

"I hate myself," he said grimly. "I wish to God I'd kept quiet about what I know. Lily, honey, please don't cry like this. You'll make yourself ill."

"I don't care!" She lifted her tear-ravaged face to his. "Do you know how empty I feel inside? How *ugly?*"

"You're not ugly," he insisted, holding her face in his hands. His voice dropped a notch, took on a husky edge that rendered it almost tender. "You're beautiful and desirable and...!"

And then he was kissing her, his mouth coming down on hers as masterfully as though, by the sheer force of his will, he thought he could undo all the pain he'd brought to her. Kissing her with a dedication and passion so fierce that it kindled a tiny flame in the cold, empty wasteland that seemed to fill her.

She felt his hand at her throat, at her shoulder. Touched her fingertips to his chest and found the rapid, uneven thunder of his heartbeat. Saw, just before her own fell closed, the smoldering heat in his eyes. And the flame grew; flickered and strengthened into a blazing torch radiating through her blood to chase away the chilling horror of the last few minutes.

As quickly as they'd surfaced, all the ghastly details he'd disclosed shriveled in its heat and left behind a rapacious need to *belong*. To be possessed and cherished as if she were the only woman of any consequence left on earth. She wanted to be loved, honestly and without reservation or secrets, if not forever, then at least for a little while.

Her hands roamed the starched front of his shirt,

searched out the pearl studs holding it closed, and tugged them loose with feverish impatience.

He caught her fingers in his, crushed them gently to his bare chest. "This isn't a good time to give in to impulse. Neither of us is thinking straight."

"I don't want to think. I want to feel…to heal." She kissed his throat softly and finished on a sigh, "Help me to do that, Sebastian."

"Be careful you don't start something you're not prepared to finish," he muttered, then floundered into a groan when, undaunted, she dipped her head and circled the tiny bud of his left nipple with her tongue.

"Make love to me," she begged against his skin.

His breath caught in a harsh, agonized rasp. "You didn't want that earlier."

"I want it now," she told him, bisecting the line of dark hair arrowing into the waist of his trousers with the tip of her fingernail.

"It won't make the truth about the past any less ugly."

"This isn't about the past, it's about the here and now. About me—" she skimmed her fingers over his flat, hard belly; toyed with the straining fabric of his fly "—and you."

"Li…ly…!" Her name hovered on the labored whisper of a man fighting a hopeless battle against overwhelming odds.

She swirled her tongue in the hollow of his throat. Massaged the heel of her hand against the rigid contours he couldn't hope to disguise. Let her palm define the shape of him. Felt the life force pulsing urgently for release beneath her fingertips.

He shuddered. Groaned again. Attempted to hold her away.

Whimpering with need, she clawed at her dress, freeing

it from her shoulders and letting it glide in a silken whisper to her waist. She wore no bra underneath; no camisole. Nothing but a tan line dividing decency from forbidden pleasures.

His gaze seared her nakedness and she knew, from the sudden flood of color darkening his face, that she'd won. Dipping his head, he kissed her ear and whispered, in language erotically explicit, how he was going to love her and make her forget. And then, he proceeded to show her.

He cupped her bare breasts and took their aching peaks in his mouth, drawing so deeply at their core that she felt her soul slip away. He trailed his tongue in a slow, tormenting path down her cleavage to dally with her navel, then toured back, circuitously and at excruciating leisure, to her mouth.

Whatever secrets she had hidden there, he discovered with deft and expert thrusts and swirls. His tongue tasted of cognac and her perfume.

With one hand supporting her back, he took his other and slid it with delicious intent to the slit in the front of her skirt. Slow torture turned to raging gratification as his finger inched up her inner thigh and slipped inside the fine lace border edging the leg of her panties. If he hadn't known before that she was hot and sleek with hunger for him, he soon discovered that, too.

He was a devil and an angel, and she was so helplessly in thrall to his fondling that the best she could manage was to cling to him like a wilting vine as the spasms of completion he induced rolled over her.

When her knees threatened to buckle, he released her side zipper and with one sweep of his hand sent her dress and panties into a silken puddle on the floor, then lifted her into his arms and carried her to one of the couches. While she lay there with echoes of pleasure still rippling in the distant recesses of her body, he stripped off his own clothes and what he laid bare to her passion-glazed eyes was awesome to behold.

Of its own volition, her hand reached out, only to be halted by his while still inches from its destination. "Let me touch you," she pleaded. "Let me give pleasure to you."

His eyes caressed her face. "I'm not finished with you yet," he said, his voice overlaid with velvet.

"But I can't...not again, Sebastian...." Limp and depleted, she closed her eyes and felt tears pool along her lashes.

He parted her thighs, found her with the tip of his tongue and when she arched convulsively, brought his lips back to hers and whispered against her mouth, "Yes, you can, my lovely Lily. And when I'm deep inside you, you'll come again."

She was sure he was wrong. Would have found pleasure and satisfaction enough in accommodating him, in holding him close to her heart as his urgent thrusts took him closer to the edge of oblivion. Instead she caught the rhythm, climbed with him past the point of no return, then convulsed around him to milk the passion spilling from him and secrete it deep within herself.

The scented aftermath of their loving permeated the night, an elusive blend of skin and heat, of aftershave and perfume and fine French brandy, of man and woman and sex. His labored breathing punctuated the silence. His weight pressed her into the cool, smooth leather of the couch. His limbs, tangled with hers, held her his prisoner. And all the while, in her most intimate and secret place, he remained joined to her, a spent warrior at rest.

How long, if they'd had the choice, they'd have drifted together like that she never discovered, because another sound disturbed the night: that of the lower door from the stables opening and footsteps ascending the winding staircase, and Natalie's voice calling out, "Sebastian, you beast, are you here? I've been looking everywhere for you. We need to talk."

Lily's breath caught in a horrified gasp. Her eyes shot open, slewed across the room to the window where her dress lay like a puddle of ink on the pale oak floor. The diamanté heel of one of her shoes sparkled gleefully in the moonlight. Sebastian's shirt lay hooked on the corner of the coffee table, shining like a beacon to advertise his undressed presence.

Her limbs, which mere seconds before, had possessed all the strength and resilience of overcooked pasta, tensed. Completely unhinged, she swung her gaze back to Sebastian still stretched out on top of her, her eyes spelling out the words that surely must've been pounding through his mind, too. *What are we going to do?*

He gave an infinitesimal shake of his head and quietly laid his hand over her mouth before she could give voice to the question. And Natalie, having reached the landing, began making her way down the hall toward the living room.

CHAPTER SEVEN

"SEBASTIAN?" Her steps grew nearer and came to a stop so close to the couch that Lily's lungs seized up in anticipation of the scene about to unfold. Oh, the indignity of being caught in so compromising a situation! The shame!

Panic-stricken, she struggled to find an explanation—something…*anything!*—which would lessen the magnitude of the embarrassment consuming her. And the best she could come up with was, *Natalie, this isn't what it looks like.*

The utter absurdity of such a statement sent her into a paroxysm of silent hysterical giggles. Feeling the ripples chasing through her, Sebastian gave a faint, admonishing shake of his head, and buried her face against his shoulder.

Then Natalie's voice came again. "Hmm…wonder if he went to pick up Penny after her shift ended? Maybe he's already back at the party with her, and I've missed my chance *again*…."

Praise heaven and a benevolent God, her footsteps were fading toward the stairs! Shortly after, the lower door thudded closed.

Sebastian waited a full two minutes before moving: a small eternity of time that left Lily suspended somewhere between acute appreciation of the narrowness of their escape, and the fact that their naked bodies still lay entwined in the ultimate intimacy. But the magic of the moment, if, indeed, there'd ever been any, had left with Natalie, and if Lily had thought to presume otherwise, Sebastian soon disabused her of the idea.

The second he deemed it safe to do so, he rolled off the couch and disappeared down the hall. Shivering for all kinds of reasons, not the least being the sudden absence of his warm body on top of hers, Lily shot across the room and attempted to climb into both items of her discarded clothing at the same time.

Not a wise move, she quickly discovered, yanking viciously on her dress and hopping around on one foot as the other became hopelessly snarled in folds of fabric.

A table lamp clicked on. "No need to ruin a perfectly good outfit. Natalie went away convinced there was no one home. The odds of anyone else showing up unannounced are negligible," Sebastian observed, sauntering back into view decently covered in a navy terry-cloth bathrobe.

Feeling at a decided disadvantage with her panties hanging at half-mast around her knees, Lily grabbed the dress and used it to shield herself from his inspection—as if he hadn't already seen his fill! "How can you stand there and calmly behave as if what just happened wasn't a near disaster?"

"Are you referring to Natalie's untimely arrival, or the fact that you and I got rather carried away in the heat of the moment?"

"Both!" she cried, her nerves so brittle she felt ready to snap in half. "You're supposed to be dating another woman, yet you don't think twice about making love to me, and when we're almost caught in the act, you just lie there and wait to be discovered."

He shrugged and picked up the brandy decanter. "Sure you wouldn't like a shot of this to settle you down? No...? Okay...." He poured himself a refill and cupped his hands around the delicate balloon glass in much the same way he'd held her face not half an hour before. "First, to set the record straight, *you* were the instigator of our sexual encounter, not I."

The truth of that allegation sent a blush sweeping through her like wildfire. "Well, you didn't exactly rebuff me."

"No, Lily," he said evenly. "I suspect not many men would have turned down such a charmingly insistent proposition. We are, after all, mere mortals, just like women. And you are a very persuasive and accomplished seductress when you put your mind to it."

"Are you so fixated on sex that you don't see the bigger picture here? *What if Natalie had found us?*"

Smothering a sigh, he paced the width of the room. "It's because I *do* see the bigger picture that I can't worry about something that didn't happen. Tonight I betrayed the trust of a man who's been father, friend and mentor to me for longer than I care to remember and who never, except for this one thing, asked for any kind of return on his investment."

"I gather you're referring to the fact that you told me about my mother?" she said, scrambling into her dress while his back was turned. "Well, if you're worried I'm going to run to Hugo with the news—"

He spun around, his glance so loaded with rage, it was a miracle he didn't self-destruct. "I don't give a damn what you do! It's what *I've* done that'll keep me awake all night, and if you think I can just sweep my actions under the carpet and forget them, you know even less about the kind of man I am than I thought. So spare me your heroics, please! Hugo will learn his secret's out, but he'll hear it from me, not you, first thing tomorrow. I might have acted unethically, but I've not yet sunk to the level of cowardice."

"And that's the only regret you have?"

"Should there be another?"

His contemptuous indifference to what the two of them had so recently shared should have burned her. Instead it chilled her to the bone. "Some might say the fact that we risked an unplanned pregnancy tonight might be cause for concern."

He drew his hand down his face as if, by doing so, he could erase the entire evening. "Thank you for reminding me that, on top of everything else, I didn't use a condom. I suppose it's too much to hope you're on the pill?"

"I'm not on the pill. Casual sex isn't a recreational pastime for me and, unlike you, I'm not involved in a serious relationship with anyone." She stepped into her shoes and tried to finger-comb into place all the loose ends which had fallen out of her elegant hairdo. "Which brings up another point—how would Penny feel if she were to find out you and I had…?"

"Had sex?" He smiled bitterly. "Well, that's one secret I *am* prepared to keep, nor do I imagine you're too anxious to broadcast your indiscretion."

"It was your indiscretion, too," she reminded him, dismayed all over again by how much his easy dismissal of their lovemaking hurt. "I might have started it, but you didn't seem to have too much trouble joining in and finishing off."

He rounded on her, the anger formerly directed at himself turned now on her. "You want me to tell you I'm swimming in guilt about that, too? Fine, you've got it! I'm the world's biggest jerk. I should be strung up by my thumbs—unless there's some other section of my anatomy you'd prefer to see surgically removed. But I'm not a magician. I can't turn back the clock. What's done is done and we're both going to have to live with it.''

"Was there nothing memorable about it, Sebastian?'' she asked, tears stinging her eyes and choking her voice. "Were you just going through the motions? Would it have been just as easy to turn me down?''

"If it had been, I'd have done that,'' he told her, a hint of tenderness warming his tone. "But I can't give you what you really want, Lily, and that's what makes sex between us wrong.''

"What is it you think I want?''

"Love,'' he said simply. "It's one reason, maybe even the chief reason, you came to Stentonbridge in the first place. The loss of your immediate family has left you vulnerable and that by itself gives you enormous appeal.'' He took a step closer and brushed his knuckles down her cheek. "It would be very easy to ignore my conscience and embark on a summer affair with you. I'd be lying if I didn't admit the attraction's there, *and* the opportunity to give in to it. But we aren't *in love,* Lily. We don't even like each other very much, most of the time. And I've seen too many lives turned into a living hell because people mistook good sex for something deeper and more enduring. I'm not about to make the same mistake myself, especially not with Hugo Preston's daughter. I owe him better than that.''

Everything he said made perfect sense. Trying to elevate lust to love was preposterous. Laughable. So why was she having such a hard time holding back the tears? Why did she feel as if she'd just found something precious, only to have it snatched away from her grasp before she could gain firm hold of it?

"You're absolutely right, of course. A summer fling

doesn't do it for me. I do want more. I want commitment from a man. Permanence.''

"And I'm not able to offer you either, not now and perhaps not ever.''

"Of course not, nor do I expect you to.'' Since looking him in the eye was out of the question, she turned to stare out of the window and called up every last iota of pride to get her through what had to be said. "I think the least damage all around would be for us to forget everything that's transpired between us in this room tonight. Don't burden Hugo with your confessions, Sebastian, and let's not burden each other with useless regrets.''

"I have to tell him.''

"No.'' She shook her head, and the motion set the tears in her eyes to shimmering and blinding her vision. "Don't risk your relationship with him because of what you've told me. It's enough that I finally know the truth.''

"I can't promise I'll abide by that, Lily.''

"Well, you'd damn well better,'' she cried, wheeling toward the stairs. "If you care about him as much as you say you do, you won't ease your conscience at his expense. You'll learn to live with what you know, just as I have to.''

She got no farther than the landing before he caught up with her. "Where do you think you're going?''

"Anywhere, as long as it's away from you!''

"I'm afraid not,'' he said. "By now, we'll surely have been missed at the party. If you're serious about not wanting to arouse everyone's suspicions, we're going to reappear, together, and act as if nothing untoward has taken place. If anyone asks, we went for a stroll by the river.''

She couldn't do it. As far as he was concerned, her acting repertoire had exhausted itself. She couldn't pretend she was fine when her heart felt as if he'd stamped the imprint of his heel on it. "You're hardly dressed for the part," she said, shrugging off his hand, "and I'm perfectly capable of making up my own lies to explain my absence, without any help from you."

"You're a mess," he said brutally. "You couldn't fool an infant, let alone anyone as perceptive as Hugo." He steered her past the stairwell and shoved her into a powder room near the other end of the hall. "Splash some cold water on your face and fix your hair while I get ready. It won't take me more than a couple of minutes."

She looked in the mirror over the sink. A stranger stared back, wild-eyed and disheveled. The chain of her pendant was snagged in a section of hair trailing down her neck. She was wearing only one earring. Her lipstick was smeared, her mascara had run. He was right: she was a walking advertisement of sated passion and grief.

Somehow she managed to repair the worst of the damage to her face, though anyone looking closely at her reddened eyes would surely know she'd been crying. Restoring her elegant, upswept hairdo was another matter, and in the end she pulled out all the pins and let it fall loose to her shoulders.

Sebastian was waiting for her when she came out and, certainly, no one would have guessed he'd recently been rolling around naked. He looked as coolly unperturbed as if he'd spent the entire evening reading law books in Hugo's library. His bow tie lay precisely where it should against his shirt which shone crisp and fresh as new snow. His jacket clung with immaculate precision to his shoulders.

"Ready?" he asked.

"No. I'm missing an earring." She scanned the floor by the window. "I must have lost it here, but I don't see it."

"I'll look for it later. With your hair down like that, no one's going to notice." He surveyed her critically. "I won't say you look as good as new, but you'll fool the people who matter. Let's go."

He preceded her down the stairs and led her out and around the back of the stables to another path, which followed the course of the river. "Gives more credibility to our story, should anyone ask," he said, tucking her hand into the crook of his elbow. "Smile, for Pete's sake. You look as if you lost your best friend, instead of just an earring."

"I did," she said stonily. "Thanks to you, I just found out my mother wasn't who she pretended to be."

"I tried to spare you, but you're the one who insisted on knowing."

"Right now, I'm not in the mood for any *I told you so's,* Sebastian."

"No," he said thoughtfully. "I don't suppose I would be, either, in your place. Does it help at all to know I didn't gain an ounce of pleasure or satisfaction from enlightening you and that I wish I could have been the bearer of better news?"

"Not much. It doesn't change anything."

They rounded a bank of rhododendrons and found themselves back on the lower lawn. The party had clearly wound down, leaving only a handful of guests remaining at the small tables on the terrace. "Uh-oh," Sebastian muttered, as all eyes turned their way. "I hoped we'd be able to merge with the crowd. Instead we're making an entrance. Just keep your smile pinned in place and leave the talking to me."

She did and wished she could admire his accounting of their absence, presenting the facts as logically and persuasively as if he were trying to convince a courtroom judge. Instead she hated him for his ability to shift gears so effortlessly. Shakespeare, she decided bitterly, had been right when he'd written, *Let's kill all the lawyers!*

After that night, Sebastian didn't see her again for nearly two weeks. He wished he could as easily get her out of his mind but his conscience wouldn't allow it. As if it wasn't bad enough that he'd spilled secrets that weren't his to share, he'd compounded matters by making love with her.

No use trying to trivialize the experience by labeling it as nothing but sex, because it had amounted to more than that. They *had* made love and in such spectacular fashion that whatever interest he'd once had in Penny Stanford had withered overnight.

Even worse, he'd betrayed Hugo a second time by taking advantage of his daughter when she was most vulnerable and even if Hugo could forgive him for that, he couldn't forgive himself.

What was it about her that made her so hard to forget? Her fragility? Her vulnerability when she learned the truth about her mother? Or was it just that he felt sorry for her?

Hell, no! It wasn't pity stirring to life down below his belt whenever he recalled their night of love, and it wasn't charity!

Then, on top of everything else, there was the latest report from the investigator. The information it contained should have vindicated his suspicions about her. Instead it sat in his gut like lead and he wished he'd never embarked on the inquiry in the first place. *Suspicion of fraud and conspiracy* were ugly words in any context. He didn't want to believe they applied to her—and if *that* didn't go to show what bad shape he was in, maybe it was time he retired from the law and went to work collecting other people's garbage!

On the Thursday of the week following the party, his mother phoned him at the office. "Just wanted to remind you we're going up to the cottage tomorrow afternoon, and spending the weekend there, Sebastian. You'll come with us, of course?"

To stare Lily straight in the eye and behave as if the most they'd ever shared was a cool handshake? To pretend he didn't know how she'd trembled beneath him and begged him with her eyes and her hands and her little urgent cries, to come to her as she hovered on the brink of orgasm? To know he could look as she paraded around in her skinny little bathing suit, but he couldn't touch? And worst of all, to act as if he didn't know she was under police investigation in Vancouver?

"I don't think so," he said. "I'm bogged down with work right now."

"But that leak in the flashing around the chimney needs to be fixed before it damages the bedroom ceiling, and I can't have Hugo climbing ladders to the roof at his age! And we've done so much entertaining since Lily arrived that I thought a quiet weekend with just the family would make for a nice change." His mother's voice sharpened with disappointment. "Honestly, Sebastian, I can't believe you forgot, though I suppose I shouldn't be too surprised since you haven't shown your face at the house in days."

"If you must know, I thought Lily would be heading home any day now and you'd changed your mind. Didn't she plan to stay here only about three weeks?"

"Yes. But her father's convinced her to stay until the Labor Day weekend since there's no pressing need for her to fly home any sooner."

Oh, terrific! One more complication he didn't need!

"So, what do you say, Sebastian? Will you join us? You can bring your work with you, if you like. You won't be the only one. Natalie's going to have to study part of the time, too, with her finals coming up soon. But it would mean a lot to Hugo to have you there. You know how much he enjoys a man's company, especially yours, and he's noticed that you seem to be avoiding coming to the house."

Because I'm ashamed to see him—or Lily!

But in the end, and against his better judgment, he agreed to his mother's request. He told himself it was because he had to face Hugo sooner or later but there was more to it than that, and he knew it. His attraction to Lily Talbot was out of control. For all that he wished it were otherwise, when the opportunity presented itself, he couldn't stay away from her.

Still, when he arrived at the lake the next evening, he tried to keep his distance and, apparently, succeeded too well. Natalie cornered him in the kitchen where she'd coerced him into helping her clean up after dinner, and wasted no time getting straight to the point. "You've told her, haven't you?"

"Told who what?"

"You've spilled the beans to Lily about her mother."

He made a big production of stowing stuff into the refrigerator. "What makes you think that?"

"Oh, I don't know!" she drawled sarcastically. "Perhaps because neither one of you can stand looking the other in the eye. Or perhaps it's got more to do with the fact that every time she opens her mouth to speak, you act as if she's not even in the room, but then, when you think no one's noticing, you watch her like a hawk hovering over its next meal. You *did* tell her, didn't you?"

He heaved a weary sigh and leaned against the refrigerator door. "If you must know, yes, I did. And I wish I hadn't."

"I don't," she said. "I think she deserved to be told. In fact, I came looking for you the night of Dad's birthday party, to try to convince you to tell her, but you'd disappeared."

And you'll never know how close you came to finding me, Nat! "Yes. Revealing family secrets with an audience of a hundred didn't seem such a hot idea, so we…went off by ourselves."

"How did she take the news?"

He rolled his eyes. For someone bent on a career in social work, Natalie could be astonishingly obtuse when it came to understanding people. "How do you think!"

"Not well. I can see in her eyes that she's pretty torn up about it. Does Dad know?"

"That I've told her? No."

"Well, if you don't want him to guess for himself, you'd better get cracking on some sort of damage control. I've thought ever since the party that she's been quieter than usual, but it wasn't until you showed up tonight that I figured out why. Heck, Sebastian, I thought she was going to faint when she saw you!"

It wasn't often that he followed Natalie's nineteen-year-old advice but, for once, she had a point worth taking. He strolled out to the porch and found Lily, with Katie at her feet, chatting idly with Hugo and his mother. Slapping the flat of his hand to his waist, he said casually, "I need to walk off that meal. Come with me, Lily, and I'll show you the neighborhood."

He saw the stubborn cast to her chin and knew she was about to refuse him. Hauling her off the wicker love seat, he marched her down the steps before she could voice her protest aloud and strong-armed her down the path to the lakefront. "Don't bother telling me you'd rather keep company with a pit viper," he informed her, when they were out of sight and earshot. "I've already received that message loud and clear. But I need to talk to you. Privately."

"I hope it's urgent," she snapped, massaging her wrist. "I don't appreciate being man-handled like this. And if you've dug up more dirt on my mother, you can keep it. I'm not bartering my self-respect a second time to hear things better left unsaid."

He caught her elbow and pulled her around to face him. "Lily, please!"

"Don't touch me!" Angrily she shrugged him off.

He raised both hands in surrender. "Okay. I won't touch you. But will you at least hear me out?"

"Do I have any choice?"

She was putting up a good front, but he could see the effort it cost her. Her eyes were glazed with tears, her voice shook. "Look," he said gently, "I can see you've gone through hell, this last couple of weeks, but if it makes you feel any better, it's been no walk in the park for me, either."

"Why? Because you broke your promise to Hugo?"

He nodded. "I should have listened to him. Respected his judgment, his wisdom. He recognized from the first that your knowing about Genevieve's mistakes would cause nothing but unnecessary trouble and hurt."

"I've come to terms with her mistakes," Lily said flatly. "She wasn't perfect, but who is? Not Hugo and certainly not you or I. Yes, I was shocked to hear what had happened, but I can live with it because there's another truth that counts for more than things that happened before I was born. Whatever her faults, Genevieve was a good mother. *Both* my parents were the best—and I'm not talking about Hugo when I say that.''

''Then why are you still so unhappy? I found your earring, if that's what's bothering you. I was planning to get it back to you but hadn't figured out how to do so discreetly. I didn't think you'd appreciate my presenting it to you in front of everyone else, and saying I'd found it between the cushions of my couch.''

She stared at him. ''You have the nerve to suggest a piece of jewelry is the reason I'm upset?''

He couldn't remember the last time he'd blushed but he knew for a fact it was well before his tenth birthday. As if to make up for the time elapsed since then, an embarrassing heat spread over his face. ''Of course not. It's because we…were together.''

''Good heavens, Sebastian, don't try to sugarcoat the facts now!'' she said scornfully. ''We *screwed!* Had a one-night stand! Isn't that how you men phrase it when you're intimate with a woman you don't care about and never want to see again, once the romp between the sheets—or, in this case, the sliding around on your leather couch—is over?''

''Stop it, Lily! I won't listen to that kind of talk.''

''Why? Am I making you uncomfortable? Speaking the truth too plainly?''

''It's not the truth, and you know it.''

''No?'' A lone tear, bright as a diamond, trembled on her lower lashes. ''Well, here's something that is. I feel cheap and dirty because of the way I behaved with you. You might not have been my first lover, but you are the first man who made me feel like a whore!''

''Don't talk like that!'' Overcoming her efforts to evade him, he grabbed hold of her again. ''And unless you want to hurt yourself, stop fighting me. Because I'm not letting go.''

''Yes, you are,'' she cried, aiming a kick at his shin and, when she missed, bursting into tears of frustration.

As it had more than once before, her mouth reminded him of a rose carelessly crushed underfoot. Her eyes wore the look of bruised pansies. When he pulled her into the shelter of his arms, the sobs shaking her body made her feel as frail as the thin glazing of ice that covered the lake in early winter and crumbled at a touch.

''You want to know something?'' he muttered, rocking her against him and burying his face in her hair. ''I wish I *had* been your first lover. I wish I'd been the one to teach you what passion's all about. And I wish we could have met under different circumstances. Perhaps if we had…''

Even though he left the sentence unfinished, she guessed the direction his thoughts had been taking. ''We might have fallen in love?'' She drew in a tortured breath. ''I don't think so, Sebastian. Love doesn't come calling only when it's convenient. It's not that calculating, or that easily controlled.''

Nor was desire! Holding her close again revived the same pulsing ache that had gotten him into so much trouble two weeks before. Rational thought dissolved into hot, urgent need. She was warm to his touch, her skin soft. So smooth and satin soft he wanted to stroke her all over. And taste her—the delicate flower fragrance of her mouth, the sweet secret honey of her femininity.

She tilted her face up to his. The fading light touched her tear tracks with gold, sparkled on her wet lashes, kissed the curve of her mouth with a familiarity he resented. ''Please let me go, Sebastian,'' she whispered. ''I can't bear your being kind to me like this.''

"But it isn't kindness." His voice became trapped in a throat grown thick with an emotion that didn't bear close analysis, something that went beyond mere passion. "God help me, I want you, Lily. More than ever. And I think you want me, too."

She looked away and refused to answer.

He gave her a little shake, slight enough, to be sure, but it didn't take much for the undulation of her body against his to increase his hunger to fever pitch. "Don't you?" he persisted urgently.

"Stop cross-examining me," she retorted. "You're not in the courtroom now, and I'm not on trial."

"Answer the question," he begged, against her mouth. "And if I'm wrong, I'll let you go."

"Oh, I want you," she said hopelessly. "And I despise myself for it."

Above them on the rise of land where the cottage stood, a sudden flood of light spilled into the dusk. Anyone standing at the windows would easily spot them, might even think to join them for the neighborhood tour he'd so flippantly come up with as an excuse to get her alone. Never mind that his reason for doing so had changed. What mattered now was that they not be deflected from a course as inevitable as the pattern of early stars pricking the sky.

"There's a dinghy in the boathouse," he said, turning back to the foot of the path that had brought them to the waterfront. "Come out on the lake with me. We'll be alone there, with no chance of anyone walking in on us."

She hesitated. Pulled away from him until the tips of their fingers barely touched, yet he felt her indecision as clearly as if he were grasping a live electric wire.

"Please," he said, increasing his hold and inching her back toward him. "Come with me, Lily."

CHAPTER EIGHT

THE lake was limpid as smoked glass. Except for the muted slap of the oars and the cry of a distant loon, not a sound broke the silence of the night. Rowing swiftly, he angled the boat to the far side of an island lying about a mile offshore.

"We used to come here as kids," he said, after they'd waded onto the sliver of beach and he'd tied up the dinghy to a nearby tree.

"And as adults?"

A simple enough question on the surface, but he heard another in her voice and said, "I've never brought a woman here until tonight, Lily, if that's what you're asking. You're the first."

He tried to catch her hand and draw her to him, but she slipped away and walked parallel to the water, head bent and footsteps whispering in the soft, white sand. She wore shorts and a cotton top. Her skin, tanned honey-gold by day, took on a richer tone in the gloom against the pale color of her clothes. Her hair, caught back in combs, spilled down her back dark as midnight silk.

Although he'd have preferred to have her close in his arms, viewing her from a distance gave him a better appreciation of her slender elegance. How had he missed it, when they'd first met? Wherever had he come up with the idea that she was unremarkable? Her kind of understated good looks put more flamboyant beauty to shame.

When she'd gone about twenty yards, she stopped and

turned to face him. Her voice carried clearly in the night. "I don't suppose I'll be the last, though," she said.

He lifted his shoulders in a shrug. "I don't know. But I do know every time I tell myself that becoming involved with you is a bad idea, another part of me doesn't want to accept it."

"I can imagine which part!"

"I'm talking about a connection that goes beyond physical attraction."

"But you can't put a name to it. Or won't." There was no missing the barbed edge in her words.

"You want me to call it love, but we both know it's too soon for that." He stifled a sigh. "We've known each other less than two months. Can't we agree to table definitions until the end of the summer, and just let things evolve at their own pace? See how things work out between us?"

"Sneak around having sex, you mean, but lead the family to believe we're just good friends?"

"Would it be so bad if friendship's the best we could manage?"

"But we won't manage that, and we both know it." The moon slid out from behind the low rise of hills to the east. Limned in its light, she looked achingly lonely and vulnerable. "When an affair goes sour, Sebastian, it never ends in friendship. It ends in pain and bitterness and regret."

He couldn't look that far down the line. There were too many unknowns. "All I really know at this minute is that I want to hold you." He opened his arms. "Come here, sweetheart, please."

She scuffed her bare toes in the sand and dragged her feet, an outward show of resistance to combat the desire she couldn't deny so exactly mirroring his own ambivalence that he almost smiled. But the way she was looking at him, the sultry curve of her mouth, the way she ran her tongue over her upper lip and let her hand trail suggestively all the way from her throat to her breast and down the length of her thigh, were no laughing matter. They spoke of passion about to be unleashed, of a magnetic pull that had her suddenly giving in to its force and running toward him.

He met her halfway and they collapsed together on the cool sand. Her mouth softened beneath his. Opened. Welcomed. Her fingers inched inside his shirt, traced lightly over his ribs, slid to his navel.

The heat in his belly raged, left him throbbing. He wanted to savor the moment, enjoy the feast she presented. Dwell in close detail on every satin inch of her. But a dozen demons drove him, savaging his control. He had to have her…now…!

Dimly he heard cotton and denim shrieking softly as they were flung aside; the protesting gasp of silky underthings too roughly handled. He felt her, hot and moist against his cupped hand, heard her inarticulate little cry when he touched her sensitized flesh.

She deserved to be loved with leisurely expertise. With finesse and sophistication, and respect. But he'd left it too late, tormented himself for too long. There was room for nothing in his universe but the sheer heaven of finding himself inside her and then, mere seconds later, losing himself inside her, utterly and completely.

Eventually he lifted his head and looked down at her. Her mouth was swollen from his kisses, her eyes luminous in the moonlight. ''I should probably apologize for that,'' he said, when his breathing allowed him to speak, ''but regret isn't the emotion uppermost in my mind right now.''

The slow, sweet radiance of her smile and the way she stroked the hair off his forehead moved him unbearably. Flirtation, teasing, sexual gratification pure and simple— these things he could deal with in a woman. But tenderness, Lily Talbot style, left him wide-open to a baffling array of emotions.

Too bad that regret sat so close to the top of the list!

Averting his gaze, Sebastian wished for the umpteenth time that he'd accepted her at face value and never started the investigative process. Just knowing that all the time they were making love, his West Coast spy was compiling an ever-incriminating dossier that laid bare every particle of her life for his inspection, made him ill.

Pursue this and send more details, he'd instructed his man, but the guy had run up against a brick wall. Police weren't forthcoming about ongoing investigations, and the odds were he'd learn nothing new until charges were laid.

"What are you thinking about?" Lily asked him softly.

Squirming inwardly at the uncomfortable shot of guilt flushing through him, he said, "That we should go swimming."

She gave a captivating gurgle of laughter. *"Here?"*

"Why not?" He circled her breast with one finger. "I seem to recall you like swimming after dark."

She laughed, a breathless, abbreviated gasp that told him how much she liked the way he was touching her, too. "I'd forgotten about that night in the pool."

"I hadn't," he said. "That was the first time I kissed you."

"You lied to me, as well. About wearing a swimsuit."

He was lying to her now, about something a whole hell of a lot more serious than being stark naked, and the knowledge was eating holes in him.

Mistaking his silence for confusion, she reminded him, "You said you were skinny-dipping."

"Well, this time I will be and so, my dear, will you."

He sprang to his feet and pulled her up after him. The sight of her, all moon-washed curves and shadows, reminded him again why he'd really brought her to this isolated spot. For crying out loud, he was worse than a randy eighteen-year-old in the back seat of his father's car with a high school cheerleader!

"Last one in's a chicken!" he taunted, sprinting to the water's edge and taking a flat, racing dive into the lake guaranteed to shock the most active libido into submission.

Her laughter chased him and when he surfaced a hundred yards from shore, he found her bobbing beside him, her hair streaming out behind her, her eyes blacker than the night except for the pinpoints of stars reflected in her pupils.

She closed her eyes, and folding her hands behind her head, floated on her back. Her nipples showed just above the surface, tiny islands of temptation just beyond his reach. She sighed blissfully. "The water's so warm, it's like a bath in here!"

"Yeah," he said ruefully, gaining a foothold on the rise of a sand bank in the shallow depths. "Where's a cold shower when a guy needs one? I'm aching for you again already, Lily."

The laughter on her face faded. She flipped herself upright and floated closer, sculling gently with her hands. Her legs tangled briefly with his, then drifted away again. Her shoulders looked as if they'd been dipped in silver.

"Why can't I seem to get enough of you, Sebastian?" she asked seriously, fixing her gaze on his mouth. "Why do I risk getting hurt by letting myself fall under your spell time and again?''

Absently he twirled a lock of her hair around his finger, plagued by another question he wished he dared ask. *How can you be so open and honest on the one hand and, on the other, capable of the kind of duplicity that my investigator's report suggests?*

She tipped her head to one side and touched her hand to his jaw. ''Sebastian? What's troubling you suddenly?''

''What makes you think anything is?''

He attempted to laugh off her concern, but she held his gaze. ''I can see it in your face.''

He wished he could tell her. Wished he could just come right out and say, *Look, I know you're in some sort of trouble back home, that you could be facing legal action. Come clean with me, and I'll help you. No one else in the family needs to know. I'm a lawyer, professionally and personally committed to protecting client confidentiality. But as long as you keep this secret, there's a barrier between us that's crippling any chance we might have of developing a lasting relationship.*

The trouble was, for him to admit he'd gone behind her back in the first place would deal a death blow to what they shared. She'd never forgive him and he could hardly expect she would.

''Rule number one—don't go looking for problems where they don't exist, Lily,'' he said, looping his arm around her neck. ''Just savor the moment.''

She bit her lip and lowered her eyes, and he knew she was hurt by his evasion.

To make up for it, he tugged her close enough to leave no doubt as to how he proposed to make that moment memorable. ''You're beautiful by moonlight, did you know that?''

Her eyes flew up to meet his. She looked almost embarrassed. "You've never said anything like that to me before."

"Then I've been very remiss. I should have told you a long time ago."

"Is that another of your rules—to flatter a woman into submission? Because if it is, you ought to know by now that you don't have to go to such lengths. I know I'm not beautiful. I'm merely...pleasant looking." She parted her thighs and trapped him between their soft inner contours. "And very...very...willing..."

He shaped her with his hands, stunned once again by her perfect symmetry: the narrow span of her waist and slender flare of her hips, the sweet, full curve of her buttocks. "Oh, you're a lot more than that," he murmured, slipping inside her and exhaling sharply as she closed around him sleek as a glove. "You're...irresistible."

Their coming together this time was slow and exquisite, the thrust and retreat in sync with the flow of the water around them. If he could, he'd have loved her like that all night, riding the gentle waves and warding off the climax lurking in the darkness like some predatory beast waiting to destroy him.

But she decided otherwise, wrapping her long, golden legs around his waist, tormenting him with her mouth, whispering in his ear how he pleased her, how she loved the power and drive of him. Begging him in a voice close to a sob to touch her "...right there...like that...oh... *yes!*"

And he was lost. Shattered. He heard himself cry out her name, his voice a razor-edge of anguish bordered with ecstasy. His seed surged free, and took his soul with it. Depleted him so exhaustively that it was all he could do to remain afloat. Indeed wouldn't have, if it hadn't been that the water was no more than five feet deep and he could anchor his feet to the sandy bottom.

She clung to him, her breath winnowing in warm, damp gusts against his neck. "Oh, Sebastian!" she murmured, drenching his name in the aftermath of passion. "*I love...*how you make me feel!"

She had been on the verge of saying something else. He knew by the subtle stiffening of her body, the way she suddenly reined in the impulsive flow of her words. And he couldn't begin to decipher his reaction; didn't have the first idea how to reconcile the chagrin that rolled over him because she hadn't said it, with the welling relief that she hadn't forced an issue he wasn't ready to deal with.

"Know what?" he said, grazing her mouth with his reply. "We'd better get back before someone at the cottage realizes the boat's gone and they send out a search party to look for us."

She didn't have to tell him it wasn't the response she'd been hoping for. The way she dropped her arms and drifted away from him, then turned and swam quickly ashore, spoke volumes of disappointment.

Following, he caught up with her as she ran up the beach to where they'd left their clothes. "Lily," he began, searching for a way to soften his rejection without compromising his sense of decency any more than he already had.

She turned to him, a too-bright smile fixed in place. "You should have thought to bring towels. How are we going to explain the fact that our hair's soaking and our clothing damp?"

If only that was all he had to worry about! "With any luck, everyone will be in bed by the time we get back. If not, I'll distract them while you sneak in by the back door."

*   *   *

The cottage was old, built some time in the late nineteenth century. Though constructed to withstand the vicious winters, its floorboards creaked and its interior walls were thin. Even if his room hadn't been next to hers, she'd probably have been able to hear his every move.

With her window wide-open against the stifling heat of the Ontario summer, though, she knew to the second when he climbed into bed. By turning her head just a fraction, she could see where the glow from his reading lamp illuminated the near branches of the pine tree in the garden.

A moth batted against the screen at her window, then fluttered off in search of the source of light. *Just like me, poor fool,* she thought miserably. *Not happy until it scorches to death on its own folly.*

Next door, Sebastian extinguished the light. The mattress squeaked faintly as he turned over. Would he fall asleep easily, the lovemaking they'd shared already consigned to the past? Or, like her, lie awake in the dark and brood over where their relationship was headed?

She closed her eyes and relived that hour on the island. The first frenzied coming together over too soon, but still magnificent enough to leave her yearning for more. And then the next time...the velvet night, the water plush against her skin...

She felt again his body, sleek, slick, joining with hers and carrying her on a current of passion growing ever more urgent. Sweeping her toward rapids tantalizingly out of reach until, suddenly, with a rush that took her breath away, he hurled her over the edge.

Goose bumps pebbled her skin. Squirming, she pulled the sheet over her. It had been perfect. *Perfect!* Until, caught up in the emotion of the moment, the words hammering in her brain had burst forth.

Oh, she'd caught herself in time, turned *I love you!*—

an admission he didn't want to hear—into an innocuous *I love how you make me feel,* but he'd guessed how close she'd come to slipping up and breaking the rules he'd laid down. Any fool would have known, when her whole heart had revealed itself in the timbre of her voice. And Sebastian was no fool.

That second time they'd made love had been different, though. In the warm water of the lake, they'd merged softly—which was an odd word to use, considering he was all steel and unyielding strength. But she'd sensed a rare gentleness in him, a protectiveness almost. Inured as she'd become to his more abrasive nature, this other side of him had taken her by surprise and stolen past the defenses she'd thought she held so securely in place.

The pity of it was, she hadn't been content with small gifts. Like a child let loose in a candy store, she'd been greedy for more. When he'd hustled her into the boat and, instead of using the oars, had fired up the small outboard motor and propelled them back to the mainland with what struck her as taciturn haste, she'd said plaintively, "Now that you've had your way with me, you seem in an almighty rush to get rid of me. A mistress—and a mistress on your terms—is all I seem to be."

He'd lifted his head and subjected her to a stare so full of frustration that she could have cut out her tongue. "I know that in all the best movies, this is the moment where the hero's supposed to announce that his intentions are honorable," he'd finally said, "but I think we've already established we're a long way from anything remotely approaching that. If you're looking for some sort of commitment, you're knocking on the wrong door. The sex between us couldn't be better, but I thought we agreed that's as far as it goes right now."

The worst of it was, he was absolutely right. They were

both long past the age where they allowed physical attraction to get in the way of common sense. But logic didn't carry much weight when feminine intuition was calling a different tune, and every instinct she possessed was sounding a clarion call that Sebastian Caine was the man she was destined to love.

Apparently she wasn't the only one nurturing such hopes. Just before noon on the Saturday, Penny Stanford showed up at the cottage. "Found your message waiting when I came off shift last night, Sebastian," she chirped, standing on her cute little tippytoes to kiss him in a way that left no doubt in anyone's mind that she considered herself at the head of the line for his attention, "and thought I'd invite myself up here for the day since I've seen next to nothing of you for the last few weeks."

"You're always welcome, Penny, you know that," Cynthia said.

"Thank you." Her smile flitted warmly over Hugo and Cynthia, then chilled noticeably as it skimmed over Natalie and then finally came to rest on Lily. "One more in such a crowd hardly makes any difference, does it? And I did pick up treats—those dear little shrimp pies from the deli that we love so much, Sebastian. And our favorite wine."

She batted her eyelashes in blatant promise of other treats intended just for him. "I was hoping we could slip away for a while, just the two of us, and catch up the news. Maybe go over to that island you once mentioned. I could use a little relaxation and if you don't mind my saying so, you look a bit peaked, too. Have you been getting enough rest?"

It was all Lily could do not to shriek out, *No, he hasn't! He was up half the night making love to me on that island*

*you're so anxious to see, and if he takes you there as well,
I'll rip his throat out!*

As if she sensed trouble brewing, Natalie poked Lily in
the ribs and muttered, ''Grab a towel and let's get out of
here before I hurl!''

She waited until they'd cooled off in the lake and were
stretched out on the sunbaked boards of the boat jetty
before asking, ''From the look on your face back there at
the cottage, Lily, I'd say I'm not the only one who can't
stand to be in the same room with Penny Stanford for
more than five minutes.''

''Oh, dear!'' Lily looked up from folding her towel into
a makeshift pillow. ''Was it that obvious?''

''You practically turned green around the gills.''
Natalie giggled. ''Not that I blame you! Imagine waking
up after an operation and finding her face hanging over
you! No wonder so many people get nauseated after an
anesthetic. As for the little TLC act she put on for
Sebastian's benefit…!''

Trying to be scrupulously fair, Lily said, ''Perhaps she
genuinely cares about him.''

''And we don't?'' Natalie shot her a scornful glance.
''Anyway, let's forget about her and talk about something
more interesting. I got some news yesterday, just before
I left the college, and I'm so excited I can hardly stand
myself. Once I've written my finals, I've been invited to
go to India with eight other students to work under the
supervision of a team of social workers and medical per-
sonnel in Bombay. If I accept—''

''What do you mean, *if?*'' Lily exclaimed. ''Natalie,
it's a wonderful opportunity and a great compliment! Of
course you'll accept!''

''I was hoping you'd say that, because I might need
some help convincing Mom and Dad. In their eyes, I'm

still the baby, barely able to cross the road without supervision. But with you on my side, I think I can talk them into letting me go. I have to give my answer on Tuesday, so maybe we can present the idea this afternoon, while dear old Penny is chasing Sebastian all over Snake Island.''

''*Snake* Island?''

''That's not what it's really called. In fact, I don't know if it even has an official name, but we've always called it that because we used to find so many snakes there when we were kids.'' She gave another infectious giggle. ''Maybe one'll bite her!''

''If it does,'' Lily said sourly, ''I guarantee its name will be Sebastian.''

Selling Hugo and Cynthia on the idea of letting their daughter spend six weeks thousands of miles away in India was no easy task, but in the end, they agreed it was an opportunity not to be missed.

''Thanks, Lily,'' Natalie said later, as the two of them drove into the village to pick up a tub of ice cream to go with the strawberry tarts Cynthia had made for dessert. ''I'm not sure I could have swung it if I hadn't had you there to back me up.''

By the time they returned, the afternoon had dwindled away and taken the sunshine with it.

''Looks as if we might be in for a bit of weather,'' Hugo observed, scanning the far side of the lake where purple thunderheads were building above the horizon. ''The dog's restless and the wind's picking up. I hope Sebastian thought to bring the dinghy into the boathouse.''

''You mean he's here?'' Lily looked up from setting

the table. "I thought he and his date were still on the island."

"No, they came back soon after you and Natalie left for the village. Penny headed back to town and Sebastian decided to follow her. It'll just be the four of us for dinner."

Wiping her hands on her apron, Cynthia came out of the kitchen. "I think we'd better put the pails out upstairs. I'm afraid we're in for a downpour and that flashing still hasn't been fixed around the chimney."

Sure enough, about nine o'clock, the storm picked up and blew across the lake with terrifying speed. One minute, the four of them were playing bridge by lamplight, and the next, Katie was cowering under the dining-room table as thunder rolled in the distance and the first blast of wind hit the house.

While Natalie helped her parents close all the windows and place pails and bowls to catch any water leaking through the ceiling, Lily ran down to the lake to make sure everything there was secured. But her flashlight showed her that although the sleek motor vessel used for waterskiing was secure inside the boathouse, the twelve-foot aluminum dinghy had been left tied to the jetty and was taking a relentless beating as the wind slammed it against the pilings.

Since she didn't have nearly the strength to haul it to safety onshore, her only choice was to lower herself into it and by hanging on to the rail edging the deck of the little dock, try to steer around to the wide double doors on the water side of the boathouse. A difficult task at the best of times, it was made that much worse by the driving rain that lashed her face and cut the already limited visibility to zero.

Before she'd even managed to cast off, she was soaked

to the skin. Freeing the dinghy from its mooring was a monumental undertaking, and only when she'd succeeded did she realize she'd merely compounded her difficulties. With nothing to anchor it, the boat tossed and bobbed like a cork, completely at the mercy of the weather.

Even sitting in the center of the seat, she'd have been hard-pressed to maintain her balance, but trying to stand, hold a flashlight in one hand and grasp the edge of the jetty with the other, was inviting disaster. Before she knew what was happening, a wave caught the side of the boat and flipped it over. In horrible slow motion, she saw the water coming up to meet her, then the dark shadow of the hull rising above her.

The painter attached to the bow snaked around her ankle. A vicious gust of wind sent the upturned boat lumbering forward and threatening to crush her between it and the pilings supporting the jetty. A wave buried her and she realized in stunned disbelief that she was in danger of drowning in ten feet of water, with land less than ten yards away. It shouldn't have been possible, but it was happening.

Well, damn it, she wouldn't allow it!

Choking and spluttering, she clung to the hull of the dinghy with one hand and with the other struggled to free her ankle from the rope. Was that what caused the boat to turn turtle again—her putting her weight too much on one side and the waves pushing too hard from the other? Or was she engaged in a losing battle from the first? Whatever the reason, it slowly heaved up like some prehistoric creature, turned slowly on its side and started filling with water.

As the painter around her ankle tightened, Lily tasted a fear like nothing she'd ever known before. A scream tore loose from her throat and, involuntarily, a name. *"Sebastian!"*

A light appeared, weaving erratically down the path from the cottage and, miraculously, he was there, racing along the jetty and flinging a lifeline to her. "Let go of the boat!" he shouted, aiming the lantern he carried so that he could see her. "Push yourself away from it and I'll pull you in."

"I can't," she gasped, sobbing the words between breaths that burned her lungs like fire. "I'm trapped in the mooring line."

"The hell you are!" In a flash, he'd dumped the lantern on the dock and was in the water beside her. The blade of a knife glimmered as he raised his hand. And then, blessedly, the awful tension around her ankle lessened and he had her by the scruff of the neck and was towing her ashore. She had never felt anything as welcome as the fine gravel scoring her knees and elbows as he heaved her above the waterline.

For the longest time, she lay in a heap, incapable of speech or movement. When she at last lifted her head, she found him kneeling beside her. "You know," he said, "you've really got to stop this business of swimming after dark. You're obviously not very good at it."

"I know," she said, and tried to smile. Instead she burst into tears. "I thought I was going to die," she wailed, burying her face against his sodden shirt. "I thought the boat would sink and take me with it, and I'd never see any of you again."

"Fat chance! For a start, it's designed not to sink. And you're not getting rid of us that easily," he said roughly.

But his hand was gentle on her hair, his arm tight and comforting around her shoulders. And when she lifted her face to his, his mouth closing over hers was warm and tender.

"You're turning into one big headache for me, you know that?" he murmured, when they came up for air. "What the devil am I going to do with you?"

CHAPTER NINE

THE storm blew itself out before midnight. The next morning, Sebastian repaired the roof, Hugo mopped up the damage inside the cottage and Natalie and Lily cleaned up outside while Cynthia prepared lunch on the screened porch.

Sebastian was the last to join them. He took his place at the foot of the table, with Natalie on his right and Lily on his left. Before he'd even helped himself to the cold chicken salad, Natalie began quizzing him. "What made Penny leave early? We practically have to evict her, as a rule."

"Natalie!" Cynthia's eyebrows rose in reproof.

"Oh, Mom, it's true and you know it! You said yourself you were surprised she only stayed a couple of hours."

"Perhaps," Sebastian said mildly, amusement flickering at the corners of his beautiful mouth, "she had to work again last night."

"That might explain *her* taking off in such a hurry, but not why you went with her—unless she needed help getting into her uniform!"

"Watch your mouth!" he said, but there was no bite in his words, and when he turned his glance on Lily, it seemed to rest on her longer than necessary and with particular warmth, before he continued, "I had some matters to attend to in town. Phone calls to make."

"On a Saturday?" Natalie snorted, disbelievingly.

"They were urgent," he said, helping himself to iced

tea. "As a social worker-in-training, you ought to know better than most that not every problem conveniently arises during normal business hours."

Ignoring Cynthia's frown of disapproval, Natalie planted her elbows on the table and wagged a finger at her brother. "Sebastian, you're hiding something!"

"Why do you say that?"

"Because you're talking like a lawyer and you only ever do that around us when you're up to something. Come on, we're your family. You can tell us. What's going on? Did you dump Penny?"

Again, his gaze drifted over Lily before he answered. "We reached an understanding."

"And…?"

"We agreed to remain friends, but otherwise go our separate ways."

In the babble of comment that followed his news, no one seemed to notice that his eyes locked with Lily's and conveyed a silent message meant only for her. Was she delusional to think he was telling her *she* was the reason? Had the fact that they couldn't keep their hands off each other whenever they were alone dealt a death blow to his other relationship?

His slow smile told her it was so.

"But that doesn't explain why you decided to come back here last night, instead of staying in town," Natalie said.

He laughed. "I think you're chasing the wrong profession, Nat. You should be studying law. You'd make a great prosecutor."

She grimaced. "Quit trying to change the subject."

"I heard there was a storm headed this way and thought I'd better come back in case you ran into trouble out here."

"And thank heavens you did! We were so concerned about the roof leaking that we weren't paying attention to how long Lily had been gone." Cynthia shuddered. "What might have happened to her if you hadn't shown up to rescue her doesn't bear thinking about."

"No, it doesn't," he said, covering Lily's hand.

A warmth stole through her at such an open gesture of affection and for the first time in many months, the hurt she'd carried inside began to ease. Gratefully she looked around the table: at Cynthia who'd welcomed her without reserve; at Natalie with whom the bonds of sistership had grown so strong in such a short time; at Hugo, who'd risked losing her a second time rather than shattering her illusions about Genevieve.

And then, last, first and always, there was Sebastian.

Flustered, she shied away from his glance. She'd lost a very great deal. Jonathan Speirs had cheated her and because of him, she'd been subjected to embarrassing cross-examination by the police. But she'd held fast in her belief in the justice system and emerged in the end with her reputation intact.

Her parents were dead, they hadn't always been quite the perfect people she'd believed them to be, and they'd lied to her, even if only by omission. But they'd given far more than they'd ever taken away.

Never be afraid to follow your heart, her mother had said. *It's the one thing that will never lead you astray.*

Nor had it. Instead it had brought her to this moment. To her destiny. She'd been avoiding facing the obvious for days, but suddenly it overwhelmed her and refused to go ignored any longer. She'd fallen in love with Sebastian Caine. Often difficult, at times *impossible,* he was the only man for her. She knew it as surely as she knew her own name.

As if the same realization had crept up on him, too, he squeezed her fingers and she looked up to find him smiling at her with that special intimacy shared only by lovers. Perhaps Hugo and Cynthia saw what was happening, but were too discreet to comment openly.

Natalie showed no such restraint. "Uh-oh! I smell romance in the air," she crowed.

Although meaning no harm, her throwing something so new and untried under public scrutiny ruined the moment. Hot with embarrassment, Lily pulled her hand free and sprang away from the table.

"Honestly, Nat, talk about nineteen going on five!" Sebastian exploded, glaring at his sister with rare annoyance. "When are you going to grow up?"

Obviously crushed, she muttered, "Sorry. I was only teasing. I didn't think—"

"You never do, that's the trouble! Your mouth's in gear long before your brain's engaged!"

"Perhaps," Hugo said, obviously hoping to defuse the tension, which threatened to turn a pleasant get-together into a family free-for-all, "it's time we thought about heading back to town. Last night was long and trying for all of us, and I know I'm feeling the effects today."

"Good idea." Cynthia dabbed her napkin to her mouth and stood up. "If everyone's had enough to eat, I'll start clearing away these dishes."

Ignoring Natalie, Sebastian came to where Lily had drifted to the end of the porch overlooking the lake. "I'm sorry about that, Lily. I don't know what came over Nat. The last thing I wanted was for you to be made to feel uncomfortable."

"It was as much my fault as hers," she said quickly. "If I hadn't overreacted the way I did, we'd all have had a good laugh and that would have been the end of it. Look at her, Sebastian. She's devastated.''

''She'll get over it. And don't blame yourself. She pulls this kind of thoughtless stunt too often and I meant what I said. She *does* need to grow up.'' He stepped close enough that his breath stirred wisps of hair on her forehead. ''Will you drive back to town with me, Lily? There's something I need to talk to you about—a lot of things, in fact.''

The urgency in his voice struck a chord, and she'd have liked nothing more than to be alone with him so that she could express all that was in her heart, too. But, ''It's more important that you straighten things out with Natalie,'' she said. ''Take her with you instead.''

He stood with his back to the others so that when he opened her hand and traced lazy circles over her palm, no one but she was the wiser. ''But you're the one I want to be with.''

Under his heated gaze, happiness swelled inside her like a flower bursting open under the sun. Past tragedy and broken trust left scars. Nothing would ever bring back her parents, or alter the fact that she'd been fooled into entering into a business contract with a criminal.

But with Sebastian looking at her like that, what she'd gained outweighed what she'd lost and she wasn't about to let anything intrude on the perfection of the moment. ''I want to be with you, too, but we're only talking about an hour. Take Natalie, Sebastian, and put things right between you. You and I can see each other later.''

He heaved a sigh. ''It'll have to be a lot later. Hugo mentioned that you're all invited next door to the Andersons' for cocktails this evening. You'll be lucky if you get away from there before nine or ten.''

He was wearing shorts and an open-necked shirt.

Taking advantage of the privacy screen his width of shoulder provided, she slid her fingers between the buttons of his shirt and rested them against his bare chest. "Would you rather wait until tomorrow to get together, then?"

"Keep that up, and you can forget waiting any time at all," he warned her thickly. "I'm likely to put on a floor show right here and now that'll send your father and my mother into orbit, never mind Natalie."

"Perish the thought!" She pursed her lips in a kiss. "So what—?"

"So as soon as you can escape the Andersons, come to the apartment."

"You aren't going to join us for cocktails?"

"Not a chance, sweetheart. I've got a party of my own to organize."

"Semi-dressy," Cynthia told Lily, when she'd asked about the Anderson affair. "Winona isn't one to stand on ceremony, but she likes to do things with style."

Style and elegance pretty much defined everything that took place in the Preston circle of friends, from what Lily could determine. "If I were staying here much longer, I'd need to buy a whole new wardrobe," she muttered, subjecting herself to a last inspection in her bedroom mirror.

The plainly cut black dress with its narrow skirt and fitted waist had seen more than its share of wear lately. But with the addition of a single string of pearls, matching earrings and the pearl dinner ring her parents had given her on her last birthday, she thought it passed muster.

However, the disfavor with which Sebastian regarded her when she finally escaped the cocktail party and at last showed up at his door, made her wonder if it was time she consigned the outfit to a used-clothing store. *Not,* she thought, noting his rather rumpled look, *that he'd have topped anyone's best-dressed list himself just then!*

"Were you sleeping?" she said, dismayed that he confined his greeting to a peck on her cheek and a wordless gesture, which she took to be an invitation for her to climb the winding staircase. "You look a bit...out of sorts."

He shook his head. "Merely anxious to clear up a few things."

But the warmth he'd shown earlier was lacking, and instead of heralding anticipation, his words seemed to clang with foreboding.

"Want something to drink?" he inquired offhandedly, when they reached the living room.

"Thanks. Perrier, if you have it," she said, not liking the situation at all. It reminded her too much of the only other time she'd been a guest in his home, except that, then, she'd wanted information and he'd been bent on seduction. Now it seemed to be the other way around.

"So, how was the cocktail party?"

"Very nice."

He served her drink and waved her to a seat on the same couch where they'd first made love, but seemed in no hurry to join her. Yet just that morning, his every gesture and glance had indicated he was eager to explore the romantic dimensions of their relationship. "Meet any new people?"

"A few. No one interesting enough to keep me there a moment longer than necessary," she said, her glance roaming over the room. No moonlight tonight to bathe it in mystery. No candles, either, or soft music filling the air, or imported wine chilling in ice.

Yet, *I've got a party of my own to organize,* he'd said, when she'd asked him why he wasn't going to the Andersons'. But although the halogen lamp spilling light on the papers spread over his desk was unquestionably efficient, it hardly made for romantic ambience. At their present rate of nonprogress, he'd be showing her the door before much longer with nothing resolved between them.

Well, she wouldn't allow it! Not when they'd come this far, and not until he'd aired whatever was preying on his mind! "What's wrong, Sebastian?" she said, placing her glass on the coffee table and going to where he stood by the window. "Is it Natalie? She begged off coming with us tonight, claiming she had to catch up on her studying, but I thought she seemed a bit down. Are the two of you still on the outs with each other over this morning's incident?"

"No," he said, the look he turned on her about as warm as April in Antarctica. "Thanks to you, we're fighting about something else."

"Me?" She almost laughed. "What have I done now?"

"Oh, plenty, not the least being your latest interference in this family's affairs! Just who do you think you are, encouraging her to take off on some wild-goose chase to India?"

"So that's what this is all about! I gather you don't like the idea very much?"

"No, I do not."

Still not able to take him too seriously despite his black scowl, she said, "Well, the last I heard, it's okay for people to disagree sometimes, Sebastian. It doesn't make them sworn enemies."

"This amounts to more than a disagreement. We're talking about my sister here—a nineteen-year-old girl who thinks the sun rises and sets on every damn thing you say or do. And I don't like the influence you're exerting over her. I'm beginning to think I was right in the first place—

we'd all have been a sight better off if you'd never come here."

"I think you're exaggerating," she said, her earlier hopes and optimism suddenly seeming as absurdly far-fetched as her misplaced amusement. If something this trivial could so easily derail them, perhaps they weren't quite as firmly set on the rosy path to romance, after all. "You're her idol, Sebastian, not I, and your influence far exceeds anything I might have to say. But do go on with your diatribe. I can hardly wait to hear the rest of it."

"Lately it's what you think that carries the most weight with Natalie. In my book, that means you're obligated to show some responsibility for the advice you dish out." Nostrils pinched with annoyance, he glared at her, the almighty Sebastian Caine conveying displeasure to a lowly subject. "You had no right encouraging her to put herself in danger."

And to think she'd been ready to lay her heart on the line for him!

"Don't be ridiculous," she snapped, all the old hostility surging to life with renewed vigor. "Natalie's going to Bombay with a team of professionals to work with underprivileged children, not setting out alone to conquer Everest. You need to get a sense of proportion here, Sebastian!"

"When I want your advice, I'll ask for it."

"I'll be sure to remember that," she said. "Meanwhile, Natalie *did* ask for my advice, and I gave it to her."

"Where are your brains, for God's sake? You've seen firsthand how immature she still is—how she acts like a kid, half the time."

"I agree. Unlike you, though, I don't see that as an indication of impaired mental ability. Natalie's bright, intelligent and eager to learn. And I happen to think this special project will go a long way toward helping her grow up.''

She headed toward the stairs, as eager to be gone as she had been to arrive. Whatever sweet promise the evening had held had long since evaporated. She thought he'd accepted her place in the family but it was obvious she was as much an outsider as ever. ''At least give me credit for being up-front and open about it. I didn't go sneaking around behind your back.''

''Not this time, perhaps.''

She flung an outraged glance over her shoulder. ''Exactly what's that supposed to mean?''

''Oh, can the innocent act, Lily! It's pretty ludicrous, coming from someone who's been covering up ever since the day she set foot in this town. It strikes me, from the mess you left behind in Vancouver, that you'd be better off attending to your own business and leaving other people to mind theirs.''

''What do you know about my life in Vancouver?'' she asked, a stillness draping over her like a cold, wet cloak.

''More than I care to,'' he shot back. ''I've known for days that your flower shop's been closed down and you're under suspicion of fraud and conspiracy. Now I learn your business cohort has links with organized crime. Nice company you keep, Lily! Just the kind of people Hugo and my mother would love to invite into their home and include in their social circle! What I don't know is when you were going to share all these sordid facts with the family you claim is so important to you.''

Shock rendered her temporarily speechless. Staggering slightly, she steadied herself against the back of the couch and finally said, ''Never, if I could help it! I'm not proud of having been so gullible and stupid.''

''But not so ashamed that you stayed out of our lives!''

"I didn't say I was ashamed. I'm not! I don't know where you got your information, but if you'd—"

"I'm a lawyer, in case you've forgotten. I know how to dig up dirt on people. All it took was a phone call to the right party to set things in motion."

"You hired a private detective to spy on me?" she whispered, all the lovely warm certainty that, with him, she'd found her soul mate, shriveling up and dying.

"That's putting it a little fancifully, but it more or less fits the description. I had your background investigated."

"When?"

"Within days of your getting here, but it's been an ongoing project." He strode to the desk and tried to shove a sheet of paper into her hand. "I received the latest report just this afternoon. Read it for yourself."

"I don't care to!" She slapped it aside, furious, dismayed and, most of all, deeply hurt. She'd been willing to trust this man with her heart! For her to discover now that, all the time he was seducing her so expertly, he'd had another agenda...!

She felt as if she'd been hit, hard. She felt battered and bruised and torn to shreds inside. "Do you know why I came here tonight?" she said, in a low, broken voice. "Because I wanted to tell you that I love you. Because I thought you were going to say the same thing to me."

"The idea had crossed my mind." He looked as haggard as she felt. "I guess it just goes to show what self-delusional fools we can be sometimes."

"I trusted you!"

"I wish I could say the same about you."

"You could. *Can!* If you'd just asked me, instead of—"

"Every day that passed, I waited for you to say something. Hoped you'd have the decency to come clean and tell me the kind of trouble you're in. Hoped the next report I received would clear your name. But you remained silent, and the investigator kept turning up more dirt, culminating in today's report. Sorry, Lily, but that doesn't exactly inspire trust.''

She could have pleaded her case. But why waste her time?

''I won't bother trying to justify my actions,'' she said, holding her head high. ''You've already judged and found me guilty. I'm sure you'd find my protestations of innocence laughable.''

''The evidence against you is pretty conclusive. You can hardly blame me for being concerned.''

''There *is* no evidence against me!'' she spat. ''Or if there is, it's entirely circumstantial, a concept you appear to have dismissed out of hand. But from where I stand, there's certainly plenty against you.''

''Oh, really?'' He sneered, supremely confident of his superiority, his unimpeachable moral fiber. Clearly it had never occurred to him the rest of the world might view him as just a little less than perfect. ''Such as what?''

''You're not the man I took you to be, Sebastian Caine, and I am *so* glad you showed your true colors before I made an even bigger fool of myself than I already have. You've been determined to discredit me from the minute you set eyes on me. As for your righteous indignation about my sins of omission, you could certainly give me lessons in underhandedness!''

He looked vaguely disturbed by her vehemence. ''Hey,'' he said, spreading his hands palms up, as if he were the most reasonable creature on earth, and she nothing but a woman in the throes of PMS or some other kind of hormonal imbalance, ''if there's something I've missed in all this, fill me in. Defend yourself. I'm willing to listen. I always have been.''

"Why waste my breath? You've already got enough ammunition to condemn me out of hand. I'm able to spend unlimited time here because I don't have a job waiting for me in Vancouver. Why? Because the police closed down my business. And why was that, you ask? Because it was a cover-up for organized crime, which naturally makes me some sort of Mafia gun moll. So why did I show up here? Because Daddy's rich as well as good-looking, and so full of guilt at having abandoned me that touching him up for money to bail myself out of my current mess will be a piece of cake for an experienced crook like me.''

Running out of steam, she pressed a hand to her chest and drew in a fresh lungful of air. "Good grief, Sebastian, how much more proof do you need that you've jumped to all the right conclusions?''

"Just hold your fire a second," he said, advancing toward her. "Something here doesn't—''

"No! I've heard enough. More than enough! You want me out of your life? You've got it! I'm gone! You'll never have to breathe the same air as me again. As far as I'm concerned, Sebastian Caine, you're history that's well on the way to being permanently forgotten. But just so there's no misunderstanding, I'm not giving up on Natalie or Hugo. They're all the family I've got left, and I'll see you in hell before I let you shove me out of their lives, as well.''

Seeing him winding up to argue the point, she spun on her high heels and took off down the narrow, winding stairs with dangerous disregard for her safety. She'd rather have broken her neck than give him the chance to have the last word.

"Tomorrow," she promised herself, sprinting as best she could through the shrubbery and across the lawns to the main house, "I'll be on the first flight out of here, if I have to charter a private jet to do it. I'll gather enough proof to show him just how far off the mark he is with his nasty suspicions! Before I'm done with him, he'll wind up with so much egg on his face that no one will recognize him!"

Hugo hauled him on the carpet the next afternoon. Or, more accurately, he showed up at the law firm, something he hadn't done in months, and after being admitted to Sebastian's office, closed the door behind him with a quiet precision that broadcast his displeasure loud and clear.

"Lily left town this morning," he began, without preamble. "And it didn't take a genius to figure out that she was very upset. You told her, didn't you? Against my express wishes, you told her the truth about her mother."

Sebastian held him with too much respect and affection to take the easy way out. "Yes, I did. Quite a long time ago. That's not why she's gone, but you're right in assuming I'm responsible for her leaving." He looked his stepfather straight in the eye. "I initiated an investigation into her past, also against your express wishes, and she found out about it."

Hugo sagged in his chair, suddenly looking all of his seventy years. "Why, Sebastian? By what right did you take it upon yourself to invade her privacy like that?"

He'd asked himself the same question a thousand times since she'd stormed out of his apartment. "Damned if I really know," he said. "In the beginning, I suppose I was looking out for you, protecting you. You were so trusting, so ready to take her at face value. I wanted to make sure you weren't going to wind up being hurt, that she wasn't a chip off the old block, out to take advantage of you. At first, all I intended was to confirm she was who and what she claimed to be, but it got out of hand...." He heaved a sigh. "Stuff turned up that put her in a pretty bad light and I felt I had to keep going. If it makes any difference, Hugo, I was hoping my source would unearth something that would clear her."

"Damn it, Sebastian!" Hugo was white around the mouth, his eyes blazing. Normally a man of temperate nature, he was formidable when roused to anger. Sebastian could count on one hand the number of times he'd witnessed it. "I've been in the legal profession a long time and I consider myself a pretty sound judge of people. I don't need proof of Lily's good character. But I am beyond disappointed in you."

Sebastian pushed away from the desk and paced across the carpet. "I'm pretty disappointed in me, too. During our last conversation, I told her I didn't trust her, but the truth is, I don't trust myself around her. She clouds my judgment, Hugo. She makes all the boundaries marking my life shift out of focus. I pride myself on being a man willing to be held accountable for his actions, yet where she's concerned, I break all the rules that normally govern my conduct."

"Are you telling me you think you're in love with her?" Hugo swiveled in his chair and subjected him to a disconcertingly probing gaze.

Jeez, if that were his only sin! But he'd had to compound his errors by making love to her. He'd had sex with his stepfather's daughter, for God's sake! What kind of jerk was he that, even now, visions of her lying hot and naked beneath him colored his mind and evoked the taste and scent of her with startling clarity?

"I think," he said, choosing his words carefully because, for the first time ever, he couldn't be completely honest with the man who'd guided him into manhood with unwavering dedication, "that any such possibility was nipped in the bud last night."

"So that's it, then." Wearily Hugo got to his feet. "I had hoped our perfect summer might last indefinitely. Instead both my daughters are flying the coop."

"Both?"

"Natalie leaves for India at the end of next week."

"I can't believe you've agreed to letting her go. Hugo, I really don't think that's a smart idea."

"You'll forgive me, Sebastian," came the reply, "if I don't hold your opinion in much regard right now. You chose to interfere in my relationship with Lily. I'm not disposed to let you do the same where Natalie's concerned. Your mother and I both feel this is an opportunity unlikely to come her way again and are encouraging her to take full advantage of it."

The silence he left behind rang with recrimination. *I've screwed up,* Sebastian thought gloomily. *And I've done it in spectacular fashion.*

The question was, how could he redeem himself, not only in Hugo's eyes, but, more importantly, in his own?

CHAPTER TEN

HE KNEW the answer, of course. And if he hadn't been able to figure it out for himself, the final investigative report arriving on his desk five days later spelled out in conclusive detail the extent to which he'd misjudged Lily. No question about it: he was going to have to swallow *all* his pride, not just selected parts.

He waited until Natalie was safely en route to her adventure and he'd cleared his desk of his most urgent cases before telling his mother and Hugo of his plans. "I'm flying out to B.C. next week. I could phone, and save myself the time and trouble of making the trip, but I figure I owe it to Lily to deliver my apology in person. I'm booked into the Hotel Vancouver if you need to reach me."

"How long will you be gone?" Cynthia asked.

"As long as it takes." He looked at Hugo. "I don't really expect her to forgive me, but I hope, in time, you can."

"I've looked on you as a son for a good number of years, Sebastian," Hugo said. "It'll take more than one mistake on your part for that to change."

He should have found the words comforting but, as he left his mother and stepfather standing on the terrace, he felt only ashamed and strangely uneasy. Suddenly they both looked old and very alone.

He was not a man given to superstition, yet the apprehension stayed with him all during the long flight west the next day. He hoped Lily would agree to see him that night, that he could persuade her to return with him to Stentonbridge as soon as possible, and spend what remained of the summer with her family.

He didn't phone ahead to warn her of his visit, figuring he'd be better off taking her by surprise. The way he saw it, that was probably his only chance of getting her to open her door to him.

She lived on the top floor of a fourteen story apartment building overlooking English Bay. It was growing dark when he arrived, and not much was left of the sunset but an orange glow behind the mountains on the far side of Georgia Strait.

He stationed himself in an inconspicuous spot among the potted palms screening the foyer from the street, certain he wouldn't have long to wait before someone opened the main entrance and he could slip inside the building.

What he hadn't counted on was that that person would be Lily. She came running up the steps from the street not five minutes later, with a sack of groceries swinging from her hand and what looked like a French baguette in a bag tucked under her arm.

She had no idea she was being watched, no sense that he was right behind her, until he touched her on the shoulder as she juggled her purchases and tried to fit her key into the lock. He thought he was prepared for her possible reaction at seeing him again—anything from her slamming his foot in the door to trying to shove him down the nearest stairwell. But her subdued shriek of alarm and the way the groceries flew out of her hand and hit the ground with a resounding *thwack* startled him almost as much as he'd obviously startled her.

"Hey," he said, patting her soothingly, "it's just me."

"*Just* you?" she echoed faintly, clutching the French bread to her bosom and turning huge, fear-filled eyes on him. "That makes it even worse than what I originally expected. What are you doing here, lurking in the bushes like some pervert?"

"Waiting to talk to you. Are you going to invite me upstairs, or shall we sit on the steps out here?"

"Neither," she said. "And stop patting me as if you were trying to placate a vicious dog."

"Nervous, perhaps, but never vicious," he said ruefully, unable to take his eyes off her. Agitation stained her cheeks a rosy pink and left her breasts heaving delectably under her lightweight summer dress. Swallowing, he bent down and stuffed a carton of peach ice cream, a bag of frozen French fries, a king-size bottle of ketchup, and a box of chocolate-covered peanuts into the grocery sack. "Still a junk-food goddess, I see," he said, handing it over.

"Not that it's any of your business, but yes. Some of us really are what we first appear to be."

Uh-oh, the way things were shaping up didn't look promising! "Look, Lily, you don't owe me a damn thing—"

"How magnanimous of you!"

"And if you insist, I won't push you to hear me out. But I've come a long way, in more ways than one, since we last spoke, so I'm asking you, please, to let me try to put a few things right." He stepped closer, hemming her into the narrow space between the intercom panel and the front door. "Please?"

"Don't you dare touch me," she warned, wielding the bread like a sword. "I don't ever want you to touch me again!"

"That's a pity," he said softly, "because I find myself wanting to touch you very badly. But it's not my primary reason for being here."

"Then what is?"

He glanced around. "Do we really have to go into it here? Isn't there someplace more private we can talk—a coffee shop or a hotel lounge?"

"I've got perishables that need to be refrigerated," she said, eyeing him narrowly. "You can come up to my apartment and I'll give you ten minutes to say your piece, then you're out of here."

Her home was spacious and as elegantly understated as she herself. "Lovely view you've got," he remarked, strolling to the balcony and looking over the treetops to the curving shoreline below.

"Ten minutes, Sebastian," she reminded him, stashing her stuff in the streamlined kitchen. "So never mind the small talk."

"Okay." He pivoted to face her. "I've been a damned fool. I know I treated you shabbily. I should have trusted you, taken you at your word—at face value, as you once said. You're furious with me, and I don't blame you. And I want you to know I'm sorry."

"Are you really? And what brought about this massive change of heart?" she inquired coldly. "Could it have something to do with the fact that you've finally got the goods my oh-so-shady past, and now have proof I'm not the reincarnation of Lizzie Borden, after all?"

"Well, I—"

"Don't bother denying it, Sebastian. You're not the only legal eagle on the planet with connections. The minute I got back to Vancouver, I contacted my lawyer and let her know exactly what you'd been up to. She flushed out your weasely little sleuth in no time flat and he, in turn, relayed to you everything he subsequently learned from her—which is that I'm really quite harmless and have no evil designs on any of the people you guard so jealously.''

''All true, every word,'' he said. ''And I apologize for having ever doubted you.''

''And is that all you came to say?''

He'd thought he could manage the rest. Admit that he hadn't been able to get her out of his mind. Tell her that she...that he...that what he felt for her amounted to...

Love: the most straightforward four-letter word in the world, and the most difficult to say, lodged in his throat and he couldn't spit it out. Instead he hedged the question with pompous, pointless evasions that he knew weren't what she wanted to hear. ''It's the most important thing, certainly. I take no pleasure in having judged you so harshly.''

''Well, hope that God can forgive you,'' she said, ''because I can't. I'm not interested in an apology made after the fact. You didn't believe in me when it counted, Sebastian, and I don't need your support now.''

''Jeez!'' he said, frustration getting the better of him in the face of her obstinacy. ''You're not entirely blameless in all this, you know, coming across as the poor orphaned little waif in mourning one minute, then parading around the next with enough clothes and jewelry stashed in your wardrobe to keep a countess on a world tour well dressed!''

''Well, excuse me! If I'd known *that* was a concern, I'd have shown you a copy of my parents' will and you could have seen for yourself that I've been left rather well-off. But even if I hadn't inherited a penny, I was never the money-grubbing impostor out to punish an old man by fleecing him of every penny, the way you implied I was. So take your injured pride and stuff it, Sebastian, along with your apology! My name and reputation are squeaky clean and I intend to pick up my life and go on— without your blessing, thank you very much.''

"You know," he said, stung by her absolute disdain, "you could have prevented a lot of this unpleasantness if you'd just come clean in the beginning. Why the hell didn't you at least confide in me about your business problems?''

"Because I'd done nothing wrong! And I shouldn't have to tell you that, in this country at least, a person is deemed innocent until proven guilty.''

"No," he said heavily. "In the end, of course, it does all come down to that, doesn't it, and saying I'm sorry hardly compensates.''

"Hardly," she said, snippily enough that his temper rose again.

"What *would* you like, then? My head on a platter?''

She regarded him across the width of the kitchen, her color still high, and her beautiful eyes suddenly empty. Despite all the things that had gone wrong between them, one thing had always been right: their lovemaking had been touched with rare perfection. He could have tried to recapture that special magic, but he knew it was no longer enough.

"Nothing quite that dramatic," she said dully, "and certainly nothing you're not able to offer willingly.''

"You're not making this easy, Lily!''

"Deceiving someone who trusted you isn't supposed to be easy, Sebastian, so if you don't like where it's landed you, go cry on someone else's shoulder. And show yourself out, while you're at it. Your time's up.''

Baffled, he swung away from that flat, empty gaze. "I know what you want to hear, but be reasonable, for Pete's sake! Don't ask me to rush blindly into something I'm only just coming to terms with.''

"Why not? You had no hesitation about rushing blindly into bed with me while your paid flunky ran a check to make sure I deserved to be welcomed into the bosom of your precious family."

"Isn't it enough that I've missed you every second you've been gone? That when I saw you tonight, what I most wanted was to take you in my arms? Can't that be enough for now?"

"No," she said, stalking to the door and flinging it open. "I've already got plenty of friends more than happy to wrap their arms around me if a feel-good hug is what I need to see me through the night. I'm sorry you came all this way for nothing."

Considering she stood nine inches shorter and weighed at least eighty pounds less than he did, she hustled him out of the apartment with astonishing speed. "Hey!" he roared, his male pride mortally offended. "I'm not finished!"

"Oh, yes, you are," she replied, from the other side of the door.

He debated thundering on the blasted thing with his fist. Better yet, aiming a good kick and smashing in the lock. But he'd made enough mistakes where she was concerned, and he'd be damned if he'd compound them by giving her the pleasure of calling the police and having him hauled off to jail for the night. He'd accomplished what he'd set out to do.

As for what didn't get done—the emotional stuff that snuck up whenever he found himself within kissing distance of her—well, that had never been part of the original game plan and a man of his experience ought to know better than to switch strategies halfway through. The day had yet to dawn when Sebastian Caine became a fool for love.

* * *

Long after he'd stomped off, she remained plastered to the door, her heart beating such a furious tattoo that she wasn't at all sure she could make it to the nearest chair without going into cardiac arrest.

She'd dreamed about him day and night in the weeks since she'd walked out of his life. A hundred times or more, she'd thought she'd seen him on a crowded Vancouver street, on the beach at dusk, across a noisy restaurant during the lunch hour. The set of a pair of broad shoulders, the angle of a stranger's dark head, a graceful, long-legged masculine stride—how often had wishful thinking led her astray?

Memory had deceived her, too. The motel where they'd spent their first night had been indescribably tacky, yet, in retrospect, became a magical place where the beginnings of a love affair had sprung to life. The scent of him, the olive tint of his skin turned darker where the sun had touched it, his thigh brushing hers in the night, his breath ruffling her hair…oh, if only she'd known how it would all end!

Ironically he'd been the last thing on her mind tonight as she'd walked home from the supermarket. Hearing earlier that her former business associate had signed a confession, which spared her the ordeal of having to testify against him in court, had lifted such a weight off her shoulders that she'd been almost happy.

Then she'd turned and found Sebastian there, warm and solid and real, and wild hope had sprung to life. But she'd been fooled again. All he'd wanted was to ease his conscience with an apology and the bonus of a little sex thrown in on the side, whereas she…

Your heart! she'd wanted to cry out, when he'd asked her what it was she wanted. *Your love—as unconditionally as I'd give you mine, if I thought you'd accept it!*

But there'd never been anything unconditional about his feelings for her, and no use fooling herself otherwise. Even when he shuddered in her arms, and his seed spilled hot and urgent inside her, and he kissed her as if his life depended on it, he held a part of himself back.

He might find her desirable, but he'd never found her irresistible, and she was smart enough not to settle for anything less. Because, she wanted *him*. All of him! Forever!

Why did he have to be so beautiful, so persuasive, so stunningly sexy? And what in the world was wrong with her, that she was crying like a baby over a man who didn't deserve her tears?

"Sending him away was the only thing to do," she wailed to the kitchen at large as she spread frozen French fries on a cookie tray and popped them into the oven. If ever she needed comfort food, it was tonight! "Count your blessings, you silly twit. You're luckier than most people who lose their parents too soon. You found a new family—a father and a sister, and a lovely stepmother. Don't ask for the moon, as well."

In the weeks that followed, the phone calls from Hugo and Cynthia, and the postcards from Natalie were what kept her grounded. If Sebastian came sneaking into her thoughts when she wasn't looking, a flurry of late-summer weddings kept her busy enough to shunt him aside, and she had Thanksgiving in early October to look forward to. Natalie would be back from India by then, and had promised to fly out to spend the holiday weekend in Vancouver with her.

The call came on the first Friday in October. After work, she'd gone shopping for pretty new sheets for the guest room, in preparation for her sister's arrival the following Thursday, and didn't get home until well after sunset. When she opened her front door, the first thing she saw was the red blinking light on her telephone answering machine.

Hugo's voice was so low and distraught that she was hard-pressed to make out his words and had to play the message over again before she caught the gist of it. "Lily, it's your…it's Hugo. We've received some bad news, I'm afraid. Please call me at home."

Sebastian! was her first thought. *Something had happened to Sebastian!*

But when she pressed the Redial button and the phone was picked up at the other end, it was Sebastian who answered.

She had wondered, if or when they spoke again, how she'd find the words; had, ridiculously, practiced what she might say—flippant, glib, meaningless remarks designed to let him know how unimportant he was to her life. How she'd managed to toss him aside. Now that the moment was at hand, though, she simply spoke from the heart.

"Oh, Sebastian, thank God you're all right! It's me, Lily. I just got Hugo's message. What's happened? Has there been an accident?"

"No." She had never believed anything could defeat this man she loved so well despite herself; never believed he could know despair. Hearing both in his voice now terrified her. "It's Natalie, Lily. She's…very ill."

"Ill, how?" she cried. "I spoke to her just the other day, and she was fine. *Fine!* There must be some mistake."

"Oh, there was a mistake, all right, and it happened the day she got on that flight to India," he said bitterly. "If she'd listened to me and stayed home—!"

"What's India got to do with anything? She came home over two weeks ago. She's resumed her university studies.

She was happy and healthy and coming to visit me in another few days.''

She hadn't recognized the shrill edge of panic in her voice, but trust him to waste no time setting her straight. ''Get a grip, Lily! We've got enough to deal with, without your falling apart. Natalie's come down with some sort of post-infection complication from some bug she picked up in Bombay, and it's not responding to treatment. She's been hospitalized and her doctors are very worried. I'm afraid it's looking very serious. Unless things turn around, her life could be in danger.''

The strength went out of Lily's legs and she fell into the nearest chair like a rag doll. *He was implying that vital, irreverent, lovely young woman with so much living to do might die!* ''Don't say that!'' she wailed. ''Don't even dare to *think* it!''

''I'm sorry, Lily. I know what a shock this is. We're all walking around in a daze. Going through the motions. Waiting for a miracle.''

''I'm coming out,'' she said, her thoughts scrambling to catch up and make sense of such a senseless tragedy. ''I'll be there as soon as I can.''

''Why? There's nothing you can do.''

''Because she's my sister and I want to be with her! And you're not going to talk me out of it, so don't even try!''

His tone softened, and a weariness crept in that brought tears to her eyes. ''Let me know when you're due to arrive and I'll meet your flight.''

The last time they'd sped through the gentle, rolling countryside, the roads had been awash with mud, the flowers in the gardens flattened from the rain. This time, the weather was indecently lovely. The leaves splashed red and gold against the soft blue sky. Chrysanthemums and purple asters lined pathways leading to cottage doors; scarlet geraniums nestled in window boxes.

She had barely slept since hearing the news. Most of the time, worry had occupied her mind. During the brief moments that she had been able to turn her thoughts elsewhere, she'd wondered how it would be, seeing Sebastian again. Except for fighting or making love, they'd had so little practice in interacting. But when she saw him waiting at the airport, she'd started to cry and they'd simply walked into each other's arms and held on to each other in wordless grief.

"How is she?" she finally asked him, as the miles spun by and the silence became too oppressive to bear. "Any change?"

"None."

"Is there no cure? No treatment?"

His chest rose in a massive sigh and he had to clear his throat before answering. "Her doctors are trying everything they've got."

Lily smothered a sob. "How did things come to this ugly pass, Sebastian? What went wrong so suddenly?"

"She picked up a strep infection in Bombay. Although she was treated with appropriate antibiotics and seemed to make a normal recovery at the time, complications set in which didn't become apparent until recently, and now her kidneys are affected."

He closed his eyes briefly, and she thought she'd never seen him look so desolate. Reaching over, she covered his hand as it rested on the gearshift. At her touch, he curled his fingers around hers and didn't let go. "I'm glad you're here," he said brusquely. "Hugo needs you, and so do I."

Why did it take tragedy to bring us together? she wondered sadly. *Why couldn't we have found trust and solace in each other before?*

"It's a rare disorder," he went on, after a few seconds. "Only about one in ten thousand comes down with it, and the vast majority usually do respond to treatment which, from what I understand, is largely confined to relieving symptoms. But every once in a while, more serious complications set in—congestive heart failure, hypertension or, in this case and unfortunately for Nat, kidney problems. The medical term for her condition is poststreptococcal glomerulonephritis, which is a mouthful by anyone's standards. Simply translated, it means the capillaries in the kidneys become inflamed and don't filter and excrete the way they should."

"People can't function without healthy kidneys," she said, cold fingers of dread crawling up her spine. "They…"

He understood exactly which path her thoughts were following. "If the condition can't be reversed, she'll need a transplant. If a compatible donor isn't found…"

His voice cracked, betraying the misery and dread he was working so hard to conceal. Devastated for everyone but, at that moment, especially for him, Lily fought to control her own fears. "Oh, Sebastian, I know how frightening this must be for all of you and I wish there was something I could do to make it more bearable."

"There isn't. Family means everything to me and the idea that I could lose my sister…!" Wrenching his emotions under control, he squeezed Lily's fingers. "But your being here will be of some comfort to Hugo, I know."

But I want to comfort you, too, she longed to tell him. *I want you to turn to me, instead of shutting me out.*

They reached the outskirts of Stentonbridge just before eight o'clock. A faint mist rose from the river, smoke curled toward the stars from the chimneys of the lovely old houses, and the smell of autumn filled the air.

"I'll drop you off and leave you to get settled," Sebastian said, turning through the elegant iron gates and up the sweeping driveway to the Preston estate. "Afraid the only ones to welcome you this time are Katie and the housekeeper, but you know your way around, so make yourself at home. My mother and Hugo will probably stay at the hospital again tonight."

"And what about you?"

"I'm going back there, too."

"Not without me, you aren't," she said. "The chief reason I'm here is to see Natalie."

He inhaled sharply, always a telltale sign that he was irritated. "I've been away all afternoon as it is, Lily. I'm not hanging around while you unpack. I want to be with my sister."

"As do I," she declared, "so instead of wasting time arguing over something we're in agreement on for a change, let's go."

"I hope you're prepared for what's waiting," he said grimly, stepping on the accelerator and speeding off again. "Nat's not the same person you last saw."

Regular visiting hours were over by the time they arrived, and the hallways were filled with that special kind of hush peculiar to hospitals at night. In the Intensive Care Unit, though, people wandered distractedly up and down the waiting area, their faces tight and anxious.

A nurse stopped them as Sebastian led Lily through a set of double doors to the main area. "Glad you got here when you did, Mr. Caine," she said quietly. "Your sister's condition has worsened, I'm afraid, and her doctors are consulting with her parents now." She indicated a small room to one side. "They're in there, if you'd like to join them."

"Is no one with my sister?"

"Not at the moment, though she is, of course, being closely monitored."

He turned to Lily and she saw the question in his eyes. "I'll sit with her," she said. "You go hear what the doctors are saying."

"Thank you. I should be there."

So should I, she thought desolately. *But even at a time like this, you still don't consider me a real part of this family, Sebastian. I'm here on sufferance only.*

But the time to press the point was not now. What mattered was Natalie and she lay so still on the narrow, white bed, with so many tubes stuck in her body, and with a face so waxen and sallow, that Lily feared, when she first laid eyes on her, that she'd come too late.

"Don't be afraid," the same nurse told her, guiding her to a chair beside the bed. "The equipment looks scary, but for now it's doing its job, and that's what counts."

Sebastian had warned her, but nothing could have prepared Lily for the shock. Unable to reconcile present reality with the memory of Natalie as she'd last seen her—laughing, teasing, filled with a zest for life, poised on the brink of a great adventure, bursting with good health and vitality—she whispered brokenly, "She will get better, won't she?"

"We hope so, but it won't hurt to pray for a miracle." The nurse patted her shoulder kindly. "Talk to her. Let her know you're here and that you love her."

"So there you have it. We hope it doesn't come to that, but it's best to be prepared. A transplant might be our only option." The head of the medical team shook his head sympathetically.

Sebastian looked at his mother, at Hugo. Despair and grief had etched new lines on their faces. Instead of young-at-heart seniors, he saw old people, too broken and frail to cope. If Nat died, they would not be long following her. Well, damn it, he wouldn't let it happen, not as long as he had breath left in his body! "And you're absolutely certain I can't be a donor?"

"You know the answer, Mr. Caine. We've run the tests, you've seen the results. Even if you'd been full siblings, there was always the chance you wouldn't be a match. As it is…" The doctor lifted his shoulders in a tired, helpless shrug, as if he'd told the same story to too many other families.

"And us?" Hugo asked. "Her mother and I—?"

"I'm afraid it's out of the question, sir. Any other medical considerations aside, your age is against you."

"I want you to alert every hospital on this continent," Sebastian said, struggling to contain the anger choking him. "Farther than that, in fact. Europe, Asia, Australia, South America. I'll personally charter a plane anywhere in the world and pay whatever it costs to get a healthy kidney here in time, if one should be needed."

"Before you go that far, there is another option," Lily announced from the doorway. Her eyes met his and he saw that she'd been crying. But her gaze and voice held steady. "I want to be tested as a possible donor."

"Oh, my dear!" his mother wept. "Oh, Lily, thank you!"

"My darling daughter, you've already given us so much. And now this…" Hugo struggled to his feet.

"No!" Sebastian said. "You will not do this, Lily!"

"And why not?" she said. "Natalie's my sister, too. You didn't hesitate to offer her one of your kidneys. Why wouldn't I be willing to do the same?"

"Because," he said.

She lifted her eyebrows in mild reproof. "You're going

to have to do a lot better than that, Sebastian. 'Because' is no answer at all.''

"There are other reasons,'' he blustered, torn between two unacceptable alternatives. He could not stand idly by and let Nat die, but the thought of Lily...*his* Lily...of her lovely, perfect body being...! "No,'' he said again. "There has to be another way.''

"Perhaps,'' one of the doctors said, "you all need to sleep on this. It's not a decision to be made lightly, and nothing's going to be done tonight anyway, so I suggest you go home and try to get some rest. People generally don't make the best choices when they're overtired and overstressed. If you're still of the same mind tomorrow,'' he concluded, addressing his last remark to Lily, "let us know and we'll arrange for you to be tested.''

"And if I'm a compatible donor?''

"If it becomes necessary—and I stress that we have not reached that point yet and hopefully never will—you and your sister will be put under the care of a urologist with transplant experience. He will perform the surgery.''

"Take Lily home,'' Hugo said, after the medical team had left. "Your mother and I will stay with Natalie.''

"You heard the doctor,'' Sebastian told him. "We all need to get some rest.''

"And you know very well that neither of us will sleep a wink away from this hospital. There are comfortable recliners in the waiting area, with plenty of blankets and pillows. I'll call you the minute there's any change, but our place is here with our child, Sebastian, and I'll rest easier if I know you're taking care of my other daughter.''

Oh, he'd take care of her, all right! If it took him all night, he'd dissuade Lily from her impulsive offer. "Okay,'' he said, "we're out of here. Come on, Lily, I'll drive you home.''

CHAPTER ELEVEN

"YOU'VE missed the turnoff for the main gates," Lily told him.

They were the first words she'd spoken since they left the hospital. Buried in her own thoughts and knowing he was just as occupied with his, she'd seen no point in trying to engage him in empty conversation.

"I know," he said.

"Why? Where are we going?"

"To my place. I use the rear driveway. It's faster."

She didn't want to go to his place. She was too vulnerable to face the memories it would stir up. "I don't think that's such a good idea, Sebastian."

"If we should be called to the hospital in the middle of the night, we'll make it there a lot faster if I don't have to stop by the main house first to collect you."

Half a mile farther down the road, he swung the car through a set of smaller gates and followed a narrow, tree-lined lane, which ended in a clearing in front of the stables. "Also," he said, switching off the engine and turning to face her, "you and I have to talk."

"Talking never gets us anywhere but into trouble." She pushed her hair away from her face wearily. "And I don't know about you, Sebastian, but I've had just about as much of that as I can take for one day."

"Fine. I'll do the talking and all you have to do is listen." He stepped out of the car and came around to her door. "Come on, Lily. This is no time for us to be on opposite sides. We've got to hang together."

She was too tired to argue and, if truth be told, afraid to be alone. Too many nightmares waited. Stoically she watched while he unloaded her luggage from the trunk, then followed him inside the stables and up the winding staircase.

His apartment had a different feel to it with summer gone. A fire snoozed behind glass doors in the hearth and threw a pale orange glow on the high whitewashed ceiling, and he'd moved the leather couches so that they flanked the hearth. Only one window stood open a crack. Although the view beyond was obscured by night, she could hear the river flowing quietly at the foot of the property and was reminded of the many times she and Natalie had walked Katie along its banks. Everywhere she turned, it seemed, there were memories that brought her nothing but pain.

Sebastian dumped her bags on the landing and went to the armoire. She heard the clink of crystal, the splash of liquid—déjà vu again. "Here," he said, coming to where she'd collapsed on one of the couches. "Stay put and drink this."

Suspiciously she inspected the glass he thrust into her hand. "What is it?"

"Not poison, if that's what you're afraid of. I'm sticking with scotch, but when I knew you were coming back, I laid in a supply of the sherry you like. Come on, Lily, don't make me hold your nose and pour it down your throat. We both need something to fortify us."

"I doubt alcohol's going to do it," she said. "It's a depressant, in case you didn't know, and I'm already feeling low enough." She tried, unsuccessfully, to bury a sigh. "What's involved in donating a kidney, Sebastian?"

He didn't answer. Instead he disappeared through a doorway at the back of the room and a moment later, she heard the sound of pots and pans clattering, followed shortly thereafter by the smell of maple-cured bacon frying.

Sebastian Caine, lawyer and lover, she'd come to know well, but this sudden display of domesticity was something new. Curiosity getting the better of the fatigue that had attacked her limbs the minute she sank into the comfort of the couch, she went to investigate.

Shirtsleeves rolled back to just below the elbow and a dish towel tucked in the waist of his dark gray cords, he was slicing tomatoes at a butcher-block island separating the working half of his kitchen from a small dining nook.

Without bothering to look up from the task, he said, "I thought I told you to stay put."

"I wanted to see your kitchen." She leaned against the doorway. Actually "wilted" was a more apt description as the sherry took effect, spreading a warm, delicious lassitude throughout her body. "Somehow, I never expected you'd have one."

A trace of amusement lightened his expression. "You thought elves came in the night and left food on my doorstep?"

"I suppose I never gave the matter much thought at all. We've always had…other avenues to explore whenever we've been together." She took a sip of the sherry. "You didn't answer my question, Sebastian."

"What question?"

"The one about kidney transplants. You've already looked into it so tell me, what do living donors face?"

He set aside the tomatoes, popped two slices of bread into the toaster and opened the refrigerator. "Sorry I can't offer you French fries," he said, "but I make a pretty mean bacon, lettuce and tomato sandwich. You like mayo on yours?"

"You can put strawberry jam on it, for all I care! Stop evading the question, Sebastian. I refuse to be brushed off like this."

"And I refuse to dwell on something that's not going to happen. Nat's going to recover on her own."

"And if she doesn't, and it turns out she needs a kidney from someone else and you aren't a suitable donor, what then? Are you still going to tell me to go away and be quiet?"

"You never know when to quit, do you, Lily?" he said savagely, slamming a head of lettuce and a jar of mayonnaise on the counter, before kicking closed the refrigerator door. "You just have to keep poking away at a subject until you've exhausted it and everyone connected with it. What will it take to satisfy you?"

"Having you treat me as a family member instead of some interfering pariah would be a good place to start. And receiving reasonable answers to reasonable questions."

"Fine." His shoulders slumped. "You'll undergo blood tests and X rays to determine if you're a healthy prospective donor and immunologically compatible with Nat." The toast popped up. He removed it and put in two more slices of bread. "If you pass that hurdle, you'll go through more lab tests and a final evaluation, including assessment by a social worker to ensure that you're genuinely willing to donate."

"And then?"

He looked up and gave her a blast from those unforgettable blue eyes. "If all systems are go, they'll cut you open and remove a kidney."

He put it like that deliberately, hoping the bluntness of his words would shock her into reconsidering. He should have known better. She'd weathered plenty of storms in the last year. One more wasn't going to defeat her.

"It will be worth it, if that's what it takes to save Natalie's life," she said quietly.

"And what about *your* life?" he raged, grabbing the second batch of toast and slapping it down on the cutting board. "What about the risks you'd be taking, the possible future restrictions you could face with your own health?"

"Life's full of risks, Sebastian. We live with them from the moment we're born. Most of the time, we're able to avoid them, but when someone we love is in trouble, we don't stop to count the cost. We do what we can to help, and if that means taking chances, well…" She shrugged. "We take them. If it turns out that Natalie needs a kidney and I'm able to give her one, I will."

He thought of himself as a man able to take whatever life dished out, but suddenly, he'd reached his limit. He hadn't slept in a week. He'd watched his mother and Hugo age before his eyes. He'd watched Nat slide deeper into illness and never doubted he'd move heaven and earth to make her well again. But he hadn't reckoned on this; on being caught so squarely between a rock and a hard place that he felt as if his heart were being squeezed dry.

Overcome, he swung away and went to lean on the dining table. Planting both hands on its surface, he stared down at them and willed his vision to clear. It would have, too, if Lily hadn't come up behind him and wrapped her arms around his waist, and said, "We are defined by the choices we make, Sebastian. At the end of the day, they are what count."

The words triggered something deep inside him that nothing she'd ever said or done before had quite managed to touch. He'd done his best not to like her, to find good reason to despise her, to forget he'd ever met her. But with those two sentences, she forced him to acknowledge the absolute decency and goodness which were so much a factor in what made her beautiful.

His chest heaved in a silent sob. Part of his mind—the proud, stupid, arrogant part that men swaggered about because it made them feel invincible—reviled him for showing such weakness. But another part gave him the courage to say what had been in his heart for months. "I love you, Lily. Too much to let you do this. Please…don't. *Don't!*"

"It's for Natalie. My sister—*your* sister." She slackened her hold and forced him to turn and face her. "How can you ask me not to do this, not to give?"

"Because," he said, his voice breaking, "if anything should happen to you, I couldn't live with myself."

She looked at him, and he saw the future in her eyes. It promised more heaven than he knew existed, if only they could find their way through the present. "You've never been a fearful man, Sebastian," she said. "Don't fail me now when I need your courage to help get me through this."

He clamped down on the moan rising in his throat but could do nothing to stem the tears suddenly clouding his eyes. Her face grew indistinct, blurred, so that all he had to guide him was the memory of how she looked. Of the way her mouth turned up in a smile; of how her eyes grew drowsy with passion, and her skin flushed with anticipation when he made love to her.

If he were to lose her, this is how it would be: memories growing dimmer each year until all he had left was the fading echo of her voice.

Blindly he reached for her and buried his face against her hair. He'd fought her when he could have been loving her and he was fighting her still because he *did* love her. More than anyone, even Nat.

"You've accused me of not accepting you into this family," he said, when at last he had himself in control again, "and you were right. I didn't want to see you in that light because family members aren't supposed to fall in love. They aren't supposed to *make* love."

"Not even when there's no blood connection between them?" She lifted her face to his. "Oh, Sebastian, you're too fine a man to hide behind that kind of subterfuge."

"Fine? Is that why I repeatedly hurt and rejected you, when all you ever asked for was acceptance? Is that why I engaged a stranger to delve into your private life, instead of having the decency to come straight out and ask you to share yourself with me in every way, and not just between the sheets?"

"I didn't say you were perfect," she whispered, her hands skimming over his features with such tenderness that he could have wept. "Just that—"

The phone rang before she could finish and, for a moment, they both froze. An hour before, he'd have shoved her away, turned his back to her while he answered, shut her out in as many ways as he could devise, just to keep uppermost in both their minds who was in control. Now, he anchored her to his side as he reached out with his other arm and lifted the receiver, holding it so they could both hear.

"Sebastian?" His stepfather's voice shook with emotion.

"I'm here, Hugo," he said steadily. "Lily and I both are. Has there been a change? Should we come back to the hospital?"

"No...no...! I—" He stopped briefly, obviously fighting for composure.

Glancing down, Sebastian saw Lily's eyes fill with tears. Hugging her closer, he said, "It's bad news, isn't it? We'll be there as soon as we can."

"No," Hugo said again. "That's why I'm calling—to tell you that the odds at last have swung in Natalie's favor. She's made a remarkable turnaround and is finally responding to treatment. The doctor was just in to speak to us. It's going to take time, but he's very optimistic she'll make a full recovery."

Sebastian dropped his forehead to Lily's and closed his eyes. "Thank God," he breathed.

"Our reaction exactly," Hugo said. "Listen, I know it's late and you must both be exhausted, so I won't keep you on the phone any longer, but I didn't think you'd mind being disturbed for news like this. Give our love to Lily, and both of you get some sleep. I know your mother and I will."

Slowly Sebastian hung up and turned to face Lily again. "You heard all that?"

Her mouth trembled and a tear rolled down her cheek. "Every word."

He wiped at the tear with his thumb. "Think you'll be able to sleep now?"

She shook her head. "Suddenly I'm not tired anymore."

"Me, neither." He drew her toward him until his mouth grazed hers. "You want to do something else?"

The emotion of the moment had built to a crescendo they knew could be satisfied only one way. Smiling shakily, she said, "It depends."

"Oh, really?" He pressed a kiss to each of her eyelids. "On what?"

"On what else you have in mind." Her hands fluttered over him, refined instruments of torture and delight.

Heat shot through him. Curling his hand around the back of her neck, he steered her down the hall toward the bedroom. "You said earlier that we get into trouble when we talk, and you were right. How about I show you, instead?"

Much later, when she'd exhausted him and he wondered if he'd ever be able to rise to the occasion again, she had the nerve to say she was hungry. "Cripes, woman, you're insatiable," he complained.

"I was thinking about those sandwiches you made. It seems a pity to let them go to waste."

He opened one eye. "You want ketchup on yours?"

Her smile flowed over him like melted honey and from the way his body responded, he decided there was still life in the old tiger, after all. "I want you," she said, walking her fingers down his chest. "With or without ketchup."

They finally ate the cold BLT sandwiches for breakfast, and washed them down with champagne and orange juice. "So where do we go from here?" he asked, watching as she loaded the dirty plates into the dishwasher he never bothered to use.

Even though she had her back to him, he saw the way she stiffened at the question and would have laid money on the doubts suddenly chasing through her mind. "I suppose, to the hospital and eventually, when I know Natalie's really out of the woods, I'll go back to the West Coast."

"How about to the altar with me, instead?"

Silence hung in the air for several seconds before she asked incredulously, "Are you offering to marry me?"

"Well, it's a lousy job, I know, but someone has to do it."

Very slowly, she turned to face him. "Well, thank you very much, but no, I don't think so."

He stared at her, dumbfounded. "Why the hell not, Lily?"

"Because you happened to come into my life at a time when I was feeling lonely and abandoned, and needed someone. Hugo has Cynthia and Natalie and, for a while, I had you. But I never really expected it would be for keeps. You're not the permanent kind, Sebastian. You've told me so yourself, more than once."

"A man can change his mind, can't he?"

"Not for the reasons prompting your actions now. I don't want the words *'For guilt, and pain inflicted, I do,'* included in your wedding vows."

"Then perhaps I haven't made myself clear. My asking you to marry me is not driven by a need to atone for my past sins." He cupped her face in his hands and looked deeply into her eyes. "Last night I told you I love you," he said, inching closer until his mouth was caressing hers. "I still love you this morning. I have loved you for weeks and I will go on loving you for the rest of my life."

"This isn't fair," she sighed. "You're not supposed to be able to seduce me like this. Not again...and not so easily. You're hard and mean and undeserving...I've told myself so a hundred times. You have...no right...proving me wrong."

But her protests were all for show. Her body and her lips and the dreamy expression in her eyes told him she no more believed what she was saying than she did that the moon was made of green cheese.

"I know," he said, backing onto the nearest chair and drawing her down on his lap. "I need a good woman to whip me into shape. Think you're up for the job?"

She wriggled out of his hold and put the safety of the work island between him and her. "I'm not sure."

A flicker of nervousness rippled through him. "Jeez, Lily, I've laid my heart on the line. What more do you want? I can give you a good life, the kind you deserve. There's nothing to keep you in Vancouver—no business, and certainly no family. Why can't you just say yes, and put me out my misery?"

"Oh, I don't know." Thoughtfully she folded the dish towel and hung it over the oven door. "Maybe because I'm an old-fashioned kind of woman who wants an old-fashioned kind of proposal from the heart."

"You mean, you want me down on one knee?"

She planted her fists on her sexy little hips and glared at him. "After all the grief you've put me through in the last few months, Sebastian Caine? You bet I do! I want roses and violins and moonlight and promises of happy-ever-after."

"That kind of promise is hard to keep, Lily. Will you settle for me promising to love you as long as we both shall live, and then some?"

She nibbled the corner of her lip consideringly. "If you'll let me do the same for you."

"Oh," he said, striding around the island and reaching for her, "I think I can safely promise you that."

"In that case, yes, I'll marry you, Sebastian," she said, brazenly pulling open his bathrobe and creating mayhem in places no well-brought up young woman would dare to trespass until the ink was dry on the marriage certificate.

"Better make it soon," he muttered unsteadily. "I don't fancy having to tell Hugo he's about to be a grandfather before he becomes a father-in-law."

* * *

They were married six weeks later, in an evening ceremony in the middle of November, two days after the first snowfall had turned Stentonbridge into a winter wonderland and one week after Natalie received a clean bill of health from her doctor.

Dozens of candles illuminated the old stone church. Giant white chrysanthemums and dark green ferns adorned the altar and hung from satin ribbons at the end of the pews.

Cynthia wore midnight-blue silk and wept happy tears all over her orchid corsage. Natalie made a delectable maid of honor in cranberry brocade. And Lily came down the aisle on her father's arm, radiant in an exquisite full-length white velvet wedding gown.

"Hey," Sebastian murmured over the dying chords of the organ, as she came to a stop next to him at the altar. "This is your last chance to run."

"I just did," she told him, her smile dazzling. "How else do you think I wound up here? I've finally come home."

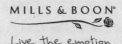

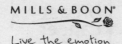

researching the cure

The facts you need to know:

- Breast cancer is the commonest form of cancer in the United Kingdom. **One woman in nine** will develop the disease during her lifetime.

- Each year around **41,000** women and approximately **300** men are diagnosed with breast cancer and around **13,000** women and **90** men will die from the disease.

- 80% of all breast cancers occur in post-menopausal women and approximately 8,200 pre-menopausal women are diagnosed with the disease each year.

- However, survival rates are improving, with on average 77.5% of women diagnosed between 1996 and 1999 still alive five years later, compared to 72.8% for women diagnosed between 1991 and 1996.

Breast Cancer Campaign is the only charity that specialises in funding independent breast cancer research throughout the UK. It aims to find the cure for breast cancer by funding research which looks at improving diagnosis and treatment of breast cancer, better understanding how it develops and ultimately either curing the disease or preventing it.

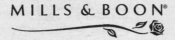

1006/01a

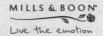

MILLS & BOON®

Live the emotion

Modern
romance™

PURCHASED FOR REVENGE *by Julia James*

Powerful tycoon Alexei Constantin has only one thing
on his mind – to destroy the Hawkwood family empire!
But Alexei doesn't realise he's just shared a passionate
kiss with Eve Hawkwood – the beautiful but innocent
daughter of Alexei's bitter enemy…!

THE PLAYBOY BOSS'S CHOSEN BRIDE
by Emma Darcy

All women love Jake Devila…except his personal
assistant, Merlina Rossi. Merlina secretly wants Jake so
much it hurts. But she knows her boss's taste runs to
skinny blondes, not curvy brunettes! Then she sees a
chance to show Jake what he's been missing…

HOLLYWOOD HUSBAND, CONTRACT WIFE
by Jane Porter

Love-'em-and-leave-'em leading man Wolf Kerrick is never
out of the headlines. This time, he has taken Alexandra, an
unknown, ordinary girl, and turned her into an overnight
celebrity, then into his Hollywood bride! But the glitz and
glamour of their wedding is tarnished by a dirty secret…

BEDDED BY THE DESERT KING *by Susan Stephens*

Zara Kingston has gone to Zaddara – to confront the
man she believes ruined her childhood. A dark, brooding
stranger proves that the desert holds hidden treasures…
But then Zara finds that the man whose touch she yearns
for is desert king Sheikh Shahin…thief of her youth!

On sale 3rd November 2006

*Available at WHSmith, Tesco, ASDA, Borders, Eason,
Sainsbury's and most bookshops*

www.millsandboon.co.uk

All you could want for Christmas!

Meet handsome and seductive men under the mistletoe, escape to the world of Regency romance or simply relax by the fire with a heartwarming tale by one of our bestselling authors. These special stories will fill your holiday with Christmas sparkle!

On sale 6th October 2006

On sale 20th October 2006

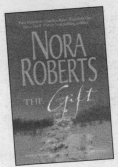